D1066087

To Mom, Dad, Mara, and Eldon:
thank you for the parts you played in making childhood full of blessed memories.

Acknowledgments

I would first like to thank my parents, Eldon and Diana, for the unconditional love, support, encouragement, and faith in their youngest child. I wish to thank all those who have assisted me with editorial suggestions and corrections through the years—South Coast Writers, Santa Barbara Literary Service, Joan Kilgore, and Doug Harms. Though they may not be aware of the impact of their words, I wish to express gratitude to those who have encouraged me to be persistent and continue writing, in particular, South Coast Writers, Lisa McKay, and Brock and Bodie Thoene.

The cover art is based upon the original work "Silent Night" created by Amol Arun Kamble, a student at Vadaketh Development Centre in Miraj, India. I would like to thank Master Kamble and Dr. V.C. George, the founder of the center, for granting use of the painting.

A word to the wise, to all the children of the twentieth century . . . There's a wondrous magic to Christmas, and there's a special power reserved for little people.

—Rod Serling

BOOK I: PRESEASON

A Nativity

1498, Florence, Italy

Few children played, or laughed, or ran through the alleys, fields, and markets. Their voices were a murmur, lost in the silence outside the walls of St. Mark's. The usual neighs of horses, shouts from coach drivers, beckons of merchants, and bargaining with the city's inhabitants were absent. The city had become nearly as monastic as those who lived within the walls of the friar's home.

He had once found joy in jarring a window or door, listening to the many sounds of Florence, its people, and its commerce. Whether it was civic pride or his desire to sense a camaraderie among its citizens or of wanting to know the struggles faced by those who lived ordinary lives, who were not protected by vows of silence, or celibacy, or service to God, he sat at his window, observing a child at play, a young man courting a Florentine maiden, a vendor making a sale. To understand them would assist in intercessory prayer and serving their needs.

There was no more time to meditate on what should be done to assist the needy, what could be done, or what must be done. The sermons had been preached, the lessons taught, the hungry fed, the naked clothed, the stranger welcomed. Still, what had been accomplished? How much progress had been made in light of all that had transpired over the last several days?

St. Mark's was his home. He ate here, slept here, worshipped, served, and sought his God within its walls. Now he was leaving the doors for what he felt certain would be the last time.

The streets whispered as he walked the graveled path leading from the monastery. He raised his eyes, canvassing the land, down to the River Arno and beyond. There could be no place like this on earth—hills were blossomed with lush trees and spotted with tops of homes surrounding the perimeter of the city; the streets converged to the many plazas; the buildings rose higher the farther one ventured in, confirming that his city was progressing and leading the world in achievements of architecture, science, and engineering.

He stopped, closed his eyes, and took a deep breath, lifting his head toward the river, imagining his feet in the Arno's waters, and trying to remember its rush against the banks, its speed under the bridges, the cool of its touch created by the newly melted snow traveling from the Apennines. If only he could cross it one last time, over the Ponte Vecchio to the Medici gardens.

A hand violently pushed him, forcing him to open his eyes and move forward. He struggled to raise his hands, hoping to shield his face from the sun's glare, but his strength would not cooperate. Instead, his arms and hands trembled. Years ago, this was the first ailment that caused him concern, making him aware of the price to be paid for outliving most from his generation. He took a step forward, and a dull ache radiated from his inner thigh up through his groin. After several more steps, the walking became less painful. When he straightened his back, his vertebrae crackled in rhythm. He smiled, grateful that he could still walk on his own efforts; grateful that he still lived.

They led him toward Via Cavour; if asked, he would have chosen to be led on Via Ricasoli. Ricasoli was a straighter route, offering more opportunities to view his adopted home. Perhaps they chose Cavour intentionally; perhaps he should be grateful they had. He would reach the domed church, and from there be led to where? Would there be someone, or some ones, waiting for him at the *Duomo* to decide his fate?

Just before they entered Piazza Giovanni, he gazed longingly at the distant Vecchio, recalling his many visits to the Medici family gardens. He'd sit on a stone bench for hours, watching the squirrels dance up and down trees and scamper across the paths and fields of green. He'd enjoy a finch's melody as it darted from the tops of fruit trees to pines, from olive trees to the vine-covered walls. Surrounded by the harmonizing aromas of lemons, apples, figs, and roses, he'd wait to witness the flight of a butterfly or to hear the occasional rhapsody of a woodpecker. He wished he had made the effort to walk the four miles one last time.

No sight, however, was as precious to him as the dome of the Duomo flanked by its tower and baptistery. He lifted his head; his heart raced.

Determined to no longer let his eyes wander, he fixed them at his feet. This was to be done nobly, with no malcontent and with no anxiety or fear. The sun radiated its warmth; though evening drew near. He felt the sting of its warm rays staring at him, accusing him, judging him, just as he was sure the two men on either side judged.

The escort on his left strode ahead, knocking on the large wooden doors of the Duomo. He glanced back, looking across at the baptistery, for a moment forgetting his predicament, and admiring the bronze doors created by Lorenzo Ghiberti. Bronze reliefs, so intricate and life-like, of Old Testament narratives: Adam and Eve; Cain and Abel; Abraham, Isaac, Jacob and Esau; Jacob and his twelve sons; Moses; David; and Solomon. He caught only a glimpse of the motif illustrating Joseph being thrown in the pit by his brothers, when he was nudged to turn around.

From inside the main cathedral, the left door was pulled open. His two escorts led him into the narthex, one in front, the other behind him. Candles burned in the front of the cathedral, providing light enough only near the altar. Long shadows crept on the walls, shifting with the tides of the flames. He lifted his head for the first time since entering, cautiously taking in the familiar scent from the burning wax.

Voices echoed through the cold, damp chambers. The scents of wood and incense mingled with the sweet fragrance from the candles, aided his attempt to remain peaceful. He had embraced this sacred building, along with its sights, its aromas, its leaders, and its parishioners. It was a place of worship and refuge, not only for the people of Florence but also for believers throughout the papacy's sphere of influence. The arrival of these men changed all that. Within a week, they destroyed the hope he had held for his city, his country, and his world.

The escort behind led him gently toward the right. These two men, who had boldly led him out from among his fellow friars minutes earlier, seemed more cautious within these walls, in the presence of those who led the proceedings near the altar. With a much greater respect than he had received since the arrival of the Rome delegation a week earlier, the younger of his two escorts motioned to a pew in the middle of the cathedral and assisted him in sitting. Fear filled the young man's eyes and perhaps just a bit of respect for the elderly that youthful pride had not yet chased from him. He returned the young man's gesture with a gracious nod.

The two escorts stood in the aisle, leaving him in the pew to ponder his fate. A deep breath. And another. This is what he told himself he must do. Keep all in perspective. Remember the path that had led him here.

Regardless of what the city endured, he never regretted his decision. There had been years of peace and prosperity. Florence was now one of the wealthiest cities in the world, but he knew all was not well. There was too much turmoil in the world and the church; and Florence was not far enough from Rome to insure protection.

It was appropriate for it to end this way. He knew this would be his destiny. And though he was apprehensive of the pending pain and loneliness, he had always hoped to be counted worthy of suffering for his Lord.

He looked up at the men gathered near the altar. They deliberated over the fate of a much younger friar. Reclined in their chairs, they grinned and seemed to enjoy the process, apparently oblivious to the somber nature of their task. It was as if they had done this so often that they grew numb to the effects on those whom they judged. All of the friars had been led from the monastery to the cathedral. Most walked back unscathed; three had not.

While he waited in the pew, the bright-colored clothing of the delegates reminded him of his childhood. He raised his hands to cover his eyes, trembling at the memories of growing up in the south German city of Constance and of the atrocities resulting from the church council that had come to town when he was seven years old. He was haunted by the similarity of what he was now facing.

> "Benjamin," his father had warned, "these are troubled times. The church may do things that you will not understand. You must find your strength in our Lord. Whatever happens, remember that your mother and I love you."

It was as though his father had known what was going to happen. The friar closed his eyes again, trying to shut out the echoing voices of the pope's delegation. Lowering his head, he tried to pray, but his thoughts returned to his early years in Constance.

The Council of Constance had wasted little time. At first, Benjamin was excited to finally see men who knew the pope, who had been in his presence. They were taller and more dignified than the clergy he had seen from neighboring villages. Their clothing was made with bright-colored fabrics he had never known existed: a crimson-red, a shining blue, a radiating gold, and a bold-green. The men were pristine, untouchable, and as they approached Benjamin's church, they appeared to be giants, their heads grazing the bottom of the clouds.

But their somber faces reflected none of the joy he regularly saw in the faces of his parents and their friends. The delegates whispered words to the priest in Benjamin's village, walked past him, and entered the church.

The men had arrived in May, declaring the English man, John Wycliffe, whom Benjamin had heard his father esteem on many occasions, to be a heretic. They ordered Wycliffe's works to be burned.

Though Wycliffe had died in England thirty years earlier, they further decreed that his body be exhumed and his bones set to flame.

Two large hands grabbed him from behind. He turned and looked into his father's eyes. "This is only the beginning," he whispered.

A month later, the council invited Jan Hus to travel from Prague, offering him the chance to discuss his theology. But when he arrived, his only opportunity to speak was to recant his beliefs. After refusing, they imprisoned him for two days.

Benjamin begged his parents during those two days to be allowed to attend the trial that would soon continue. Though they refused, he disobeyed and followed an older friend into the church in which the proceedings were held.

"I am prepared to submit to the council's judgment," Hus began, "but only if by doing so, I do not offend God or my conscience."

Again, Hus was sent to prison.

One month later, Hus was brought before the council again, enrobed in priestly vestments and given one last opportunity to recant. Once more, he refused. They bound his hands with ropes and tightened them behind his back. They placed a paper crown on his head, inscribed with the word *Heretic*. They wrapped a chain around his neck and attached the other end to an iron stake that was pounded into the ground surrounded by wood, straw, and writings of John Wycliffe.

A fourth opportunity was given to recant.

"God is my witness," Hus announced, "that I have never taught that of which I have been accused by false witnesses. In the truth of the gospel which I have written, taught, and preached, I will die today with gladness."

The executioners lit the flame and set the fire to Hus.

"Christ, thou Son of the living God," Hus sang, "have mercy upon me. Into thy hands I commend my spirit."

Benjamin was lost. The man admired most by his parents was declared an enemy of the church and executed.

"A man like Hus," his father mumbled over and over, shaking his head with a look of determination. "Hus sought nothing but that all men come to know God. Why else does the church exist? Still, he dies like this at the hands of those who claim to be God's church. I cannot stay here, witness these acts, and do nothing."

Three weeks later, Benjamin's parents were declared heretics. His mother's Jewish lineage only added to her crime and that of his father's. Their stance cost them their lives and left Benjamin an orphan to be raised by members of the congregation. By his tenth birthday, it became clear much was expected of the son whose parents had died for their beliefs.

But his parents were great speakers, bold and charismatic. Benjamin began to stutter following the trial and executions. Though his writings and performance in the classroom exceeded his classmates', he was shy and solemn. He loved his parents, but if he were to accomplish anything for the church, he would have to leave Constance.

An understanding benefactor approached Benjamin, offering to pay for travel and education, so he could continue his studies at Oxford. Excited by the opportunity to travel to the land of Wycliffe, Benjamin gratefully accepted. He arrived in England at the age of fifteen and excelled in his studies. Still, his stutter remained.

As his studies drew to a close, he feared what lay ahead. When he thought of the pending decision of what he would do next, following his completion of studies at Oxford, he wept, feeling he had nothing to offer. He needed respite from the growing turmoil and anxiety.

Hoping to find inspiration in the town where Wycliffe had lived during his final years, he traveled the sixty miles northward to Lutterworth.

Two days after his arrival, he was awoken by large shouts in the streets. He looked from his window, seeing in the distance a horse-drawn carriage, flanked by church officers. Benjamin rushed from his room and pushed his way to the front of the gathering crowd, expecting perhaps the pope, or some other important official, to step from the shining black carriage door.

The driver jumped from his seat and handed a piece of paper to another church officer. The officer read the message on the paper and then pointed to the back of the carriage. With the assistance of two other men, the driver opened the back of the carriage and lifted an old wooden coffin. They struggled to carry it through the thickening crowd to the center of town several hundred yards away.

"Men and women of Lutterworth. Children of God. Listen to me," the man with the paper announced.

He spoke with a dreaded tone. His eyes were lowered, his chin raised. Benjamin's eyes widened. He held his breath.

"Loyalty to Rome is rewarded. Obedience to our Lord and the pope is esteemed, and proper, and essential for our communities, our nations, our world. Those who do not share these beliefs, and who teach and encourage others to disrespect the church, will suffer."

At that moment, the nails of the coffin were pried open. The wooden box was set upright and propped up by a large wooden pole in the ground. The lid was thrown down by one of the delegates who quickly ran from the coffin as the lid fell. A cloud of dust formed and cleared seconds later, revealing a skeleton.

"The English man, John Wycliffe," the leader announced. "A heretic. A blasphemer. An enemy of the church of our Lord."

The leader dropped his hands to his side, turned to a man holding a burning torch, and signaled him to begin with a determined stare.

"This is the end of God's enemy. This will be the end of all God's enemies."

Within seconds, flames engulfed the coffin, the yellowed bones of the skeleton remaining oblivious to the heat. Benjamin turned and searched the crowd, hoping to find someone he knew, someone who could explain what was happening.

But upon further thought, he knew what was happening. It took thirteen years, but they finally carried out the orders from the papal delegation in Constance.

He finished his studies in Oxford, and though he had decided to return to his hometown, as he approached Constance, he felt God telling him to travel further south. So he did, past the Alps and into Italy.

He chose Florence because it was far enough from Constance to avoid his name being known yet near enough to return if he failed in his efforts. He was drawn to St. Mark's, recalling the words he had heard from a fellow student at Oxford, "The friars at St. Mark's are independent from Rome. They are free from corruption and strive to serve our Lord."

Unable to explain how the church could condemn good people, such as Hus and his parents, Benjamin entered St. Mark's a cynic. For too long, too much had gone wrong: Fifty years had passed, and still, two men claimed to be pope; during ten of those years, three men had claimed to be the head of the church. There were common practices such as nepotism, simony, and the selling of indulgences. If the church in Rome needed money, they increased the price for an indulgence and a commoner was forced to pay the inflated cost for his sins to be forgiven.

These practices made Benjamin and those with whom he served at St. Mark's ashamed. The friars wondered how men of God could bring themselves to do such things. But they were faithful in their prayers, and none as much as Benjamin. Three times each day, they convened to seek God's guidance as to how they could serve Him, combat the vile practices of those in authority, and aid the poor.

In 1490, their prayers were answered when a thirty-eight-year-old Dominican monk from Ferrara arrived.

Lorenzo de' Medici had heard of the monk and found his teachings entertaining. "We must invite Savonarola to join St. Mark's," Lorenzo shared with Benjamin and other select friars.

Benjamin was suspicious; he knew of Lorenzo's reputation. His main task in life was to impress others and to raise the grandeur of Florence. It was this drive that helped make the Medici family prosperous and Florence a beneficiary of their success. Benjamin surmised that Lorenzo's ulterior motive in inviting Savonarola was to secure for Florence a charismatic preacher, adding to the city's prestige and appeal.

Savonarola was greeted with as much pomp as Benjamin could remember. It was the largest gathering in the city's history—shops closing, farmers riding fifty miles, and travelers coming from distant villages, all to see and hear the great preacher.

Lorenzo stood near Benjamin, and his proud grin of satisfaction grew larger with each eloquent word the preacher spoke in his inaugural sermon. A bolt of jealousy hit Benjamin. His whole life he had endeavored to be like this preacher. Never had he heard anybody speak as clearly, intelligently, and emotionally as Savonarola, not even his father. Benjamin lowered his head, ashamed of his failures in measuring up to the attributes of his parents and ashamed of his envy.

At the friars' first meal with Savonarola, Benjamin observed the downcast expressions of some of the other friars; their eyes lowered in humility. Others were aflame with anger, and a few enlarged like those of a child with free reign in the local baker's shop. Benjamin chuckled, coming to realize that all three reactions he saw in the faces of his fellow friars were battling within his soul.

Following the meal, Savonarola cleared his throat, wiped his mouth with an embroidered napkin, and spoke: "On the evening Jesus was betrayed, on the evening our Lord was denied, on the evening the Christ was deserted by His twelve trusted followers and friends—on this night, our Lord arose from supper, took off His outer clothing, wrapped a towel around His waist, poured water in a basin, and washed all twenty-four feet, one hundred twenty toes. Atop. Below. All twelve disciples. Peter, who would deny he knew the man who stood at his feet. And Judas, who hours later would betray our Lord with a kiss.

"Presumptuousness dictates that I now follow in our Lord's steps, that I bind myself with a waistcloth, kneel, and wash your feet. Doing so would be a parade, an attempt to illustrate my great humility and service to my brethren. But neither you nor I have the intimacy with one another that our Lord had with His disciples. The acts of our Lord must not be taken lightly. The words of our Lord must be held in highest regard. Manipulating His words or using Him as a device for my own ends is a disservice to the mandate to which He has called us all.

"I will not follow, nor will I teach, what is proper if it runs contrary to the words God has revealed to us in Scripture, or contrary to the integrity with which our Lord desires each of us to live. Proper in man's eyes does not equate with proper in God's."

Benjamin glanced around the table, his heart resonating with approval at each word he heard. All of the friars were now wearing the same expression, resembling the child in the bakery.

Savonarola continued, "Our task is to serve under our Lord, to worship Him, to seek Him, to serve our brethren within these walls and without. We are His lights, His hands, His feet to all those in Florence. Let us represent our Lord faithfully."

The friars were dismissed in silence. Benjamin remembers lying in bed that evening, unable to sleep and filled with excitement and thankfulness for the preacher's arrival.

Over the next eight years, Savonarola, with the support of St. Mark's friars, sold church property and gave the proceeds to the poor, reformed the inner life of the community at St. Mark's, helped Florence develop into a republic, and entered into a treaty with King Charles VIII of France that saved Florence following the death of Lorenzo. But it was this same treaty that led Savonarola into conflicts with Pope Alexander VI. It was Alexander who had sent the five-man delegation, in front of which Friar Benjamin would soon stand.

Benjamin's hands shook more violently as he lowered his head further. Only two days had passed since these men condemned Savonarola, hung him in the town's center, and burned his body. Benjamin thought of the hours, the countless days, weeks, months, and years that he had spent praying for a man who would help change the church. But just as they had done to his parents and to Hus, they murdered a man whose greatest fault was his intense desire to introduce more people to God.

The delegates condemned only two other friars. One was to be banished; the other burned at the stake. Benjamin was certain he would receive the council's condemnation as well. He was the oldest friar at

St. Mark's. Savonarola therefore relied on him to motivate the others to participate in acts of charity. Benjamin did so, not with words but with actions. He was the first to lift a crate of fruit to feed the poor, the first to pound a nail in a new house, and the first to teach at a new school. If any friar was deemed by the pope's council as being a threat to Rome's authority, it was he.

The cathedral fell silent. Benjamin raised his head and saw his fellow friar walking toward him. The young man walked upright and fast; his shoulders were no longer slouched, as they had been an hour earlier. He grinned at Benjamin and tried to offer some words of encouragement, but his escort led him outside the cathedral before he had a chance.

Benjamin took a deep breath. Everything in his life had led him to this point. Finally, he thought, he would live up to the expectations those in Constance had held for him. Finally, he would do something tangible for the kingdom of God. His moment of triumph over evil had arrived. He stood up, straightened his shoulders, and raised his head. With resolve, he walked to the front of the cathedral until he stood before his accusers.

"Friar Benjamin?" one of the papal authorities asked. Benjamin lowered his arms and wrapped his left hand within his right. "Yes," he answered.

"You are from Germany? Constance it says here."

Each of the men leaned toward the man holding the document, glancing at the paper once they heard of Benjamin's birthplace. Benjamin observed each man with caution, unsure what their intent may be with these questions. "Yes," he answered once more.

Another of the delegates looked up. "You are advanced in years, Friar. Do you recall the council that convened in Constance eighty years ago?"

Benjamin glanced at the man who asked the question. He hesitated to look for too long at any one of them, afraid of offending their sense of authority. Already he was doing what he hoped he would not do. He felt his shoulders rise and the tension around his neck tighten. Perspiration formed on his lips. He tapped his foot. To be strong was his aim, as his parents had been, but he was not up to the challenge. It wasn't that he was afraid of what might happen as a result of his meeting with these men, but it was the meeting itself. He hated confrontation; he hated speaking in public, even if it was before five fellow clergy.

The same council member continued, "Ironical, isn't it, Friar?"

Benjamin remained silent, unsure how to answer.

The member cleared his throat. "Don't you find it curious? As a lad, you witness the death of those challenging the authority of God's church, and now again, near the end of your life. Things have not gotten much better. It would seem our efforts have been futile."

Benjamin shrugged his shoulders and lifted his eyes to watch the delegate who spoke.

"Do you not speak?" another of the men asked.

Benjamin's eyes opened and closed rapidly. He could feel his throat tighten. It would worsen if he did not speak soon. "No, sirs," he began. "The . . . the . . . irony of . . . of it . . . it . . . it all, is . . . is that . . . that . . . Rome still does . . . does not rec— . . . rec— . . . recognize those who . . . who . . . who . . . are the true . . . true . . . church."

The five men eyed each other. Benjamin could see their amusement. Regardless of how firm a supporter of Savonarola he had been, they would not see him as a threat. He was old, could not speak eloquently, and was near death. It dawned on him that these men might perceive making a martyr of him more detrimental to their cause. Why, then, did they call for him?

One of the men lifted a wooden box and set it on the table in front of the others. "I believe this belongs to you?"

Benjamin looked at the man, unsure of his intentions. He saw no reason to hide the truth. "It . . . it . . . was. I mean, it used . . . used . . . to be."

"And now? It belongs to your preacher?"

"Last Christ— . . . Christ— . . . Christmas Eve. We ex— . . . exchange gifts af— . . . after mass."

The man smiled, opened the box, and took out its contents. "You made these?"

"Yes. Yes, Your Ex— . . . Excellency."

"Well crafted, old Friar," another of the men said. "It seems you missed your calling. You should have been a carpenter."

The five delegates chuckled while Benjamin wondered where this was heading.

A minute later, all the contents were removed from the box. "What do we have here, old Friar?" the leader asked.

The question confused Benjamin. It seemed obvious to him what these pieces of wood represented. And if he was as good as the other friars had always told him, then it must be obvious to these men as well. But arguing this point would get him nowhere, so he answered. "The . . . the . . . na— . . . na— . . . nativ— . . . tiv— . . . ity."

"The nativity?" the leader repeated.

"Yes. You see," Benjamin inched forward and stopped, making sure it was acceptable to approach. The men were reclining and did not seem bothered by his movement. Benjamin continued as he pointed to each of the figurines. "This . . . this . . . this . . . is the Vir— . . . Virgin Ma— . . . Ma— . . . Mary. This is . . . is . . . Jo— . . . Joseph. And these are . . . are the wise men and . . . and . . . the shep— . . . shepherds."

Benjamin paused and looked at the men. He saw a hopeless stare that he knew reflected the emptiness of religious conviction in Rome. It flooded him with the despair he had felt the day his parents were killed. For thirty years, he had labored over these wooden figurines. Under the tutelage of some of Florence's leading artisans, he had embraced the art of carving and sculpting. It was more than a hobby; it was part of his devotional routine. Regardless of how often he thought of the Christ child's birth and the significance it had had on each of those symbolized by the wooden sculptures, he still felt a surging shiver run though his body as he carved their expressions. It amazed him how many emotions the birth of a child fifteen hundred years earlier caused him to experience.

But these men were unmoved by the wooden pieces and apparently unmoved by the nativity itself. Their faces reflected none of the appreciation of that special night. They, like Benjamin, had heard the story from their youth. But it was obvious to Benjamin they had forgotten the unique nature of the child.

This was inexcusable. These were men of the church, sent by the pope. If anyone should rejoice in the birth of the child, it should be men such as these. Benjamin could not let this moment pass. He looked his accusers in the eyes and pointed to the remaining wooden figurine. "This is the baby Jesus, the Christ child, the Son of the living God—Emmanuel, God come to dwell with us."

The five men looked at one another. Benjamin assumed his clear-spoken phrases surprised them into a momentary silence.

"Whatever the church stands for," he continued, "it must stand for this above all else: that this child is God and that this God willingly became a man to provide salvation for all men. *All* men. Not salvation for only those who can afford it or for those whom the papacy favors . . ."

"Enough!" shouted the leader. "We did not call you here for a sermon, old man."

Benjamin stepped back from the table. He noticed his shoulders and neck relaxed, and smiled. He raised his head.

The leader continued. "These pieces you have made, old Friar, may have spiritual meaning to you. But for us, they served a more practical purpose, and that is why we called you here."

"To thank you," another said as he began gathering the strewn documents on the table.

Benjamin looked at each member, shifting his gaze and searching for further explanation.

"Your nativity is evidence, evidence of the preacher's idolatry. It may not have led us directly to his conviction, but it was one of many accusations that helped lead us to the punishment we had come to administer."

As Benjamin lowered his eyes, the scenario grew clearer. Savonarola worshipped God, these men worshipped power. Here they were, gloating over the fact that they condemned Savonarola wrongly. Not only did they not deem Benjamin as a threat worthy of martyrdom, but the confession of their successful plot revealed how harmless they felt he was.

Benjamin's knees weakened. Falling backward, he grabbed the front pew behind him, raised himself, and sat. He had been used and humiliated, failing once more to suffer for his Lord.

He remained still, looking into the darkening recesses of the cathedral, not aware of the delegates' departure. He looked behind him, toward the front doors, uncertain as to how long it had been since they had left. The five men were scheduled to depart town the next morning, and Benjamin would have accomplished nothing more for the church than when they had arrived.

Yes, he helped Savonarola win the approval of St. Mark's other friars. Yes, he had served the poor, ministered to the hopeless, and cared for the sick. These were the comforting words he heard again and again while praying. But there was nothing he had done that would be remembered: no act, no children, no sermon, and no martyrdom.

Defeated, he rose from the pew and walked to the table on which the nativity pieces still stood. He looked at them, staring. He thought back to when he had spoken so eloquently to the five delegates. His conviction of the truth carved into each of the pieces had inspired him to speak as boldly as he had.

He folded his arms, hoping to find comfort in his own embrace. A shuffling, whistling sound from behind the altar startled him. He walked to the altar and glanced where he thought the sound originated. There was nothing.

When he walked back to the table, a rush of air brushed past, causing him to straighten and look behind.

He saw no one.

"Hello?" He turned toward the cathedral's entrance. "Is anyone there?"

There was no answer.

Again, the breeze rushed past, turning him back toward the table. "Hello?"

He stopped and touched his head, his chest, and his legs. Something was strange. He hadn't felt like this since he was a child. He drew in a deep breath. His legs felt fresh; his hands and face warm and full of life.

Then as unexpected as the surge of life came, it was gone. Benjamin looked at his wrinkled and decrepit hands. He felt weak and nauseous; his bones ached, and his head pounded. He heard the wind approaching from behind, increasing in strength until it rushed past and drove him to his knees.

His heart raced, perspiration dripping on the cathedral floor. He tried once to raise himself but hadn't the strength. Turning himself toward the altar required several seconds of shuffling on his knees until he could look into the eyes of Christ nailed onto the cross.

Benjamin coughed and coughed. He cupped his hand over his mouth, coughed once more, and caught a spray of blood. "Please, God," he muttered, "what is happening? Are you speaking? Is this you? Is this the end?"

Then a stillness emerged, calming his anxiety. Another cough brought a flow of blood that washed down his chest.

"Why, Father?" Benjamin pushed with his legs, struggling and coughing until he stood. "Why, Father, am I here? Why, Father, was I here?"

Another surge of wind passed, leaving him shaking in its wake and turning him toward the table on which the nativity rested. He was face-to-face with the wooden pieces he had spent carving for over thirty years.

Now he knew.

He was wide-eyed and grinned, the corners of his mouth reaching heights they had never known. He raised his arms, sheltering the nativity, and lowered his head.

"May these pieces," he whispered, "be used by You to teach, to encourage, to guide those who will come after. Help them to see what these shepherds and wise men saw. Help them to feel what our Blessed Virgin and Joseph felt. Help them to know what each discovered."

Holy Days

1685, Paris, France

The sun had almost set, a fluorescent red radiating on the horizon. Still, most families had lit evening candles, their faint glow illuminating the darkening streets of Paris. On occasion, a bird could be heard singing, flying from a tree to the perch of a neighbor's home and seemingly unaware that soon it would be night. A light rain had fallen hours earlier and filled the winter air with a fresh scent of hope. It was Christmas Eve, and the streets were still. There was no movement and no sign of human life except for the solitary candles burning in each home.

Charles Thurmanier opened the window of his children's upstairs bedroom, eyes downcast and face saddened. He turned his head to the left and right, hoping to find some evidence that things were not as bleak as they appeared. "Papa," one of his children called out.

"Yes, Francine," he answered, still gazing out into the streets below, trying to disguise his anxiety.

"Why are we in bed? Last year we didn't go to sleep until after church."

"Don't be foolish, Francine," her older brother, Philippe, interrupted. "I've already explained it to you. Don't bother Papa."

Charles turned, uncertain how to address his daughter's question. He glanced at his wife seated in the chair near their children's bedside.

She held a Bible in her hands. He looked closely to see if they trembled; they did not, not even now. How fortunate he was to have her.

Charles shut the window, lowered the curtains, and turned to his daughter. "This year, Francine, Saint Nicholas will be delivering to the children of France first. Then England. Then Germany. That is why you must go to bed so early."

"And Russia, Papa. Will he visit Russia?"

Francine's voice warmed him. He walked to his daughter, placed his hand on top her head, and gently kissed her cheek. "Yes, darling, even Russia."

"And America?" Philippe asked, raising his head from the pillow.

Charles smiled. "Yes, children. He visits any place where children live."

The children raised their bodies from the bed and smiled at their father and then at each other. Charles wished to share their innocence and eager anticipation of Christmas morning.

Charles kissed Philippe and walked outside the bedroom. He closed his eyes, breathed deeply, and attempted to control his fear as his wife began reading the narrative of Christ's birth to their son and daughter.

He walked downstairs and sat in a chair near the family's dinner table. Looking out the front window into the darkening streets, he wondered how different tomorrow could be.

He stood up and slowly walked toward the front door of their home. He opened it and looked in all directions. Two neighbors to his left and one to his right stood as he did. He smiled, hoping to express some sign of encouragement. They returned the gesture.

Charles was startled when someone laid a hand on his shoulder. His wife gently wrapped her arms around his chest, resting her head on his back. "The children are asleep," she said softly.

Charles looked into the darkening sky, hoping to find some relief. "Do you think they know?"

"The other children talk, Charles. Philippe's heard things from the other boys."

Charles braced his arms on the doorposts, releasing his wife's tight embrace.

"I'm staying up with you, Charles," she announced. "We will get through this together."

Though his back remained facing her, he felt his wife's stare. He turned, glanced down, and received a surge of strength, losing himself within her determined eyes.

"You make something to eat. I'll get things ready."

Charles walked to the wardrobe in the corner of their home and raised a floorboard. He reached inside, lifting out two flintlocks. Sitting a careful distance from the fireplace, he cleaned and loaded each one, also inspecting to make sure that the earlier light rain did not moisten the flints needed to trigger the gunpowder. Within four hours, they may be all that would stand between his family and death.

He finished cleaning the guns and walked to the front door. He opened it, looked out, closed the door, and walked back toward the guns. Pacing the floor, he mumbled and cursed. How could he have been so naive, thinking things were going so well? They had been, until months earlier when the king issued his latest edict.

Various scenarios, conflicting scenarios, competed for his attention. He could not focus on any. There were endless possibilities of what may happen, yet one frightened him more than any other.

He wanted more than anything to hear the voice of his father, ensuring that all would be fine and that he had nothing to fear.

His father, his grandfather, his great-grandfather, his great-great-grandfather—did any in his family have it easy? His eyes wandered his home, collecting the sights of his family history: the wall clock from Geneva, the leather-bound Bible from Germany, and the shelves his grandfather had made. Charles walked toward them, caressing the aged hickory. He closed his eyes and tried to imagine what advice his great-grandfather might have. Bending to the lowest shelf, he opened a large wooden chest and removed a thick pile of letters bound with a string. He held them gently, wondering why it had taken him so long to come back to these writings. Was he afraid of his ancestors' disapproval of what he was about to do?

It had been too long since he read his great-grandfather's journal. When he was a boy, the words served as a tale of great adventure and heroism; when he was a young man, they were a warning of betrayed trust. For a father with children, they would be the measure of his own faith.

Filled with anticipation, he yearned to read the words of his great-grandfather, but he was unable to untie the string holding the papers together, the knot stubbornly holding fast against his anxious fingers. Frustrated, he raised the manuscripts to his mouth and gnawed at the string until it broke and the papers fell to the floor. He reached down to pick up the top page. Barely legible and darkened with age, the writing was that of a child. Charles breathed deeply, his eyes widening as he read the words his great-grandfather had written over one hundred years earlier.

> Papa and Mama died two years ago. I'm still not sure why. The sisters tell me they meant well, but that I must not be what they had become. When I ask them what had my parents become that was so horrible, they tell me I'll understand when I get older.
>
> Sister Jeannette says writing my feelings might help me feel better. She says writing can be a friend to those without friends. I think Sister Jeannette's a little vacant upstairs. Why would writing about what makes me so sad make me happy?

Charles grinned. For a moment, the memory of his great-grandpapa eased his anxiety. In the midst of adversity, even as a child, he had found a humorous way to describe suffering. Charles picked up a large stack of papers strewn to his left and continued reading.

> It was August 24th, the year of our Lord 1572. The neighbors rushed into our homes and killed my papa, Augustine Thurmanier, and my mama. All our homes. It was St. Bartholomew's holiday. Each of us unsuspecting that it would come to something as drastic as this. There was our neighborhood, perishing in flames. Only embers evidence that our families once lived there. We were chased into the streets of Paris—our fathers dead, our mothers scrambling to protect their children.
>
> How many of my friends survived? I do not know. I was brought to the abbey at La Rochelle and have yet to recognize a face from my home. Still, so many children with whom I now share meals and with whom I fall asleep are orphaned for the same reason as I. They come from northern, central, southern, eastern, and western portions of our beloved country. All of us love our mother France. Why then did France take away our parents?

Charles looked up, damning the tears he felt building within his head. He stood up and lit another candle on the desk. Before sitting, he bent over and tried to organize the letters by date. He grabbed a handful of pages, stopping to read a section of an older, more mature writer.

> Who would have known that, after all that has happened, my father and the Queen Mother were good friends? I will not speak of such nonsense, afraid of what my colleagues would do. The very thought of the queen having a Huguenot as confidant would be deemed heresy.
>
> I've learned to hide my origin quite well. Sister Jeanette was correct in asserting that writing is good for the soul. But she failed to mention the economic benefits. A well-read

> youth that can write and do arithmetic is in high demand. The sisters helped me enter the university, and now the orphaned Huguenot is teaching history to Catholic children around Paris. Perhaps I am teaching children whose parents killed my own. I do not know, nor do I any longer hold my countrymen in hatred. If there is one thing in my studies of history that I have learned, it is this: that all societies, no matter how sophisticated, can be frightened into believing and therefore doing anything. Examples abound—Cain and Abel; Pharaoh and the Israelites; Herod's determination to kill the Christ child; the fall of the Roman Empire; the Crusades; St. Bartholomew's Day.
>
> I am convinced that only God can redeem us from our self-destructiveness. If I were to respond to my parents' murder with hatred, I would myself be entering that endless cycle of self-destruction. Hatred destroys; vengeance is never satisfied. But love ends all disputes. Forgiveness begins the healing.

Charles looked away. The guilt grew with each of his great-grandfather's written words. Forgiveness, love, unsatisfied vengeance—it was clear what his great-grandpapa would say of his plan.

The floor was still not clean of papers. He grabbed another handful, unable to keep himself from reading its contents.

> Papa had a cunning, sharp wit. I remember it well. He often made Mama and me laugh for hours on end with one of his stories. His ability was a coveted quality, I've come to learn, especially in those days within the affluence of Paris. The gift of laughter was precious, and he who could produce much of it was often invited back to share in royal suppers. He was Queen Catherine de' Medici's favorite and thereby frequented the palace, entertaining nobles and royalty.

The Queen Mother grew aware of my father's religious beliefs, yet she did not seem to mind. After all, she was a daughter of Florence, a great-granddaughter of Lorenzo de' Medici, the city leading Europe in discoveries and wealth. She was open-minded, at least when they first met.

There was a day, I remember Papa coming home from court with a sadness I had never seen. It was the day the Queen Mother, after years of pressure from Rome and France's Catholic nobility, gave in to their demands. It was St. Bartholomew's Day. In his arms, Papa carried a box. "A gift from the queen," he announced.

When I asked Papa what it was, he smiled and said, "A gift from a friend who is sorry."

"What do you mean, Papa?" I asked.

He clarified, "Forgive me, Son. It's from Florence. The queen received it from her mother who received it as a gift from the friars at St. Mark's almost eighty years ago." Papa walked to the box and opened it. "She'd often talk about how precious it was to her."

I knew there was something Papa was not telling me. I'm not sure if I would have understood, had he explained it to me then. But I know now that the queen's gift was a guilt offering. For it was that same night she allowed French citizens to murder their Protestant neighbors with the support of her soldiers.

I cannot hate our queen. In her defense, she was a puppet to the nobility, who was feeling threatened by our growing

> independence and wealth. We received a reprieve when Henry of Bourbon took the throne as King Henry IV. He did not take long to ensure our safety and rights via his Edict of Nantes.
>
> But it was not long after his death that Cardinal Richelieu began limiting our freedoms again. We will not surrender. They can plow us down until they feel they have accomplished their task, but our ashes will rise as testament to our God. It is He whom we worship; it is He for whom we work; it is He who will one day use our lives as a phoenix to those who come after us. They will reap the benefits of our losses. And we, with them, will rejoice together at the foot of His throne.

Charles closed his eyes and threw the stack of papers back to the floor. "I'm a failure, Father." His head sank. "But what else can we do?"

For years, he had searched for solutions, alternatives to fighting, and courses of action that his father, his grandfather, his great-grandpapa would endorse. He knew he was not following in their steps. But it was time for someone in his family, for someone in his church, to stand up for their rights.

He remembered sitting at his great-grandfather's feet alongside of elder and younger cousins, his grandfather seated to his great-grand papa's right, his father to his left, aunts and uncles seated and standing along the walls of his childhood home. His great-grandpapa was near death and had vowed Charles' grandfather to gather the family. Charles had heard the stories of his family prior to this gathering, but on this occasion, there was a message by which they must never stray. "Stay the course," he encouraged. "Follow the words of our Lord. Things will improve as years and generations pass."

Such was the message passed on by his grandfather prior to his death. And so it was when Charles's father died six years later.

But in Charles's mind, they were not progressing. One hundred years had passed, and still the Huguenots were ostracized, persecuted, and threatened.

Though Huguenot artisans and merchants were again thriving in French society and intellectuals were entertaining the royal court and securing positions at universities, as their wealth increased, so did their threat in the eyes of their fellow countrymen.

Charles was certain that this limited success was what convinced the grandson of Henry IV, King Louis XIV, to abolish the provisions made by his grandfather. No longer would the freedoms guaranteed by the French monarchy a century earlier be granted to French Protestants.

It was the common belief among Charles and his friends that an agreement had been made among the king and his advisors that another massacre, much like that on St. Bartholomew's Day, would soon be carried out. Since the worst massacre in their history occurred on a holy day, they feared what might be in the minds of their Catholic neighbors on the most celebrated day of the Christian calendar.

Charles shuddered, gripping the neck of one flintlock and wringing his hands around its cold metal. It was not his wish to shoot another Frenchman, only if it was necessary in defending his family. Once more, Charles shut his eyes and took deep breaths. He set the gun aside and walked to the fireplace mantle where he and his family had arranged the nativity pieces given to his great-great-grandfather, Augustine Thurmanier, by Queen Catherine.

Solemnly, he studied each piece, remembering what his father told him about the set, how it had been carved by a friar who witnessed the execution of Savonarola. How appropriate, Charles thought, that his family had come to own the wooden figurines. His family, like the great preacher, was at the mercy of those in power. The set of pieces was a constant reminder of choice—God's choice to come and dwell among man and man's choice to believe in God regardless of the cost.

Weeks prior to each Christmas, Charles would set aside minutes each day to spend in front of the wooden set, finding the expressions carved on the faces and the angles of heads tilted helpful in illustrating and teaching him of God's love. At times he would be drawn to the carving of Joseph, contemplating the fear he must have felt and questioning whether he was capable of raising his adopted son. Other days he studied Mary; a content gaze was crafted into her wooden face. Sometimes he studied a shepherd, sometimes a wise man, and sometimes the child. As his eyes canvassed the manger scene, he felt a sharp pain in his chest and his eyes grew wide. Two of the pieces were not on the mantle. Before he could begin looking for them, he heard a knock on the door.

In a daze, Charles walked across the front room and waited for a second knock.

"Charles," a voice whispered, "it's me, Anthony."

Charles opened the door slowly, verifying the identity of his brother-in-law. There were three men with him.

"Charles, we must talk," Anthony urged quietly.

Charles opened the door wider, eyeing the other men. They appeared harmless. He waved them inside.

Anthony pulled Charles aside, breathing heavily. "I know what you're thinking, Charles. You think I'm out of my mind bringing them."

Looking at the three other men, Charles immediately recognized one of them. "Samuel I know," he whispered, "from La Rochelle. But the other two I've never seen."

Anthony angled his body away from the others and whispered more softly. "Charles, you must listen to them. This whole idea of yours is insane. We cannot fight the French Army."

"We've been through this. I'll do what I must. Your sister is more determined than I. We will not let them destroy our family."

"Listen to me, Charles." Anthony grabbed hold of his shirt and moved closer. "These men met with the elders of La Rochelle. Samuel traveled here with them, knowing of our predicament. They have a plan."

Charles gently pushed Anthony aside to get a better look at the two strangers. One was tall, taller than any man he had seen, but thin.

He was dark-skinned and broad-shouldered. The other was short and ruddy and had rotting teeth. They were a peculiar couple, and Charles was curious to know how they came to be in each other's company, much less having devised a plan together.

He focused his attention back onto his brother-in-law. "You've searched them?"

"Yes, Charles," Anthony answered.

Charles looked sternly into the eyes of his wife's brother. "They have no weapons?"

Anthony leaned in close again. "If they meant us any harm, Charles, they'd have done some already. They've met with over a thousand Huguenots between here and La Rochelle."

Laying his hand on Anthony's shoulder, Charles whispered, "All right."

He approached Samuel and the two strangers. "Samuel, blessings. How are the brethren in La Rochelle?"

"As good as can be expected, Charles."

Samuel tilted his head, shrugging. "Charles, we're in desperate need of guidance. We're looking to you."

Charles embraced Samuel.

Samuel stepped back, extending his arm toward the two men Charles did not recognize. "This is Joshua," he announced, motioning to the shorter of the two. "And this is Kamal."

Charles folded his arms. "I understand you've a plan. It has something to do with the king's edict?"

Samuel moved closer to the two strangers. "It does."

"Please. Sit." Charles pulled out chairs from the table. "My wife is preparing supper. Are you hungry?"

"Perhaps some tea for everyone?" Anthony suggested.

Charles tilted his head toward the other end of the home. "Let Felicia know, Anthony. We've three guests."

Anthony left for the kitchen as Charles looked into Samuel's eyes and started, "Now, what's all this about?"

The three men looked at one another. Charles's curiosity grew, wondering what these men could say that would bring Pastor Samuel all the way from La Rochelle.

"Fighting is pointless," Samuel started, "We'll only see more bloodshed. We cannot afford another St. Bartholomew's Day."

Charles shifted his weight and tapped his foot under the table. He'd been through this discussion numerous times with numerous individuals. His patience was wearing. "With or without our fighting, there will be bloodshed, Samuel. Do you suggest we lie down, do nothing, and let them commit another massacre?"

"Jesus did teach, 'Turn the other cheek,'" Samuel said.

"No," Charles spoke in a soft, determined voice, lifting his body from the chair and leaning forward, "He said, 'When someone strikes you on the cheek, turn to him the other.' We have turned to our enemies the other cheek, not once, not twice, not three times, but countless times. We have no cheeks left to turn."

"May I?" Kamal, the taller stranger asked. He spoke in an eastern accent Charles recognized as *Indian.*

Samuel extended his arm, inviting him to proceed.

"*Wee* are not suggesting you allow another massacre to destroy *yoor* families. *Yoo* are correct; the spilling of more blood will not quench the royal family's thirst for political power. It will not end for a long while."

Charles furrowed his brow and sat back down. "What are you telling me? 'Yes, they'll keep pushing us; yes, they'll kill our men, imprison our wives, and make our children orphans, but fighting back is not the answer, nor is turning the other cheek'?"

The three men remained silent.

"Then what else are we to do?" Charles asked as his wife and Anthony emerged from the kitchen carrying cups of tea.

"We will leave, Charles," his wife announced.

Charles turned in his chair. "Nonsense! Leave France? Never!" He quickly turned his gaze on Anthony. "Is that what this is about? You want us to run away, leave, give them what they have wanted for the past two hundred years? A country free of those who refuse to bow to the pope? A country free of those who seek release for all men from the burdens placed upon them by Rome?"

Reaching his arm out to Samuel, Charles begged. "And you, Samuel. Of all men! What of our fathers? Did they die to see us retreat? Did they die in vain?"

No one answered. He felt betrayed and helpless. An emptiness entered his chest. "And where are we to go? To Germany, where Protestants are persecuted as much as our people in France? To England? The Anglican Church is as ardent as the Catholic here."

Still no one spoke.

"Even Switzerland," Charles continued, "and the Netherlands. Wherever we go, there will be men who hate us. We cannot escape."

The shorter guest cleared his throat.

"Yes, Joshua, you may speak," Samuel said.

"There is the other option," he announced. "Other than Europe."

Charles froze. Secretly, he had considered this possibility.

"You mean America?" Anthony shouted.

"Shh!" Felicia whispered. "The children are sleeping."

Emotionally, Charles embraced the idea, but logically this could not be done. It would cost too much, and not everybody in the congregation would agree. It was true; many could be talked into moving to Switzerland or Germany. But America?

"Why me?" Charles asked quietly. "Why come to me?"

Samuel leaned forward. "Brethren throughout France look to you for guidance, Charles. Your family is well respected. You take this step, and thousands will follow."

Charles felt his shoulders droop. He motioned toward the two strangers. "And you, this was your idea?"

"They came to me asking for you, Charles," Samuel answered. "For you. They wanted to speak to you. In all the villages between La Rochelle and Paris, they ask for you, to convince you that leading our people across the Atlantic is our best hope. We need you, Charles."

Felicia walked to her husband and placed her hands on his shoulders. "I think you should all go. Charles is weak. He needs his rest. Time to think."

Anthony clasped his hands together and whispered urgently, "This isn't something that we can think about, Felicia. We must decide—now!"

Charles looked at his wife. The determined stare he saw an hour earlier was more intense. He knew what she wanted.

Samuel stood up, whispered to Joshua and Kamal and led them outside. "Monsieur and Madame Thurmanier," Samuel said as he held the door open, "we are sorry to have disrupted your holiday. We understand the enormity of what we are asking. But, Charles, you must consider how few options we have. We will return in the morning."

Anthony followed them to the door.

"Gentlemen," Charles announced as he stood, "if there is a morning, I'll have an answer for you when you arrive."

"I'll be outside for just a minute," Anthony said before walking the three men to their horses.

"Felicia—" Charles started.

"Don't speak, Charles. Sit down."

"Listen to me," he ordered as he raced toward the fireplace. "Come here."

"What is it? What's wrong?"

Charles's eyes watered as he picked up one of the manger pieces from the mantle and handed it to Felicia. "When I was a child, Grandpapa told me a story about his father's childhood, when the massacre occurred."

Charles read the confusion in her eyes.

"I know all this, Charles," she said, "you've told the children—"

Charles started again. "It's the crèche, Felicia."

He went to the floor where papers from his great-grandfather's journal were still strewn. Collecting them all, he blew out a candle and placed the candlestick on top of the papers to hold them down. "The night my great-grandfather's parents were killed, the house was burned. Somehow it survived.

"The following Christmas, he realized three pieces were missing. He wandered outside the orphanage looking for them and ran into three strangers with whom he spent the entire day. The sisters at the abbey thought he had run away or gotten hurt, but when he returned that evening, he explained to the nuns that he had met three men who described to him the first Christmas.

"The nuns, of course, did not believe him. They dismissed his story as the imagination of a lonely child. But that next morning, the nuns found the three missing pieces of the nativity outside on the porch."

Felicia put the nativity piece she held, back in its position on the mantle. She turned toward Charles and ran her hands over her hair. "What are you saying, Charles?"

Just then Anthony reentered. In his hand he held two objects. "Well, Charles, what do you think? It beats fighting the French Army."

"What are those?" Charles asked, pointing to the two objects Anthony held.

"Excuse me?"

Charles trembled. "In your hand? What are those?"

"Just a couple of carvings. Kamal handed them to me just before they left. Funny thing is, they remind—"

Charles grabbed the two wooden figurines from Anthony's hand and turned, holding them out for his wife to see.

"Just before the four of you arrived," Charles said, "I discovered these two pieces missing."

"Kamal must have found them outside." Anthony shrugged and sat near the dinner table. "The children must have been playing with them. Left them out in the garden."

"No, no," Charles muttered. "I've been preoccupied. I haven't looked at the crèche since Philippe and Francine set it up two weeks ago. I'm sure they've been missing that long, enough time for them to travel to La Rochelle."

"Enough time for them to what?" Anthony asked.

"Shh!" Felicia silenced her brother as Charles turned toward the mantle and placed the two pieces near the manger.

"Charles," Felicia asked, "what does this all mean? What are you trying to tell us?"

"Mean?" he repeated. "It means we are going to America."

Exodus

Margaret Thurman Smith prayed. She prayed with her eyes shut and pressed hard, her hands gripping the pew in front of her tightly. What she prayed was a mystery to her nine-year-old daughter sitting quietly beside her in the pew at the Christmas Eve service at First Baptist Church of Baltimore. She stared with open eyes at her mother as the congregation prayed silently. During the war, when her father was overseas, she understood why her mother had spent so much time here. But even after V-J Day, after her father's safe return, Katie would arrive home from school and inadvertently disturb her mother kneeling by her bedside, her lips moving without making a sound.

A war, Katie understood, had kept her father far away. But what she could not understand was why her mother spent so much time praying once the war had ended.

The silence in the church continued, and Katie still studied her mother and tried to understand how she could stay in this position so long. Katie had previously tried to emulate her mother at church or at home, but it was no use. There was always something—an object, a sound, or a thought—that disrupted her concentration.

As the Christmas Eve service neared its end, Katie thought of the candy and toys she hoped to discover under the family Christmas tree. She tried to pray, but her mind could focus only on the sandy-blonde doll, almost a foot tall, that her father had promised. Katie was nine; she understood how the gift-giving process worked while her father was overseas—instead of writing Santa a letter, she pleaded with her mommy. Now that her father was home, she'd plead with him too.

As she dreamed of cradling the doll, the choir bellowed the opening words of "O Come All Ye Faithful." Katie followed her mother's movements, grabbing a hymnal that rested in a rack attached to the pew in front of her. The melody grabbed her attention. The looks on the faces of her mother and the others around her suggested the song was special. Her smile grew, and her anticipation heightened as she sensed the end of the service.

Finally, it was over. The pastor offered the benediction. Her mother remained motionless for thirty seconds, her head bowed. Katie counted the seconds as though she had been betrayed. They were sure to be the last ones out the church doors.

A light snow fell as Katie and her mother walked the half mile back to their home. She grasped her mother's hand and skipped until she had to stop. Her mother could not keep up.

Since Katie's father had returned from the Pacific, her mother gradually became less lively. Though they had raced home on occasions, Katie could tell her mother was not in the mood to play. Sure, she was humming the melodies of the carols sung minutes earlier, but her eyes seemed distant.

Warming herself against her mother's side, Katie's excitement grew as they neared their neighborhood.

When they arrived home, the house was dark. Katie suspected her father had turned down the lights to surprise her with an early Christmas present. The family tradition was for each of them to open one present on Christmas Eve. She hoped that the present she chose to open would be the doll. That way, she could sleep with it on the most exciting evening of the year.

Her mother flipped the switch next to the front door, but there was no light. She told Katie to stay at the door until she could find a light that worked. Katie heard her mother bump into objects in the kitchen, as though the floor was strewn with pots and pans.

Once the kitchen was lit, Katie could see the living room in disarray: chairs on their sides, a broken lamp, and several empty beer bottles.

"Katie, go to your room, Sweetie. I'll be there in a minute."

This was not right, Katie thought. Had they been robbed? This was Christmas Eve, the happiest day of the year. Katie did not want to know what was wrong; she just wanted to go back outside, open the front door again, and hope that the house this time would be in order and that everything was all right.

Katie walked slowly to her bedroom, maneuvering past the objects on the floor. While pulling her pajamas' top over her head, she heard an object crash against her parents' bedroom wall and the dull thumping of flesh against flesh echo through the hallway.

At first, Katie placed her hands over her ears. But as the sounds grew louder, she rushed out of her bedroom and into the hallway where she found her mother kneeling. When Katie inched closer, she noticed that her mother was crying. She froze. Her mother's right eye was swollen, blood trickling from some broken skin just beneath it.

The commotion and arguing, as well as the loud crashes, were common occurrences once her father had returned from the war. But her mother always explained it hours later: "Your father is clumsy. He dropped a plate, a book, a radio, the iron on the floor." At first, Katie wondered how the objects her father broke were repaired so quickly when she saw them unscathed the next day.

Eventually, Katie's innocence gave way to awareness. She told herself that all her mother suffered must be normal. Otherwise, how could her mother be so happy and loving? She chose not to ask her classmates at school whether they too experienced what she did at home, fearful that her theory might be wrong.

As Katie stared at her mother, her father stumbled out of the bedroom, stepped over his wife, yanked Katie by the arm, and pulled her back into his room.

"Mama," Katie screamed as her father slammed the bedroom door and threw Katie on the floor. Katie wrapped her arms around her head, unsure of what was happening. She looked up; his eyes were wild and red. A mist seemed to cover his face. She shrunk back as he inched closer. He grinned, offering Katie some hope that she was safe. Katie jerked her head toward the bedroom door. It shook but would not give way to her mother's efforts. Katie closed her eyes, waiting and hoping this was not happening. All she wanted was to see her doll and hold her mother.

Her mother banged and kicked the door, screaming, "Don't hurt her. Please, don't hurt Katie."

Katie opened her eyes. Her father's grin erupted into laughter. He leaped forward and grabbed Katie by the ankles. Terrified, she recoiled as his cold grasp gripped both her arms. As she turned in disgust at his terrible breath, he raised his hand high and slapped her across the face.

"The doll," she heard him say. "A ten-dollar doll. Is that all my sweet little Katie wants for Christmas?"

Katie touched her right cheek, feeling the blood trickle. As her father raised his hand again, Katie leapt on her parents' bed, tumbled across, and raced toward the door. Her father rose, tripped on one of the bed legs, and struck his head against the bureau.

Now what? Was she safe? Was he okay? Should she try to help him?

She walked carefully to his side and reached toward the large gash on his forehead. He rolled over, smiled, and belched. "Your stupid little doll," he rasped. "A stupid little doll for my sweet Katie."

He belched again, looked into Katie's eyes, and laughed. "It's always been somethin' round this house. Ya all be the death o' me. First your mother, then our little angel, the war, now the dolly. Can't a man have any peace?"

She looked in fear as her father closed his eyes. She placed her hand in front of his mouth. His warm breath sent shivers through her body. Shaking, she got up, opened the door, and crept back, bracing herself against the wall until she got to her room. There, like she had seen so many times, her mother knelt.

Now she understood.

Her father's stupor gave Katie and her mother the time to pack their necessities and leave. By the kitchen's light, Katie's mother instructed her to lay her suitcase at the front door and help with something in the living room. Katie followed her to the Christmas tree. Beside it was an empty hatbox from Gimbels.

Her mother knelt beside the table on which she had arranged the family's nativity. She carefully placed the figures into the box, wrapping each in its own protective tissue. Katie breathed deeply. She knew some of the history of the set and that it held a special meaning for her mother's family; how far back, even her mother was not certain. Each piece was noticeably aged, but they were intact and had no breaks and few scratches.

Katie felt her heart race. She looked toward her parents' bedroom. What if he awoke? Why was her mother, in the midst of all that was happening, going out of her way to pack this family heirloom? Other than their two suitcases, this hatbox was the only luggage they would carry.

Her mother finished placing the figures in the box. Katie looked up, hoping her mother was finished. Once she placed the lid back on top of the box, Katie's mother jumped to her feet, grabbed her suitcase with one hand, braced the Gimbels box underneath her arm, and led Katie out into the darkened Baltimore streets.

Twelve hours later, Katie and her mother were resting, well-fed guests at a countryside inn in northern Virginia. The light snow from the evening before had produced a white Christmas. Katie could tell her mother was doing all she could to brighten her spirits. At the inn's gift shop, she bought Katie so much candy that Katie felt she would never have a need to ask for sweets again for the rest of her life. After handing the bag of candy to Katie, her mother guided her toward the shop's exit. Katie looked through the bag, grateful for the candy, but disappointed that she would not be opening a box with a doll resting inside. She stopped at the book display next to the door and looked up. She pointed excitedly, "Look, Mama!"

"What? What is it, Sweetie?"

"That book. I want it. Please!" Katie begged.

"Which book, Katie?"

"That one!" Katie moved closer to the stand as she touched the front cover, "*A Doll's House*!" she exclaimed. "Please, Mama, please!"

"But Katie. This is for adults, not children. You're not old enough." Her mother stopped as Katie lowered her eyes.

Her mother purchased the book and wrote inside the cover:

> *To my Katie:*
> *Within a year, you will have your doll.*
> *Within a year, we will have started a new life. God bless you.*
> *Love,*
> *Mama*

Katie sat beside the window of their room that evening, watching the falling snow. On the table next to her was the nativity scene. Katie turned her attention from the snow to the crèche, studying it. "Mama," she called out.

"Yes, Sweetie," her mother answered from the bathroom.

"The manger set. Why is it so special?"

"Special?" her mother repeated.

"Last night. You went out of your way to bring it with us. Why?"

Her mother stepped out of the bathroom. Katie grinned as she reached to pick up the Virgin Mary.

Her mother placed the towel she held on a nightstand and walked to Katie. Picking up a brush, she lifted Katie's thick hair and brushed it gently.

"I've told you many times, Katie."

Katie reached back and held her mother's hand. She turned, looking straight into her eyes. "But Mama, if it's as special as you say, you must never get tired of telling me."

She grinned, beginning the narrative with their ancestor, Charles Thurmanier, leading his family and others to America in the late seventeenth century.

Katie cherished the stories, losing herself in the drama, playing with the figures as though they were dolls, and listening to her mother recount those in their family who had faced potential catastrophes and survived. There were farmers threatened with foreclosure, clergymen accused during the Salem witch trials, landowners who had freed their slaves and fought for the freedom of others slaves, and businessmen attacked by their competitors. And there was her mother, who at fifteen had lost her parents and five siblings in a boating accident off the New England coast. All the stories were inspiring; all attested to the family's resilience, fortitude, and faith.

Her mother's soothing voice and the gentle motion with which she brushed her hair helped Katie fall into a peaceful slumber.

Promised Land

Katie's mother kept the promise she had written on the inside cover of Ibsen's novel. The next morning, she and Katie started their new life. They boarded a train for California, leaving their past and her married name behind forever.

The following Christmas, Katie received the doll she had wanted. After a month of dressing it, feeding it, putting it to bed, and rocking it to sleep, Katie grew bored. Playing with a doll did not make her as happy as she thought. Instead, she was homesick, half wishing that she and her mother could move back home, but knew that was not possible.

Her mother got a job cleaning homes and eventually found full-time office work. As those first two years in California passed, Katie wondered whether her mother was happy and whether she too thought of returning to Maryland.

She sensed that finding a replacement for her father was not a priority for her mother. It was nice coming home after school to an empty house, having full reign, before going outside to play with the other kids in the neighborhood. Katie had more chores than her friends and classmates and always was the last outside. While the other kids spent most of their free time playing, Katie shopped, cooked, cleaned the house, and watered the lawn, anticipating how pleased and relieved her mother would be after a full day's work.

"Katie," her mother begged, "play with the other children. You're young. Enjoy yourself."

Katie was unsure how to respond. Didn't her mother realize this is how she wanted to spend her free time?

"It's not that I'm not grateful," her mother would add, "but I want to see you happy."

"But, Mama, I am happy." Katie paused, unsure how to say what she felt.

"What is it, Sweetie?"

"The other kids."

"Yes. What about the other children?"

Katie kicked the floor. "They bore me, Mama." She looked up, hoping she had not disappointed her mother.

"I don't understand."

"They talk about Superman, comic books, TV shows, movies, cartoons, who likes whom, and what candy bar each of us likes best."

"But you have fun. I've seen you playing with them. My goodness, Katie, you're better than all the boys, even those who are older. You hit the ball farther, throw it harder, and run faster."

Katie stood silent, smiling inside at the words she heard. None of the kids told her how good she was; maybe they were jealous. After her first week playing with them, she began to be picked first, before any of the boys. That her mother recognized her talent confirmed what Katie felt.

Still, her mother did not seem satisfied. She looked down at Katie, making her feel uncomfortable. "Don't you have fun with the other children?"

Katie lifted her shoulders, bit her lip, and tried hard not to divulge the truth to her mother, afraid of how she might respond. "I guess so," she answered.

"Then how can you say you're bored?"

Katie kicked the ground again, hoping her mother would grow impatient and give up the inquisition. But it was too late. Looking up into her mother's eyes, she saw a curiosity that would not be appeased. "I can't talk to them, Mama. I mean, about the books I read. I've tried.

I listen to them jabber about, 'Oh, how cute this boy is,' or 'Isn't that horrible about Little Orphan Annie?'"

Katie stopped. She noticed a strange look on her mother's face. It was not an expression of disappointment but of pride. It encouraged Katie to continue.

"But when I try to ask them what they think about one of the books I'm reading, they shrug their shoulders, laugh, and say, 'How should I know?' They've never heard of the books; don't know they exist. They don't know the writers or the history behind them. They don't even seem to care that they don't know."

"Have you tried talking with your teachers?"

Katie looked up at her mother with surprise. "About the other kids?"

"No, Sweetie. About the books."

Katie was confused.

"I'm sure they'd enjoy talking with you." She paused, placing her hand gently atop Katie's head. "You can talk with me too."

Why hadn't she thought about that? Of course her teachers would like to talk with one of their students about something more interesting than the mundane information they teach daily. But her mother? Tell her mother about the ideas that had been racing through her head for the five years since they had settled in Southern California?

Never.

The gift Katie received from her mother on the Christmas day in northern Virginia had started it all. Initially, Katie accepted the book with joy, feeling triumph and surprise when her mother agreed to purchase *A Doll's House* for her.

During the following year, Katie kept the book on her dresser in their apartment in Fullerton, California. Her mother's written promise inside the front cover was a constant reminder that she would receive the doll for which she yearned by the next Christmas. After receiving the doll, Katie still read the message regularly, finding comfort in the fact that she and her mother had begun a new, peaceful life on their own.

As Katie approached her eleventh birthday, she ventured past that page and began to read the words of Henrik Ibsen. Although there was much she could not understand, the words enticed her. She read and reread Ibsen's work, trying hard to understand the point he was making. She concluded that Ibsen's characters had relevance to her and her mother.

If the play's main character, Nora Helmer, had reason to leave her husband and children, then Katie felt her mother had a greater reason. Katie came to revere Nora as a role model, as much as she did her own mother. Nora's motivation to depart stemmed from her desire to discover herself, regardless of society's guidelines; Katie felt her mother's motivation was to protect the two of them from further physical harm.

The new life she and her mother enjoyed was not a result of her mother's faithful prayers, but a consequence of her mother's courage in leaving their home. Likewise, Nora had to muster enough courage to leave her husband in *A Doll's House*. Katie concluded that human efforts are tangible and effective but that, with God and religion, nothing was tangible and nothing was effective.

The set of nativity figurines also came to hold a special place in Katie Thurman's life. Following college, marriage, and the birth of her first child, she received it from her mother as a Christmas present. Katie had been taught its history and the legends surrounding it but kept her children from learning it's fabled past, knowing they'd learn enough from their grandmother. The crèche was a paradox for Katie: it symbolized the courageousness of her mother and the uselessness of religious faith. For it was on that Christmas Eve of 1947 that Margaret Thurman had boldly left her abusive husband; but it was also the evening on which Katie had discovered her mother kneeling in prayer to a God too busy or too weak to rescue them from an abusive home.

Table Talk

The school yard's large grass field was still moist from the light morning rain. A rich scent of newly cut blades surrounded him as he shuffled his feet, kicking clumps left by the John Deere mower just hours earlier. Reaching inside his backpack, he took out his graded spelling test, stopped to confirm the words he missed, lowered his head, and slipped it back inside.

"A B isn't bad," his friends consoled, but try telling that to his parents. Sure, they'd appear satisfied and pleased that their only son was above average, but he knew what they really wanted. He saw it each time one of his two sisters brought home their tests and papers from school.

In thirty minutes, his friends in the neighborhood would meet for the afternoon's football game in the cul-de-sac across the street from his home. That did not leave enough time to complete his assignments due the next day. Biting his lip, he sighed and lowered his head further. Why did he stress over homework and grades? Why couldn't he just have fun when playing at recess or with his friends after school? When he caught a touchdown pass, instead of celebrating, he thought, "I should be studying for that history exam tomorrow." Upon getting a base hit, he rested on the bag for a couple seconds before taking inventory on the list of assignments to be completed that evening. And when he slid safely into home plate, he anticipated the drama to unfold at the supper table, fairly certain that once again he would have little to contribute to the family dialogue.

But, for the last five evenings, he had a plan. He had written an outline on a three-by-five index card and placed it in his right front pocket each night before racing downstairs for supper. It had to be implemented at the perfect moment. He knew his sisters' tendencies, the topics they most discussed, and the lines of reasoning they most utilized. So he waited.

The outline on the card was based on the report he had just turned in on President Richard Nixon. It would be two to three weeks before he received the graded report from his teacher, but he was sure this time he earned an A.

Such certainty was rare. Just yesterday he got a B on the math test; today it was the spelling test; last week it was the B on his science quiz. "Just a little better than Charlie Brown," he muttered. "I'm doomed to mediocrity."

His eldest sister, Carolyn, frequently rebuked him for moping. "Carter," she'd say, "you don't realize how fortunate you are. Stop feeling sorry for yourself and just do it."

With reluctance, he took a deep breath, raised his head, and began a slow jog through the schoolyard toward the street leading to his home.

The spring weather was mild. A cool breeze from the nearby Pacific carried with it the subtle fragrances of Southern California's budding jasmines and gardenias. He smiled. The scents reminded him that a new baseball season had begun just one month earlier; that meant six months remained.

He walked through the front door of his house. "Mom," he called out, but there was no reply. He looked to the table, and a snack was set out for him—two graham crackers, a couple apple slices, and a tall glass of orange juice. Next to the plate was a note, explaining that his mother went to the supermarket to get some ingredients for dinner and that he could go outside to play.

"Carolyn!" he shouted, to see if his eldest sister was home.

There was no answer.

"Shannon!" he shouted once more.

Again, no answer.

Sitting at the table, he pulled another of the chairs closer to him and kicked his feet on top of it, reclining as he ate his apples and crackers.

He couldn't rest too long; his friends expected him to be outside shortly. He glanced at his mom's note, confirming that she had given him permission to go outside once he had finished his snack.

He ran upstairs, changed his shoes, and walked to the nightstand next to his bed. He opened the drawer and took out the note card on which he had written the outline of Nixon's life. He looked at the clock on the other side of the bedroom wall and sat on the edge of the bed. There were still fifteen minutes before his friends would meet in the cul-de-sac.

He had memorized most of what was written on the front side of the card: Nixon's birth in Yorba Linda, his education at Whittier College and Duke University, his early law career, his service in the war, his marriage to Pat Ryan, and his quick rise in political life from representative to senator to vice president.

Carter swung his feet onto the bed, grabbed a pillow and placed it behind his head, bracing it against the bed's headboard. He turned the card to study Nixon's loss to Kennedy, his failed attempt to become governor of California, and his subsequent retreat from political life.

Carter lifted his eyes from the card and raised his nose, confirming that his mother must have done her thorough house cleaning. The smells around the house were always pleasing. He had spent lots of time in the homes of his friends and quickly learned how fortunate he was. He wasn't sure of the reason—whether it was the handmade furniture crafted by his father, the lemon-scented carpet freshener, the furniture polish that his mother used to clean, or that his family had no pets—but it was a fact that his house was cleaner and smelled better than any other in the neighborhood. Why else would his friends agree to play indoor games or get a snack at his house rather than any of their own? "We'll watch the game at your house, Carter," they would unanimously decide. "There's more room there."

Content to know that his home and the atmosphere inside, more than any other in the neighborhood, was the most coveted, Carter sighed and closed his eyes. He took another deep breath, anticipating aromas soon to be created by his mother's cooking.

Carter's mother never used a written recipe. He had never seen a cookbook in their home. He wasn't sure whether she had memorized the recipes earlier in life or whether she created the meals using her imagination and common sense. Even when she made a dish similar to one the family had previously eaten, it would never taste the same, only better. So Carter believed it to be her creativity that made the meals so good.

"Your parents are so . . ." one of his friends would start to say and then, following a pause, continue their thought: "Different . . . talented . . . strange . . . smart . . ." Whatever word they chose, it made no difference. He knew what they meant because he felt the same.

Carter tilted his head, burying it into his pillow. He felt the index card in his left hand and rolled onto his side, making sure to keep it within his grasp. Though he had yet to memorize most of the notes on the back, he needed rest before playing outside with his friends.

Anticipating what meal his mother may prepare, he smiled and buried his head further into the pillow. His thoughts turned to his father. The mahogany furniture around the house was all handcrafted by his dad. Within the dining room, there was the supper table along with its eight chairs. He had made the writing desk in the den for Carter's mother, the cabinet that held the television, the six-foot bureau full of family pictures next to the front door, and the set of bookshelves in the library. Each evening he and his sisters enthusiastically vacated the supper table, rushing to the library's tall doors. Carolyn would dig into her pocket, searching for the key, and after turning the knob, swing the doors open. The three would rush inside and open the book they were currently reading.

By the time Carter's imagination migrated to the worlds created by his favorite writers, he had fallen asleep.

"Carter," he heard a whisper.

He opened his eyes. Shannon was leaning over him, smiling, and ready to poke him in the chest. Carter held out his hands. "Don't," he whimpered. "What time is it?"

"Five thirty," she answered.

"Stink," Carter pushed his head off the pillow. "I missed the game." He rubbed his eyes, stretching his arms and letting out a long yawn.

"What's that?" Shannon asked, pointing at the card still held between the fingers of Carter's left hand.

"A report."

"Really?" She appeared curious, and though she didn't press on with questions as she often did, she narrowed her eyes and glanced down at Carter and then at the card. "Hmm," she continued, "dinner in five minutes."

Carter slowly moved his legs from off the bed, dangling them over the edge. "Thanks."

It smelled delicious downstairs. He placed the card into his right pocket and walked to the staircase.

As he descended the stairs, he noticed a bright reflection from the glass-encased bureau next to the library. He looked behind; the setting sun was entering the window above the stairwell and hitting the glass at just the right angle to cause the bright glare. He walked to the bureau and looked at the pictures of his parents when they were younger and the few black-and-white photographs of his paternal grandparents and maternal grandmother. There were framed newspaper clippings of his father crossing finish lines, alongside of ribbons, trophies, and medals. On the shelf just above rested his mother's trophies earned as the most valuable player on her college softball team.

On the very top shelf were three pictures of his parents' wedding day. In one of these pictures, Carter's father embraced his bride, his slim stature rising slightly higher than hers. Carter's mother was radiant in all three pictures: wide hazel-blue eyes; thick, black hair rolled into a bun under her veil; and gleaming teeth encased by cherry lips. There was a joy about her, captured in the pictures, as she fixed her eyes upon her husband. As handsome as he may have been, Carter's father showed few signs of reciprocation. It seemed to be just another life event. He was content. As Carter's sisters would say, "That's just Dad."

Next to the bureau, nailed onto the wall, were hung his parents' college degrees. Although he had yet to understand all the words, he dreamed of seeing his name in place of his father's:

> *The Board of Trustees of Boston University upon the recommendation of the Faculty, hereby confers upon*
>
> *Douglas Anthony Mason the degree of Bachelor of Arts in*
>
> *Civil Engineering with all the rights, privileges and honors thereto appertaining.*
>
> *Given under the seal of the University at Boston, Massachusetts this seventh day of May in the Year of our Lord one thousand nine hundred and sixty.*

To the right was his mother's diploma:

> *Radcliffe College and its Board of Trustees recognize the completion of requirements and confer upon*
>
> *Katherine Melody Thurman the degree of Bachelor of Arts in Western Literature.*
>
> *Given under the seal of Harvard University at Boston, Massachusetts this twelfth day of June in the Year of our Lord one thousand nine hundred and fifty-nine.*

Carter often heard Carolyn question their mother in regard to her choice of profession. According to his eldest sister, their mother was overqualified. Being a housewife was wasting her skills, her intellect, and her prestigious education. She could utilize these skills as an educator, or a business executive, or an orator of sorts, but to limit oneself to the status of housewife was incomprehensible.

He could not understand this sentiment. It made him aware that his mother had other options, and he therefore made it a point to thank God each night for his mother's choice of profession. Besides, she wasn't wasting all her talents. "She's gone back to school," Carter once countered, "to get a master's degree in literature."

"We'll see, Cart," he recalled Carolyn saying. "Being a mom is a full-time job." She paused, grinning, "When she's the mother of Carter."

Carter walked to the dining room; only Shannon was there, placing the silverware around the table. "Need help?" he asked.

Shannon held out her fist wrapped around three knives and forks. Carter took them from her and began placing them in the vacant spots.

"You have the card with you?" Shannon asked.

Carter looked up.

"I was once in your shoes, Carter," she said. "You understand?"

Carter shrugged.

He placed the last fork and knife he held and looked down, ashamed that he was not able to conceal his plan from all in his family.

"Don't stress it," she continued. "The others don't know. Okay?"

He looked at Shannon, and that feeling reappeared, that feeling of shame and inadequacy that he didn't belong in this family. He reached down toward one of the legs of the supper table and ran his fingertips across the surface of the carving made by his father. On each leg was etched the scene from an American novel. It was a gift his father had given to his mother on their tenth wedding anniversary. The left front leg, at which Carter stood, portrayed Captain Ahab harpooning the great whale Moby Dick. The right front leg showed an old man with a long beard asleep. On the third leg, his father had etched the profiles of a Native American man and a woman of European decent. The fourth leg was a scene of a boy steering a river raft.

His father emerged from the kitchen, pushing the swinging door and carrying a plate of dinner rolls. He placed them on the table, looked at Shannon, and jerked his head toward the kitchen, signaling her to join her sister and mother.

Shannon patted Carter on the back, rubbed his head, and ruffled his hair. "Say 'Hi' for me," she instructed as she skipped into the kitchen.

His father walked around the table and sat in his chair on the far end facing the kitchen door. Carter sat next to him, on his left.

They bowed their heads.

"Our Father in heaven," his father began, "thank you for your blessings—for life, for all you provide, for our health, for our family. Thank you for the nation in which we live. Thank you for the schools we attend and the lessons we learn. Help us to be obedient and live the way you want. Amen."

"Amen," Carter echoed. He peeked from his left eye, noticing the kitchen door slightly open, Shannon's eyes meeting his.

She pushed the door and entered with the main entrée, chicken cordon bleu. Carolyn followed close behind with a bowl of white rice. Shannon sat next to Carter, on his left; Carolyn, across from Carter, to her father's right. Finally, their mother entered, carrying a bowl of mixed carrots, peas, and green beans.

"So," his father began, "anything interesting being taught in our schools today?"

Carter looked at Carolyn, assuming the normal routine to occur. "We're studying the colonies," she announced.

Listening attentively, Carter hoped to find an inviting avenue into which he could enter the dialogue and utilize the preparations he had made. He reached inside his pocket and placed the index card under his right thigh.

Carolyn continued: "Mrs. Jackson asks us, 'Why were only one-third of the colonists in favor of rebelling against the king? Why not two-thirds? Why not one hundred percent?' I answered, 'It's because you either want freedom or you don't. Some people want no change, because they are content with the status quo. It's the same as today.'"

Carter glanced between his parents and Shannon; they all seemed in agreement. He understood most of what she said because he had heard Carolyn previously use these words, and asked Shannon to explain them to him. It seemed Carolyn was moving in the direction for which he was waiting the past five days. He reached under his leg, verifying the card was still there.

"The colonists were divided into roughly three equal groups of dissenting opinions," Carolyn continued. "One group, the Tories, remained loyal to the crown. The second group was made up of those who wished to rebel against the king and no longer remain colonies. And the third group was comprised of those who felt comfortable enough not to complain, unless of course they were convinced that there was something to complain about. And it dawned on me—nothing has changed. It's no different today. The groups are called by different names, but it's the same old game. Today, you have three basic groups, just like the colonies did."

Carter studied his parents. They seemed pleased with Carolyn's reasoning. But somewhere she lost him. He wasn't sure what she was talking about or how he could enter the discussion.

"Go on," their father invited.

"They may not be of the same proportional size as they were back then, but the principles are the same. What I'm trying to say is that the Republicans are the Tories of today, the party of tradition, the party to bring back the good ol' days—prayer in schools, more discipline in the classroom, more morals in the Capitol, less government control of the economy. Sort of like you, Dad.

"The Democrats, however, are today's rebels. They fight for social change, for civil rights, for the rights of women and minorities, for protecting the environment, to get the government out of the bedroom. Sort of like you, Mom."

Carter raised his eyes, hope reappearing. Carolyn had just spit out some of her key rhetoric, words upon which Carter could capitalize if he decided to participate in tonight's dialogue.

She continued, "Then there are the rest of the people who are unsure of what side to take. The Tories' job two hundred years ago was to convince colonists who were in this third group that their lives would be better under the British Crown; the rebels, that life would be better without it. Today it's the same. The two parties find themselves trying to convince Americans that if they agree with their particular stance on an issue, then their lives will be better."

"Time out!" Shannon held out her hands, forming a T. "Let me see if I understand this. Carolyn compares Dad to a Tory, a current-day Republican, based upon the assumption I presume that Dad prefers the government to stay out of the way. Out of the way of what? is my question."

"Well, Carolyn?" their father invited.

"Business, of course," she answered. "Dad and his friends want the government to have no business in their business!"

"All right then," Shannon continued. "The Republicans of today want government out of our business lives. Then Carolyn goes on to describe Mom as a Democrat based partly upon her belief that the government should stay out of our private lives. Therefore, in both political parties, as well as both our parents, we have a paradox, a hypocrisy really. On one hand the Republicans want the government out of business and into the realm of controlling the moral fiber in our schools, in our cities, and in our homes; the Democrats want the government involved in business but to have no control over an individual's choices."

Carter narrowed his eyes, studying Shannon. He could not believe what he was hearing. He couldn't have prepared a more perfect script. He had to enter the discussion soon, before it changed course.

"And to what do you attribute this hypocrisy?" Carolyn asked.

"Human nature, I suppose," Shannon answered. "Everyone is looking out for number one. They'll vote whatever serves their interest best—Democrat or Republican."

Carter raised his hand.

Shannon stopped speaking.

From across the table, Carolyn stared at him with disapproving eyes.

Carter braced his risen right arm with his left arm, cupping his left hand underneath the right elbow, increasing the height of his right hand.

"Carter, Honey," his mother started, "I've told you, there's no need to raise your hand."

"Sorry." Carter reached under his leg, grasped the card in his right palm, and glanced at it briefly.

"So what do you have to say, Son?" his father asked.

Carter looked up. "Nixon," he began. He looked back down at the card. "Nixon is a Republican."

There was no response from anyone. Just looking at Carolyn increased his anxiety; so again, he looked back down at the card.

"He's a Republican, yet as a senator, he voted numerous times in favor of civil rights legislation."

This time, when he glanced across at Carolyn, she appeared interested.

He continued. "And as vice president, where he served as president of the Senate, he utilized the filibuster in order to increase the passage of Eisenhower's civil rights bill in 1957."

Shannon patted him on his left knee and gave him a thumbs-up underneath the table.

"Even after he became president, he fought to pull troops from Vietnam; he increased government aid for individuals, increased welfare assistance, decreased defense spending, established the EPA and OSHA, endorsed the Equal Rights Amendment, and fought tirelessly for integration of public education. He even said that racism was the greatest failure in our nation's history."

Carolyn cleared her throat. "What's your point, Cart?"

"You mean, I didn't make any sense?"

"All these facts you have written on your card, what do they mean? What are you trying to tell us?"

"Your sister—" his mother began.

Carter held up his hand. "Nixon's a Republican. You all hate those guys, right?"

Shannon smiled. So did his mother. Carolyn shrugged.

"*Hate* is a strong word, Son," his father said.

"Well, not you, Dad. I know you like Nixon. But not you three," Carter said, swinging his arm in front of him.

"So," Carolyn said, "what if we do hate Republicans? Still, what's your point, Cart?"

"Look at all he's done!" Carter raised his hands, the index card falling and floating to the floor. "I mean, seriously, look! All these things I hear you say every night, the things for which our government should fight: cleaning the environment, helping the poor, giving everyone a fair chance regardless of their skin color. He's fighting for all these things, just like you say a politician should. Yet he's a Republican. The guys you hate!"

His two sisters and parents were looking at him. They seemed to be expecting more. But he was finished. He had no more to add. His aim was to impress, to show that he belonged around the same supper table as his two sisters, but all he saw in each of their faces was a blank stare.

"I think," Carter began, hoping a significant thought would pop into his head, "I think Richard Milhous Nixon is the best president our country has ever had."

Immediately, Carolyn began coughing, Shannon giggled, and his mother cupped her hand over her mouth.

"Carter," his father asked, "haven't you been watching the news? Haven't they discussed in your class what's going on in the capital?"

Shannon tilted her head toward him and whispered, "We've been talking about it for the past month."

Carter looked up, shocked and calculating what he could have missed that apparently should have been so obvious.

Shannon whispered more softly, "'Tricky Dick.'"

Carter's mind raced over the many recent discussions centering on the man who had been caught cheating and was probably going to be removed from his elected position. Around the supper table, this cheater was always referred to as "Tricky Dick," never Richard Nixon or President Nixon. Until now, he had never considered that there was a connection between the two. How could the president do such things? How could such a man become president?

He sunk his head, realizing the intense stupidity he had just displayed.

"Carter," his mother asked, "don't you read the paper?"

"Hah!" Carolyn blurted. "He reads the paper, sure! The sports page."

Carter looked up, rage building. Humiliated at his failed attempt to prove his intelligence, he was not going to be further humiliated by his sister's attack of his strength.

"Sure, I read the sports page," he shouted, "and look where it's gotten me! I am hands down the most knowledgeable sports fan within this house!"

"Really!" Carolyn contended. "Would you like to make a wager on that?"

"Two weeks of chores!"

Carolyn reached across the table to shake his hand.

He pulled it away and added, "The subject is baseball."

"Fine."

They shook.

"Who's first?" Carter asked.

Shannon pushed herself up in her chair, sitting on her knees, "You, Carter," she said. "You go first. Whoever misses the first question looses!"

Their mother cleared her throat.

"We're fine, Mom," Shannon assured. "We do this all the time."

"Go on, Carter," Shannon instructed. "Your turn."

"All right." Carter looked to the ceiling, trying hard to think of a good question. "Who is the only player to hit more home runs than Babe Ruth in a single season?"

"Roger Maris, sixty-one in 1961, on the last day of the season while playing for the Yankees. My turn." Carolyn said it all in one breath, took a bite of a dinner roll and, with her mouth full, asked, "Who has the most career saves in major-league history?"

"Elroy Face," Carter quickly answered. "Hah! I read that just last week in a *Sports Illustrated* article."

"That's wonderful!" She swallowed the roll. "Ask your next question."

From then on, the questions and answers were rhythmic.

Carter: "Who are the only two men to manage the Dodgers since the late 1950s?"

Carolyn: "Alston and Lasorda. Whom did the Angels trade for Nolan Ryan?"

Carter: "Jim Fregosi. Who was the last switch-hitter to earn American League MVP?"

Carolyn was silent for over thirty seconds. Carter was sure he had won.

"Vida Blue," she answered. She grabbed the glass of water in front of her.

"Stink," Carter muttered.

Carolyn finished her drink and slowly placed the glass back down on the table. She looked squarely into Carter's eyes. "Who is the only player to have over four thousand career hits?"

Carter bit his lip. He had heard the name before but could not remember it at the moment. After a minute of silence and an additional minute of stalling, he gave it his best shot. "Ty Coon."

His parents and sisters simultaneously began laughing.

"What?"

"His name is Ty Cobb!" Carolyn announced.

"Well, I was close, wasn't I?"

No one responded.

"Shannon, you'd give it to me!"

She shrugged.

"Mom? Dad?"

He was desperate. "Carolyn. Please!"

"No way, Cart! Trash, lawn, and dishes this week and next!"

"What a stupid, corny name—Ty Cobb. C'mon, Carolyn, give me a break. Please?"

Just then the phone rang. Carolyn jumped from her chair, ran to the phone, and picked up the receiver after the second ring.

"Hello. Mason residence." There was a pause. "Certainly. I'll get him for you." Carolyn turned to their father and covered the receiver with her right hand. "Dad, it's that guy again."

He pushed himself from the table and stood up.

"What guy?" Carter asked.

Carolyn's eyes told Carter not to speak.

Shannon turned toward Carter, leaned to his ear, and whispered. "You know, that Barney guy. From back East."

He knew the name. Somehow his calls put his parents in a somber mood. Carter lowered his head, raised his eyes to watch his mother, and lowered them again to finish his meal.

Their father slowly rose from the table. "I'll take it upstairs. Hang up when you hear me."

"Sure, Dad," Carolyn answered softly.

His father's eyes had narrowed, creating "the valley" as Carolyn had named the crevasse between their father's eyebrows that formed whenever he grew uncomfortable or was on the verge of an explosion of anger. Most times, the explosion did not come, but "the valley" remained well into the following day. Carter would often look in the bathroom mirror at night, trying to mimic his father's facial creation, frustrated he could not even form a wrinkle of skin. He felt it made his father, who otherwise looked quite young, appear more distinguished and scholarly.

Carter looked at Shannon, who seemed a bit more concerned about this than Carter. He relied on her to be the lighthearted savior of his family. But there she was—no smile, eyes downcast, studying their mother.

It seemed his mother's beauty had vanished. If a face could show no expression—no anger, no happiness, no emotion at all—that was the expression he saw.

Carolyn hung up the phone and sat back down.

She turned to Carter. "Well?" she asked with an intimidating stare. "When are you going to start?"

Carter held up his fork. "I'm not done with my rice."

He felt like a coward beneath Carolyn's stare and was relieved when her eyes shifted toward their mother. She stayed seated and silent, as if she was contemplating what to do next.

Finally, she stood up. "Don't assist him," she ordered Shannon.

"I'll be right there. Don't worry. I've got some algebra to finish up."

Shannon's plan to depart for the library as soon as she finished her meal saddened Carter further. He had hoped that she would assist with the chores he had inherited from losing the bet.

He frowned and studied Shannon and his mother. Neither seemed to notice the sagging expression on his face. He was alone. He made the bet; he lost the bet; he inherited the chores. Nothing was to be gained by sulking at the table.

He stood up and quietly stacked the dishes.

Life's Road Map

Carter cursed himself for losing the bet. "I should have known," he muttered, placing silverware into the dishwasher. "She tricked me into betting two weeks' chores."

He closed the dishwasher, pushed the button to start the wash cycle, and walked past the supper table toward the doors of the family library. The doors were not locked and slightly ajar. He peaked inside. Both sisters were intent in their studies. How did they do it? Why were they so successful in the classroom, so wise, and so eloquent? Why was he not?

He pushed the door slowly and entered, closing it softly behind him.

"What are you studying tonight?" Shannon asked as he entered.

Carter held up a history textbook, angling it in Carolyn's direction. He glanced at Carolyn and smiled. Behind it, in clear view for Shannon to see, he held a copy of Robinson Crusoe from his school's library. He jumped in his chair, opened his history book and, while carefully watching Carolyn, maneuvered the paperback within the tall bindings of the textbook.

He hadn't read two pages when he felt a tug on the two books he was holding.

He looked up. It was Carolyn.

"When are you going to learn, Cart? You've got to do your schoolwork first. Let me have it." Carolyn held out her hand.

"I was just going to finish this chapter—" Carter started.

Carolyn turned the book toward Shannon. "He's on page two."

"I was on page two until you stole it."

"Read your next history chapter. Shannon and I will ask you the questions in the back. If you can answer at least ninety percent of them correctly, then you can go back to the islands with Mr. Crusoe."

Carter eyed Carolyn, resenting the authority bequeathed upon her by his parents when the three of them studied in the library. He sank in his chair and read of California's early history.

An hour had passed. He finished the history reading, answered his sisters' questions, and reentered his world of adventure. He reached page 5 when his mother knocked lightly, cracked open the door, and announced it was time for bed. "I'll never finish this book," he muttered. "You guys don't let me read anything I want." He swung himself out of the chair and followed his mother upstairs.

Carter had not seen his father since dinner. "Your father went for a run," his mother said as she pulled the covers over Carter's chest and tucked them tightly under his chin. It tickled Carter, but he enjoyed the sensation and felt silly for looking forward to it each night.

"But that was over two hours ago!" Carter announced.

"Your father can run a long way."

"How long?"

"Very."

"So, he's all right?"

"He'll be fine."

He looked up at his mother and felt comforted by her certainty. It was a curious thing, Carter thought, how much fun he had in his house. He knew all his friends did not feel the same about their families. Yet there were prices to be paid and expectations he was obliged to meet. His failure around the table just a couple hours earlier was testament to the costs involved.

"What's wrong, Dear?" his mother asked. "You don't seem yourself." She brushed Carter's hair away from his eyes. "What's on your mind?"

"Nothing," he answered, turning away his head.

"Carter. I'm your mother."

He could not figure out how she knew these things without his saying a word.

"Carter!"

"It's supper tonight."

"Yes?"

"I made a fool of myself. Not connecting the dots, figuring out that Nixon and 'Tricky Dick' is the same guy. I wanted to impress you all and . . . and . . . I just made myself look more stupid."

"You mustn't let that bother you, Carter. Keep listening. Keep trying to understand. Ask questions. Realize that they were once in your position. They were once your age."

"Carolyn says she was smarter than me when she was half my age. Is that true? Am I the idiot of the family or something? Did they get all the brains?"

His mother looked at him like she had just heard something ridiculous, something so far from the truth that she couldn't believe it was said. "No, Carter. It's not like that at all."

"Then what? Why don't I get it?"

"You just have to read more, like your sisters."

"But I do read!"

"Yes, Carter. Yes, you do. But—"

"But what?"

"The books you spend time reading are not the most rewarding."

"I don't get it. I thought you and Dad like seeing us read. What difference does it make what book I read?"

"Carter, Dear, it's all right to read about make-believe worlds full of dragons, knights, and wizards, but in order to learn more, you need to start reading other types of books."

"You mean like Shannon and Carolyn?"

She tugged on the blanket and tucked it under the mattress, making Carter feel more snug and secure. "If you spend all your time reading about a make-believe world, Carter, you will think and live as though you were in a make-believe world. If you read about the real world, you'll understand the real world. You'll understand what your sisters are talking about each night at the dinner table. Carolyn and Shannon read the newspaper, magazines, history books, literary dramas, things about life, real life, not about a world of make-believe."

"But I read about history. I read those storybooks about stuff in the Bible. That's history."

His mother sighed and took a deep breath. He had never noticed such a strong resemblance between her and Carolyn. Something told him that her next words would further confuse him.

"I know this is difficult, Carter. It's not easy to understand. It's not easy for me to explain. Your father likes you to go with him on Sundays. Carolyn and Shannon went with him when they were younger. But your father and I agreed that when our children were old enough, then they would make their own decision."

"Decision?"

She got up from the bed, walked over to Carter's desk, and pulled the desk chair near his bedside. She crossed her legs, leaned forward, and cleared her throat. "Some people believe the Bible is history, Carter, but not all people. In fact, most people believe it is not history at all. It's, well, it's like one of your fantasy books."

"But, but, Dad reads it! He goes to church!"

"Your father has his reasons. When you're old enough to understand, just like Carolyn and Shannon, we'll let you decide."

Carter shook his head. "But I still don't get it. Why can't someone just explain it to me? Why do you always say I have to read about it before I can understand it?"

He looked up at his mother. She had stood up from the chair, bent down, and ruffled his hair. "You know the answer to that, Carter Anthony."

He followed her cue as she began to speak, joining her in unison: "Because if I read something, I'm more likely to remember it. Reading is the key to understanding. It is the road map of life."

"Always remember this, Carter Anthony. If you dream, dream about reality, about how it is, the good and the bad, how it can be different, how it can be changed, how you can help change it. That is how our imaginations ought to be used, to help make this world more enjoyable for those less fortunate, to help awaken others who do not care for those who are less fortunate. Dreaming is good, Carter, but dream about changing our world, not about another world entirely. Do you understand?"

Carter tilted his head, burying it into the pillow. He did understand some of what she said, but he wasn't sure he liked it all.

"Do you feel better?"

He was tired. He was frustrated. He needed to sort this out. "I guess so."

"That's my boy. Love you, Carter." She kissed him good night and turned off the light, leaving him in the dark.

That night, Carter found it difficult to sleep. How could his mother be so certain that his father's beliefs about God were not true? Who was right? They couldn't both be, could they?

And what about the Bible being a book of fantasy? Was his mother correct about that too? If she was, then how holy could the Holy Bible be?

Carter had wondered why he and his father always attended church alone. He had not known it to be any other way. Now he was beginning to understand. There was a point at which his sisters learned what his mother knew—that God was a fairy tale. If he were to reach their status around the dinner table, he too would have to start reading the books they read, studying as hard as they study, and discover what they discovered.

Carter shut his eyes, pressing them hard. What was he to do about his father and Sunday school? He still wanted to go; he liked the stories they told and the way they made him feel. It was as though the people in the stories were real, and if they were alive, they would teach everyone of the lessons they learned, the things God had taught them.

He would continue to go, he decided. Maybe he could discover a way to please his mother and still attend church with his father. Maybe he'd be the first in his family to discover that both his parents were right but that both were also a little bit wrong.

Independence Day

To play baseball every day was Carter's dream. He couldn't imagine being good enough to play in the majors and how nice it would be to get paid for doing something that was so much fun. Regardless as to whether he won or lost, Carter loved the game and was glad he lived in a neighborhood with five boys who felt the same.

Because there were only six of them, they played a different brand of baseball that was taught to them by Stuart Hardaway, the oldest of their gang. He had learned it from his elder brothers and called it "Over-the-Line." It only required one infielder stationed between second and third base and two outfielders, one in center and the other in left. Right field was considered foul territory. The batter would toss the ball in the air, similar to a coach hitting groundballs or fly balls to his players. To make an out, any of the fielders had to either catch a fly ball or liner, or field a grounder and throw it over the imaginary line between second and third base before any runner arrived safely at a base.

There were days they played twice, once in the late morning hours and again in the early evening. And even then, Carter came home anticipating that either Shannon or Carolyn would play catch with him underneath the dim backyard light.

The early months of the year were dull and filled with nothing but work—school five days a week, papers to write, assigned books to read, and no vacation time except for a couple presidential birthdays. Carter often wondered if historians had been as kind to other presidents as they had been toward Washington and Lincoln, whether he'd get more days off from school. Those two days in February were little relief during the first three months of the year. Finally spring arrived, bringing with it an extra hour of daylight and the onset of America's treasured pastime. Once the professionals began playing, he and his friends could begin their daily battles on the ball fields of their neighborhood.

At first, Carter was not comfortable playing with the older kids. His sisters, whose skills outmatched most of their male classmates, spent hours teaching him how to stay in front of grounders, watch the ball into his mitt, and follow through with his throws. "Stay with it, Cart," Carolyn would encourage. "Just keep your eye on the ball."

It was paying off. Though he had just turned nine, Carter was still the second youngest among his friends. But they were beginning to pay him more respect when he was at the plate. And they no longer singled him out when he was in the field; he could catch and throw just as well as any of them.

He savored the feeling of exhaustion, the sweat dripping from his hair into his eyes, the heavy breathing, and the walk with a limp. It was all part of the wonderful feeling baseball brought him. It was as though he were a real athlete, nursing his injuries, coming home with bruises and scrapped knees.

As Carter and his five friends walked home from their afternoon game on the nation's 198th birthday, Carter threw his mitt into the air and kicked it just before it hit the ground. "When we playing again?" he started.

"We'll get you guys next time," Chuck DeSanto interrupted. "There ain't no way you're going to beat us again! It was luck. You'll need even more tomorrow."

Stuart Hardaway threw a ball into the air and caught it with his mitt. "Give it a rest, Chuck. Face it, you just can't handle losing."

"Yeah, right. I just can't handle losing to losers. You guys stunk out there."

Carter looked to his other friends who had played on Stuart's team, wondering whether they'd defend themselves.

"We stunk?" Stuart repeated. "Yet we won. Hmm?" He glanced at his teammates, Allen and Tony, "If we stunk so bad, guys, how do you think we beat Chuck, Hector, and Carter?"

Allen shrugged his shoulders.

Tony, Chuck's younger brother, shouted, "'Cause they stink more!"

Chuck pushed Tony. "Shut up, you little jerk. I wasn't talking to you."

"Tell you what," Stuart said, "we'll have a rematch this afternoon. In the pool."

Chuck sighed. "No way. I'm too tired."

Hector Romero, the tallest in the group, just finished eating a second bag of potato chips. With his mouth full of half-eaten fragments, he announced, "I'm in."

Allen sighed. "I've had enough for a day, too, Stuart. Sorry."

"I'm with Stuart," shouted Tony. "Man, you guys are wimps. Look, I know we're all tired, but once we get home, get something to eat, we'll all feel like jumping in the pool. And then if we feel like it, we'll play!"

All five faces turned toward Carter. It was three-to-two in favor of playing again. Chuck lobbied first, "Well, Carter, which is it?"

By this time, the six friends had reached the fork in the road that led to their homes. Carter could tell by the tone in Chuck's voice that he was in no mood for hesitant decision-making. First, Chuck had lost in baseball for the third consecutive day; second, his younger brother was standing up to him. Chuck gave Carter "the look."

"Come on, Carter. I'm beat," Allen blurted.

There was silence and what seemed to Carter an eternity when Hector announced, "Man, I got to go home. I got to go bad!"

"Hold on, Hector," Chuck said. "We'll be done in a minute. We're waiting for Cart."

"No, I mean . . . I've got to go bad!"

Chuck turned in disgust. "Geez, Hector! Why didn't you go at the park?"

"He hadn't digested his bags of chips." Allen nudged Hector as he said it, beginning a friendly shoving match. Carter eyed them with envy.

Chuck kept hounding, "Well, Carter."

Tony joined Hector and Allen in their fun. He shouted back to his brother, "Give it a rest, Chuck. Leave Carter alone."

Chuck pulled Tony away from Allen and Hector, and pushed him hard with an open fist against his left shoulder.

Tony rapidly swung his arms, entangling them in Chuck's. "You just can't handle being the loser! Don't give us this crap about being tired! You're mad about losing again!"

Carter felt he had to act fast, before Chuck had a chance to destroy his younger brother. "Listen guys. I'm all for playing in the pool later, say, maybe in a couple of hours when it cools down."

But his words were too late. Chuck slugged his younger brother in the chest and was in the middle of his second swing when Stuart grabbed Tony with his right arm and stopped Chuck's swing with the other.

"That's enough," Stuart warned as he escorted Tony toward the DeSanto home.

Chuck followed them, cursing under his breath as Hector ran to his home. Allen and Carter were left alone.

Carter shrugged. "Call me if they decide to do anything."

Allen smiled, "I'll see you around four. My house. They'll be there."

Carter's mother and two sisters had left for the beach around eight in the morning. He wondered whether they were home, hoping they weren't so he could plop himself onto the sofa and watch the annual *Twilight Zone* marathon on television. He was relieved to see that the station wagon was not in the driveway or at the curb in front of the house.

His father would be home, but Carter knew he'd be busy in the garage. As he reached the front lawn, Carter heard a power saw's engine rumble. He raced to the driveway, hopped on top of a planter adjacent to the garage, and studied his father, who was in the process of maneuvering the tool over a piece of wood cradled between two sawhorses.

Carter slid off the planter, tiptoed to the worktable on the other side of the garage, and pulled himself up. His father turned off the saw a few seconds later. He placed another piece of wood between the sawhorses.

Carter scratched his head. "Hey, Dad."

His father turned to his left. He was wearing protective goggles and denim overalls. He removed the goggles. "Son. I didn't see you come in. What was all that fuss about?"

"You heard that?"

"I did." His father looked up at Carter, his stare communicating that some explanation was required.

"You know the guys. Making a big deal about nothing. Can't decide whether or not to play more ball this afternoon."

Picking up a clamp from the floor, Carter's father tightened its grip on the piece of wood. "That's it?" he asked. "It sounded more animated than that."

Carter hopped off the work table and walked closer to his father. "What are you making?"

"You'll have to wait."

"Wait? Wait 'til when?"

His father turned and grinned.

"Is it for tonight?"

His father's grin grew, confirming Carter's assumption.

"Cool! What is it? It looks like a box."

"It's a podium."

"A podium? A podium for what?"

The neighborhood's annual Fourth of July block party began in less than eight hours. If his father was building a podium, he'd better have completed whatever would be on top of it.

Carter reminisced of last year's block party—the clear summer sky, the sparks and smell of burning powder, an endless supply of hotdogs and soda and potato chips and ice cream and popcorn and baked goods that were brought by the neighbors. The experience was surpassed only by the annual holiday decoration competition that was held three days prior to Christmas. The family that produced the most entertaining fireworks display, or the most decorative light display during the holidays, was awarded an all-expense-paid dinner at their favorite restaurant by the other participating neighbors.

Carter's family was a perennial favorite on the Fourth of July, but they did not win last year. This year would be different.

He could tell his father was determined to win. For over two weeks, before school got out, his dad wouldn't talk much during dinner, as though he were thinking of the work waiting for him in the garage. But nobody, including Carter, knew what it was.

Carter glanced at the garage floor, searching for anything in his father's vicinity that might help him determine what his father was making. But all he could see was the wooden box that his father called a podium.

"You'll find out tonight," his father said as he began sawing another board.

A couple minutes later, his father attached the boards he had cut to the box on the floor. Now it resembled a podium. He began to sand its surface. "Would you like to help?"

"Sure!" Carter lowered to his knees and crawled next to his father.

He handed Carter a piece of sandpaper and directed him to the opposite side of the podium on which he was currently working. Carter observed his father's sanding strategy and did his best to imitate it.

"So, tell me, how are things with the guys?"

His father's question caught Carter unprepared. All he wanted was to sand with his dad, help him prepare for tonight. He didn't want one of his father's probing inquisitions.

He reluctantly started, knowing any hesitation may fuel the fire to his father's questions. "Fine," he answered. "All right, I guess. Allen and

I get along. Stuart never gets on my nerves. You know, he minds his own business and all."

"Tony and Chuck?"

"They fight a lot. We're all used to it. Stuart had to separate them just now. That's probably all the commotion you heard."

Carter kept sanding. There was one friend his father had not mentioned.

"And Hector?"

Carter remained silent.

His father stopped sanding, moved to the other side of the podium, and sat next to Carter. "What's wrong? What's going on with you two?"

"Nothing." Carter stopped, knowing eventually his father would get it out of him. And then he'd have to deal with the lying as well. It was best to get it all out, into the open, to be honest, just like he knew his father wanted him to be.

"Well," he continued, "I guess it was something I said a couple days ago." Carter looked up to see if he had stunned his father or made him ashamed. His face was unchanged; he was still Dad. It was safe to reveal more.

"You see, Chuck was complaining again about his dad: 'He's too this . . . he's too that . . . he doesn't let me do this . . . he doesn't let me do that . . . he makes me take out the trash while all he does is sit around on his fat . . . ' well, you know. I get sick of hearing him complain, and I figure if I get sick of it, well, shoot, it must really get Hector upset! So, a couple of days ago when Chuck was shooting off his mouth again, I said, 'Well, at least you've got a father!' I meant it to help Hector, but as I said it, I realized how stupid it was."

His father rubbed his chin. "How did Hector take it?"

Carter mumbled. "His eyes lowered. He didn't seem himself the rest of the day. You know, joking, laughing, playing."

"And today?"

"Well, he's playing better, and he's joking with the guys, but we haven't said more than hello or good-bye for a couple days."

Carter felt warm inside. Spilling this out to his father was helping. His father placed down the sandpaper he held, inched closer, curled up his knees, and wrapped his arms around them.

"What can I do?" Carter asked.

His father did not answer immediately. For a moment, all hope of regaining Hector's friendship seemed to hang on a thread. He had stepped on the soul of the only boy in the neighborhood without a father.

On the walk home from the park, while Hector was eating his chips, he seemed preoccupied. Hector had these episodes often, so maybe his musing was not about Carter. Most times, he was working on an algebra or geometry problem, talking to himself and motioning with his hands. Though Hector was also in third grade with Carter, Chuck, and Allen, his mathematic aptitude was on par with a high school freshman. The school had arranged for Hector to attend high school math class two times each week.

His father's eyes shut. When he reopened them, he looked as lost as Carter felt. At the moment, it did not look promising. Carter turned his attention to the melody of birds chirping, hoping they could calm the guilt he felt.

Finally, his father spoke. "Sometimes we say things with good intentions, Son. But somehow our bad intentions get mixed in with the good intentions and make the end result of what we say a worse situation than if we had said nothing at all."

Carter winced, curling his lip.

"You see," his father continued, "you wanted to silence Chuck almost as much, if not more, than you wanted to assist Hector. If you had understood that beforehand, you could have come up with a better plan of attack. However, all this may still turn out for the best."

"Really?"

"Has Chuck complained the last two days?"

"Well. No!" Carter said, feeling some relief.

"There, you see. Maybe that's all Chuck needed to realize his foolishness."

"But, but, what about Hector?"

"You apologize." His father made it sound so easy.

Carter looked up. This sort of thing was not done within the circle of six. Among his friends, Allen was the only one from whom he had heard the words "I'm sorry," but he would say it so often that neither Carter nor the rest of the gang would think anything of it. *We're too cool to participate in the ritual of apologizing and forgiving one another*, Carter thought. In the past, the memory of ill will faded with time and the relationship continued; no apology was necessary. This concept of sincerely apologizing that his father was suggesting, was foreign enough to make Carter squirm but logical enough to make him consider its value.

"I guess I'm lucky," Carter said, hoping to change the course of conversation.

"Lucky?" his father asked.

"First of all, to have a dad at all. And second, to have a dad like you."

His father stood up and frowned. "I don't know about that," he muttered and then returned to sanding the upper portion of the podium. On his face, the deepening crevasse of "the valley" had emerged.

Carter looked down, focused on his side of the podium, and continued sanding.

Twenty minutes later, they had finished the podium. Carter went to the kitchen, drank a tall glass of orange juice, turned on the television, and sat on the sofa.

His father woke him an hour later, tapping him on the shoulder. "Carter. Son, get up."

Carter shrugged him away.

"Carter, it's Allen. Do you want to talk to him?"

A few moans and what-does-he-wants later, Carter shuffled to the phone.

He picked up the receiver. "Hello?"

"Carter?" Allen sounded surprised as if he did not recognize his voice.

"Hi, Allen. Yeah, it's me. What's up?"

"We were right. I just got a call from Tony. Chuck's ready to play. Hector's in. Stuart said he'll be here. Now all we need is you."

Carter was drowsy. All he wanted to do was to fall back onto the sofa and resume his nap. He knew if he did, he would regret it later. Instead, he asked Allen, "What time and whose pool?"

"Boy, you sure sound excited about this."

"I just woke up."

"Oh. Well, uh . . . I'm sorry. I mean, waking you up. I'm really sorry, man. You still want in? We need you!"

"Of course," Carter answered.

There was a pause for about ten seconds until Carter realized Allen had not answered his question concerning logistics. Carter let out an audible yawn and asked, "When did you say we're playing?"

"Tony said three thirty."

"I'll see you then." Carter began to hang up the phone.

"Oh, Carter," Allen shouted.

Carter pulled the phone back to his right ear. "Yeah?"

Allen continued. "We're playing at my house. In case I didn't tell you. Did I tell you? I forget. Well, anyway, three thirty. See you then."

Carter and his friends gathered for their second baseball game of the day. It had always been a mystery to Carter in figuring how the six of them were able to begin any of their games since it was such a chore, and at times as great a battle as the game itself, to choose teams. As it happened on this occasion, part of Chuck's stipulation in playing was he chose his teammates. He wouldn't play unless he, Hector, and his younger brother, Tony, were on the same team.

When Carter arrived, Chuck, Tony, Allen, and Stuart had already jumped into the pool and were splashing one another. Carter lingered along the pool's perimeter, waiting for Hector to arrive. He pulled off his T-shirt, taking his time, when Allen shouted, "Hurry up, Carter! What's the holdup?"

He continued moving as slowly as he could. The guys started splashing water on him and then resumed splashing one another. Finally, the gate opened and Hector appeared around the corner.

Carter's eyes met his.

Hector lowered his gaze toward the ground. He began to undress.

Carter walked toward him. "I'm sorry," he whispered. "I'm sorry for what I said. You know, about your dad and all."

Hector looked up, smiling. "Thanks, Cart," he said. "I wasn't sure what to think."

Carter felt something inside, something he had never felt, a mixture of happiness and relief bouncing in his chest.

He and Hector finished undressing to their trunks. Just before they jumped in, Hector turned toward Carter and said softly, "At least you got Chuck to shut up!"

The six friends had invented a new format of baseball during the prior summer; "Baseball in the Pool," they called it. It was still in its early stages of development by the middle of the summer of seventy-four, but Carter and his friends had gradually perfected ground rules, base-running rules, best positions in which to play on each hitter, and the most effective fielding and base-running techniques.

The rules were dictated by the change of venue from a traditional dirt-and-grass baseball diamond to a swimming pool. Rule changes followed from there. First, the pitcher and hitters both stood in the shallow end of the pool. Each team had two fielders: a rover who played between second and third base while treading water, by far the most difficult position, and an outfielder who roamed on the deck of the pool or perched on the diving board in order to catch Texas Leaguers.

The second rule change evolved when the boys discovered how difficult it was to make outs against the opposing team. To resolve this they decided to limit each half-inning to two outs rather than three. Finally, there was the change in equipment. The ball used was a white practice golf ball made of plastic and full of holes, which gave the pitcher the ability to throw out-of-the-ordinary breaking balls. The normal twenty-eight-to-thirty-inch bat that kids used was substituted with the twenty-three-inch wooden souvenir bats that their parents had bought them at Dodgers and Angels games.

The most challenging aspects of this brand of baseball were hitting the ball solid enough to get it into fair play and swimming the bases. Especially difficult was second base. It resided in the middle of the pool where it was five and a half feet deep. Treading water was necessary until a teammate successfully advanced the occupant further. Throwing a base runner out created another difficulty since there were not enough players to occupy each base. The solution was thought up by Stuart: If the defensive player can successfully throw the ball in the general vicinity of the base without it going out of the pool, prior to the runner arriving, then the base runner is out. If there is not a force at home plate, then the pitcher must cover home and attempt to tag out the runner.

Each team was participating in a slugfest that afternoon. Chuck, the best pitcher among Carter's friends, decided to take the day off and play outfield. Tony was stuck in the middle of the pool, and Hector's pitches were not fooling any on Carter's team. Stuart, Allen, and Carter were hitting line drives to the left and right of Chuck. The three of them each had a home run and at least seven hits. By the end of the seventh inning, they had scored thirteen runs.

Carter pitched for his team. He only allowed one run during the first six innings. In the seventh inning, however, his pitches were no longer fooling Tony, Chuck, and Hector, as they scored eleven runs to make the score thirteen to twelve.

To all their amazement, nobody scored in the eighth inning. Then came the ninth.

Tony led the inning off with a long line drive that hit the backyard fence on the fly. By the time Allen retrieved the ball and threw it to Stuart, Tony reached third base. Hector came up next and, after falling in the count zero to two, launched a long fly ball toward Allen. Allen had a great jump on the ball as he hopped off the diving board and gave chase toward the fence. In bare feet, he ascended the wall in a desperate attempt to steal Hector's glory. Allen reached over the fence and, with a surge off his left leg, lifted himself several inches higher, high enough to slap the ball back into fair territory. He did not catch it, though.

Tony began swimming toward home plate once the ball started falling. Chuck screamed for Tony to go back to third as Allen dropped to the ground and shuffled toward the diving board, reaching as far as he could while still laying on the pavement, and caught the ball before it hit the ground.

Carter started to celebrate, but Stuart raced toward home plate from his infield position as Tony tagged from third. It was Carter's job to cover home, but he was so excited about Allen's catch that he forgot his duty. Stuart got there in time to have the plate covered. Allen jumped to his feet and fired a bullet throw straight toward home. Tony used his agility, bending and twisting around and under Stuart's tag. He was safe, and the game was tied.

Carter's team needed only one more out to keep the score even. But before they could bat, Carter had to face Chuck. He cringed as he looked into Chuck's face. Carter knew he was toast. Why test fate? He threw Chuck an ordinary pitch. Chuck hit the ball, and it sailed five feet over the fence. Allen did not even give chase. Carter had just surrendered a twelve-run lead. His team was losing, fourteen to thirteen.

After striking out Tony, Carter and his teammates took their places behind the plate, ready to face Hector, but Chuck had replaced him. He hadn't won a game in almost four days, and Carter could not blame him for this strategy. Victory was within his grasp. He was the best pitcher out of all of them, and there was no better way to insure a victory then by taking the mound himself.

Carter's pulse raced as he stepped to the plate. He swung at Chuck's first pitch and hit a line drive far to the right of Hector, who was now playing outfield. He swam into second base safely. Stuart then singled him to third base. With runners on first and third, hope reappeared for Carter and his teammates.

Allen struck out on three of Chuck's nastiest curve balls. They were down to their final out, one last chance to prolong the game into extra innings. Allen took Carter's place at third. Carter was face-to-face with the fiercest competitor in the neighborhood. He was up against Chuck, just as Chuck was up against him minutes earlier.

Chuck's first pitch was way outside—ball one! Carter took a deep breath. His second pitch hit the water in front of Carter—ball two. Now Carter could relax. He was way ahead in the count and could draw a base on balls, placing Stuart in the unenviable position he now found himself. Chuck's next pitch sailed over Carter's head—ball three! The next pitch once more hit the water before reaching the plate—ball four! Carter was walked. As he began to swim toward first, it dawned on him that Chuck did not come close to pitching a strike. It was as if he intentionally walked him, Chuck's way of saying, I respect you, Carter. Now go to first and shut up!

As Carter wondered this, he looked across at his friend. Chuck cocked his head and winked. Carter beamed inside. He valued Chuck's compliment more than anybody's because it was honest and sincere. Regardless of how the game would end, Carter had won!

None of this would get by Stuart, though. What was for Carter a pat on the back was for Stuart a slap in the face. These two hardly talked but held each other in respect, for each had put the other in his place. They stared down one another for thirty seconds before Chuck appeared to think about throwing a first pitch.

Finally, Chuck hurled a fastball, and Stuart swung straight through it. The whoosh from Stuart's swing caused Allen and Carter to look at each other in hopelessness. The next pitch had the same results—strike two!

"If I was Stuart, I'd be looking for more of the same," Carter told himself. "Chuck is in no mood to fool around with his junk pitches. He wants to win!"

Stuart must have been thinking along those same lines because Chuck hurled another fastball that Stuart tipped at the plate. The next ten pitches were all the same—one fastball after the other, all of which Stuart fouled, each foul becoming a more solid hit. By the ninth and tenth foul balls, Stuart was lining Chuck's pitches against the side of the

Stanowitz home. This had become a battle of pride. Chuck was going with nothing less than the hard stuff; any less would be "un-Chuck."

Pitch number thirteen was another fastball. Stuart waited a moment longer than he had on the previous pitches. As his bat connected with the ball on the thick of the butt, Stuart turned his wrists and lined the ball into the shallow part of the outfield, into the deep end of the pool. This was no man's land usually.

Hector was perched on the end of the diving board. As clumsy and awkward as he may appear in everyday life, he was the most sure-handed, reliable clutch athlete among them. This made Stuart's otherwise sure base hit into a drama. First, Hector bent his knees and sprang into a parallel position to the water. He appeared to fly across the surface of the pool, his lanky torso, legs, and arms gliding through the air and hovering just above the playing field. Hector was to the left of the ball's path and was in flight when he reached out with his left hand, cupped the ball, and wrapped it with his long fingers just before it hit the water.

The five friends waited to see if Hector had retained control. They had never seen such a remarkable athletic feat in real life. Could he have really held on to the ball?

As Hector and the ball plunged into greater depths, the friends were overtaken by an even greater shock when Hector's trunks surfaced. The blue-and-yellow bathing suit danced upon the waves created by Hector's dive. The silence created by Hector's catch was broken with bursts of laughter.

Hector joined in the joy after he emerged with the ball tightly gripped in his hand, jumped from the pool, and wrapped himself in his towel. The game was over. Carter had lost again. But he had regained a friend.

That same evening, the neighborhood gathered to pool their resources and create an unforgettable Fourth of July celebration. Each family had purchased its own supply of fireworks, but Carter and his friends began a black market of sorts, creating assortments of fireworks they liked best.

The box Carter helped his father sand that day turned out to be a podium upon which stood Lady Liberty. Carter's father placed in her hand the largest firework fountain he could find and arrayed the wooden statue with an assortment of other fireworks that lit her silhouette for all the neighbors watching. His presentation was the best in the neighborhood, and Carter knew his family would win the prized dinner.

But the greatest surprise of all was a result of something Carter's father could not have planned. Near the top of the hills overlooking Anaheim in Southern California, the torch in Lady Liberty's right hand was almost extinguished and the neighborhood darkened when the sky lit up behind her with the firework display from Disneyland. Their perch atop the hills in Fullerton gave Carter, his family, and friends a clear view of the Magic Kingdom's most spectacular firework show of the year.

As the group of neighbors watched, their enjoyment was interrupted by a high-pitched scream. Everybody turned, looking in the direction from which it came.

Carolyn stood motionless with a terrified stare as her father approached.

"What happened?" a voice in the crowd inquired.

"Carolyn, Dear, are you all right?" Carter's mother asked.

A murmur of questions arose among the neighbors until Carter's father begged for silence and asked Carolyn what had happened.

Carolyn hesitated before explaining how she and Shannon had decided to ignite their final firework, a ground bloom flower, a gadget that radiates and twirls at a speed so fast that it appears to be a sphere of light. This particular one twirled and skipped off the street's surface as it approached a driveway and climbed the curb. The incline, combined with the firework's natural power, lifted the flower a little over five feet into the air, straight toward Shannon's face.

"It just seemed to stick there!" Carolyn explained while still shaking.

"Carolyn, where is your sister? Where is Shannon?" her father asked.

"There she is!" Allen Stanowitz shouted as he pointed toward a silhouette further down the street.

Carter's father motioned for his neighbors to remain calm as he and his wife approached their daughter. Carter followed in their wake. As they drew nearer, Carter could not tell if Shannon was all right. She seemed calm, her head tilted back as though she were studying the stars.

As Carter's parents reached out to embrace her, she turned. Directly beneath her right eye was a thick, crooked, black streak. Carter noticed a strange expression on her face, like she wasn't sure where she was.

Carolyn later explained that Shannon seemed undaunted by the whole event, as though she fully expected it to happen. It was Carolyn who had produced the frightening scream, not Shannon.

As it turned out, she was fortunate to not have any injury to her right eye. "Another half inch," the doctor informed, "and she may have lost all vision."

However, she was left with a quarter-inch scar. She was more solemn than before and did not participate as enthusiastically around the supper table after the incident. Carter wanted to ask her why but was afraid Carolyn might tell him it was none of his business.

Other than Shannon's scar, that day was the highlight of the entire summer. Carter's renewed friendship with Hector and his father's victory at the Fourth of July block party filled him with a peaceful gratitude that he was a part of the Mason household. But his father always told him that good things come to an end. "They have to," he told Carter. "Otherwise, future good times would never arrive."

Carter came to accept the fact that each summer was split into two sections: pre-Fourth of July and post-Fourth of July. The passing of the first three weeks was fine, since there were still nine more to follow. Besides, those twenty-one days went by somewhat slowly, as Fourth of July is anticipated. The next nine weeks were a different story. The days disappeared as quickly as the morning dew became part of the hot summer air. Soon his mother would be escorting him and his sisters to department stores in the attempt to beat the Labor Day weekend rush for school clothes and supplies.

There were three saving graces to school's annual arrival in September. First, Carter, Carolyn, and Shannon were taken to Disneyland, just about six miles from their home, the Friday before school began. This insured a relatively light crowd at the park, since most tourists had returned to their homes for the new school year. It was a wonderful way to end the summer, and it salvaged an otherwise depressing weekend.

Second, the beginning of the school year marked the two-week countdown for the annual family vacation. Carter's father always reserved his vacations for the last two weeks of September. As much as the teachers may have disagreed with the decision, his mother's insistence that her children's homework would be completed and that each of them would be more than happy to write a report about their experience, convinced school administrators to grant the Mason children the additional two weeks.

The third and final saving grace of school's arrival was that it ushered in the beginning of fall, which would eventually develop into winter, in which the greatest, most wonderful and mysterious of all days occurred—Christmas Day.

Sam

"Not necessary? It's an insult. What am I supposed to think?"

Carolyn's words echoed from the bedroom of Carter's parents. He and Shannon waited in the hallway, leaning against the wall, fairly certain that Carolyn's efforts would be futile.

"She'll convince them one day," Shannon said in the midst of blowing a bubble with the gum she chewed.

Carter pushed off against the wall, turned, and stared up at Shannon. "You think tonight?"

Shannon shook her head.

"Why not?"

"If it was Mom's decision, she'd probably win. But Dad will stick to his guns. Not until she's sixteen."

"Then why even try? Why does she always have to make such a big deal about it?"

Carter kicked his feet through the thick carpet, wishing the three of them were still in the backyard throwing grounders and playing catch. Shannon slid down the wall onto the floor.

"What do you think, Shannon?" He paused, collecting his thoughts. "Carolyn sets herself up for such disappointment whenever they go out. And what good does it do? She's just living in a world of delusion when she thinks she can win. We could be playing more ball. Instead she had to march into our parents' bedroom, act like she's reached an acceptable level of maturity, and defend her pride."

Carter stopped when Shannon looked up with a look of skepticism.

"What? What's so funny?"

"Come here, Carter." Shannon patted the carpet beside her.

He thumped onto the floor next to her.

Shannon wrapped her arm around his neck, grabbed hold of his shoulder, shook him, and whispered, "Don't try to impress me. I like you already. You're Carter; so be Carter."

Carter looked up at her, dismayed that once again he failed to impress. His parents would respond with a patronizing smile and Carolyn with a demoralizing comment; but Shannon was the only one who seemed to appreciate what he was trying to do and who understood how stupid he felt.

Carter jerked his head when he heard his parents' bedroom door open. Carolyn walked out and closed the door behind her.

Shannon stood up. "Well?"

Carolyn frowned and shook her head. "Sixteen," she mumbled. "You'd think something magical will happen the day I turn sixteen. I'll become more mature. I'll have reached some mythical well of wisdom, making me more capable of the task. Sixteen, what's that got to do with anything?"

"We could hear you," Shannon said. "You sounded more convincing."

"I look after you guys in the library or in the backyard when they're not around. What's the difference?"

Shannon placed her right hand on her hip; her left hand pointed at Carolyn. "The difference is one year, Dear."

Then Carolyn turned her face solemn. She hiked up her pants, raised her shoulders and eyebrows, and lowered her head in a masterful imitation of their father. She even narrowed her eyes, successfully creating "the valley." "Yes, Honey," Carolyn said in a deep voice, "your mother and I have determined by mutual consent that a girl your age should not be held responsible for the behavior of her two younger siblings in the absence of her parents. We want you to enjoy yourself tonight without having to worry about what your brother and sister are up to."

Carter held his hand over his mouth, muffling laughter. "Besides," Carolyn continued, "how can I trust a girl who doesn't believe in God?"

"He didn't say that?" Shannon gasped.

Carolyn motioned Shannon to follow her as she walked toward their bedrooms. Carter, his hands in pockets, followed silently.

"He didn't have to," Carolyn continued. "I know how he feels about the two of us."

Their parents' bedroom door opened again. "Carolyn!" their mother shouted. "Are your dinners out of the freezer? Your grandmother will be here in a few minutes."

"See, Mom knows I can do it." Carolyn turned and walked toward the stairs. Carter saw fury in her eyes. He moved against the hallway wall and looked away.

Shannon cleared her throat, catching Carter's attention. She set her eyes on Carolyn's back, pushed her chest forward, raised her head toward the ceiling, and jerked her head away with disdain. It was too much. Shannon could mimic Carolyn to perfection. Carter's hand failed to silence his laughter as Carolyn passed by. She turned, but Shannon had already retreated to her bedroom.

It had become clear that his parents would not budge when it came to choosing a babysitter. It was always Nana Thurman, his mother's mother, and Carter had no complaints. He loved being under the supervision of his grandmother who didn't seem as concerned as to what he was accomplishing at school but as to how much fun he was having. Carolyn and Shannon acted differently, too. They didn't try to impress Nana like they did their parents. The four of them would eat dinner, play games, and watch television. No one had center stage.

Carter loved these nights most because he knew he would be the last in bed, an impossible feat on any other evening. It was as though she intentionally planned it that way.

This particular night was like any other under the supervision of their grandmother. They ate dinner, watched television, and headed to their bedrooms.

Nana turned off the light in Carolyn's room and led Carter into Shannon's bedroom. "Kiss your sister good night, Carter," she whispered.

Carter hurried to his sister's bedside, anxious for his time alone with Nana. He bent to kiss Shannon on the cheek when he noticed her moistened eyes and her sniffling nose. She raised her hand to clear the tears.

"It's all right, Cart," she whispered. "Do as Nana says. Give me the kiss. I'll be fine."

Her stern voice soothed the uneasy feeling he felt. He bent down and kissed her.

"You're a good kid," she said as she turned her body further from him.

He stepped back slowly, uncertain of what to do next when he felt Nana's hand on his shoulder. "Go to your room, Carter. I'll be there in a minute."

Carter hesitated as Nana gently pushed him outside Shannon's bedroom. He fixed his eyes on Shannon until Nana turned and motioned him to leave.

He left reluctantly, put on his pajamas, and sat on the edge of his bed, waiting for Nana. She didn't come.

He got up and peered down the hallway. He saw Shannon sit up in bed, listening intently to Nana, shaking her head, and arguing in an excited whisper.

Shannon climbed out from beneath the covers and sat on the edge of her bed. Motioning with her hands, she said something that caused Nana to gasp and throw her hands to her mouth.

"I'm sorry, Nana," Carter heard Shannon say, "but I must be honest."

Nana bent down and kissed the top of Shannon's head. She closed Shannon's door as Carter jumped back onto his bed.

"Carter," she called out, "come downstairs."

Carter smiled and rushed to follow Nana into the family den. Dimly lit by the distant lights of the surrounding homes, the objects around the house appeared dull with shades of black and white. Nana sat in the rustic yellow-stained rocking chair, and gingerly raised Carter upon her knees as he wrapped himself in her sweater.

She didn't seem herself. Usually, her rocking was more lively and her embrace tighter.

At first, the only noise he heard was the chirping of crickets and the friction of wood against tile as Nana tried to rock him to sleep. The aroma of mothballs from her aged clothes provided a powerful scent, keeping Carter awake in spite of her gentle rocking. Her soothing voice, while she sang nursery rhymes and hymns, failed to move Carter closer to slumber. Something was wrong. Carter felt it. And regardless of Nana's efforts to conceal it, Carter could tell she was distraught over the conversation she just had with Shannon.

On previous occasions, Carter found it difficult to stay awake in her arms. But after what he witnessed in Shannon's bedroom and how it was affecting his grandmother, the last thing he wanted was to fall asleep. He knew what Nana would resort to after her singing and rocking had failed.

A few minutes later, Nana led him upstairs, turned off his light, and tucked him into bed. She carried his desk chair outside his room, placing it a few feet from the doorway. A minute of silence passed as he waited with anticipation. He knew that if she left the hall light on, he would soon hear the distinctive sound he had grown to love—Nana Thurman raising the leather Bible from the wooden hallway cabinet.

Carter held his breath when he heard the cabinet open and Nana turn the crisp, thin pages. There were nights when she would read a passage from another portion of Scripture, but Carter's favorite was of Samuel, the boy prophet. Once, when he sat through a long sermon with his father, he occupied himself during the service by searching through the Old Testament, finding the story in the first fourteen verses of I Samuel's third chapter. Somehow, when he read it, the power of the story was not as great as when Nana read it to him.

> *Now the boy Samuel was ministering to the LORD under Eli. And the word of the LORD was rare in those days; there was no frequent vision.*
>
> *At that time Eli, whose eyesight had begun to grow dim, so that he could not see, was lying down in his own place; the lamp of God had not yet gone out, and Samuel was lying down within the temple of the LORD, where the ark of God was. Then the LORD called, "Samuel! Samuel!" and he said, "Here I am!" and ran to Eli, and said, "Here I am, for you called me." But he said, "I did not call; lie down again." So he went and lay down. And the LORD called again, "Samuel!" And Samuel arose and went to Eli, and said, "Here I am, for you called me." But he said, "I did not call, my son; lie down again." Now Samuel did not yet know the LORD, and the word of the LORD had not yet been revealed to him.*
>
> *And the LORD called Samuel again the third time. And he arose and went to Eli, and said, "Here I am, for you called me." Then Eli perceived that the LORD was calling the boy. Therefore Eli said to Samuel, "Go, lie down; and if he calls you, you shall say, `Speak, LORD, for thy servant hears.'" So Samuel went and lay down in his place.*
>
> *And the LORD came and stood forth, calling as at other times, "Samuel! Samuel!" And Samuel said, "Speak, for thy servant hears." Then the LORD said to Samuel, "Behold, I am about to do a thing in Israel, at which the two ears of every one that hears it will tingle. On that day I will fulfill against Eli all that I have spoken concerning his house, from beginning to end. And I tell him that I am about to punish his house forever, for*

> *the iniquity which he knew, because his sons were blaspheming God, and he did not restrain them. Therefore I swear to the house of Eli that the iniquity of Eli's house shall not be expiated by sacrifice or offering for ever."*

Nana Thurman would go on to read how Eli's two sons died in a battle and how Eli himself died that same day. But on most nights, Carter fell asleep before this tragedy occurred. The privilege granted to Samuel was enough of a dream for him to ponder. Though he had heard many speak audibly to God at church and Sunday school, nobody he knew had heard God speak audibly. Samuel was special. Carter wished to be like him: "Samuel, Samuel," he'd imagine. "Carter, Carter . . ."

The few times Carter did remain awake left him troubled. *What was it that Eli's sons did that got God so upset? And could it be so bad as to let all three of them die on the same day?* Sometimes, God didn't seem fair.

On that fall evening of seventy-four, Carter decided God was not fair. Carolyn and Shannon had fallen asleep, and Nana had started the narrative from the book of Samuel. Suddenly, she stopped during God's first beckoning of the boy prophet. Carter thought it strange; possibly a stomach problem or some other ailment people her age endure.

Seconds passed and then a couple minutes.

Still she did not resume the story.

Carter crawled out of bed and peaked down the hallway. Nana's head hung loosely, her eyes closed. Thoughts raced through his mind: Had Nana suffered from a heart attack? Was it too late to help her? Had this anything to do with what Nana and Shannon were talking about minutes earlier?

His heavy breathing and rapid heartbeat awoke him from his stupor. He raced to Nana's side and shook her gently, attempting to wake her.

She remained motionless.

He rushed to Carolyn's bedside. "Nana. Something's wrong," he anxiously whispered.

Carolyn did not hesitate. She shot out of bed into the hallway. It was just in time. The paramedics claimed that another minute and she would have died.

"It's sad, really," Carolyn later told Carter and Shannon. "Instead of resting peacefully in a wooden box, she's stuck in a five-by-ten room, not aware she's alive."

Nana's new home was a convalescent hospital a few miles from their house. Carter visited her once each month with his mother and sisters, but she did not appear to recognize any of them, not even Carter's mother. Nana's eyes would open, but they seemed to fix on something far beyond her visitors. She could not speak and had to be fed by a nurse. The memorable aromas Carter once associated with his grandmother, mothballs and TV dinners, were replaced by the unpleasant odors that infiltrated the halls of her new home.

Carter wondered about the words Carolyn had spoken. *Would Nana have chosen to die rather than live in an awful-smelling hospital? Was she even aware that she was alive?*

In bed, at school, at church, even while playing football with his friends, Carter pondered Nana's situation. He concluded that God just was not fair. It was his father's God who allowed this to happen. It was no wonder his mother felt the way she did about the Bible and going to church. Why believe in such a God?

He decided to continue attending church, but only because he had no desire to see how his father would respond if he told him otherwise. Increasingly, the stories he heard each week were just that, stories, or fantasies as his mother called them. He enjoyed them for pure entertainment while becoming more aware of how ridiculous it was to have ever believed them to be true.

The Pickle

Carter was certain he knew what his friends were doing: watching cartoons, playing a pickup game of football outside in the cul-de-sac, or maybe hitting some balls to one another in the grass field of their school down the street. They'd be sweating by now, in the thick of competition, concerned only with the outcome of their game.

Saturday mornings were meant for such things. His friends' parents appeared to understand this. Carter's parents did not. Or perhaps they did, Carter thought, and didn't care. Leave it to them to devise the cruel practice of insisting that their children invest their weekend mornings in the family library, preparing for school the following week.

Carter looked across the table at Carolyn. She jostled a pencil, using both ends equally, attempting to solve an extra-credit math problem her teacher had given the best students in class.

Shannon reclined on the sofa at the base of their father's towering bookshelves, turned on her side, and read a book she held with both hands. She looked intent, but perplexed, as she turned pages back and then returned to the page she was reading previously. Carter narrowed his eyes, focusing on the front cover. "*The Stranger*," he muttered to himself. He wrote this on his paper, hoping that it may give him a start on his English assignment.

He looked down at the sheet. The words he had just written were all he saw. On Monday it would have to be full of words. These could not be just any words but words that made sense and told a story, a story he would have to make up using his imagination. He shook his head. It had been over an hour since they had finished breakfast and started their Saturday morning homework. He had hoped to be finished by now so he could start his math problems.

Math was easy. It was fun. All those numbers made sense once his father helped him recognize the relevance they had to baseball. Division was not the numerator over the denominator, but the total number of hits over the total number of at bats. Most of his peers were still struggling with division. Third-grade math failed to be a challenge any longer. Whereas Hector attended high school two times each week, Carter was allowed into the sixth-grade classroom to learn the basics of algebra. He was lost at first but soon began to appreciate how everything seemed to fit nicely into formulas. Even if he could not understand a particular lesson, it was better than sitting in class, solving problems he already knew how to do.

This writing assignment was an entirely different proposition. It was tedious. It was boring. Placing his hands over his eyes, Carter wished he had done his math assignment first.

He would not ask his sisters for help. Carolyn would give him a dirty look if he disturbed her and then suggest things that he would not understand. She made him feel stupid. Maybe that was her plan, Carter thought, so that he'd not ask the next time.

Shannon used to be his greatest asset in times such as this. She'd help him study for spelling tests and make up math problems for him to practice. Lately, she didn't seem to put the effort into it she once did. It wasn't long ago that she would take Carter by the hand and sing a "song of remembrance," a popular tune with lyrics from the topic Carter was studying. Or she might take on the persona of a historical figure and prod Carter to react to her dialogue and actions as another historical figure he was studying.

No such enthusiasm accompanied her tutoring techniques any longer. It seemed her mind was elsewhere, perhaps in the book she was reading, when he had asked for help. He knew she would not refuse to help, but her assistance was becoming increasingly incompetent. She'd be no use here.

In two days, the paper would have to be full of words. Dad was at work. Carolyn and Shannon were not an option. Carter rose from the table and sighed. He looked at both his sisters. Carolyn was undaunted by his movement. Shannon glanced up, smiled, and returned to her book. It was hopeless. He had only one choice.

The interrogation would begin as soon as he entered the kitchen. "What are you doing here, Carter?" she would ask. "Finished your homework already?"

Carter stopped midway between the library and the kitchen, next to the supper table. He glanced behind, wondering whether he should give it one more shot on his own. He looked to the floor and then at the legs of the table. Hadn't his father carved these legs for his mother, each leg portraying a famous American novel? Did she not love to read literary works? Is that not what she had studied in college? If anyone could help him begin to write, would it not be she?

Carter was certain that any idea of his would not measure up to the standards Carolyn and Shannon had set. He had made a habit of going to his father for help, frightened by the possibility of his mother's disapproval.

The clock chimed; it was ten forty-five. He had wasted enough time. Carter raised his head and walked to the kitchen.

He pushed open the door and stepped inside. His mother was sitting at the counter, sipping coffee, and reading a book. Carter looked to the floor and then at the piece of notebook paper he held in his hand. He read the words he had written minutes earlier, "*The Stranger*."

"What is it, Carter?" his mother asked. "Not feeling well?"

She placed the book next to her mug of coffee and walked to him. She placed her hand on his forehead. After several seconds, she ruffled his hair. "You don't have a fever."

Carter looked up and smiled.

"What's in your hand?" she asked.

Carter raised the paper.

"*The Stranger*?" his mother read. "What is this, Carter? A story?"

"It's a book," he answered.

"You are writing a book report on *The Stranger*?"

His mother sounded impressed. He felt an urge to lie.

"No," he answered. "Shannon's reading it in the library. I just saw the words and wrote them down."

Carter could see the questions form as his mother's eyes narrowed. The interrogation was about to begin.

"You have an English assignment due on Monday?" she asked.

Carter looked up, grinding his teeth.

She walked back toward the kitchen counter. "How long have you been working on this?"

"Uh, well, just a little while."

She looked skeptical.

Carter lowered his head. "All morning. I've done nothing else. Just sat there and thought. Nothing comes out. Nothing."

She sat down and had another sip of coffee. She waved Carter to sit next to her. "It's not easy," she explained, "writing a story."

Carter studied her, waiting. She seemed eager to help. "Would you like some suggestions? Something to get you started?"

Carter's eyes widened. "Sure," he answered, wondering why he had hesitated coming to her. He raced to the stool next to his mother and hopped on top.

She opened a cabinet drawer and took out a pencil. "Tell me, Carter, what are the parameters of the assignment?"

Carter wasn't sure what she meant. It was as though Carolyn were helping him.

"Let me ask it another way," she said. "What did Mrs. Reed say you were to write about?"

"She played this record in class. It was music without any words. She asked us to close our eyes and imagine what the music was telling us. After the music was over, we wrote down what we thought of. I'm supposed to write about that."

"And what did you think of?"

"The music was kind of neat, like it was from a movie or cartoon. It reminded me of a chase scene, like maybe some little people being chased by a giant or something like that."

"Is that what you wrote?"

Carter shook his head. "Another kid thought that up. I don't want to copy him."

"Did any other thoughts pop into your head during the music? Anything special you remember?"

Carter shrugged. "Sure. I guess."

His mother placed the pencil on the sheet of paper. "Draw me what you were thinking."

"But don't you want to know what I was thinking first?"

"You told me about the giants. Now I want you to draw your other idea," his mother explained.

Carter hesitantly picked up the pencil. His artistic abilities were the worst in his class. He wondered if he could portray what was in his mind onto the sheet of paper. But explaining this to his mother would get him nowhere.

He began to draw three men. They were stick figures. He looked up out of the corner of his eye, trying to determine from his mother's reaction whether he was on the right track.

"Go on," she said.

Next, he drew caps atop each of their heads and baseball gloves on the two men on the left and right of the third man in the middle. "They're chasing—"

"Shh, Carter." She placed her hand on his shoulder. "Keep drawing. Show me. Don't tell me."

Carter drew two bases and a baseball in midair tossed from one of the men with gloves to the other. By the time he was finished, there was an umpire in their midst, making his decisive motion; a base coach with an expression of anticipation; and a fan screaming, his hands forming a megaphone over his mouth.

Tapping his pencil, Carter wondered whether that was enough. He looked at it further and smiled, anxious to return to the library and begin writing his story.

He looked up.

"Now you're ready," she said as she smiled at his drawing.

"Thanks, Mom." Carter pushed his chair back and ran to the library. He threw open the doors and leaped into his chair. Breathing heavily, he grabbed some papers and wrote.

Carter was not conscious of time. The words flowed through his body—from his brain, through his arms, to his fingers. He caught himself smiling as he approached the end, astonished that within such a brief span of time he had journeyed from two words of meaninglessness to two pages of a story. As he finished, he held his pencil high and lowered it with force toward his paper to produce his final period. His smile grew, and he looked up, ready to share his accomplishment. Carolyn was already staring. "What?" he asked.

Carolyn tapped her pencil's eraser on the table. "What are you doing?"

"Writing," Carter said with pride.

"Don't be a smart ass, Cart," Carolyn warned. "What were you writing?"

Carter gulped. He hated to anger anyone in his family. Next to his mother, Carolyn was the most relentless. "My English assignment," he said with less enthusiasm.

Carolyn stood up and walked behind him. She reached out for the paper. "Shannon," Carolyn asked, "when was the last time Carter wrote anything without first whining for a half hour about having to write it?"

"Maybe he's been awakened," Shannon said as she turned a page in her book.

Carolyn read the first page and then handed it back. "It's about baseball of course."

"This family is about baseball," Shannon muttered.

"Listen to her, Cart," Carolyn announced. "It's as though she no longer reveres our nation's pastime."

"Oh, I know its worth," Shannon said as she closed her book, placing it beside her, "but like anything in life, worth diminishes once we are so full of it that there's no desire to want any more of it."

"Nothing in excess you mean?" Carolyn asked.

"Something like that," she answered. Shannon rose from her reclined position and stretched her arms and yawned.

She leaned forward. "Nothing in excess," she repeated.

Carter looked at Shannon, wanting to ask what she and Carolyn were talking about. If he understood correctly, it sounded as though it was possible to have too much of baseball. Too much food, sure, Carter knew what that was all about. All too often he'd be at a restaurant and order more than he could consume. But baseball? How could one ever get tired of it? It sounded like maybe Shannon was.

"Are you guys done with your assignments?" Shannon asked.

"I can breeze through my math later tonight," Carter announced.

"Carolyn?" Shannon asked.

Carolyn closed her book and sat next to Shannon on the sofa.

"Good." Shannon reached inside her backpack and took out an unopened box of baseball cards.

"Wow!" Carter cautiously got out of his chair and walked to the sofa. "Can I hold it?"

Shannon smiled. "Of course. But we're not opening them yet. These are going to be our bargaining chips."

"It all went smoothly?" Carolyn asked.

"The guy at the store went for it. I couldn't believe it, Carolyn. I was holding my breath the whole time, waiting for something to go wrong. Waiting for him to change his mind."

"So what you give him?"

"That's the best part. At first I offered him five Reggie Jacksons, three Mike Schmidts, two Gaylord Perrys, and one Nolan Ryan. But he wouldn't have any of that. I thought it was over until he asked if we had any Luis Tiants, Mike Marshalls, or Steve Garveys. I held my breath and tried to hide my excitement."

"Well, what you end up giving him?"

"Ten of our Tiants, ten Garveys, five Marshalls, and ten Joe Rudis."

Carolyn raised her hand. Shannon slapped it. "We scored, Cart," Carolyn almost sang. "Shannon does all our dealings from now on."

"Now, this is what we'll do." Shannon looked at Carter, waiting for him to hand back the box of new cards.

Carter held the box away from his body and raised it just under his nose. He knew better than to open it without permission. Closing his eyes, he took a deep breath, inhaling the aroma of the bubble-gum sticks wrapped inside each wax pack of cards. He pictured the blue, red, and yellow wrapping and anticipated the joy of ripping the paper and flipping through the pictures on each card.

"Carter," Shannon said again, "we need to start before Mom opens that door and chides us for playing the market with the cards they've given us."

Carter handed the box to her.

"Now, these are the rules," Shannon started. "We'll split the packs evenly into thirds. There's twenty-four. That's how many for each of us, Carter?"

Carter frowned and eyed Shannon with disappointment. "C'mon. That's too easy. Eight."

"Good." Shannon removed the cellophane from around the box, opened the lid, and dumped the individually wrapped packs of cards on the floor. "Each of us grab eight. Now!"

Carter reached out and grabbed three. By the time he was ready to get more, there were only five remaining. He looked up at his sisters, both smiling. He shrugged and pulled the final five packs toward him.

"Now what?" Carter asked.

"Now we use these along with our current collections for bargaining chips."

Carter no longer envied his friends. He had finished a dreaded English paper and was now on the verge of partaking in a card-trading frenzy with his sisters. The trading process was pleasant enough—nostalgia and stats of old and young ballplayers mixed with bubble-gum aroma—as cards changed owners two, three, four times.

After ten minutes of trading, Carter was pleased with the collection he now possessed. He had a cornucopia of players from the late fifties through the seventies, Hall of Famers and guys with colorful names, such as Blue Moon Odom and Boots Day. He was most proud of the gains he had made and the small sacrifices he had paid to obtain them.

Once the session was over, Carter rushed to his seat and placed his cards on the table, admiring his savvy in obtaining Pete Rose, Reggie Jackson, and Ferguson Jenkins for players whose names he did not recognize, all of which Shannon seemed more than eager to obtain from him. He raised his hand over the glossy pictures, careful to touch only the edges of each card.

"You didn't leave yourself with much of a collection," Carter heard Carolyn chide Shannon.

Shannon shrugged. She dropped her cards into the empty box, picked up her book, and reclined on the sofa.

"Does this bore you?" Carolyn continued.

Carter looked up. It sounded as though Carolyn was upset.

"This isn't good enough for you anymore?"

"I didn't say that, Carolyn." Shannon stared at her book. It seemed to Carter she had not begun to read but was only staring into the pages.

"You're better than us now? Is that it?" Carolyn asked.

Shannon turned her head, looking at Carolyn, "What are you talking about?"

Carolyn raised her arms. "What just happened here? You just gave your most valuable cards to Cart and got nothing in return."

Shannon shook her head. "I've got plenty more in my room."

"Not those you don't."

"Don't I?"

Carolyn's eyes narrowed. Did this mean Shannon had been holding out on both her brother and sister? Carter wondered what other cards Shannon had, why she was hiding them, and from whom or where she received them.

"Are you jealous? Is that what this is about, Carolyn? Carter's younger; I was just helping out his collection a bit."

Carolyn shook her head. "I don't care about Cart."

She stopped and looked over at Carter. "I mean I don't care about Shannon giving you the cards."

Carter nodded in quick thrusts, not wanting to make a commotion or become entrenched in what appeared to be brewing into a confrontation between his two sisters.

"It's like you don't care anymore." Carolyn pointed at the box holding Shannon's cards.

"About cards?" Shannon seemed to ask for clarification.

"About anything," Carolyn said.

"Things change. They evolve," Shannon answered. "I'm evolving."

Carolyn stood up. "Mom walks in and hears you say that, she applauds. She heralds you a genius, intellectually sound beyond your years. But she's not here, Shannon. It's just the three of us."

"Mom's got nothing to do with this."

"Like hell she doesn't. Do you have any idea what she'll say when you tell her you're quitting?"

Carter raised his head. "Quitting? Quitting what?"

"There you see," Carolyn pointed to Carter.

"Carter will understand," Shannon said.

"Really?" Carolyn turned toward him. "Cart, Shannon told the coach yesterday that she's not going to play softball this year."

Carter looked at Shannon in shock. She shrugged and grinned.

"How does that make you feel, Cart?" Carolyn asked.

"I'm sad," he said without being conscious of trying to say anything.

Carolyn turned back toward Shannon. "Mom will be less understanding. I promise you."

"I'm not living my life for Mom, Carolyn. Since we were little, we've always seen her as the one to please. Never Dad, never a primary concern to please a teacher or a coach, or a friend, or even ourselves. Only her. Have you ever thought about that?"

"What happened to you?" Carolyn asked. She no longer seemed angry but somewhat defeated and remorseful. "We were so close. We talked."

Shannon shook her head and looked up at her sister. She said nothing. Placing her book facedown, she sat on the edge of the sofa. She looked forward to the far end of the library, as though she was not sure how to answer Carolyn. "I think it all started that night, on the Fourth of July, with that firework. It happened so fast, but I remember it as though it happened in slow motion, like it was supposed to happen, that it was ordained."

She paused and walked to the table near the center of the library, across from Carter. "I'm trying to figure things out," she explained, "and the more I try to figure them out, the more questions I begin to ask myself. The more questions I ask, the more books I read to try and find some answers. The result, more questions. It's endless."

Carolyn dropped herself on the sofa. "Call it sisterly love, or whatever you want to, but don't go overboard, Shannon. If you think baseball gluttony is bad, I don't suppose philosophical gluttony is any better."

"There's gotta be something, Carolyn. Something that never gets tiresome, old, or faded. Something to get excited about. Right now, it's these books."

"That's because they're still new to you. Give them time."

Shannon shook her head. "I don't think so. I hope not."

Carter scratched his head.

"See," Shannon said, "Carter understands. That's it in a nutshell. Scratching my head each day, wondering whether Mom's ideals or

Dad's or some other combination are what we should use to govern our lives."

"All this from a firework?" Carolyn asked softly.

Shannon smiled wryly. "I've seen the light."

Color Blind

"Have you ever thought about how our brain works, Carter?" Hector Romero asked as they walked home from school in early September. "I mean, think of it. I say the word apple, and you probably picture it in your head—a red apple, not green. But I ask the same question to some kid in China, and he thinks of a green apple, not red. Why?"

Carter scratched his head.

"I suppose," Carter answered, "because the first apple I saw was red. The first apple a Chinese boy saw was green."

"Exactly!"

Hector seemed pleased.

"So?" Carter asked.

"Yeah?"

"What's your point?"

Hector shrugged. "Perception."

"I don't understand."

"Look at me Cart. What do you see?"

Carter shook his head. "A boy. My friend. A tall, skinny kid who asks too many silly questions."

"I'm a spic, Carter. A no-good, low-down, greasy-haired, Mexican loser."

Carter frowned. "Who told you that?"

Hector's head lowered. "I saw it on television."

"You were on TV?" Carter asked with excitement.

"Perception, Cart. That's what I'm talking about. That's how they portray us. That's how they make me feel."

"But you're Hector. You're not any of those other things. You're just Hector."

Hector smiled. "You don't understand because you look like they do."

Later that night, Carter thought about Hector's comments. He wondered how long Hector had felt this way, how long it took for him to discover that he was not like all the rest.

"Not like all the rest." Carter knew what that was like inside his home. Finally, however, he was beginning to sense a change in tide. There was another family member he could consider an ally, someone on his side of the fence. Before, it was Dad on the right and Mom, Carolyn, and Shannon on the left, Carter doing all he could to survive on the edge separating the two. But now Shannon was climbing up from the left side to join him atop.

He'd let Hector know tomorrow, in some way, maybe by just a pat on the back or a smile, that there's room on that fence for him too.

Horses, Plains, and Punch on a Train

"My Vacation Journal" by
Shannon Mason
P.3/English

September 16, 1975

Hmmmmmmm . . . Our tires met the steel grating on one of the bridges crossing the Mississippi River. My younger brother, Carter, began counting to himself softly. Counting what, I did not know; I only heard him mumbling, making sure not to wake the rest of us. "One, two, three, four, five, six, seven, eight, nine . . ."

My mother was driving. "Carter, what are you doing?" she asked. "Counting cars?"

Carter shook his head. "Seventeen, eighteen," he continued.

"Buildings?" our mother asked again.

Carter shook his head. "Twenty-three, twenty-four."

Carter and our parents were in the front of the station wagon. My father was asleep. Carolyn, my older sister, was sleeping beside me. Mom and Carter must have presumed I was sleeping also; otherwise I don't think they would have entered into the senseless chatter that followed. But since I like things that appear meaningless, I paid careful attention and preserved the contents of their dialogue to bore you to tears for making me write this assignment while on vacation.

I could see my mother look at Carter inquisitively out of the corner of her eye. Carter kept counting as she resumed her guessing, "Bridge beams?"

Carter shook his head.

"Birds?"

He shrugged his shoulders. I could see his reflection off the front windshield. He was suppressing a grin.

Mom let out a sigh of frustration. She enjoyed playing these games with us, but Carter was always so far in left field that none of us could guess where he was coming from. We often played them to fill the time before a movie at the theater, between innings at a baseball game, and in the car or airplane during vacation.

Mom went on guessing. "Not cars. Not bridge pillars. Birds, no. Boats? Is it boats? No, not one in sight."

As she mumbled, Carter kept counting all the way to the other side of the bridge. "One hundred seventy-two, one-hundred seventy-three, one-hundred seventy-four . . ."

Once our rear tires left the steel gratings, Carter stopped.

"That was it?" my mother asked. "You were counting how long we were on the bridge? For goodness sake, Carter, why didn't you use your watch?"

Carter didn't speak.

"Well?"

I could see his grin growing in the windshield's reflection.

"Thank goodness we are not in the South," my mother said, "travelling from Louisiana to Mississippi. You'd be counting forever!"

Carter jerked his head toward her. "You mean there's a longer bridge?"

"So that is what you were doing?" My mother, always wanting to be the one who breaks the code, spoke loudly. I quickly shut my eyes when I saw her eyes shift to the rearview mirror. I've grown tired of these family games. I think my mother believes that they make us special somehow, that they illustrate how creative and intelligent we are. But my brother still enjoys them, so for his sake, I still play along.

"I didn't say that," Carter protested.

There was a pause. I know Carter. He was done with his game. Now, all he wanted was to know more about this alleged long bridge in Louisiana of which my mother made reference.

"Tell you what," Mom said, "I'll make a deal. There is no way you were counting the time we were on that bridge. There were too many uneven pauses between your numbers. You tell me what you were counting, and I'll tell you about the bridge in Louisiana."

Carter scratched his head and then turned to look back at Carolyn. Again, I shut my eyes, knowing he'd look my way next. Dad was snoring in the front seat beside him. Carolyn began fidgeting beside me. I turned my head toward the window and reopened my eyes once I felt Carter had turned back around. We had just left Saint Louis, and I could see the distant skyline and the Arch fade in the early morning haze.

Carter tilted his head upward. It appeared he was pondering his predicament, the embarrassment, and the utter helplessness he would feel if he told our mother and she laughed. But I know my brother. His curiosity regarding the bridge in Louisiana was eating him alive.

"Horses." Carter blurted.

My mother looked down at him.

Carter continued, "Horses, Mom. I was counting horses." She looked at him as if she were questioning the validity of his confession.

Carter began his explanation before she had the opportunity to ask. "There we were, still in the hotel parking lot. I heard a blast behind us. We had to hurry. You started the engine. They were gaining on us; I could hear the rushing sound grow louder with each passing second. I didn't want to glance behind, afraid of seeing what I knew was there. But you were brave and pressed onward, crashing through the barricade they had created across the entrance of the bridge."

Let me stop here to say that I was very tempted to reach into my backpack and write my brother's words in my journal. I was stunned to hear my little brother express himself so eloquently. And I felt a strange emotion I had not felt before; I guess it was pride. You see, my brother has struggled for so long to gain my parents' recognition that he is as scholarly as his two sisters. He strives so hard but often fumbles over words and phrases with which he tries to impress. Many times he makes matters worse. I feel sorry for him because I think my mother is disappointed with his development. Anyhow, I felt this was a crowning moment for Carter, and I wanted to keep record of it.

But to make any sudden movement might have disrupted his flow of thought. I decided to use my keen memory to record his words and write them later.

Carter continued, "All around us were gunshots. Arrows flying." Carter placed his hand on my mother's shoulder and looked into her eyes. "Mom," he said with a serious brow, "you saved us from the cavalry. I counted just under two hundred horses. By the time we had reached the bridge we were surrounded. Horses of all shades and sizes. Brown, speckled, shiny black, white, and grey. But you drove on, undaunted by their presence, unmoved by the pending doom."

"*Lawrence of Arabia*," she sighed. "You three watched it last night."

I wasn't sure at this point whether I was going to kill my brother or recommend my parents taking him to a doctor to examine his sanity. He lowered his head in mock shame. He looked up at Mom with a grin. I could have strangled the little monkey!

Mom had not yet shown her reaction. Her gaze remained focused on the road. Carter finally answered, "Yes, ma'am."

"How late did you and your sisters stay up?"

Carter turned around. I quickly shut my eyes. I sensed his betraying stare. I knew he did not want to answer, in fear of getting us, his two best friends on the trip, in trouble. I opened my eyes and grinned as Carter shrugged his shoulders and said, "I don't know."

"That's a long movie, Carter Anthony. When did you start watching it?"

I could read through my mother's ploy. I hoped Carter would not fall for it. "About ten thirty," he blurted.

"Ten thirty!" My mother shouted before realizing how loudly she had spoken. She studied Carter, taking her eyes from the road.

She whispered, "Ten thirty! Was that the beginning or near the middle? Never mind, I don't want to know."

Turning her attention back on the road, she did not seem angry but shook her head in disbelief.

She didn't say a whole lot the next twenty minutes, just commentary on passing landmarks and interesting billboard advertisements. I contemplated dramatizing my arrival of consciousness but refrained from doing so in hopes that more enlightening dialogue would begin. Mom finally did tell Carter, and me, about the bridge in Louisiana. She said that it was the longest water bridge in the world and that it crosses a lake named Pontchatrain that divides Mississippi from Louisiana. She and my father had crossed it on their honeymoon while traveling by train. Dad kept calling it "Punch-on-a-Train" because he enjoyed the mixed drinks the bartender had served.

I finally "woke up" so that I could enjoy the scenery. The horizon seemed endlessly the same. Dad and Carolyn were still asleep, and I could tell that Mom was tired of driving. She kept encouraging Carter to talk about something, anything, in order to keep her awake. I busied myself with recording what you are now reading (if you really do read this junk you assign to us). I told her and Carter not to disturb me, that I was doing homework. Actually, I finished writing about their previous conversation when more dialogue began. From then on, I was simply taking dictation.

Carter's attempts at initiating conversation to keep my mother awake were hopeless. Mom's head began to bob up and down, trying to stay awake. It was becoming painfully clear that he was not up to the task.

"How much gas do we have left?" he asked.

"Quarter of a tank," she answered.

"When do you think we'll stop to get more?"

"Another hour, hour and a half."

"Which state do we come to next?"

"Iowa."

"Whom did they name Iowa after?" he asked. "An Indian tribe? And what about California? I know who Washington is named after. That's easy! And Louisiana was named after Louis the XIVth. Illinois, Mississippi, the Dakotas—they're all Indian tribes. But most of the other states, I have no clue. Like Texas, what was a Texas before there was a Texas? And Kansas, what is that? What in the world is an Oregon, a Maine, a Tennessee, or a Kentucky? Is Maryland where all the mayors happened to colonize? Was Virginia named because it was considered to be virgin land? But it wasn't, the Indians were living there! Maybe there was an Indian named Virginia. I remember Massachusetts; that was the name of a company. But what was the origin of the company's name?"

As Carter continued the barrage of questions, my mother grew increasingly perplexed. Whether she was confused about the questions themselves or hearing her son babble, I am not sure. Whatever it was, it was keeping her awake.

"Think about it, Mom," Carter continued. "It's interesting. Don't you think?"

"Maybe you should ask Mrs. Reed if you could do that for your project." (Carter has to do one of these stupid projects also. Do you teachers get together and plan on how to make our lives miserable?)

"Maybe," Carter said.

"What's a great idea?" My father mumbled as he reached forward, stretching his arms and his back. "Why are you two shouting? And Carter, what on earth were you just blabbering?"

"You heard that?"

"Carter's going to write his project on how each state was named," I announced. "He knows some of them already. And we'll be passing through at least ten more."

My father digested this data, rubbed his eyes, and asked my mother how she was feeling.

"I'd feel better if I could sleep in a bed for a full night."

"It was your idea to get out of Saint Louis before seven."

She did not speak—no response, not even a slight movement of her head. I could read a hint of impatience. Something was bothering her, and she didn't seem too happy about my father now being awake. "What time is it, anyway?" she asked.

Dad dug into his loose-fitting blue jeans and pulled out his antique stopwatch he had used for timing laps when he ran in college. He despised all jewelry and, except for his wedding band, refused to wear anything around his neck, wrists, or fingers. His rusty stopwatch served as his timepiece. "Quarter till eight. How far have we gone?"

"About a hundred miles."

"We've made good time. You need a break?"

I could tell Dad's offer was not sincere.

"We'll see. We can stop for breakfast in about an hour. I can last that long. After a few cups of coffee, I should be all right."

My father turned to his left, and looked straight at me. "What are you doing?"

I didn't answer. I simply held up this lovely notebook into which I am writing.

"She's still sleeping?" his eyes focusing on my sister.

"She needs her beauty sleep," Carter teased.

"She looks beat. I thought for sure you'd all be up. What time did you get to bed?"

Neither Carter nor I answered. I eyed Carter who winked at me. I winked back. Mom kept a straight face, "They're just tired, Dear. Why don't you help Carter figure out some of the states?"

Mom to the rescue! Yippee! Take lessons, Mrs. Carmichael, for when you have teenagers! Rarely had she salvaged us from Dad's discipline. Usually, it was Dad who rescued us from Mom. One thing neither of them could endure was their children staying up too late. Somehow, Mom felt it necessary to overlook our mistake. Still, something told me she just didn't want to argue with Dad.

"So," Dad started, "What's your first state, Son?"

"How about Oregon?"

"That's easy. I'm surprised at you. Oregon's named after the Lewis and Clark Expedition and the path the settlers followed."

Carter returned Dad's reply with a blank stare. My father clarified, "You know, the Oregon Trail."

"Shoot, Dad, I know about the Oregon Trail and all that, but why did they call it the Oregon Trail in the first place?"

Carter didn't mean to stump him; he just wanted an answer.

"Well," my father continued, "I suppose those are the types of questions you'll need to research when we get home."

Mom looked at my father skeptically. He smiled back. Maybe I was wrong. Maybe everything was all right between them.

Dad rolled down his window to let in some fresh air. I was relieved; the air in our station wagon had become stale during the two-hour drive out of the city. A minute later he rolled it back up. The faint staleness remained. I closed my eyes, trying to imagine the pleasant aromas I had experienced the previous day at Busch Stadium where the five of us saw the Cardinals beat the Philadelphia Phillies. This was one of the highlights of our vacation. Both Carolyn and I are huge Philadelphia fans. Carolyn has a crush on their young third baseman, Mike Schmidt, and reveres their first baseman, Dick Allen, for his uncompromising pride and stance on political issues. My favorite player is "Lefty," the silent, but deadly, craftsman on the mound, as Dad calls him. I believe he's the prime example of what intellect and determination can accomplish. Carlton is so overpowering because he outthinks and outprepares all of his opponents. He is always a step ahead of them. Unfortunately, he was not pitching this game. Even though the Phillies lost the game in the bottom of the ninth, Carolyn was pleased with the performance of her two favorite players: Schmidt hit his thirty-third double of the season, and Dick Allen hit a three-run homer in the first.

I awoke from the memories of yesterday by the odors filling our car—morning breaths mingled with stale, humid, drenched socks and feet. I closed my eyes again to relive the hearty aromas at the ballpark. The scent from roasted peanuts served by vendors reached our noses as we walked the streets of Saint Louis leading to the stadium. The smell of hotdogs sizzling on grills graced the corridors within the stadium as we entered. There was the brewed coffee for my mother, the ice-cold bitter smell of beer for my father, and the scent of cherry tobacco rising from the pipe of an elderly man sitting near us, the sweet aroma of which made me wonder how anything that smells so enticing could be so harmful to the chimney that exhaled it. And finally, the most wondrous fragrance of all, the unsurpassed bouquet of freshly cut grass. We could not have experienced this most wonderful of baseball's fragrances (since the Cardinal's home turf is artificial) if Dad hadn't pulled a bag full of grass from his backpack and spread it generously under each of our seats. The fans seated around us thought we were a bit strange at first, but when we moved from our seats near the end of the game to get closer to the field, I saw a couple kids rush over to where we had been sitting and begin to dance on the pieces of grass Dad had brought. And they thought Californians were strange!

The first three days of our vacation had already been full of pleasant memories. I smiled as I recalled them. It seems that we operate best as a family when we leave home. So many times during the past year, I've felt a haunting loneliness and desperation within the walls of our house. Mom's mapped out all our lives. I didn't mind so much before, when Carolyn and I were content to let our parents decide which decisions we should make. I can understand when we were children; they protected us from making foolish choices. But I feel equipped to make choices of my own now, and unless they are in line with my mother's plans, I feel that any choice I make is the wrong one.

For Carolyn, it's not a big deal; she's a carbon copy of Mom. I fear to think of what explosive exchanges would occur if the two of them ever disagreed. And poor Carter, he's no freedom to be himself. I love that kid; he's so funny and caring. He loves the world of make-believe, something our mother drilled into all of our heads is not a desirable trait. His creativity is being stymied.

And then there's me. Where should I start? My friends are not acceptable, because they do not perform well in class; they have no future according to Mom. The fact that I quit playing softball has my whole family against me. Even Carter bothers me once a week, asking if I've reconsidered my decision. And the hypocrisy of Mother—boy! It's blinding. "Read. Read. Read," she drilled into our heads. Now, when I am desperately seeking for some explanation for existence and why any of us are here, I find it almost impossible to find a piece of literature that addresses life's meaning that does not include, as part of its theories and philosophy, some belief in a deity. The only books I've brought home lately of which she approves are ones by Satre, Camus, and Engel. Any other, and she'll make a comment, subtle but poignant, that I'm wasting my time.

The car's stale scent was strong enough to again bring me back to reality. Dad rolled down his window once more, letting in fresh air. I smiled as Carter's wearied head gently came to rest on Dad's left side. Our father pulled his arm out from behind Carter's back, hooked it around him, and pulled my brother close to his chest. Carter had the finest pillow in the car.

September 17, 1975

Saint Louis is the farthest city to the east we visited. Mom was not so much interested in us seeing the big cities as the great national parks and monuments. This is not because she does not like the big cities of our country but because we had traveled down the East Coast for our vacation last year while visiting museums, libraries, and of course, ballparks as far north as Boston and as far south as Raleigh, North Carolina. In order to give Carolyn, Carter, and me an opportunity to see another angle of American life, history, and geography, she decided that this year we would travel via Interstate 40 and 44, through the Great Plains, then head back west and visit the majestic national parks of the great Northwest. We had left Saint Louis, traveling north through Illinois toward Iowa City. From there, we'd move west.

On all our trips, Mom and Dad would plan activities that interest each of us. Some activities would interest Carolyn more than Carter and me, like visiting the sites of Woodstock or the student uproar at Kent State. Some would interest my brother more than either Carolyn or me, like visits to museums specializing in prehistoric relics. And some would interest all three of us, like a visit to the Baseball Hall of Fame in Cooperstown, New York, or a visit to any major or minor league ballpark. Mom was a wizard at creating the assortment of activities, and Dad served as the engineer. He would labor for a week or two before we left, finalizing our travel arrangements: where we would sleep, the most efficient roads to take to get to all the attractions and sites Mom wanted us to visit, and gathering schedules from all the minor league teams in towns we would happen to pass.

The three of us had no worries. Our parents had figured it all out. This year's vacation was no exception. If only I didn't have to write this journal!

September 18, 1975

If something does not proceed as planned, as is often the case, my parents have a brief argument on how to resolve the conflict and create an adventure that turns out so exciting that the three of us could hardly imagine anything better that we could have possibly done.

The only wrinkle during our annual family vacations centers around my dad's driving. The problem is, he doesn't! The only time I remember him behind the wheel was three years ago when my mother got so sick from a greasy breakfast that she had to stop every five miles to relieve herself at a café, gas station, or whatever else might serve her purpose. It was horrible!

Dad drives himself to work each morning, so none of us can figure out why he doesn't drive during our vacations. Mom says it's because he needs the rest. Whatever the reason, we soon discovered that riding with our father as the driver was not a pleasant experience. The year my mother got sick, we were traveling through Texas. Carolyn and I decided to sing the chorus to "The Yellow Rose of Texas." Suddenly, my father shouted for us to stop. His outburst was horrifying. None of us had ever heard him so upset. Carolyn and I immediately quit singing, and my mother shook her head. I thought a heated argument would ensue, but all we heard the next two hours were the sounds of passing cars. There were no tears, no giggles, and no whispers.

That evening, Dad did apologize to all of us and specifically to Carolyn and me. Since then, Dad has not driven during any of our vacations.

Now we return to this year's trip. The previous tangent was necessary for a full appreciation of what would soon happen. By the afternoon of September 18, we had passed most of what looked like the Great Plains. Dad said that the plains extend from Central America all the way into the northernmost parts of Canada. Carter began writing down this fact into his notebook for his writing assignment. I must have made Carter jump when I screamed, "There it is!" for his pencil flew out of his hand and hit Carolyn in the eye—fortunately the eraser end.

Next to the Philly-Cardinal game we had seen three days earlier, this was the most exciting part of the trip for me. Emerging from the flatness of the plains rose a small range of hills. We were driving through South Dakota on our way to Yellowstone National Park and the Grand Tetons. This small range of hills in South Dakota was the first protrusion from the earth's surface that we had seen in two days. What a welcome sight!

"There they are, Dad, do you see them?" I said as I sat at my mother's side in the front seat. Dad, Carolyn, and Carter were in the backseat, soaking in the beauty around us. "Can you see it, Mom? Oh shoot, they're gone."

"Don't worry, Honey, they'll be back," my father said. "We'll have plenty of views before the day is over. Look to the right when we turn again at that bend. They'll be there."

"I can't see!" Carter whined. "Where? Where are they?"

"Oh, pipe down, Cart," Carolyn said, "We're going to be right in the park. You'll see them up close."

Carter could not believe it. "Really? How close? Can we touch them? Can I climb on top? Oh, I can't wait. Hey, Shannon. Did you hear that?"

He sounded almost as excited as I felt. This was the event of the vacation that Mom had planned especially for me. I had suspected that Carter would be as enthused. One freedom my parents had granted me was to stay up when I discovered in the television listings one of Alfred Hitchcock's films. I find his insights into the human mind and spirit fascinating. It has been with his aid that I've begun to question much of what I had previously assumed to be true: that we will be safe from harm if we follow the rules; if we work hard, we'll reap the benefits; we can trust those closest to us; we can trust our senses. Hitchcock illustrates to us how wrong we can be. I for one do not want to be duped like one of his characters in any of his films.

And the film of his I enjoyed most, as you can probably guess from my excitement over entering the Black Hills of South Dakota, is *North by Northwest*. As for my brother, he had discovered that he could sneak downstairs unnoticed on those nights my parents had given me the okay, and watch one of Hitch's films with me.

I edged up closer to the car's window. Carter got my dad to hold him on his lap so that he could get a better view out of the right rear passenger window.

"There, Carter, on the right above those trees!" I exclaimed.

There they were. I was in awe. My jaw fell. A few seconds later, they disappeared again as my mother turned around another curve in the road.

At this point, Carter shouted an expletive that I shan't repeat here. Let's just say that its letters are contained in the word *shirt*; and if you remove the *r* from such word, you then have the word my brother exclaimed.

"They're gone again," he lamented.

Mom looked back at my brother in disbelief. Carolyn stared at my brother, shaking her head. I tried to keep my attention focused on the four faces of granite that would any second reappear. Immediately, Dad pulled Carter off his lap and fastened his seat belt around his small waist. In all his excitement, my brother had forgotten family etiquette.

After about ten seconds, Carolyn spoke, "Well, is that it? Your son uses profanity, mind you one of your least favorite words in the English language, and all you do is pull him from the window? What kind of punishment is that? He's going to see those goons in a few minutes!"

I kept my eyes fixed on the horizon. Carter later told me he couldn't move but kept his eyes focused on the car mats, hoping Dad would not pay heed to our elder sister.

Before Dad had the opportunity to scold him, the four presidents on the side of the mountain reappeared. "Oh my! Isn't it beautiful." I must have sounded like a fool! "Hurry, Carolyn! Hand me my camera!"

"Give me a break," Carolyn muttered. "Here," she said impatiently as she handed it to me.

I had already taken six pictures before Mom parked the car. I was the first to leap from the station wagon and stretch from the long drive. Carter tried to jump out to join me but was restrained by my father's arm. "One minute, Son." Then he directed his gaze toward our mother, who was still in the driver's seat. "We'll be out in a minute."

"All right. I'll take the girls up near the ridge. You can meet us there."

"We'll only be a minute," he said.

Before Mom escorted Carolyn and me toward the four Presidents, she reached back and rubbed the top of Carter's head. "Don't be too hard on him, Douglas." She shut the front door, and there was silence.

Or so my brother told me. The following events are the eyewitness account of Carter Anthony Mason. I have never understood my parents when it comes to discipline, and this situation only confirms my parents' ambiguous nature. The older I get, the less I understand them. And how many times have my teachers told me that when I get older, I'll understand my parents better? When do I cross that line which marks the point when I begin to understand?

"What was that word you used several minutes ago?" my father asked. Carter was confused. Did he want him to say it again?

"C'mon, Son—the word. What was the word you shouted so enthusiastically as we drove up the mountain?"

Carter was frightened by the motives with which the question was asked. "You mean back there? When you pulled me back?"

"That's right."

Carter shrugged. Fearful. Bashful.

"Yes, Son. That word."

Carter stared at the car mats, fearful of looking at his father. He said the word again, only much more softly.

"What was that? I couldn't hear you."

Carter did not believe what he was hearing. Did he want him to say it a third time? He looked at Dad, hoping that this would soon end and that he didn't have to repeat the word again.

"I'm waiting, Son," he repeated. "The word."

Carter said it a third time, in a whisper.

"Again," our father instructed.

Carter gritted his teeth and said it a fourth time.

"Louder."

Although Carter did not shout the word, he said it with enough volume to appease our father.

"All right, Carter. Calm down. You said it with more exuberance originally; I didn't recognize it when you said it with less gusto." Dad paused, hoping his observation would make an impression. "What does it mean?" he continued.

Again he caught Carter by surprise. Carter shrugged his shoulders and mumbled, "Poop, waste, dung. Something like that."

"You're ashamed of those words?"

Carter shrugged again. "Well, yeah. In a way, I guess."

"Why?"

"They smell."

"Remember that before you use the word next time."

And that was Dad's discipline of my brother. "Ridiculous," you might say, but I've never heard him use the word since.

The two of them joined us on the cliff overlooking Mount Rushmore. Each of us had a reason for excitement during our visit to the national park, and we invested our time accordingly. Carolyn and Mom read the four biographical sketches on each president and debated their perspective on which was the most influential; which served America with the greatest fervor; which was the greatest leader, had the most integrity; and which was the least dispensable.

Dad was intrigued by the task accomplished by Gutzon Borglum, the designer and constructor of the monument. He kept muttering to himself, "Unbelievable," as he read details of the work Borglum and his men had performed. He gazed at the mountain face for minutes from different angles with his mouth wide open.

Carter and I separated early from the rest of the family. Our goal was to retrace the footsteps of Cary Grant, aka Roger Thornhill, and Eva Marie Saint, aka Eve Kendal. Although Mount Rushmore fit in nicely with my parents' planned package of national parks and monuments for this year's family vacation, the detour was made primarily on my behalf. As difficult as it has been over the last year with my mother, she is still Mom. There are fewer and fewer things over which we agree, but one thing is certain: my mother loves her children.

After a couple hours of ooing and awing, Carter, Carolyn, and I climbed into the backseat of the Oldsmobile station wagon as our parents discussed the issue of who would drive next. Mom was beat! That was obvious. But my father seemed set in his ways; he would not drive! The three of us waited in the car as our parents discussed the driving arrangements several yards away.

A few minutes passed before Carolyn opened her side door and walked slowly toward our parents. They did not notice her for at least a minute. She looked over at us in the car and shrugged her shoulders. Finally, she tapped Dad on his right elbow. He turned around and listened to what she had to say. A few seconds later, he shook his head violently and pointed fiercely between my mother and Carolyn. Mom abruptly intervened, calmed Dad down, and took control of the conversation. Minutes later, the three of them turned back toward the car. Carolyn was excited; Mom was serene; Dad was dumbfounded. He made his way to the side door that Carolyn had left open. As he sat down and closed the door, he leaned over and whispered to Carter and me, "Put on your seat belts. You're in for the ride of your lives!"

Carolyn seated herself in the driver's seat. Carter and I quickly reached for each other's hand and held on tightly. We looked at one another with uncertainty.

"You two in the back," Carolyn announced with assurance and a grin, "relax." She tilted the rear view mirror at an angle that gave me a clear view of her face. She winked. Suddenly, all the tension I felt was relieved. If Carolyn was confident, that was enough for me; I was in good hands. I turned to Carter and whispered into his ear that all would be fine. He returned my words of comfort with a dumbfounded stare, as though I was insane.

Mom now had a backup driver: a seventeen-year-old, blue-eyed brunette with a driver's license two months old.

If One Should Rise

September 20, 1975

Carolyn drove us out of the Black Hills and back onto the Great Plains until we arrived at the Montana border. We slept in a small motel just outside of Billings and continued westward the next morning. Mom was well rested, and though Carolyn had done an excellent job, I could tell Mom wanted to drive again. I don't think she feels comfortable not doing something.

Carolyn, Carter, and I are expected back at school in nine days. How Mom and Dad think we are going to travel through Montana into Idaho and on through the Cascades is beyond me. We still would have about a thousand miles back down the Pacific coast. I think they're crazy. But I guess they know what they're doing. They've been orchestrating these vacations for over a decade.

Although I began this exercise cynically, I am growing to recognize the value of writing about my daily activities and thoughts. Granted, life in Fullerton will not match the excitement of being on the road, but I do plan to continue these tidbits of my wandering wonderings, though I have no intention of allowing anyone to read them.

I have learned that journal writing is an avenue through which I can iron out my thoughts. I am digesting opinions and theories of so many different people each day that I find it therapeutic to have an opportunity to comment on what I find ridiculous and ponder what I believe has value. Whether it be a long-held belief I have had instilled into me by one of my parents, a discussion with one of my siblings, a conversation with a friend, or a line of reasoning by Hume, Sartre, Rousseau, or any other of the great philosophers throughout history, writing my reaction allows me to discover what I truly believe. There are no threats of blank looks from peers who have no idea what I am talking about, nor is there the likelihood of my parents' anxiety increasing over questions I may ask. It's just me and my subconscious, attempting to untangle the cosmic questions running through my head.

We spent the day sightseeing, hiking, and camping in Yellowstone National Park and the Grand Tetons. Carter and I agree; we both prefer Carolyn's driving to Mother's. She drove faster and did not swerve as much. But, like I mentioned earlier, except for the afternoon following our visit to Mount Rushmore, Carolyn was assigned a passenger seat in the back.

As we approached Idaho's panhandle, our mother invited Carolyn to drive. She was sleeping at the time, so I nudged her to wake. She awoke in time to hear Mom's question a second time.

Carolyn smiled, straightening her posture.

We had witnessed memorable sites up to this point, and I felt the best of our trip was behind us. But as Carolyn made a turn on northern Idaho's roads, what I saw, well, I'm not sure if any words any writer has ever written could express the matchless beauty before us.

We were in a world of emerald green. Trees full of growth seemed to occupy all available square footage of land. In the midst of the rolling hills was a valley, and within the valley, a sparkling, crystal-blue lake that bent around each hill, leaving behind the impression of overflowing abundance. It was the combination of these blue and green shades that struck a chord within me. If heaven existed, it must look something like this. It was as though beauty had unbridled itself before my eyes. Adding to this spectacle were the sun's rays dancing upon the lake's surface, and the lake's perimeter surrounded by quaint homes, boats, and docks.

When we arrived in downtown Coeur d'Alene, the lake's namesake, Dad checked us into a lakeside hotel where we quickly unpacked our luggage and headed down toward the lake's shore. Carter, Carolyn, and I played in the water while our parents rested peacefully on the sand, Dad reading the book he had bought about the construction of Mount Rushmore and Mom rereading an anthology of short stories written by Mark Twain. Each was doing what he or she enjoyed best. We ate a hearty dinner at a steakhouse and relaxed on our hotel room's shoreline porch until midnight, playing cards.

The moon was full, creating a path of light on the lake's surface. Mom and Dad had their own room. I could sense romance between them as we kissed them good night and they closed the dividing door connecting our two rooms.

The three of us decided to sleep with the curtains open to enjoy the atmosphere. I record a wish I think my brother and sister would share:

"Let it be made known, O Mighty Diary, thou Majestic Journal from beyond, that I hereby request my wish to be granted. Please let us stay another day."

September 21, 1975

What a day!

Dad woke Carter at seven thirty. Sunday.

Leave it to our father to find the times for worship services while we're on vacation. And he drags Carter along every time.

I've always thought my father a bit different, or strange, or weird. I'm not sure what word can best describe him. Why on earth would he have chosen to marry a woman so opposed to his beliefs? And for that matter, why would she agree to marry him? It seemed to be the one thing they could not and would not ever agree on. With regards to everything else, they seemed a perfect match. But what a crucial issue on which to have such diametrically opposed foundations!

I'm still surprised at how few arguments arise between them. They must have some agreement to never talk about such things in front of the three of us, or they realize how pointless it is to bring it up as a point of discussion.

Although Carolyn and me attended church when we were younger, both of us made the decision not to accompany Dad when we turned seven. All we had to do is tell him we no longer wanted to go. I think Carter has the same option, but he has yet to decide. When I heard my father enter the room and ask Carter if he'd like to join him, I wanted to hear my brother say for the first time no. But instead, he climbed out of bed quietly, brushed his teeth, combed his hair, and put on his nicest clean clothes from his suitcase. And he did it with a modest smile on his face.

I felt a piercing in my heart, a stirring within my stomach. "He wants to go?" I asked myself. All this time I had thought he was doing it just to please Dad. Maybe, I began to think, Carter had discovered something that neither Carolyn nor I had while attending Sunday school. Then, my cynic side replied, "Or, Dad's got him so mixed up that Carter doesn't know the difference between what he enjoys and what Dad wants him to enjoy."

And then I thought, "Is that any different than my relationship with Mom?"

Carter knocked softly on the dividing door. Dad opened and let him in.

I tried to go back to sleep, but all I could think about was the apparent joy with which my brother prepared for church. I sat up from bed and scratched my head, looking at my image in the mirror. I shook my head at myself. What a mess I'd become. I once thought myself pretty, but now I was just another ordinary adolescent female struggling with acne and unruly hair. And my inside turmoil was becoming unmanageable. Once upon a time, I could go to my parents, ask their opinion, accept it as gold. Now, I can't trust my mother's biased opinion, just as I learned years ago that I could not rely on Dad's.

I giggled, thinking that perhaps my younger brother discovered something that got past his two "wiser" siblings. I rose from the bed and headed to the bathroom. By the time I had washed my hands, I had already reached for the tube of toothpaste. Within five minutes, I was dressed; for what, I did not know.

I could hear my parents' door open. I darted toward the window and pulled the curtain cautiously. Carter was walking next to Dad, narrating some event with excitement. Dad was laughing.

I closed the curtain and looked back at Carolyn still sleeping. I looked back out the window. Dad and Carter were barely in sight, turning right at the hotel's entrance.

I reached for the doorknob, my heart racing. What was my problem? The door was open. I closed it cautiously and then ran in the direction they were headed.

I saw them turn into a typical church structure. The sign read The First Methodist Church of Coeur d'Alene. I waited a couple of minutes after they entered, not sure whether I should sit with them, not sure why I would decide not to. To be quite frank, I'm not sure what I was thinking at that moment. Just the fact that I was there is unexplainable.

I was in awe, not at any unusual beauty of the church's appearance but at my own consciousness of how out of the ordinary all this was. Surreal it seemed. Perhaps this was all a dream.

I held some type of program or church bulletin. I didn't remember receiving it by the time I realized it was in my hand. An usher was walking in front of me; he seemed intent on leading me to the front. I tapped him on the shoulder. "Excuse me, sir," I whispered. "This will be fine." I slid into an aisle seat in the second-to-last pew.

He looked disappointed.

I smiled.

He still did not seem satisfied.

I looked down at my bulletin, feeling uncomfortable and hoping he would walk back to the rear of the church.

He did.

"Whew," I muttered as all those around me stood up.

"Now what?" I thought, my heart racing still. I looked for Dad and Carter. They were on the outside aisle in the middle of the church. Typical Dad—hidden in a crowd.

Boom! The organ bellowed and then sprang into what I considered a rather nice melody. I began tapping my foot as I reached for the hymnal and opened it to the same number as the woman in front of me.

And can it be that I should gain
An interest in the Saviour's blood?
Died he for me, who caused his pain,
For me, to him to death pursued?

Amazing love, how can it be
That thou, my God, shouldst die for me?
Amazing love, how can it be
That thou, my God, shouldst die for me?

The words were succinct. No dillydally here. They got right to the point. I wrote the words into the margins of the bulletin with a pencil I found in the pew, so I could read them again later.

After several stanzas, a page full of announcements, and an offertory solo, the minister stood and spoke. I'll recap as best I can. I finally figured halfway into the sermon that taking notes was not sacrilegious; many in the congregation did so.

The pastor began: "This morning's lesson comes to us from the sixteenth chapter of Luke, verses nineteen through thirty-one.

'There was a rich man, who was clothed in purple and fine linen and who feasted sumptuously every day. And at his gate lay a poor man named Lazarus, full of sores, who desired to be fed with what fell from the rich man's table; moreover the dogs came and licked his sores. The poor man died and was carried

by the angels to Abraham's bosom. The rich man also died and was buried; and in Hades, being in torment, he lifted up his eyes, and saw Abraham far off and Lazarus in his bosom.

And he called out, "Father Abraham, have mercy upon me, and send Lazarus to dip the end of his finger in water and cool my tongue; for I am in anguish in this flame."

But Abraham said, "Son, remember that you in your lifetime received your good things, and Lazarus in like manner evil things; but now he is comforted here, and you are in anguish. And besides all this, between us and you a great chasm has been fixed, in order that those who would pass from here to you may not be able, and none may cross from there to us."

Then the rich man said, "Then I beg you, father, to send him to my father's house, for I have five brothers, so that he may warn them, lest they also come into this place of torment."

But Abraham answered, `They have Moses and the prophets; let them hear them."

And he said, "No father Abraham; but if some one goes to them from the dead, they will repent."

Abraham said to him, "If they do not hear Moses and the prophets, neither will they be convinced if some one should rise from the dead."""

Following the scripture reading, the pastor began his sermon: "Brethren, we are all the rich man. We are all the poor man, Lazarus. Which of us can deny that we have turned our attention elsewhere, like the rich man, when we see a fellow human in need? A fellow church member? A friend? A parent, a sibling, a child? Which of us can deny that we have felt lowly and oppressed, perhaps not to the extent of Lazarus, but nonetheless, downtrodden and hopeless?"

The pastor continued his preaching for thirty minutes. I was intrigued by his questions and wondered to whom of the two men in the passage I related to most.

"Finally,"—this word from the Pastor awakened Carter, I could see his head jerk back and hit the pew. He rubbed the back of his head. I smiled and then turned my attention back toward the pastor.

"My final point deals with the rich man's request that Father Abraham send Lazarus to warn his family of the awful situation in Hades. Brethren, Abraham's reply is applicable to each of us here this morning, for we are members of that rich man's family. We have heard the words of Moses, just as his family had. We have heard the words of the prophets, just as his family had. But we have one thing they did not: we have heard the words of him who has come from the dead, just as the rich man wanted his family to have the opportunity. Do not miss this point: the very man who told this story to the crowd, he is the one who conquered death and offers us an escape from the tortures of our rich older brother.

"We have been granted the privilege that the rich man desired for his brethren. We have the testimony of one who has risen from the dead. He has risen, and He has warned us of the torturous state of being separated from his presence. The rich man had requested that Lazarus be sent, but God has sent to us His son, Jesus Christ.

"Brethren, this man, Jesus—accept his words. Accept his testimony. And, like Lazarus, you will be comforted. Let us pray."

All heads bowed. I stood and looked over my shoulder. Those standing in the back of the church had their heads lowered, their eyes closed, including the usher who had "led" me to my seat. I rushed to the rear of the church and looked back, my departure unnoticed. Running down the steps I raced toward our hotel.

Sunset

September 21, 1975

One entry was all I planned for today. But some days are destined for suspense and activity. Such was the twenty-first of September.

As I arrived back from church, my mother was standing outside, in front of our hotel room, her eyes full of fury. "Where have the three of you been? Where are your brother and father?"

"Church," I answered.

My mother looked at me curiously. I sensed her condescending disapproval. I didn't care. Not now.

"I followed them," I said, "It was a nice service."

"How long ago did it end?"

"Ten minutes," I answered.

She shook her head. "Is this part of your search?"

I was a bit surprised that she asked it with what appeared to be genuine concern. I expected some hint of sarcasm, but there was none.

"I suppose you don't approve."

"My approval has nothing to do with it. Disappointed? Yes. But do I disapprove? No."

"C'mon, Mom," I said before thinking to hold back my emotions. "What's the difference? My decisions are grand only when they follow the agenda you have for me."

Her eyes widened; a red hue filled her cheeks. "This is why we should have left this morning."

"This was inevitable, Mom."

"Excuse me?"

"If it didn't happen this morning, I mean, then some day soon after. I'm no longer convinced of your we-can-get-it-right-ourselves philosophy.

My mother stood motionless, just staring at me. I had no idea what thoughts could be racing through her head at that moment. I hoped I hadn't dashed her world in pieces.

Before we could continue, I heard Carter and my father approaching from behind.

"We'll talk about this later," she whispered.

Carter looked up at our father to see if our mother's disturbing appearance warranted concern. They were still about ten yards from the room when Dad lowered his head, struck up the pace of his gate, and attempted to enter through the door my mother was blocking.

He stopped. "Katherine," he spoke calmly, "I need to put the suitcases in the car.

"They're already in," she announced.

"Oh?" Dad said as he looked back at our car. "Then I'll just go to the bathroom, and we'll leave."

"How was church?" she asked tauntingly. I cringed at her childishness. I could sense this would get ugly.

"Not now, Katherine."

Carter remained outside as Carolyn popped her head out of our room.

"We agreed to leave at eight. Instead you let us sleep through the alarm while you go off to church."

"So we leave a couple hours later."

"It would have been nice to have been told when to expect your return."

Our father watched her out of the corner of his eye. I suppose he knows when it's best to let her blow off some steam. He tried to remain composed as he went into the adjoining room to see Carolyn. He leaned over to kiss her on top of her head and then sat next to her on the bed. "You and Shannon slept well?" he asked.

"I slept fine. Shannon was gone when I woke up," Carolyn answered.

Carter and I remained outside, unsure of what would happen next.

Our mother looked at both of us with disappointment. For Carter's sake I was glad. Though he did not yet know, he would soon learn that I too was at church and that Mom's glaring eyes shifting between the two of us was a consequence of our presence there together. I was confident that he was intelligent enough to later deduce this meant he now had an ally.

"We're not done, Douglas," our mother warned as she entered the room.

Carter and I stepped closer to the doorway, following Mom, but remained outside, my eyes studying Carolyn. Her expression reflected the questions I had, wondering where this was headed.

"Not done?" he asked. "Not done with what? We're late, Kate. You wanted to get an early start. It's already after ten; let's get going."

"Why were you so late?" Mom inquired with a strained calm. "You left before eight. Shannon got home ten minutes ago."

"Shannon?" he repeated. "What's she got to do with this?"

"I was there, Dad," I answered. "Near the back."

His eyes widened. Things were beginning to make sense.

Mom continued, "Was it a moving service? So moving you stayed to talk with the pastor?"

Dad shook his head.

"And the sermon? Was it so profound that you decided that you needed to pray an extra ten minutes? Forget about your family waiting for you back at the hotel?"

My father stood quietly. He did not seem uncomfortable, as though they'd been through this before. It was the first time any of us had witnessed such an occasion.

"Carter," my mother almost shouted, "how was the sermon?"

Carter began shaking and replied in a crackling tone, "I don't know. I was daydreaming. All I remember was this rich guy died and wanted someone . . ."

"Why do you drag him along, Douglas?" she continued. "You don't think he enjoys it?"

"Ask him. He's now older than our daughters were when they decided no longer to attend."

This was becoming as infantile as I could ever imagine. My parents, the two people I admire most, were using their own children as evidence in their debate. It dawned on me then that perhaps that's all any of us were to them: evidence that they were right. Mom had been leading two to one. Now, it wasn't so clear that she was winning. I hoped I was wrong, but I feared I was closer to the truth than I wanted to be.

"He goes because he thinks you want him to go," she said, "you'll think less of him, you'll be displeased, you'll look down on him. You're raising him to be just like you, Douglas."

There she goes again, I thought to myself. *Look in the mirror, Ma. Look in the mirror!*

"Why are you doing this?" our father asked, shaking his head. "Nothing has changed. We're still a family with different beliefs, accepting one another, regardless."

"Nothing's changed?" my mother's voice rose. "Have you spoken to your daughter? The one who followed you to church? The one who stays up all night reading books by philosophers and theologians? The one who has quit softball, no longer dresses with any dignity, and associates with the scum of her campus?"

That did it for me. My suspicions were correct. My value in Mom's eyes had dropped considerably. I could not hold back the tears. I raced into our room before the torrent began, closed the bathroom door, sat on the toilet, and cried.

Several minutes passed when I heard a gentle tapping on the door. It slowly opened and almost simultaneously the heads of my two siblings emerged through the crack."

"You survive?" Carolyn asked.

I nodded.

"Dad told us to stay in here till he gives us further instructions. Something's brewing."

"Where are they now?" I asked.

"Next door," Carolyn answered.

I got up and walked toward the adjoining door. I could hear them arguing. Carter brushed passed me on his knees and placed his ear against the door. I followed suit, and eventually, so did Carolyn.

"I want an explanation, Doug," our mother said.

"You know why I go Kate. My reasons haven't changed. Whenever you act like this, something else is up."

"How am I supposed to act? Tell me. I don't understand. How am I supposed to act?"

"You've never understood, Kate. You've never tried to understand this part—"

"And is it so difficult for you to understand why? Are you blind? I'm your wife. Each time you go to church, I'm not sure if you go to remember her or to redeem the guilt you feel. Reliving it over and over and over again! You've done your penance; let it go. It's killing you. It's killing me. It will kill the children. It's killing our son!"

Carter looked up at us and began feeling himself for any defects. "I feel all right," he whispered.

"Shhhh!" we sounded simultaneously.

My heart skipped when I heard our parents' door open. The three of us scurried backward and tried to assume positions that would feign our innocence. Dad entered our room and handed Carolyn a twenty-dollar bill. "Your mother and I have some things to work out. The three of you go into town. Buy some lunch, some ice cream. See a movie. Be back by seven."

We stood motionless, at first wondering what could take nine hours to work out. I knew Dad was in no mood for an argument; so did Carolyn. After a few moments of silence, she grabbed Carter's hand and led him out the door.

I followed, my mind racing, trying to piece together what my parents had just discussed. Who was the lady my mother referred to? It seemed as though she had something to do with my father's religious zeal? And what happened between this lady and my father that could get Mom so worked up? And how long ago did it happen?

Carter, Carolyn, and I remained silent as we walked to a nearby park in the center of Coeur d'Alene. Without saying a word, Carolyn sat at one end of a park bench. Carter spotted some swings and looked to her for approval. She didn't seem to notice Carter's request for permission, so I signaled him that it was okay. Then I sat on the opposite end of the bench from Carolyn.

Carter eventually joined us and sat on the grass near the bench. The three of us still had not said a word since leaving the hotel.

Carolyn kicked off her sandals. "Are you hungry?" she asked, staring at the grass in which she massaged her bare feet.

Neither of us answered.

"Cart?" she asked. "Did you guys eat before church?"

"No," he answered softly.

"Then let's get something." Carolyn stood, placed her feet back into her sandals, and started for the center of town. "What you guys feel like?"

None of us knew. So we wandered. We walked into the town center and then back out, through the athletic fields of the local community college, and down onto the shore of Lake Coeur d'Alene. Nothing appealed to us until we discovered an ice-cream parlor on the other side of the street that led back to our hotel. Carolyn took hold of Carter's left hand, and I held his right, cautiously escorting him across the town's busiest street. We entered Henry's 35-Flavors Ice-Cream Parlor.

The shop was empty except for the one employee reclining behind the store counter, reading an old copy of *Life* magazine. On the cover was a picture of Nixon being sworn into office. The man reading the magazine seemed to be in his early to mid-twenties. He was a tall blond with a swimmer's physique. Carolyn and I grinned at one another; we liked what we saw.

He had not noticed our arrival since the store's front door had already been open.

"That's an old edition you've got there," Carolyn observed.

He looked up. His eyes were piercing blue. As he stood up, my heart raced.

"Excuse me?" he said in a high-pitched voice that did not seem appropriate for a man of his stature.

"The magazine," I explained. "She was talking about the magazine you're reading."

Carolyn quickly elbowed me in the side.

"Well . . . yes. You do what you can to avoid boredom."

"Aren't you in school?" Carolyn inquired.

"Finished. Last May."

"How about college?" I inquired. "Aren't you going to go to college?"

Carolyn elbowed me once more.

"Past tense. I've graduated. Just finished."

"And you're here?" Carolyn asked incredulously and, after a moment, said apologetically, "Oh . . . I'm sorry."

"That's all right. I get a lot of that around here. Problem is there's not much out here except jobs like this. I'm lucky to have a job at all. They say things may get even worse: the oil crisis, coal being the dying industry that it is. Engineers come a dime a dozen these days."

"Is that what your degree is in, engineering?" Carolyn asked.

"It is," he answered. "Now, what can I get you two?"

"Oh, no. There are three of us!" I said. Carter was on the other side of the shop inspecting the variety of choices. "Carter?" I called.

"Oh, yes. I didn't see the little guy. What can I get for you three?"

Carter placed his order first: "I'd like a triple cone. Bottom scoop: lime sherbet. Middle scoop: vanilla. Top scoop: rainbow sherbet. And I'm not a little guy."

"Apparently not," he answered. "And what can I get you two ladies?"

"Go ahead, Shannon," Carolyn said, "I haven't decided." As I studied the menu, I could tell Carolyn was trying to think of something intelligent to ask him. I waited, hoping that her efforts would offer promising material with which Carter and I could later tease her.

"Are you Henry?" she asked.

"No. Henry's the owner. My name's Scott."

Carolyn frowned.

"Are you ready?" he asked me.

"I'll have as much ice cream and dark chocolate syrup with as much whipped cream and sprinkles as possible, in the largest container you have."

"Okay. Any nuts?" he asked.

"No. Too many in the family already," I answered.

He laughed genuinely. Carolyn grimaced at our exchange. I smiled.

"And you?" he asked Carolyn.

"What's your most exquisite and intriguing flavor? Wait, don't tell me. Surprise me with two scoops of that. All right?"

"Sure," Scott said with a quizzical look. I turned my head downward toward Carter. Smirks grew on both our faces.

"So," Carolyn continued, "what about graduate school? You'd be more marketable with a master's or a PhD"

"That's why I'm here. Can't go to school with nothing to pay for tuition. My bachelor's degree broke me."

"How long before you go back?"

"Couple of years."

He handed Carter and me our orders. We began to devour them and were entertained by Carolyn's ongoing efforts.

"What about your parents? Can't they help?" Carolyn continued.

"Look, I don't know where you three are from. But around here, things are tight. My father is worse off than I am. He's a farmer, has nobody to sell to except the government. And when he does sell to them, he mutters under his breath. He's humiliated, having to rely on the government to purchase his crops that his fellow Americans don't need. He has no money to loan me. That's why I'm here."

"Oh," Carolyn murmured.

He handed Carolyn her ice cream. Carolyn handed him the twenty-dollar bill.

Scotty placed the twenty in the register and returned some change while making a comment of which I now must make another parenthetical paraphrase. Suffice it to say that he blamed his unemployment on two racial groups (Hispanics and African-Americans) of whom he used derogatory words to describe. He finished his commentary by stating, "All this affirmative action stuff is crap!"

I believe it was the words he chose to describe Hispanics and African-Americans that caused my sister, Carolyn, to just about choke on her ice cream. I stopped eating mine too. One minute I was enthralled by this charming young college graduate, and then, like a bolt of lightning in a clear sky, he speaks these words.

Carolyn spewed out the ice cream she had just consumed and threw her cup into the trash.

"Look," Scott said, "the truth is the truth, as ugly as it sounds. You might as well face it when you're young!"

"Let's get outta here!" Carolyn ordered. "I can't believe they let people like you graduate. They actually gave you a degree?" Carolyn said coldly.

"Thank you. It was nice meeting you too," he offered in return.

"What a jerk!" Carolyn muttered under her breath as we left the store and headed back toward the hotel.

"What's wrong?" Carter asked. "What happened in there? Why are you so upset?"

I needed to control my brother's inquisitive nature so I could focus my efforts on soothing Carolyn's temper. I placed my hand on his shoulder. "Not now, Carter."

"Can you believe that guy?" Carolyn fumed. "And I thought he was so great."

"Is that why Mom's upset at Dad?" Carter asked.

I looked at him for clarification.

"At the hotel this afternoon? Their fight, or argument, was it about money?"

"No, Carter. That's the stupidest thing I've ever heard!" Carolyn blasted.

"C'mon Carolyn. That's not necessary," I defended. "It's not his fault."

She looked back toward the ice-cream store, shook her head again, clenched her teeth, and let out a long sigh. "No, Cart," she said, "it may have something to do with money, but I imagine it's got more to do with Dad's religious beliefs."

"And Mom's lack of them," I added.

Carolyn angled her head, seeming to consider the validity of my assessment.

"You know, Carolyn," I started, "I'm beginning to think—"

I stopped, attempting to collect my thoughts.

"What?" Carolyn asked.

I continued, slowly, making sure to say exactly what I meant to say. "That Mom may have other reasons for disagreeing with Dad than her mere principles. I think there may be something she's not telling us."

"About Dad's past?" Carolyn asked.

"Maybe," I answered, "but I've always wondered, how could a woman as religious as Nana, raise a child as agnostic as Mom?"

Carolyn stared at me. I knew this was something that hadn't escaped her either.

We walked in silence back toward the park in the center of town. It was still too early to return to the hotel. We were frightened of what might be transpiring there. We arrived back at the community college and sat on benches across from a softball diamond. The air was cool, and the mountain breeze helped relieve the turmoil I was feeling.

I broke the silence, "How did they meet?"

"Mom and Dad?" Carolyn repeated, "I'm not sure. They've never said."

"Do you think it was like today?" I continued. "I mean, was it beautiful, romantic? Was the sun setting? How do you know when you're in love, Carolyn?"

Carolyn looked at me strangely. I suppose she hadn't expected to hear such a question from me. Over the past year we had grown distant, sharing little of our attractions to classmates. But she's been in a relationship for over a year now, and I'm sure she's got a better idea of what love might feel like than I do.

I could tell she wasn't in love with Kevin, the guy from back home she had been going out with. Otherwise, she'd have answered my question already. I suppose she was coming to that same conclusion right about then.

"Like that guy in the ice-cream shop today," I continued, hoping to redirect Carolyn's thoughts, "How did you feel? I mean, I could tell you liked him."

"Oh, please!" Carolyn protested.

"Fess up, Carolyn. Even Carter was on to you!"

Carolyn glanced over at our brother.

He smiled cautiously.

Carolyn surrendered. "Well, sure. He was attractive. But I could never go out with a guy like that."

"That's my point. You say that now, after what you heard him say. But you liked him before you had a chance to talk with him. You based it solely on his looks. What if Mom and Dad were the same way? A stranger you had never met, with whom you suddenly fall in love? Twenty years later, after you've been married, the two of you are still strangers."

Carolyn gave me a frightful stare.

"It can happen," I said. "I bet it happens every day. I bet it's happening somewhere in Coeur d'Alene right now, as we speak."

The sun was setting, causing the shadows to lengthen in the valley. We got up from the bench and walked up a steep hill that led to a cliff overlooking the lake. Our silhouettes hung over the precipice looking down upon the north side of town. Birds were singing, children playing in the water below, a boat's horn blowing in the distance, families laughing, a ball crashing against a bat on the ball field from below, and the sound of it impacting a fresh leather glove.

"Is there any meaning, Shannon?" Carolyn asked, turning and looking into my eyes. "Does life amount to any greater value than simply existing? I mean, you look at Mom and Dad and wonder whether love is worth it? If it isn't, then why bother?"

I studied Carolyn, unsure if her question was rhetorical or if she really wanted me to answer.

Carolyn continued. "You've got to know something, something you've read in all those books."

"Many of them say there is no existence," I commented.

"And," Carolyn asked further, "is there?"

I waved my hand through the air, "It's all nonsense. Our emotions today prove all those theories wrong. The spectacular beauty we see this very minute proves those theories wrong. This rail that supports our weight, our weight that increased by eating the ice cream, the ice cream that satisfied our hunger, our hunger that tells us we have needs—all of these prove that we exist. All the education and reasoning and doctorates that convince great thinkers otherwise are vanity, are meaningless. So many years of education wasted!"

"Then what is the reason? Why are we here?" Carolyn repeated.

"When I discover that, I'll let you know. I'll let Carter know. I'll let the world—"

I stopped my soapbox sermon. Something far greater was unfolding before our eyes.

The sun had hidden itself behind the rolling hills of northern Idaho, leaving enough of its light to outline the peaks and sparkle on the lake's surface. A gentle breeze whisked behind our heads as we leaned forward to behold the most beautiful sight in Coeur d'Alene that evening—a man and a woman embracing one another as they strolled down the lake's shoreline.

They were in love.

They were our parents.

The Sissy and the Giant

Within a week of returning from vacation, Carter yearned for another significant event, something to which he could look forward with excitement. The baseball season was within its final week and the Dodgers appeared to be going to the National League Championship against the Pittsburgh Pirates. Although his father would probably not be able to obtain tickets, all of the games would be televised; and the games that were played during a weekday afternoon, he would listen to on the transistor radio he'd smuggle into school.

Still, the fall season had more promise of work than of fun and excitement. Besides postseason baseball, Carolyn's high school career offered some respite from the autumn routine that Carter learned to dread.

Following her freshman year, Carter noticed the special treatment and respect Carolyn received from those outside his family. Strangers whom he had never met would stop them in the store and say, "Good job yesterday, Mason," or, "Are you guys going to wallop Fullerton High tonight?"

She was earning the best grades in her class, was the star of the softball team, and was growing more beautiful each day. Carter was beginning to notice the positive attributes of females and recognized that his sister far surpassed most of her peers in those attributes he liked best.

With all her success, Carter was dumbfounded as to the transformations with Shannon. Her appearance continued to deteriorate: drooping eyes with dark circles underneath, clothes worn two to three days consecutively, her hair beginning to resemble an unkempt shrub in the backyard, and the smell of tobacco that followed wherever she walked. Carter imagined a cloud of dust following her, similar to the cloud that shadowed Pig-Pen in the *Peanuts* comic strip.

Two or three nights a week, Shannon would be summoned into her parents' bedroom. Carter's curiosity tempted him to eavesdrop, but he felt the cost of being caught too high. Besides, he had a pretty good idea about what was being discussed. The talks wouldn't last long and were actually getting shorter as time passed. They were also getting louder.

As the end of fall approached, Shannon was returning home later each night, a vain attempt, it seemed to Carter, to avoid the confrontations with their parents.

She continued to read those weird books and, at times, tried to explain them to Carter. He'd politely listen, try to communicate comprehension with a studious look, or ask a simple question to feign his grasp of what she was talking about. But Carter valued the times she tried to teach him. It was becoming a rarity that he saw her on any given day, much less talk with her. So he'd take any time offered to him. He missed the old Shannon, but there was something he liked about the new Shannon she had become.

The times Carter enjoyed most with her were at Carolyn's softball games. The two would meet in the grandstands and cheer for their sister while Shannon read a book between innings, and if the game grew boring, during the innings as well. The action of most games held Carter's attention, but there were occasions when, much to his surprise, he was more interested in Shannon and her book than the game.

When Carter asked Shannon why she talks to him about the books and to no one else, she answered, "Mom and Dad would make me see a shrink."

"But why me?" Carter asked. "What about Carolyn? Or a friend at school?"

Shannon smiled. "I know you, Carter Anthony. You're loyal. You won't go blabber any of this to Mom or Dad."

Carter lifted his eyes cautiously. "I can't talk about it, 'cause I don't . . ."

Shannon held out her hand. "You understand more than you realize, Carter."

Not wanting to press the issue, Carter sat silently, trying to appear that Shannon's comment did not surprise him.

"And Carolyn's got no time," she continued. "Besides, I figure that if I can explain this stuff to a nine-year-old, and help him understand it, then I've got the material pretty well mastered."

The lecture, or story, Carter enjoyed best was about the Greek mythical character Sisyphus. Shannon had mentioned the myth in reference to one of the books she was reading,

Albert Camus's *The Myth of Sisyphus*. She had been digesting; that's what Shannon liked to call her reading and rereading of a book, for over a week. Carter could not remember the last time he had seen the same book in Shannon's hand for such a length of time. It was especially intriguing since the book was quite thin, smaller than most of the stuff he had been seeing her read. He found the Greek character's name humorous. "What parents would name their son *Sissy*?" Carter said in laughter.

"It's Sisyphus, not Sissy," Shannon corrected.

"Oh, right," Carter scoffed, "I forgot. Sissy!" he repeated, losing himself in laughter.

Carter and Shannon reclined on the top tier of the softball bleachers. The autumn sun was relentless. Fortunately, a cool breeze blew in from the foothills to issue some relief. They were comfortable in their shorts and T-shirts, grateful not to be on the softball diamond in fifty-percent-polyester pants and jersey. Poor Carolyn!

They watched the first inning to see Carolyn's first at bat. By the second inning, Carter was bored, growing restless with each pitch. At times he wondered why he liked this game so much; it moved too slow compared to other sports, and it seemed the same things just keep happening over and over. He would not share these thoughts with anyone for two reasons: First, it would serve no purpose but to alienate him further from his mother and would cause a needless gap in his relationship with his father. Secondly, something always occurred in this seemingly boring game that would startle him, that would wake him just as he was about to give up on it—a home run, a double play, or a diving catch. The game was full of routine but spattered with surprises.

This day was no exception. Shannon had given up long before Carter. He heard her begin flipping the pages once Carolyn got a double in her first trip to the plate.

"Listen to this guy, Carter," she began, "See if you can guess what he's talking about:

> *The only true solution is precisely where human judgment sees no solution. Otherwise, what need would we have of God? We turn toward God only to obtain the impossible. As for the possible, men suffice." (Myth of Sisyphus, Albert Camus, Vintage Books, 1955, p.25)*

She flipped forward a few pages and read more:

> *"What I touch, what resists me—that is what I understand . . ." (p.38)*

Shannon looked into the sky.

"Listen, Cart. Tell me if this makes any sense. When people understand something, anything, they feel in control. They are confident of their knowledge and ability. Like us and baseball: we Masons understand the game, so we feel comfortable out there on the diamond."

"Especially Carolyn," Carter added.

Shannon continued, pointing at the book, "But when a man or a woman, or even a child, confronts an event, concept, or idea that seems illogical or difficult to understand, he or she turns to their god. It is at this point that the individual realizes his or her need for a power greater than himself. It is not that an actual god exists, but that the idea of a supreme being is necessary because of our human frailty."

Carter knew his questioning eyes did not escape Shannon's notice.

"Let me explain it this way," she continued, "The guy who wrote this, Albert Camus—"

"Albert the Camel?" Carter repeated with a grin.

"No. Camus. He's French."

"Oh." Carter was disappointed his humor did not impress.

"That was cute, Carter," she said, lightly punching his upper arm, "but this is important stuff. You've got to try to understand."

Carter rose from his reclined position on the bleacher behind him, looking up at Shannon. "Okay."

"Camus believed there is no god. Therefore, for him, life has no meaning. It is absurd and futile. He was intrigued by this prospect: what would a logical man do when he comes to the realization that life has no meaning? Obviously, it would be to take his own life. To prove his point, he chose to use the Greek mythological character Sisyphus as a type of parable.

"Sisyphus had done some things on earth that had upset the Greek gods Zeus, Pluto, and others."

She turned to Carter. "You've heard of those guys, right?"

Carter was excited. He could honestly answer yes.

"Good," Shannon said. "As a punishment, the gods assigned him to the task of pushing a large stone up a steep incline for eternity. Sisyphus would stand at the foot of the mountain and begin pushing the stone upward. As he grew closer to the top of the mountain, he fantasized about his moment of success. However, whenever he would get just a few feet away from completing his divine task, the stone would roll back to the bottom of the mountain. Sisyphus would begin the long trek back down; immersed in his utter hopelessness and loneliness, arrive once again at the foot of the mountain; and start the whole process again.

"Bummer!" Carter said.

"Camus's whole point in telling the story," Shannon continued, "is to discover a rational for living. Sisyphus's toil appears to be the ultimate example of meaninglessness; he is destined to never succeed. Camus contends that it may be best for humans who discover themselves to be like Sisyphus, to strongly consider whether it is worth living any longer."

Shannon paused to see if Carter understood. He felt he did but didn't like what he thought he was hearing. Was Shannon comparing herself to this guy? Was she contemplating his suggestion of killing herself? Besides, this whole story sounded a bit similar to another of the books Shannon had read months earlier, and Carter's mind turned, trying to remember the details of that other book and how it might relate to this Sisyphus character.

"This might help you understand it better, Carter. Our lives, in a way, are futile: We go to school to get good grades. We get good grades so that we can go to college. We go to college so that we can get a good job. We want a good job so that we can buy a house and raise a family. But what is it all for? The children we raise will just enter into the same cycle of toil, thereby only adding to the meaninglessness. It may be better to have never been born!"

"You really think that?" Carter said, his head resting on his hands and his arms propped on his knees. He raised his eyes, hoping to hear that she didn't accept Camus's theory.

Shannon shook her head and looked back to her book. "Not yet. He hasn't convinced me. I think he missed something somewhere. Listen to what he says here:

> *Beware of those who say: 'I know this too well to be able to explain it! For if they cannot do so, it is because they don't know how to explain it or they are too lazy to search for the real truth.'" (Myth of Sisyphus, p.62)*

She turned a couple pages and read some more:

> *"All churches lay claim to the eternal. Yet, happiness, courage, retribution, and justice are all secondary priorities for them. But I have no concern with the ideas of the eternal. The truths that come within my scope can be touched with the hand." (p.66)*

Just as Shannon had begun reading the passage, Carter heard an aluminum bat hit squarely the pitched ball. He turned his head just in time to see Carolyn dive to her right and snap it out of the air, shooting the white chalk of the foul line into a cloud.

He looked up at Shannon. "Nice catch."

Shannon said nothing; she was turning pages in the book, backward and forward.

"I didn't hear anything you just said," he announced.

"Let me paraphrase," she said. "Camus thought the church was made up of a group of individuals who huddled together dreaming about eternity to comfort themselves in the midst of their Sisyphus-like toil while, at the same time, denying the reality around them. They were so consumed thinking, or dreaming, about what heaven would be like that they ignored the pain of society and the world around them. They were wimps. They were no-brainers. It's no wonder Camus believed that the absurd made more sense than the god many of his contemporaries believed existed!

"The whole point is this, Cart: Life must have a meaning. If it doesn't, Camus is right—why go on living? I haven't reached that point yet. Nothing I've read, no theory or idea has convinced me that there is anything greater to do than search for that meaning. Until I discover that, discovering *it* is my life's meaning."

"It was a giant," Carter muttered, still attempting to recall the other story similar to Sisyphus scaling the mountain. He turned to Shannon, hoping she knew what he was talking about.

A giant?" she asked.

"Yes. A giant."

"Here?" Shannon questioned. "From San Francisco?"

Carter burrowed his eyes. "Not baseball. This has nothing to do with baseball."

"Oh?"

"It's your story," Carter continued. "I remember you reading another like it earlier this year."

"And there was a giant in the story?"

"No!" Carter answered emphatically. "He wrote it."

Shannon raised her hand toward her temple and covered her right eye, peering at Carter. "A giant wrote a book I was reading?"

"Exactly! I just remember thinking that I had learned about him in school and didn't think he was a real person. How could you be reading a book written by someone who didn't exist?"

Shannon reached into her backpack and held out a paperback. "Is this it?"

Carter's eyes widened. "That's it!"

Shannon opened the book. "Imagine—assigned reading for my British Lit class having an impact on my younger brother. Go figure."

"Hey," Carter announced, "it says 'John Bunyan'. He's not the guy with the blue ox!"

"No, Carter, that's Paul Bunyan. He's the giant. And you were right; he's not real. He's a mythical character."

"Like Sisyphus?" Carter asked.

"That's right."

"Oh yeah. Now I remember," Carter started. "It was at night, in the library. You were reading excerpts to Carolyn. The two of you were laughing at most of it. As usual, I didn't understand the jokes or why it was so funny."

Shannon lowered her head. "Do you remember what part?" she asked quietly as she began searching the pages.

Carter stood and stretched. "That's just it. It was just like this Sisyphus guy. Someone was climbing up a hill, only he wasn't pushing a stone; he was carrying a burden, a heavy burden he wanted to get rid of. He fell asleep; lost his only valuable possession, a book; went back to look for it; and then began climbing the hill again."

"That's good, Carter. You remember all that?"

"Now that I talk about it, they are kind of the same but not really. I mean, they both go up a hill, they both have to either push or carry something heavy up the hill, and this other guy in the other story goes back down, like Sisyphus, for something; but unlike Sisyphus, it was because he lost it, not because it was his punishment by the gods."

Carter looked down at Shannon, for he was still standing, using his arms to narrate what he remembered of the story. She was smiling. "Go on," she invited. "Do you remember any more?"

"Yes. Wait a minute. Yes." Carter paused, collecting his thoughts. "He was a pilgrim, right?"

"That's right."

"He reached the top of that hill, right?

Shannon looked down and curled her lip. Her smile faded.

Carter shook his head; he felt confused. "It's not the same at all," he announced. "Sisyphus just kept going up and down, up and down, forever. This pilgrim got to the top, but that wasn't all. It wasn't as though it were a finish line or anything like that. That's right, it wasn't over at all. Later he met lions, slept at some kind of inn, and continued his journey."

There was silence. Carter sat. He grew conscious of the sounds he loved so well: a ball whacked by an aluminum bat and a ball smothered by worn leather and then smothered by another piece of worn leather, followed by scattered applause and shouts of, "Good play," "Nice hustle," and "Two outs."

"I don't remember any more, Shannon. I think that was all you had read to Carolyn. What happened to the guy?"

Shannon opened to the pages describing the pilgrim's ascent of the "Hill of Difficulty":

> *This Hill, though High, I covet to ascend,*
> *The difficulty will not me offend,*

For I perceive the way to life lies here;
Come, pluck up, heart; let's neither faint nor fear;
Better, though difficult, the right way to go,
Than wrong, though easy, where the end is woe.
(Pilgrim's Progress, John Bunyan, Penguin Books, 1987, p.39)

Through the fall and into the winter months, Carter yearned for these talks with Shannon. His ability to grasp the concepts she explained was still far from satisfactory as far as he was concerned, but he began to notice something in his sister. The stuff she was now teaching him was no longer dark and gloomy. She spoke to him with a gleam in her eyes, like on Christmas morning, anticipating the opening of her first gift.

Carter also recognized that she had been citing biblical texts either to prove a point she was making or to show how ridiculous a particular religious belief is. Regardless as to her use, it meant that she had been reading the Bible. That was perhaps the greatest relief, for if Shannon saw some value in it, then he could rationalize that believing in it was not as infantile as his mother contended.

"The church," Shannon once told Carter, "seems to have forgotten about what the Bible really does teach. Instead, they spend their efforts adhering to traditions that are not biblically based and at times contrary to common sense and scientific facts.

"Do you realize," she explained, "that Galileo was excommunicated by the church because he claimed that the sun was the center of the universe? The church back then believed and taught that the earth was the universe's center, primarily because the Bible taught that man was God's most important, central creation. So, Galileo's discovery of a natural fact was deemed unacceptable because of an erroneous church tradition that was based not upon the Bible but upon man's ideas of what the Bible taught. There's some good stuff in there, but the church just seems to screw it up by emphasizing points it doesn't even make!"

"Carter, sometimes I feel like Galileo!" Shannon said. "All I want to know is the identity of the stone Sisyphus is pushing. What is that mountain he is ascending? I'm almost convinced that there is some god out there. But the god of a church that refuses to make sense? That, I cannot accept! I think some god has something to do with discovering a meaning to life, but Carter, just like Galileo, I cannot accept the god of a church which embraces a concept or idea that refuses to accept reality. Dad's god just doesn't make sense."

Falling Stars

Nixon had been run out of office. Suspicions and accusations of widespread use of performance-enhancing drugs were overshadowing Olympic athletes and their accomplishments. Professional athletes from the NFL, NBA, and MLB were reported to have weaknesses for liquor, loose women, and drugs. Carter's father told him it had always been this way, even before there were football fields, ice rinks, courts, and diamonds. "Heroes have holes," he'd say. "If you want a hero without holes, a holeless hero, a holy hero, then look to God."

"God," Carter thought, "a hero? Is the guy even real?" To hold him as a hero would be like having Santa Claus or Easter Bunny as his role model. He'd be the joke on the playground.

Carter wanted someone tangible, someone he knew and could look to for guidance—an older brother-type, someone he would be able to talk with on a regular basis.

The first time Carter saw Kevin Hatch walk into his home, he knew that he was the one. Within a week of their first encounter, Carter not only shook his hand but had talked at length of sports and wrestled with him on the living room floor.

The time spent with Kevin grew each week, raising Carter's certainty that Kevin was the real deal. He noticed the envy in the eyes of his peers, especially his friends in the neighborhood. Carter's value on the playground increased. It was as though all his classmates, all his friends, believed that, since he was spending so much time with the most talented athlete to come out of Fullerton since Walter Johnson, he somehow had increased his own athletic prowess.

The local newspapers toted Kevin's athleticism monthly, brimming with anticipation as to which NCAA Division I schools would pursue him. He appeared on the front page of the local newspaper's sports page, in the editorials, and in the beat articles written by reporters covering high school athletics. The front-page feature about him, just before his senior year at Sunny Hills High, detailed the evolution of his career:

> Kevin Hatch, the pride of Fullerton, has been performing his magic for three years, awing audiences amid cheers coming even from the opponents' sidelines.
>
> It all started during the second game of the 1973 season, Hatch's sophomore year. It was the home opener, hopes high for the Lancer's senior quarterback, John Stuart. But after an early first quarter sack, Stuart was forced to leave, opening the door for Hatch. He never looked back.
>
> Three hundred seventy-two yards and five touchdown passes later, the Sunny Hills Lancers had beaten their first opponent of the ''73 season . . .

Kevin was the quarterback on every play of every quarter of every game for the next three seasons and set CIF Division I records in all major passing categories. For three consecutive seasons, the Lancers were CIF champions.

As soon as football season ended, Kevin joined the basketball squad, averaging twenty points per game during his junior and senior years.

But it was on the baseball diamond that Kevin displayed his greatest talent. During his four years at Sunny Hills, he roamed the Lancer outfield, errorless, while maintaining a .588 batting average and hitting a cumulative total of thirty-six home runs. College recruiters attended each of Kevin's football and baseball games during his junior year, and offers began arriving in the fall of his graduating year. His only handicap was his performance in the classroom.

Although his scholastic shortcomings did not deter most college recruiters, Kevin was left to make scholarship and commitment decisions on his own. His father had abandoned the family when Kevin was in sixth grade, and Kevin's two older brothers each followed their father's example once they graduated high school. His mother had been diagnosed with cancer a year earlier, leaving Kevin to be the primary caregiver for his mother and two younger sisters.

In the end, he committed to attend the local state university in Fullerton to the dismay of his coaches and local sports enthusiasts. But as soon as Kevin began playing on the field, court, or diamond, he forgot about the frustrations and what-might-have-beens and did what he enjoyed best—play. Carter admired Kevin most for this quality. He performed with seeming effortlessness and competed with an intensity hidden by his endearing smile.

He did not gloat in the interviews that Carter read in the newspapers, and the times Carter and he talked, Kevin always seemed to search for a way to divert attention from himself to Carter or one of his sisters.

He was six feet three inches tall, weighed slightly over two hundred pounds, and had broad shoulders, huge arms, brown hair, straight white teeth, and a country-boy smile. One fall day, during her freshman high school year, Carolyn could not stop talking at supper about "this amazing guy" in her geometry class. "He is a year older," she announced, "is a marvelous athlete, handsome, down-to-earth, and needs a geometry tutor."

Carolyn volunteered her services, and Kevin accepted. He obtained his best high school mark that year, a B-, and also secured his first girl friend—Carolyn Mason.

Their relationship was not one of those mushy high school romances Carter envisioned from the television shows he had watched, but rather a relationship in which both seemed quite satisfied regardless as to whether the two were alone, with a group, or apart. They shared their moments of fun, and Carter could tell that they both were fond of one another when they began holding hands and Kevin would wrap his arm around her while they watched television, Carolyn resting her head on his shoulder.

And Carolyn changed. She was less stern, more lighthearted it seemed. "How was your day, Carter?" she would ask during the dinner discussion. She would volunteer to edit his writing assignments. "I read your paper, Cart. Your vocabulary is improving. The way you express yourself; I'm impressed," she wrote on one of his book reports.

Wow! Now, if only he could find a way to bring the old Shannon back, life would be perfect.

Carter's parents took a liking to Kevin. Two to three times each week, he'd stay for dinner and participate in the family discussions. He surprised Carter at how he could hold his own with the rest of the family. For someone who did not do well in school, Carter thought, he expressed his views with clarity and eloquence. Even Shannon seemed impressed. Whenever he ate supper at the house, Shannon would eventually break into a smile.

"Kevin made a spectacular catch yesterday," Carolyn announced one evening. "It was awesome!" she said as she looked at Carter and then Shannon and then their parents. She swung her hands, "The guy at the plate whacked the ball, line drive, headed for deep center, over Kevin's head."

Carter looked at Kevin, maneuvering his salad and rice with his fork, his face growing a tint of red. He didn't look up during any portion of Carolyn's narrative.

She continued, "Kevin turned, back toward the rest of the field, sprinting toward the chain-link fence. He looked over his right shoulder, then veered a bit more to the right before extending his arms, his whole body leaving his feet, and catching the ball at the base of the fence."

"Almost Mays-like," Shannon said.

Kevin looked up.

"Only you peeked," Shannon grinned.

Kevin chuckled, smiling at her, "I guess so."

But, as Carter's father taught, all good things must come to an end. Such was the case with Kevin and Carolyn. When Kevin chose to remain local and attend Cal State Fullerton, Carolyn chided him for the decision late one night in the family library.

Carter was finishing some math homework when Carolyn asked him to leave. Carter obeyed, but once he closed the library door, he cautiously reopened it seconds later, leaving a crack wide enough for him to witness the proceedings.

"You must think long-term," Carolyn instructed Kevin. I know you care for your family; that's admirable. But don't you think your mother—"

Kevin held out his hand. Carter recalls the serious nature of Kevin's expression, so foreign to the carefree calm Carter usually saw. "You have no idea, Carolyn," he started, "this is my decision. I've told you before, my family comes first."

"This has nothing to do with family, Kevin. You're using them as an excuse. I know you. As bold as you are on the field of athletics, you are terrified on the field of life, of venturing into unfamiliar territory."

Carter could read the hurt in Kevin's eyes. He shook his head as he sat on the sofa.

"This immaturity on your part," Carolyn continued, "I can no longer endure. I think it would be best if we stop seeing each other."

A long period of silence followed. There were no sounds of sobbing; there were no more words exchanged. Carter yearned to run into the library and yell, "Wait! Hold everything! Don't listen to her, Kevin. She's wrong! Don't leave. Don't let him leave!"

But he knew such presumptuousness would get him into more trouble than he'd be willing to endure.

Minutes after Carolyn broke the news to Kevin, the front door closed and Carter heard Kevin start the engine of his '67 Mustang. As the sound of the car faded into the night, Carter surrendered to the reality of never again seeing Kevin.

Two days later, just after Carter had finished playing a game of football with his friends, he heard a knock on the door. It startled him, the unique rhythm resembling Kevin's. Tap, pause, tap-tap, pause, tap-tap-tap, pause, tap-tap-tap-tap, the first tap signaling a single; the next two taps, a double; and so forth.

Carter grinned. "They must have made up," he whispered softly. He raced to the door and opened it.

"Hey, Cart."

"Hey, Kevin." Carter wanted to shake his head. Was he dreaming? Carolyn would not change her mind about anything. Once her mind was set, that was it, no turning back. But this was Kevin, Kevin Hatch.

"Is Shannon home?" Kevin asked.

Carter's eyes shot open. He stood motionless until he realized how stupid he must look. He turned and rushed upstairs, skipping one step with each stride. He looked down, back toward the front door. There Kevin stood, hands folded behind his back, the way he looked when Carter first met him, the night he came to pick up Carolyn for their first date.

Carter lightly taped on Shannon's door.

"Yes?"

He slowly opened and peeked in. Shannon was doing something he had not seen her do in over a year. She was brushing her hair. She looked pretty.

His eyes widened. He gulped, trying to hide his excitement. "Kevin's downstairs."

"I'll be right there."

"Carolyn's not home yet . . ." he started to say.

Shannon turned her head and smiled. "I'll be down in a minute."

Carter closed the door, raised his arms, moved his hips, and punched at the air. "Yes!" he whispered as he turned to go back down the stairs.

"This one better last," Carter muttered with subdued excitement. "This one better last."

The first indicators of a lasting relationship were not promising. Carter never saw Shannon and Kevin hold hands or embrace. He even saw Shannon hold Kevin back when he tried to kiss her good-night. She was not rude but always welcomed him at the house with a smile.

Kevin called the house, wrote letters, sent flowers, and would visit the house most nights after practice. The look on Carolyn's face showed little signs of remorse or envy. Carter wondered whether she was just acting.

It was about this time that Carter's parents started to enforce a curfew on Shannon, and the arguments between Shannon and their mother grew more volatile.

"He's using you," he heard his mother say. "They teach you things in health class?"

"Things, Mother?" Shannon asked.

"Hormones—"

"Please, mother. I can handle it. I don't even hold his hand."

"Don't ever underestimate him, Shannon. Always have an out," Carter heard his father say. "Protect yourself. Don't put yourself in a situation you can't escape."

Carter understood none of his parents' worries. Had they not seen the way Shannon distanced herself from Kevin? Compared to the times Carolyn and he held hands and embraced, what was all the fuss about?

And then there was Carolyn's advice: "He's a child, Shannon. Don't waste your time."

"None of you understand Kevin," Carter contended. "He likes Shannon. That's all. What's wrong with that?"

Carter could see it in his eyes, his awkward behavior, and his smile when he would first see Shannon while waiting downstairs, none of which were observable reactions when he had come calling for Carolyn. Though Carter recognized his elder sister's beauty, her harsh personality caused him to question how anyone could be attracted to her; not so with Shannon—he understood why Kevin smiled each time he saw her. Each day her beauty grew; the scales of her gloomy nature that had accumulated over the past twelve months gradually began to fall away.

Tuesday night, December 23, the day Carter affectionately named Christmas Eve's Eve, had found Carter and his family unprepared. It was as though all the school activities, all of Carolyn's softball games, all of Dad's meetings and Mom's chores had left no time to get ready for Christmas. It was disappointing to have the holiday sneak up on him so suddenly. Only a tinge of the excitement and anticipation he recalled from prior years was present.

Carter and his mother returned from the mall at which he bought the presents for his family. His father had returned from work earlier in the afternoon, suffering from the flu. Carter joined him on the couch to watch a news program *The Year 1975 in Review*. Shannon was not home, probably at the local public library, Carter assumed, reading more of her obscure books.

When Carolyn arrived home, she rushed upstairs to dress for a date with a guy who graduated the previous year and was a linebacker at UCLA. As his mother fixed dinner, Carter left the sofa in front of the television, grabbed the gifts he had just purchased, and hoped onto the sofa directly across from the Christmas tree. His father turned off the television and walked upstairs.

Carter watched him carefully, not wanting him to see any of the gifts he was about to wrap. He finished wrapping Shannon's present, paused, and briefly enjoyed the dancing, twinkling lights and the smell of fresh pine. Next he picked up Carolyn's present and began wrapping it.

Ten minutes later, he had wrapped all but his father's gift, a desk calendar for 1976. After placing it into an appropriate-sized cardboard box, he wrapped it and placed it into another box a bit larger. He wrapped that box and placed it into a box slightly larger still. He continued this process six times.

While tying a yellow ribbon around the final box, a deep sigh and brush against his back startled Carter. Carolyn had finished dressing and sat on the sofa's top edge, admiring the manger scene next to the front door window.

"What was that for?" Carter asked before he turned to see where she was staring. "Oh, that," he continued. "I don't know why you guys get all worked up about that thing. It's so plain looking. We should buy a new one."

"It's the memories, Cart."

"I know, I know," he interrupted. "I've heard it a thousand times."

Besides the sentimental importance the crèche had for their mother, its pricelessness had increased one year prior to Carter's birth. Shannon was five years old and was so excited about the tricycle she received that she bumped into the table, knocked over the baby Jesus, and split it in half by riding over it with one of the rear wheels. After being scolded by her parents, she sobbed endlessly. She felt such remorse for the mishap that when she created a Christmas list the following holiday season, she listed a new cradle as her number-one priority. Their parents were so moved by the gesture that they decided not to replace the broken piece but went to a local jeweler and made arrangements to mend the Christ child, overlaying it with gold. A small box, no larger than a bar of soap, was placed in Shannon's stocking, the first gift she opened that morning.

"It was awesome!" Carolyn recalled. "If you could have seen Shannon's face. I still remember—"

"But you don't even believe that stuff!" Carter said.

"Don't you remember all the stories Nana told us? About our ancestors who passed it down from one generation to the next? It's a symbol of our family being able to make the best of difficult circumstances."

"I guess so."

"Just because I don't believe in what it commemorates, Cart, doesn't mean I can't appreciate the special meaning it has for our family."

Carter bit his lip and looked upward. He sighed and then placed his father's present under the tree. Returning to the sofa, and reclining near Carolyn, he scratched his head. "How long have we had it?"

Carolyn shrugged.

"Hundred years?" Carter asked.

"At least."

"Two hundred?"

"It's possible. What's your point, Cart?"

"We just studied a bit of the crusades in school. The Brits and some other Europeans wanted to control Jerusalem because of the historical significance, right?"

Carolyn tilted her head toward Carter, her eyes inviting him to proceed.

"That's a thousand years ago. And we know they were fighting against the Muslims who looked to Muhammad as their teacher. But even Muhammad recognized and respected Jesus, and he lived and wrote in the six hundreds.

"Then there's the Roman Empire, persecuting Christians up through the third century. You follow enough years back, you eventually come to Jesus who started it all. I mean, how can we deny that?"

Carolyn brushed her hair behind her ears, the sign Carter had learned meant she was thinking, contemplating, and calculating a response. "How can I deny that?" she asked.

"Exactly," Carter said.

"I don't. I don't deny he lived, Cart. I don't think many people do or can. Like you said, there's too much evidence for anybody to seriously deny it. But accepting that he lived is very different than accepting what people have come to believe about him."

"You mean what we learn at church? What's in the Bible?"

Carolyn's eyes fixed on Carter. "That's right."

Carter sighed. "But why? Why do you believe other historical documents are genuine but not the Bible? Why hold it to a higher standard than, say, Aristotle or Plato?"

Carolyn's eyes narrowed. "You and Shannon been talking about this?"

Carter felt there was nothing to hide. "Sure."

"I never thought she'd take it this far. Now she's got you more confused."

Carter crossed his legs and sat up in the sofa.

"With your vulnerability, Cart, you need to be more careful. I'm not sure what's going through Shannon's head these days, but you've got to make your own decision."

Carter lowered his head, frowning. "Now you're sounding like Mom."

Carolyn was silent. Was she taking this as a compliment or an insult?

"Besides," Carter continued, "I understand more than I feel I've ever understood. The stories Shannon tells me—"

"Stories!" Carolyn scoffed. "Listen to yourself, Cart—stories, not facts. You've always chosen fantasy over reality. Some day your imagination is going to get you into trouble."

"Life's too boring without imagination. Why be careful about using it? It doesn't harm anyone?"

"You ever hear of *The Boy Who Cried Wolf*?"

"That's a story. Not real life!"

"So?"

"That's my whole point. Stories help us see things more clearly. They warn us better than some teacher or politician telling us what we can or can't do."

"That's astute for a Carter."

He smiled. "I just thought it up right now."

Carolyn got up while rubbing the top of his head, "I've never quite thought of it that way."

The front door opened and Shannon rushed in, breathing heavily and both arms full of books. Carter turned, looking right into Shannon's eyes. Something was different. She seemed agitated, excited, but she was smiling, not somber. Her smile widened as her eyes met Carter.

"Where have you been?" Carolyn asked.

"At the library, I bet," Carter said.

"Again?" Carolyn gasped. "Were you studying or just reading more of those books?"

Shannon shrugged and grinned sheepishly. She turned back toward Carter, "I've got great news, Carter! We've made some real progress!"

"What is it?" Carter asked.

"You're never going to make it to a university at this rate," Carolyn interrupted. "You just don't get it."

"Tell me!" Carter begged Shannon. "What is it?"

"All you used to do was study," Carolyn continued, "so much so that you got the best grades in class. Now you don't even care!"

Carter slouched into the sofa, knowing were this was headed. Since Shannon began going out with Kevin, arguments would erupt instantaneously between his two sisters. Seldom had Kevin's name been mentioned during their shouting matches, but something told Carter that didn't matter. It was too much of a coincidence. It seemed Carolyn was determined to subdue Shannon, to find anything about which she could criticize.

"My priorities changed," Shannon explained.

"Changed! Changed to what? What are you going to do with all this theory and philosophy and crazy religious ideas you've been filling your head with the past year?"

Shannon placed her books on the sofa next to Carter and began taking off her jacket. Although her smile's intensity had lessened, remnants remained. She bent close to Carter and cupped her hand over his ear, "I'll explain it to you later," she whispered.

Carolyn continued, "How did you do on your SAT? Let's ask your teachers if any of these books you've been reading have helped improve your GPA."

Shannon seemed to agree with Carolyn's commentary, standing quietly, her eyes attentive. Usually more vocal, these were not normal responses in her debates with Carolyn. She dropped herself on the sofa, next to Carter. "Which one's for me?" she asked as she picked up the gifts, shaking each one gently.

"This one." Carter pointed to a small square box under the tree that was wrapped with white-colored paper spattered with pictures of candy canes and teddy bears.

Shannon picked it up and shook it. Then she placed it next to her right ear and shook it again.

"You know," Shannon said to Carolyn, "I realize I've made some foolish decisions the last couple years. But it's me who'll pay the price. I'm not asking for sympathy. You know, I did take some work from school to the library. I do every day. But I get bored with it! None of that stuff excites me. It's all so pointless. Memorizing math formulas I'll never use, names of politicians who ruined the lives of their constituents, diagramming a sentence, dissecting a frog. I can't relate to any of it. But when I read a novel or a book about what you call "crazy religious ideas," I'm stimulated. It all begins to make sense. All the irrational events in our world somehow fit into this crazy puzzle I'm trying to complete. I even begin to see the relevance of why I should solve the math problem, study the politician, and diagram the sentence. Only, by the time I realize it, it's time to go home or go to class."

"It's just that I'm concerned about your future," Carolyn said.

"You mean my *college* future."

"Well, yes."

"College isn't my dream, Carolyn. It may be yours, but it's not mine. At least, not now."

"You are such a fool! It's no wonder you and Kevin get along. You both have such great talent, so many gifts, but you're both letting them waste away!"

"Just because we've decided not to take the path that leads to fame, money, and power does not mean that we aren't utilizing our talents," Shannon contended.

"What is that supposed to mean? Is that what you think I'm about?"

"Isn't it?" Shannon straightened her posture and crossed her legs. "You may say that your life's goals are to protect the rights of the oppressed, speak for the unheard, and empower the poor, but all you really want is the admiration of those you help, the praises of society, and the warm-fuzzy feelings you think you'll get because you've done your good deeds."

"You little bitch!" Carolyn shouted. "How dare you."

Carter heard a pan fall and the kitchen door pushed open with such force that it slammed against the wall on the outside kitchen wall and returned to slam the wall on the inside.

Carolyn continued, not aware of the alarm she had created, "You don't even begin to understand my . . . my . . ."

"Your what?" Shannon stood up.

Carter backed away to the other end of the sofa opposite of Shannon.

"You are all about *you*," Shannon continued. "Carolyn Mason: homecoming queen. Carolyn Mason: CIF All-American, Scholastic All-American, valedictorian, Harvard freshman, the most wonderful civil rights leader of her generation!"

"So that's it! You're jealous!"

"Jealous? Huh. You're the one who can't keep her eyes off Kevin every night he comes over. You're the one who wishes she had never broken it off. You can't stand the way he looks at me and how I'm able to control myself, not letting him hang all over me. And you know what? It makes me even more attractive that way. You only wish you had such control and had never given in to your passion. You lost your pride, your greatest possession. Your virginity!"

Carolyn grabbed Shannon by the shoulders and threw her to the floor. Carter raised his knees to his chest and wrapped his arms around his legs, inching further away on the sofa.

On the floor, at the base of the Christmas tree, his sisters wrestled, Shannon, dressed in torn jeans and a worn gray flannel shirt, struggling against Carolyn, adorned for her date. Carolyn raised her left arm and swung it at Shannon's face.

Their mother rushed past and caught Carolyn's fist before it made contact.

Shannon raised herself from the ground. "What was that?" she shouted, raising her arms in the air.

Their father raced down the stairs. "What's going on down here?"

He looked at Carolyn and Shannon. They did not answer.

He turned. "Carter?"

Carter looked at his mother, afraid to speak. Afraid to move.

She shook her head and raised Carolyn from the floor. "Now, tell us what caused this."

Carolyn said nothing. Her eyes seemed on the verge of popping from her head.

"I said some things I shouldn't have," Shannon said. "I've been keeping them in a while. They spilled out. I'm sorry."

"Carolyn?" their mother turned.

"You two do nothing," Carolyn announced. "Look at her."

"You're stepping out of your bounds, Carolyn," their father announced.

"I'll step out then. Someone's got to. She's throwing away everything."

"I've been digesting," Shannon interrupted. "Throwing away implies I don't even consider the value of an entity."

"Carolyn," their father started, "your mother and I are fully aware of what Shannon is going through. We care for each of you."

Carolyn frowned.

The doorbell rang. Their father opened the door. It was Carolyn's date.

"Well, Carolyn?" their mother asked.

Carolyn shook her head. "Giving us freedom to choose is one thing; allowing us to keep making choices that will destroy our future is something else entirely."

She walked toward the hallway mirror and straightened her hair. "Bob," she addressed the college freshman waiting on the porch, "I'm ready."

Carolyn picked up her purse and walked toward the door. She turned back toward her family. "Shannon, in my opinion you've wasted this last year. Get your act together, or you'll destroy most of the paths Mom and Dad have tried to ensure we'd have the freedom to choose from. You've let us all down. I never thought I would say this, but right now I'm ashamed to be your sister."

She turned back toward the door, firmly held Bob's hand, and locked her arm with his. "Let's go," she commanded.

Bob looked uncertain. Carter had never seen him, and felt sorry for him, having to witness the remnants of chaos.

Carolyn nudged him to start walking to his car. "Good bye. Merry Christmas," he offered. "Nice meeting you . . ."

"Merry Christmas," Carter said. He looked at his parents, both studying Shannon.

The door shut.

No one spoke.

Carter looked at Shannon; her head lowered.

Carter heard one car door shut and then the other. A few seconds later, the engine started and he could hear it fade as Carolyn and Bob drove away.

Still, no one spoke.

Carter gulped, fearing that each passing moment of silence was leading to greater drama.

"What was this all about?" their mother finally asked.

"I see," Shannon answered. "I'm easier to deal with than Carolyn. You let her go, but you're going to put me through the inquisition."

"Carolyn has a date. We'll talk," their father said.

Shannon looked hurt, her eyes shifting between her parents.

"Carter, go to your room," his mother ordered.

"No, Mom," Shannon said. "If you're going to talk with me, I want Carter here."

"How's that?" their father asked.

"I want him to know," she paused. "I want him to know what I discovered."

"You can tell him later. Your mother and I wanted to talk to you about Kevin."

Shannon tilted her head. "Kevin and I are going to a party tonight."

Carter stood next to the sofa, waiting for further instruction.

"Shannon," their mother said, "you know how your father and I feel about him."

"Yes. And I know how Carolyn feels. None of that matters. I know Kevin. None of you do. He'd never harm me. He's never held my hand. We're friends. That's all."

Carter looked at each parent; neither seemed convinced.

"Look. If you don't trust Kevin, fine. But at least trust me. He's attractive, fun. I'm flattered at the attention he gives me. Imagine, Kevin Hatch going out with me. It's almost humorous. But I have no feelings beyond the flattery, Mom. I have not, nor am I on the verge of taking this relationship to the next level. None! He's a friend. We have fun together. We understand one another."

"Yes, Honey, but Kevin may not feel the same," their mother said.

"That's not my fault. Look, I don't want to leave here angry with you two, also. Kevin's going to be here in a few minutes."

"He's using you, Shannon," her father warned. "He's after only one thing. He'll hurt you like he hurt your sister."

Shannon laughed. Carter caught himself smirking. The very thought of their elder sister being vulnerable to such feelings was unbelievable.

"Carolyn dumped *him*, Dad," Shannon said.

Their father shook his head. "You're not listening. We're not allowing you to see Kevin any longer."

Shannon looked at her mother, tears filling her eyes. "I have not even held his hand. What's wrong with him?"

"We know about him and Carolyn," their mother said. "Your sister told us."

"I understand," she said. "I'm giving you my word; I will not allow that to happen."

The confidence with which Shannon spoke surprised Carter.

Their mother looked at their father. Carter could tell his mother was now on Shannon's side.

"I'm not approving this," his father announced, "I understand kids like him."

Shannon looked at her mother. "You guys beg me to go out more, to socialize. Kevin's my best avenue."

Carter smiled as his mother walked to Shannon and embraced her. "You know our concerns. We trust your judgment. We'll talk about you and Carolyn in the morning."

"Thank you," she said, hugging and resting her head against her mother as though she were a little child. She walked to her father and embraced him. "Dad?" she whispered.

Their father shook his head. "That kid so much as steps in this house . . ." he left off, mumbling something unintelligible.

Minutes later, Kevin arrived and Shannon left with him. Shannon's new discovery, which Carter yearned to know, would have to be revealed the next morning.

A few minutes after one in the morning on Christmas Eve, the phone rang, waking Carter. He walked slowly to his parents' bedroom door. Less than a minute later, both his parents rushed down the stairs with street clothes haphazardly pulled over their pajamas.

"Oh, Douglas! Where is she?" his mother asked.

"At Saint Jude's," Carter's father answered.

Carter followed his parents into the garage and sat in the backseat of the station wagon. He looked at his hands and legs. They shook.

"Carter, Son," his father said. "Oh, my God. My God. How can this happen? How can you let this happen?"

Carter's mother turned and put her hand on Carter's knee. "Carter," she said, "your sister has been in a car accident."

Which sister? Carter wondered. "Carolyn?" he asked, feeling guilty for having asked it with hope.

He could see his mother shake her head. Carter lowered his head, warm tears filling his eyes.

They arrived at the emergency room at one thirty. They were directed to Shannon's room. A doctor met them a few feet from the door. "Mr. and Mrs. Mason?" he asked.

Carter's father stepped forward, holding his wife's hand tightly.

The doctor looked at the eyes of Carter's father and then his mother's. "I'm sorry. There was little we could do."

Carter's mother let out a screech, filling the corridor. Currents of tears flowed from her eyes onto her hands she had raised to both sides of her face.

His father's knees buckled; he lost his balance and fell to the floor. He remained in the center of the corridor as a nurse approached his wife from behind and placed her hand on her shoulder, but she briskly brushed it away. "No. No. No," she screamed as she ran past the doctor, swung open the door, raced to Shannon's side, and rested her head upon the lifeless body.

Carter looked down the corridor. He saw Kevin Hatch sitting, bent over on a bench, his face buried in his hands. Carter walked toward him slowly, then stopped when he noticed a policeman standing near him. Kevin had cuts and large gashes on his arms and face. He had a sling around his right arm.

The policeman was speaking into a walkie-talkie.

Carter looked back at his father. He was still on the floor, resembling a praying monk with his hands pressed against his face and his elbows resting upon his thighs. Eventually, the doctor assisted him up and guided him toward Shannon's room.

As they approached the door, his father looked at Carter and then turned his head toward Kevin. He turned again, looked inside Shannon's room, stopped, and lowered his head. "Carter," he muttered, "go to the lobby."

Carter walked away slowly, but turned before reaching the lobby doors. The policeman reached for the handcuffs attached to his belt as Carter's father walked toward Kevin, placed his hand on the officer's shoulder, and spoke with him for about a minute. The officer nodded, granting what his father had requested.

Kevin did not appear to notice any of the commotion around him. His face was still buried in his hands. Carter's father clinched his fists and stepped back. He took deep breaths and inched closer. He wondered whether his father was going to hit Kevin and why the officer would allow that to happen.

His father placed his hand over his mouth and began to shake. The shaking grew more violent until his knees buckled again, but before he hit the floor, he balanced himself by grabbing onto Kevin's broad left shoulder.

At first, Kevin seemed startled, not realizing whom it was that held him. He moved over to make room on the bench and then helped him sit.

Kevin looked back to the floor. He raised his left arm to wipe tears from his face.

Carter was stunned when he saw his father wrap his arms around Kevin's back. Kevin's head lowered further as he began to tremble with each surging sob, eventually burying his face into the embrace of Carter's father.

Carter saw his mother leave Shannon's room, turning her head, searching for his father. Both hands were clinching Kleenex; her face was moist. Her eyes met Carter's. He stared at her and then back at his father.

Wasn't there a way of making this all go away? Of starting the whole day over?

The dull, deep, heavy sensation growing in his chest and pulling his heart, it seemed, toward his stomach led him to conclude that things would never be the same.

BOOK II:
'TIS THE SEASON

Night Visitors

A Christmas Commentary
by Carter Mason
English/Miss Carson
December 7, 1977

Dashing through the snow
In a one-horse open sleigh
O'er the fields we go
Laughing all the way
Bells on bobtail ring
Making spirits bright
What fun it is to laugh and sing
A sleighing song tonight!

It's eighty degrees outside. The closest snow around here is seventy miles to the east in the San Bernardino Mountains. And that was over two weeks ago before the Thanksgiving holiday weekend.

We don't have fields over which we can ride a horse-drawn carriage in Southern California—only dirty highways, polluted streets, and congested freeways. No snow. No sleigh. No bells; that is, no sleigh bells. We still have dismissal bells, the only heartwarming sound on campus!

The best scenery we see during the holidays—the brilliant assorted lights; the luscious, green Christmas trees; the decorations set up by neighbors—are hazed by our smog and clouded by our commercialism.

And what can I say about our winters? They are full of dreadfully dry high-speed winds that we named after a Mexican general who killed thousands of Americans. Go figure!

There are no sleigh bells jingling, so my sprit ain't bright. The smog makes us cough and wheeze, so don't give me any of this "We'll have fun tonight!" Please! I ain't laughing, and I ain't singing. I'll just lie in bed and listen to more of this miserable music.

Chestnuts roasting on an open fire,
Jack Frost nippin' at your nose,
Yuletide carols being sung by a choir,
and folks dressed up like Eskimos.

Everybody knows a turkey and some mistletoe
help to make the season bright,
. . .

Hold it! Hold it! Hold everything! What is this nonsense? Chestnuts roasting? Well, that sounds good for what it's worth, but it hardly salvages the rest of the lyrics.

Who is this proverbial Jack Frost? Is he related to that guy who interviews Nixon on television? Or maybe he's related to one of those Carols of Yuletide about whom people have such an urge to sing.

Why are these folks dressed like Eskimos? You don't expect me to believe that they are actually roasting chestnuts and singing outside in thirty-below weather! And if they are actual Eskimos, is that why this Jack Frost was nipping instead of kissing?

Finally, what's all this nonsense about a turkey and mistletoe making my season bright? If I had my druthers, I'll take Becky Alford in row two, third seat back, but I ain't kissin' no turkey!

God rest ye merry gentlemen,
let nothing you dismay.
Remember Christ our Savior,
was born on Christmas Day.

In the past, whenever I've heard the phrase *God rest* . . . I have subconsciously completed it with the word *soul*, as in *God rest your soul.* So as I understand it, some dope is asking God to kill all the happy people. Then he offers these formerly merry men some helpful advice: "Don't be dismayed because Christ was born." Great! First he asks God to kill them and then he thinks Christmas will make them happy!

'Twas the night before Christmas, when all thro' the house
Not a creature was stirring, not even a mouse;
The stockings were hung by the chimney with care,
In hopes that Saint Nicholas soon would be there;
The children were nestled all snug in their beds,
While visions of sugar plums danced in their heads,
. . .

Why on earth would any person in their right mind hope that Saint Nicholas soon would be *there*? Unless, of course, *there* is someplace other than your home.

First, children are resting and having pleasant dreams. Even the parents are resting. And the guy who wrote this wants this peaceful state disrupted?

Just look at the chaos Mister Nicholas brings with him. (Please note that I refer to him as "Mister," not "Saint," for a holy person would not put anybody through what he is about to do to this previously peaceful family):

- "When out on the lawn there arose such a clatter"
- Sleigh on roof—just think of the damage
- "Eight tiny reindeer"—who will clean-up their refuse?
- Down the chimney he falls—liability costs
- Smokes in the house—enough said
- "He was chubby and plump"—indication that he will take liberties in your kitchen

And perhaps the worst disruption is the fellow he brings with him inside your home. Oh, Mister Nicholas may be "a right jolly old elf," and though he may wink, giving you indication that you have "nothing to dread," still you have no idea of the mischief that other fellow may cause. For after Mister Nicholas does all his work, he then fills the stockings and turns "with a jerk." Who gave him the right to invite this jerk inside your house?

After all the commotion he causes, he has the nerve to say, "Merry Christmas to all, and to all a good night."

Jingle bells, jingle bells,
Jingle all the way.

Oh! What fun it is to ride
In a one-horse open sleigh.

A year or two ago,
I loved our Christmas tide,
But soon my sister bright,
Had vanished from our side.
The house grew cold and dark;
Misfortune was our lot;
We got into a deep despair,
And fun our home was not.

Jingle bells, jingle bells,
blah-blah-blah-blah-blah . . .

Carter rested his head on the desk, humming the tune from the carol he revised. He had finished writing his Christmas essay, read it in search of grammatical errors, and reread it in hopes of convincing himself that Miss Carson, his sixth-grade teacher, would find it acceptable. Maneuvering the pen between his fingers, he contemplated whether he should write a more upbeat essay. He hoped the one he had finished would suffice to earn him a decent grade, but Carter was not sure whether Miss Carson would misinterpret his feelings toward Christmas. He had written what he felt, and in the end, that's what mattered most. Besides, as much as it might appear that he loathed the holidays, December was still his favorite time of year. He would leave the assignment as it stood. He dropped the pen and sighed.

The house was still and silent, the way it had become most nights during the last two years. Carter would arrive home a little after three in the afternoon and was alone on weeknights until after nine or ten. His mother worked full-time as a speechwriter for the city's mayor and attended graduate school on a part-time basis at night. His dad was rarely at home during Carter's waking hours. His office had secured major building contracts for new subdivision tracts within the city of

Irvine. He was working over seventy hours per week and considered to be one of the more valuable employees at the office.

Carolyn was away at college. She had received scholarship offers from Harvard, Yale, and Dartmouth but decided to attend the University of California at Berkeley.

Carter learned to appreciate the blessings of an empty house. He could watch the television shows he wanted; he could eat pretty much anything he craved; he did his homework on his own timetable. He understood that his parents' busy schedules were a way for them to deal with Shannon's death, and though he did regret their absence, he accepted it with an equal amount of relief.

It was hard to recall what the house was like when it was full of Masons, full of discussion, full of life. He avoided the library and could not recall the last time he had opened its doors, studied on its center table or sofa, or removed one of its books from the shelves. It had a haunting feel to it. If he dared enter through its doors, he'd be alone, fighting the memories of his two sisters and the ghost of Shannon.

He didn't need anyone except his friends—Chuck, Hector, and Allen. What need did he have for his parents but to supply the necessities of shelter, food, and clothing?

He found little humor in life. What made him laugh most was the irony that he no longer felt pressure from his mother to succeed at school. She was too busy with her career and continued education.

Still, he missed his mother's expectations. What made things worse was his feeling that any progress he had made over the past two years had gone unnoticed. Carolyn was at Berkley; Shannon was gone. He had no one to congratulate him except the psychiatrist he had been visiting twice a month for the past eighteen months.

Carolyn and Shannon had taken an IQ test at the age of ten; Carter had anticipated the day he could prove equal to their performance. But his tenth birthday came and went. He was now eleven, and there were no signs of his mother's interest in his intellectual status.

The one time he brought it up, his mother shrugged. "I don't know, Honey," she said. "What value is there in taking the test?"

Carter felt her hesitancy was testament of her lack of confidence in him, that taking the test would do him more harm than good. He was not as capable as his sisters

Certain that he would perform well on the test, Carter yearned to prove his mother wrong and make her proud. He anticipated the day his father would sit him down and explain that his performance did not make him any better or more important than his friends or classmates. He could recall when his sisters had received this word of advice. Their father's speech helped Carolyn and Shannon retain an outward air of humility, but Carter noticed a new level of confidence in each of them. When the girls discussed issues with their parents, they did it as peers. Carter longed to feel like they must have felt.

As Carter's confidence in his intelligence grew, his parents' interest seemed to lessen. He could not understand why neither of them had mentioned anything about him taking the test. "It is only a couple months away," Carter informed his mother. "I know we had this talk a while back, but I'd like to take the test."

"Ask Dr. Hayvenhurst. He'll be able to arrange it for you," she answered.

And that was it.

This had become the cure-all remedy for any problem. Dr. Hayvenhurst had become Carter's best friend next to his three buddies in the neighborhood. For over a year, he had been seeing him to help deal with what his parents called "deep emotional turmoil."

"You need someone to talk to, Carter," his father had told him.

But Carter knew what he was really saying: *We're too busy to bother with your problems, Son.*

As a result, Carter resigned himself to the fact that he would not be taking the test. To help ease the disappointment, he convinced himself that it was not necessary. If he was as intelligent as his two sisters, he did not need some stupid test to tell him so.

He had finished Miss Carson's English assignment and had no intention of working any more on it. He yearned for another task.

Moving to the corner of his bed, he considered books he could read or a show on television that might interest him. He sighed heavily when he came to the conclusion that what he really desired was some company. Burying his head into his hands, he resigned himself to prepare for bed.

As he began unbuttoning his shirt, he heard an object strike the bedroom window. He jerked his head toward the sound, expecting to see a bird or cricket. There was nothing. He was pulling off his worn T-shirt when he heard the noise again. Carter walked over and pulled open the window.

"Hey, Cart," a voice whispered from the large avocado tree in the backyard.

"Carter," a different voice spoke louder.

Carter peered into the dark, figuring to see Chuck, Allen, or Hector, or any combination of the three. He put on the glasses his eye doctor prescribed several months ago and turned off his bedroom light. Relying on the glow of the full moon to get a clearer view of the tree, he recognized Allen and Chuck.

"Hey, guys! What's up?" Carter asked, genuinely surprised.

"Is . . . is . . . is anyone home?" Allen whispered.

"No. Come down. I'll get the door."

Carter raced down the stairs, opened the door, and greeted his friends.

Chuck maneuvered himself through the doorway and walked straight toward the reclining easy chair reserved for Carter's father. Allen stood at the doorway.

"Come in, Allen," Carter invited, "Make yourself comfortable."

"Yeah, Al, sit down, man. You're making me nervous." Chuck kicked his feet into the air as the chair tilted back. He rocked several seconds and then folded his arms behind his head, closed his eyes, and smiled.

"So, Cart," Chuck said with his eyes closed, "what have you been doing all night? Me, Allen, and Hector went to the galaxy far, far away. There were these junior high chicks at the theater, Cart! Man, we were checking them out. Mmm! Sixth graders don't hold a candle to these girls!"

"Again! How many times have you guys seen that thing?"

"Sorry you missed out," Allen said, "For the fifteenth time, maybe; I've lost count. You can never see *Star Wars* too much. It's always a blast. Even Hector was with us. If you had been there, it would have been perfect."

"May the force be with you," Chuck announced with a somber face.

"I was busy," Carter muttered.

"Busy?" Chuck shouted.

"What did you end up doing?" Allen asked.

"Finished Carson's Christmas project."

"That stupid thing?" Chuck turned to face his friends. "Man, I haven't even started mine. I'll do it during math tomorrow. How much time could it take?"

Carter wanted to change the subject. He was jealous of Chuck's ability to procrastinate and still maintain good grades. He turned to Allen. "How about you, Al? Did you finish?"

"I turned it in last week," he answered.

"Geek!" Chuck blurted.

"Has she graded it?" Carter asked.

Allen shook his head.

"How do you think you did?"

"I don't know. I mean, I wrote about Hanukkah."

"That's all right," Carter assured.

"But what if she doesn't like it? I mean, she's probably not Jewish. She might penalize me, you know, for writing about Hanukkah instead of—"

Chuck interrupted: "All you guys are the same, Al. Sheesh, I guess my dad is right about some things! You have this martyr complex: 'Oh, we are always treated as scapegoats . . . nobody understands us . . . all we try to do is be good citizens. And all we get in return is harassment.' Give me a break!"

"Cut it out, Chuck," Carter ordered. "Allen's not like that. He can't help it if he's—"

Allen bit his lip, looking with hurt at Carter. "Gees, Carter. It's not as though I mind it or it's a disease or something!"

"Then say it," Chuck teased.

"Say what?" Allen asked.

"Your heritage. I'm Italian. Cart's, well, a European mutt. Hector's Mexican."

Allen lowered his head. He shuffled the carpet, rubbing his foot across its surface. He looked up at Carter and then glanced at Chuck.

"If you are so proud of it, then say it. I don't know why I put up with you guys," Chuck announced, waving his hand at Allen. He jumped off the chair and stood up. "Are we going to smoke or what? Here." Chuck reached into his pocket and held out an unopened pack of Camels.

"Yeah," Carter sighed, relieved that Allen had escaped the latest of Chuck's awkward ramblings. "Why else do you guys come over?"

"So, Al. You in?" Chuck invited.

Allen reached into his back pocket for a matchbook and handed it to Chuck.

"All right!" Chuck shouted as he lit his first cigarette.

"Hey, hey, hey!" Carter shouted. "Not in here!"

"C'mon, Cart. You don't think they know?" Chuck teased.

"Uh-uh. No way. They don't have a clue. Outside. Outside. Now!" Carter was determined not to leave any evidence for his parents to discover his year-old habit. He knew his mother would not approve of the effect the smoke had on his health; his father would condemn it as one of the vices God most disdains.

Chuck gave in, and the three friends went outside, climbed the avocado tree near Carter's bedroom window, lit their first round, and remained perched until they had finished half the pack.

The night was clear and cool. Carter could feel the smoke flow through his lungs, warming his body. It relaxed him. The three boys did not talk much. Carter was just glad to be with his friends.

He stared up through the leaves and the avocados, mesmerized by the number of stars in view. He felt so small, so helpless, hopeless, and alone. Here he was, with two of his closest buddies, and still he felt the pain of loneliness deep within his chest, a pain that he had only minutes earlier thought to have escaped.

"It's unusually clear," Carter muttered.

"What?" Chuck asked.

"The stars, they seem so bright."

Carter's tone prompted his two friends to exchange glances at one another.

"You didn't cockney that, Cart. You feeling all right?" Chuck asked.

Carter was in no mood of arguing or trying to explain what he was feeling. Chuck was right; he should have done what his group of friends had mastered over the past year—speak in the British accent over which they had grown fond by watching Monty Python episodes on television. Hector was the first to use the dialect when describing their sixth-grade teacher after the first week of class: "I say, chaps, you bloody well watch that tutor of ours at the academy. She may right be a pleasant sight to one's eyes, but it ain't no surprise to this here fellow, she have the heart of a mouse."

There were only three scenarios in which it was acceptable to use the accent. Though none of his friends actually verbalized the rules, once any of them made the faux pas of breaking one, he would learn to never do it again. Otherwise, he risked the looks of disdain, displeasure, and being ostracized for an hour or more. The cockney could be used when making a keen observation, but this was perhaps the most risky of the scenarios, for if the listeners were not impressed with the insight, the sour looks and disapproval would be that much stronger. The second scenario, which up to this time, had also been used sparingly, was to make fun of a third party. To use the cockney with a joke could ruin the intent and spontaneity, thus limiting the potency of the humor. By far, the most common scenario was when Carter or one of his buddies felt the need to express sadness or failure or hurt. By speaking in the accent, it somehow released the uncomfortable feeling of divulging too much emotional turmoil to one another, thus assisting each of them to feel the freedom to share without the risk of being made fun of.

Chuck was right. To speak of the stars, as he had seconds earlier, warranted use of their cockney's first scenario. But he didn't care tonight. He was too tired. Too sad. He looked up again at the stars, releasing a ring of smoke. Allen cleared his throat. "Carter?"

"Yeah," Carter answered.

He waited for Allen to continue. He seemed to have something he wanted to say. "Yeah?" Carter asked a second time, looking at Allen.

Allen looked down. "Nothing."

"You wimp, Allen," Chuck announced.

"What's all this about?" Carter asked.

Chuck tapped his cigarette, dropping ashes to the grass below. "The three of us have been talking, Cart. You know, Allen, Hector, and I. We all agree you're not the same. You know?"

Carter eyed Chuck suspiciously. It was a curious, almost foreign, idea that Chuck had within him the ability to have genuine concern about another's welfare. Carter found it humorous. He grinned. "I'm fine, guys."

"Well," Allen started, "with Shannon's death and all."

Chuck elbowed Allen in the side.

"It's all right." Carter finished his cigarette and rubbed his face with his hands. "Of course it bothers me still. But it's been two years. I visit that shrink; he helps. And I've got you guys."

"You're not as lively," Chuck said, "you know, when we play ball. You don't joke around as much."

Carter grinned. "I guess that's supposed to happen when we grow up."

"You think?" Allen asked.

Carter shrugged as he swung himself back from the branch on which he was seated, and grabbed it as he began to fall. He held on to the branch, his feet dangling a few yards above the ground. It was a ritual motion he had long ago mastered. "Hey, guys, look. I'm a smoking monkey." Carter reached into his shirt pocket and placed an unlit cigarette into his mouth, released one of his arms from the branch, and began to scratch his armpit.

"Cute, Cart." Chuck jumped off his branch to the ground.

"Hey. Wait for me, guys." Allen was still smoking. He took a few more puffs, extinguished the butt by rubbing it against the trunk, and leapt from the branch on which he was perched.

Carter was still hanging from the tree. He released his grip and tumbled onto the grass.

"Thanks for your concern, guys. But really, I'm okay."

Chuck did not appear convinced.

Carter stood up and brushed himself off. "You guys better go before one of my parents get home. I'll clean up the butts."

"You sure?" Allen asked.

Carter raised his hands. "You guys get going. I'm fine."

Chuck turned toward the backyard fence, motioning Allen to follow. "Thanks, Cart," he said, "we'll see ya tomorrow."

Carter waved as he bent down to search for cigarette remnants. He went into the kitchen and placed the collected butts into a plastic sandwich bag. Using a wired tie, he sealed the sandwich bag and placed that bag into a brown lunch bag. Then he went into the backyard, lifted the lid on a trash can, and hid the bag in the midst of other garbage. He reentered his home, stripped off his clothes, placed them in the washing machine, started the wash, walked upstairs, put on his winter pajamas, and climbed into bed. He sat up minutes later to draw the curtains from the window. The stars he had seen from the tree were now hid behind clouds moving in from the Pacific coast.

Carter closed his eyes, hoping that on this particular night he would find it easy to sleep.

Sugar Plums

Dr. Hayvenhurst's assessment was that Carter worried too much and that this worrying got in the way of his ability to enjoy childhood. According to the good doctor, as Carter liked to call him, Carter's preoccupation with issues a boy his age should not be considering was paving a road toward a myriad of health problems.

Hayvenhurt's warnings increased Carter's anxiety. It was at night, while he lay in bed unable to fall asleep, that Carter most agreed with the good doctor's diagnosis.

"It wasn't always like this," Carter would mutter before narrating a past event to Hayvenhurst or retelling a memory of a more pleasant past.

Hayvenhurst recommended that Carter think of good memories whenever he struggled to sleep. Carter named this solution the counting-sheep remedy. He had nothing to lose. He was tired of lying in bed, tossing and turning two to three hours each night. He was willing to try anything, so he followed the good doctor's advice and discovered that it worked fairly well. Through trial and error, he determined that the best technique was to daydream about a recent, pleasant event. Following his friends' departure, Carter's initial attempt to fall asleep centered on his writing project for Miss Carson's class. He considered whether his theme was too cynical. He smiled as he thought of how his teacher might react to his satirical commentary of Christmas carols.

Although he loved the poem "'Twas the Night before Christmas," he concluded that using it in his assignment was testament to how he felt. His mocking tone hid the original love affair he once had with the unfolding events in the poem's narrative—"while visions of sugarplums danced through their heads."

Carter had not seen or tasted a sugarplum, but by the high esteem given them in the poem, he knew they must be delicious. When Nana first read the poem to him, he envisioned the treats as similar to candied apples, an actual plum, coated with a caramelized covering. Nana subsequently corrected his misconception, explaining that they were a type of hard candy, shaped as a ball.

Nonetheless, he preferred his imagination's original creation and held it as the preferred treat. He considered how the words of the poem had come to portray the bittersweet memories of his family's past Christmases. At first, he would recall the good Christmases, the holiday celebrations before Shannon's death. But then, there were the rotten sugarplums—the bad Christmases. For the previous two years, Carter had already had his fill of them. He feared that this year would be no different.

Bad sugarplums were like bad Christmases. Both appeared to be a delight to the senses only to leave disappointment and a sour aftertaste. The sweet coating of a mushy sugarplum hides the treat's poor value. Carter imagined biting into one of these plums. It would leave him never to desire another as long as he lived. Enduring one more holiday season similar to the previous two would leave him vowing to never again look forward to this time of the year. Whether it be a candied apple or one of Carter's imaginary sugary plums, one bad treat can spoil the bushel; one bad Christmas can spoil an entire year.

Carter fell asleep by nine o'clock. The weather had grown warmer as bursts of wind blew out of the dry California desert into the rich regions of Orange County. Leaves and strewn papers were carried along the path of the wind. At the Mason home, Carter had just entered into his most recurring nightmare . . .

Carter stood at the foot of an enormous mountain range. He did not know the reason nor who had given him the orders, but he was required to climb this vast range of mountains in search of a lost item.

The item could be anything: the cat down the street, a little girl in the neighborhood, a school assignment, or a piece of clothing one of his sisters had misplaced. Whatever the object was, Carter felt it was his responsibility to find it.

Sometimes he traveled alone; other times one of his friends from school or the neighborhood would accompany him. The only time he enjoyed this particular nightmare was when his attractive sixth-grade teacher, Miss Carson, accompanied him. It did not matter with whom he was traveling; by the end of the dream, he would be left alone. He could not remember how his traveling companions disappeared or if their departure was voluntary or involuntary. He suspected the former, since the remainder of the dream was full of terrible monsters, avalanches, earthquakes, blizzards, steep crevasses in which he would fall, and a bitter-cold wind, all of which his partners must have been aware of, thereby explaining their abrupt disappearance.

The most hideous portion of the dream occurred the moment before Carter would awake in fright, with sweat heavy on his brow and saturating his pajamas. Emerging from another deadly battle against a beast or the elements, he entered the final scene of the nightmare—a plain of darkness. The bitter wind would cease for only a moment, making him aware of the emptiness of his surroundings.

He wanted only one question answered at that moment: Where am I? But there was never anybody present whom he could ask. He certainly could not have seen such a person, for he could not even see his hand when he held it in front of his eyes. But he never heard a sound in that plain once the wind had ceased howling. Never, that is, until this particular early December evening.

That was when Carter shot up in his bed. The crisp sound of footsteps on pavement awakened him. He was infuriated that he was no longer dreaming. He wanted to know whose feet in the dream had made the sound. Then he realized that the sound he had heard was what awakened him. He pulled his pajama top away from his chest; it was soaked with perspiration. He pulled it off, threw it in the corner of his room, and replaced it with one of his T-shirts. He was about to hop back under the covers and attempt to continue the nightmare when he heard the footsteps once more.

Carter froze. He looked at the clock. It was 9:30, late enough for one of his parents to be home. He jumped from his bed and ran to Carolyn's room, looking out the window. Neither car was on the driveway, and of course, Carter told himself, half wishing that it were a possibility, neither car would be in the garage that was full of his father's tools. He felt his heart's pounding grow within his chest. He wasn't sure whether to trust his senses or to dismiss the sound as being produced by what Carolyn had called his overactive imagination. Another wave of perspiration deluged his body. He questioned whether he was still dreaming, whether the steps were real. He had always wanted to find someone in his dream in that plain of darkness. Now that he had heard footsteps, the sounds frightened him more than the silence they replaced.

The steps grew louder as they seemed to approach the garage. Carter scurried downstairs, being careful to make as little noise as possible. As he approached the kitchen that led to the garage entrance, the sounds of the steps came to an abrupt halt.

Carter heard objects moving. Whoever it was, he or she was too close. Carter raced to the kitchen's telephone and called 911, informing the operator that "there's somebody in our garage."

Six minutes later, Sergeant McCaskey was knocking on the front door. Carter cautiously peered through the peephole to verify who it was. He released a deep sigh and opened the door.

"Good evening, Carter," the burly six-foot-five officer greeted.

"You don't know how glad I am to see you." Carter looked up toward McCaskey, feeling security.

"I got here as soon as I could," the officer explained.

Carter was still trembling.

"Are you all right, Carter?" the officer asked.

Carter wrapped his arms around himself.

"Can I come in?"

Backing from the doorway, Carter looked toward the kitchen, wondering what may be transpiring in the garage.

"Your parents aren't home?"

Carter shook his head. "No, Sir."

"Any idea when they'll be back?"

Carter looked behind him at the antique clock on the staircase wall. "About an hour ago, sir."

McCaskey grinned. "Alone again? They must trust you a bunch, Mr. Mason."

Carter stood back with some trepidation as he awaited the officer's next move.

McCaskey stepped past Carter. "Where did you hear the intruder?"

"In there." Carter pointed toward the kitchen.

He followed the officer as he walked through the kitchen and entered the garage. McCaskey found nothing suspicious. He exited through the garage side entrance into the backyard.

Carter gradually replaced the fear he had felt earlier with the anxiety that McCaskey might not find any evidence.

"Oh, shoot," Carter mumbled as he saw the officer approach, shaking his head.

"Nothing?" Carter asked.

McCaskey did not respond. He walked straight past Carter into the family room and sat on the sofa across from the television. "Sit down, Carter," he ordered. "We need to talk."

Carter nervously swallowed and sat in his father's chair, as far away from McCaskey as he could manage and still obey the order. He stared at the floor.

"Did I ever tell you that I grew up in an orphanage?"

The question took Carter by surprise. He looked at the policeman.

"Sure. Fifteen years. From a little tyke of three to an obnoxious eighteen-year-old. Can you imagine?"

Carter shook his head.

McCaskey continued. "Well, I think you can. The two of us aren't that different, Mr. Mason. I remember playing tricks on the other kids:

pouring warm water on their hands while they were sleeping, putting their socks in the freezer, cutting their shoelaces." McCaskey chuckled and then continued, "I often was able to come up with some plan that would leave my teachers at school with no option other than making a house visit to the orphanage. I would tell you what I did, but I don't want to give you any more ideas than you already have. Let's just say they came to get explanations, or to give explanations, for my disruptive behavior. No explanations were necessary for me however. I knew what I was doing. I knew why I was doing it."

The officer allowed an interlude of silence. If he was trying to make a point, it wasn't necessary, but Carter was in no position to tell him this.

"Do you see what I'm saying, Carter?"

"Yes, sir. I think I do," Carter said with an intended mixture of fatigue, sorrow, and sincerity, hoping to satisfy his guest.

The officer rose from the sofa and walked toward the front door.

Carter followed him and opened the front door.

"So, no more calls?" McCaskey asked as he strolled toward his patrol car.

"No, sir," Carter whimpered from the doorway. "But I really did hear something this time," Carter said more quietly. "I really did."

Carter slowly shut the front door. He went into the garage, turned on the light, and did a quick survey. Nothing. No signs of disruption. He shook his head, flipped the light switch, turned, and closed the door behind him.

He dragged himself back upstairs and into his bedroom. As he lay down, he saw headlights shine against the backyard fence. Racing into Carolyn's bedroom, he caught a glimpse of the approaching car. It was his mother.

Officer McCaskey had not yet driven away in his car. Carter gulped as the officer got out and waited for his mother to pull into the driveway.

His mother parked, and Carter imagined her collecting work and school assignments that had been strewn onto the floor and under the passenger seat.

From Carter's perspective, McCaskey was pleading for her attention. He walked toward the driveway rapidly as though perhaps his mother was about to enter the house without acknowledging his presence.

Carter unlatched the window, hoping to eavesdrop on the ensuing dialogue.

"Mrs. Mason," the officer called out softly. "Please, can I have a moment?"

"I'm not going to endure another of your sermons, Jim," his mother declared. "Doug and I were a bit offended last time you were here."

"I apologize for that. I'm sorry. I can get emotional about things sometimes."

"It's comforting to know that we have officers protecting our community who find it difficult to control their emotions."

Carter grimaced.

"My only concern is for the boy. He needs—"

"We know what he needs. He is our concern, not yours, Jim!"

McCaskey cleared his throat. He crossed his arms and looked down at Carter's mother. "Well, actually, he is. You see, Mrs. Mason, these little excursions we make here two to three times each year cost the department over a hundred dollars. We can't let this continue."

"Fine!" Carter's mother said as she withdrew a checkbook from her purse, "How much do you want?"

McCaskey shook his head and looked to the ground. He raised his hand toward his head. "Listen, this has got to stop. I've written up a citation. Next time we'll have to ticket your son, Katherine. I'm sorry."

McCaskey handed the slip of paper to Carter's mother.

As he drove away, Carter nervously eyed her. She stood on the driveway reading the specifics of her son's misdemeanor. She looked up at Carolyn's bedroom from where Carter was still peering. Their eyes met. They remained fixed for only a second before Carter left Carolyn's bedroom and walked slowly to his own room. He sat on the edge of his bed, grabbed a pillow and hugged it.

He waited for his mother to storm into the room, half wishing that she would. He heard the front door open and then shut quietly. He heard her ascend the stairway and enter her bedroom. He waited.

His father returned home twenty minutes later. Carter listened as he walked up the stairs and entered the bedroom. "It wasn't always like this." Carter muttered. "It wasn't always like this."

He used it as his mantra: "It wasn't always like this. It wasn't always like this. It wasn't always like this . . ."

And as if he were counting sheep, he fell asleep.

Of Carter's Discontent

A Christmas Commentary
by Carter Mason
P.3—English: Miss Carson
December 7, 1977

The holiday season is full of songs and carols that, upon closer examination, leave much to be desired. Take for example the popular "Rudolph the Red-Nosed Reindeer." This song is an ancestor of subliminal rock lyrics of the sixties and seventies. Cowboy Gene Autry, if he really did write this song (my dad says he did not), was attempting to provide an excuse for getting tipsy over the holiday season, thus the red nose. Shame on you, Mr. Autry! No wonder your Angels never win!

And all the songs about the pleasantness of being home during the holiday season does not take into consideration those who do not have pleasant homes, live with dysfunctional families, or have no family at all. So let's do away with the classics "I'll Be Home for Christmas," "Home for the Holidays," and "There's No Christmas Like a Home Christmas," to name just a few.

But enough of my rambling. The best way to show what is wrong with the soundtrack of the season is by analyzing the lyrics, one carol at a time.

Let's start with "Midnight Clear."

It came upon a Midnight Clear,
That glorious song of old,
From angels bending near the earth,
to touch their harps of gold;
. . .

If angels are of any value, and if they exist as I have been taught at Sunday school, then their value must be far greater than the act of bending toward the earth so we can "touch their harps of gold."

Joy to the world, the Lord has come!
. . .

Joy? What joy? Wherever I turn, I see hurt. There is more evil than good in this world. More pain than healing. More sorrow and weeping than joy and laughter.

Why be joyful? Because the Lord has come? Is that why? If he came, then why is this world in such a mess? He either came and failed to bring the joy with him, or he never came at all!

Good Christian men rejoice
With heart and soul and voice!
. . .

Deck the halls with boughs of holly,
Fa la la la la, la la la la.
. . .

Jolly Old St. Nicholas,
Lean your ear this way!
. . .

We wish you a Merry Christmas,
We wish you a Merry Christmas,
We wish you a Merry Christmas,
And a Happy New Year.

Does not matter how many times you say it or in how many different ways you say it. Doesn't matter if you say it with words of nonsense, like "fa-la-la-la-la" or "ho-ho-ho." If horrible has happened, then there is no jolly, there is no merry, no happy, no rejoicing, no fa-la-la-la-la.

Carter daydreamed while Dr. Hayvenhurst read the graded English assignment, anticipating laughter from the good doctor when he neared the end of the essay. Arriving minutes before his scheduled appointment, he had hoped to hear from this man, whom he had grown to trust and respect, that his "Christmas Commentary" deserved better than the C—Miss Carson had awarded it.

Carter's father chose Hayvenhurst because he attended the same church and their pastor recommended him. His mother had felt a secular psychiatrist would better serve Carter's needs, but after meeting and questioning the doctor for over a half hour, she concluded that Hayvenhurst was one of the best in the profession.

Carter liked his doctor from the start and could tell that Hayvenhurst felt the same about him. It was fun spilling his guts, telling someone things that he never dared speak to anyone else.

He was a large man—Carter guessed he was close to three hundred pounds—and tall, at least six foot five. He spoke in a deep, gentle tone, had isolated strands of gray in the midst of his deep-black hair, and subtle sideburns, not too long, but just enough to convince Carter that his doctor was hip with the style of the day. His nose was rounded and his eyes deeply set, seeming to soak in all information around them. He dressed in the finest suits but always had the top button of his shirt undone, releasing the tension of ties around his enormous neck.

He often wondered whether Hayvenhurst enjoyed his job. He seemed to. He seemed to enjoy life. He was in his mid-forties, had been married twenty years, and had five children. Two of the doctor's children, identical twin boys, were in Carter's Sunday school class. Carter liked the twins. They went to a private school and seemed quite intelligent when they spoke. They were indiscriminately kind to the other kids in the class: the girls and the boys, the cute and the ugly, those who got picked on and those who did the picking. Carter distantly admired them and now understood how they came to be such a likeable pair.

Carter had not thought highly of the psychiatric profession before his first visit. His parents had once said psychiatrists exist only because families and friends in society had failed to care and protect their own. Hayvenhurst and his colleagues were reaping profits as a result of humans failing to do their duty. Carter looked forward to the sessions, fully aware that although his parents may have been right about their estimation of the psychiatric profession, they were now as guilty as those they once criticized.

Hayvenhurst shuffled papers on his desk. He picked up Carter's graded assignment. "Are you surprised by the grade?" he asked, handing it back to Carter.

"Sure!" Carter replied. "I worked over an hour on it. I should have gotten at least a B."

"It's interesting. You write well for your age. I'm assuming your teacher did not approve of the theme?"

Carter frowned and then shrugged. "I guess."

"You really feel this way?" Hayvenhurst asked. "About Christmas?"

"I didn't use to. I mean, I still enjoy December. It's my favorite time of the year. You know, the excitement, the memories, and all. Believe it or not, I do like most of the music."

Hayvenhurst chuckled. "Tell me about what you're looking forward to most."

Carter straightened himself in one of the four chairs in the office. Each chair was so soft that Carter found it difficult to stay awake while

Hayvenhurst's deep, melodic insights lulled him into a subconscious state of mind. "I'm decorating the house tonight!"

Carter could see the doctor was interested, so he detailed his plans further. He inched near the edge of the chair's soft leather. "You see, my parents don't know this yet. I haven't told anyone, except you. I've saved up all my allowance money to win this year's Christmas contest. I'm going all out."

"Christmas contest?"

"Well, sure. You see, each year, three days before Christmas, our neighbors judge each other's homes. We base it on the lights on the houses, the decorations, and all that stuff. The house that wins gets a free dinner."

"And where will you go if you win?"

Carter shook his head and waved his hands, "I don't know." He paused. "I don't care."

Carter caught his breath and continued. "Straight from here, I'm riding my bike to that Christmas store at the mall. You know the one? Oh shoot, I forgot the name. But you know the one."

"I do," he replied. "Very expensive."

"I've already reserved three of their motorized Christmas figures. You know, the ones that move their hands and their eyes. Tonight I'm giving them the money. I hope they'll deliver them to our house tonight while I'm setting up the lights."

"That sounds exciting. Which figures did you buy?"

"Oh, that's the best part! I got one figure that I'm going to put on our lawn next to our singing snowmen. It's a teeter-totter with a boy and girl on each end. Up and down they go . . . up and down . . . up and down . . .

"The other two robots I'm putting up on our roof next to the chimney. One is Santa. He's waving with one hand and holding a bag of toys in the other. The third one's Rudolph. He has a bright red nose; he's wiggling his tail and moving his head back and forth."

Carter inched up a bit more in the chair, tapping his foot. As far as he was concerned, this session was over. He wanted to leave, go do the work he had just described.

Hayvenhurst was silent. It seemed as though he were waiting to hear something more. Carter grew impatient and tapped his foot more rapidly.

Hayvenhurst pulled on his collar and looked across at Carter. "Why are you going through all this trouble and expense?"

Carter looked at Hayvenhurst with caution, not wanting him to pursue this line of questioning further.

"A minute ago you said you don't care about winning the free dinner. Why then are you so excited about winning the contest?"

Carter remained silent, looked at anything in the office except the doctor, and then slid back in the chair.

"Is it pride?" Hayvenhurst asked.

Carter looked up and shook his head.

"Are you bored, and this just gives you something to do?" Carter shook his head again.

Hayvenhurst stopped asking questions, but it was obvious he would wait for a response.

Carter looked past Hayvenhurst to the garden behind his office window. "I don't know," he finally said.

Still, Hayvenhurst didn't speak.

Carter raised his arms. "I don't know. I tell you, I don't know."

Hayvenhurst reclined, not appearing convinced, not appearing uncomfortable, and not appearing annoyed.

Carter sighed. "I'm the only one who'll do it. All right? If it wasn't for me, it wouldn't get done."

"But why are you looking forward to it?"

"I don't want to do this. Please. I've told you, it doesn't help."

Carter looked away, frustrated that he would have to stay and discover something more about himself. Something that would probably keep him awake at night while worrying about how he got to this point. Now Hayvenhurst was making him angry. He looked at him with a heated stare.

"The memories," Carter confessed. "I do it because I want it to be like it was. It makes me happy, I guess. Is that what you want to hear?"

The doctor shrugged. "We're not here for me to hear something that convinces me we've made a breakthrough."

Carter looked up at the doctor, confused. Then he recognized the gentle rebuke.

"I don't enjoy doing it. I mean, it's like I can't help it. What am I supposed to do? Forget about Shannon? Forget about how much better our family was?"

Carter shifted his weight in the chair, digging in to find a more comfortable position, and finally crossed his legs, placing his right leg atop his left, extended his hands, and wrapped them around his right knee.

"Sometimes when I think about how it used to be, my head begins to hurt. I lose control and start screaming as loud as I can. It's as if there's a heap of water inside of me waiting to break through and I can't hold it in. What am I supposed to do?"

"You keep letting loose those blood-curdling screams."

Carter's eyes widened.

"When the pressure gets too great, let it out. If your parents give you any trouble, have them call me. I'll talk to them. Let the flood out by hitting a pillow; run sprints in your backyard. Go to the batting cages and take your anger out on the balls."

Carter understood the potential benefits of such actions but doubted he would go out of his way to do any of them. It was much easier to yell or hit something, even himself. But telling the doctor about that would open up another avenue of dialogue, an avenue on which Carter did not wish to travel, especially not today.

"But," Hayvenhurst continued, "you must stop the pranks at school. These will only make things more difficult."

Carter looked to the floor, shameful of the escapades he had performed on his campus. A few months following Shannon's death,

Carter started to flip through the books Shannon had been reading, hoping to piece together the puzzles she left behind. He searched through her notebooks and diaries, anticipating the day he'd discover what it was Shannon had wanted to tell him the night before she died.

He grew frustrated at his inability to grasp the concepts he was reading in Shannon's memoirs and began to pull out a word, a phrase, anything that made sense. A common message he understood was the meaningless nature of life. He found these words written frequently in Shannon's journal: "If there's no meaning, then make it as interesting as you can." The best way Carter figured to make life interesting was by disturbing the peace of others, a surprise that caused fright, or joy, or laughter in the classroom, among his friends, or in the house.

"Remember, Carter," Hayvenhurst continued, "eventually you need to outgrow this stage. You need to find other outlets for your anger, your hurt, and your confusion."

"I know," Carter said, looking at the floor and uncertain he could find a way to immerge from all he felt inside.

"Listen, Carter. Live today. Decorate the house, but decorate it because you find enjoyment in the act of doing it, not because of the memories it brings. Living is present tense. Don't let yourself get lost in the past. You've lived a haunting life during the past two years, but today is new. Today you must live anew."

"Today is the first day of the rest of my life," Carter mimicked skeptically.

"It's an overused cliché, yes. But you obviously understand its meaning; otherwise you would not mock its usage."

Carter grimaced.

"You don't like clichés?" the Doctor asked.

Carter paused a moment, half thinking of how to say it and half thinking whether he should say it at all. "They're like Sunday school."

Hayvenhurst did not appear offended but inquisitive.

"There's always an answer for everything," Carter continued. "It seems they have an answer for every problem you may have. You know, 'Because God knows best,' or, 'It will all work out,' or 'just pray about it.'"

"And?" Hayvenhurst asked.

Carter took a moment to gather his thoughts. "And . . . and . . . and none of it, the clichés or Sunday school, makes any difference. They're just there to make us feel good, nothing more. No stupid cliché or pat answer can bring back my sister or make my family normal again. It's like the people who say those things are just slapping me in the face. They don't know what they're talking about!"

"Then why do you go each week?" Hayvenhurst asked.

Carter gazed at his doctor suspiciously and then at the ceiling. He had asked himself this question many times.

He decided on his answer, though he knew it to be untrue: "My dad makes me."

"You've told me before that your mother would prefer you not attend."

"Yeah, about my sisters. I've told you all about that stuff."

"If your sisters decided not to attend church and your father still loved them, and did not show any signs of disapproval, then you must know that your father will still love you if you decide not to go."

Carter shrugged his shoulders, conceding the point.

"Then if you don't see any value in church, why keep going? It can't be that your father makes you. I've seen you there on Sundays when he's out of town on business."

Carter had been caught! His eyes widened. Hayvenhurst actually noticed his presence at church. He was aware of this contradiction, but had not confronted his patient with it.

"Carter," he said sternly. "Look at me."

Carter obediently raised his head.

"You are my youngest, and probably most intelligent, client. If some of my older patients had your smarts, they would have no need to visit me."

Carter bit his lip, trying to prevent a smile.

Hayvenhurst continued. "Your problem isn't intellectual. It's not so much emotional. Yes, you have a lot of emotional turmoil within you, but you will emerge healthy. All signs of how you are dealing with the pain of Shannon's death are natural; you have nothing to feel ashamed about. Just keep being honest. The problems you are facing now, that are tearing you apart, were brought to light by your sister's death; they were there all along. It is these struggles of yours with which you must deal. It is with these struggles that you must take some action."

Carter had heard this before, many times, from the good doctor.

"I realize you are young, much younger than any patient to whom I have suggested this action, but you must begin to consider what you believe, not what one of your parents believes. You must decide, Carter, whether you believe attending church or seeking God is of any value for you; not based upon what your father or mother says but based upon what your mind and heart are telling you. Do you understand?"

Carter shrugged his shoulders. "Sure. I knew that already. I've made my decision. I just haven't told my father because I don't want to hurt his feelings and all."

Carter spoke with a feigned assurance. The doctor was right. Since Shannon's death, he had begun to realize his life was aimed at pleasing either one or both of his parents. All he wanted was their approval. But the harder he tried, the more disinterested they seemed. Increasingly, he felt like Sisyphus, pushing his rock hopelessly up the steep hill.

"Is there anything else you'd like to talk about?"

The question startled Carter from his imaging of the Greek myth.

Hayvenhurst looked at his watch.

Carter looked at the clock behind the doctor's desk. There were still five minutes before extra billing time would accumulate. *Great*, Carter thought, *my friendship is based upon the time remaining until his next appointment.*

"There is one thing that is beginning to bother me."

The doctor motioned for him to continue.

"Mom is getting on my dad's case again about spending time with Kevin."

"But you told me that was no longer a problem."

"I know," Carter replied.

"Are you having a problem with your father spending time with him?"

"Well, that's why my mother's getting on his case again. I told her last week that I wished Dad and I could spend more time together, like we used to. Don't get me wrong, I've always liked Kevin, and in a way, I feel sorry for him, but I can't understand what my father is trying to accomplish by spending so much time with him."

"I'm sure you father has his reasons."

Carter looked at Hayvenhurst inquisitively. Why was he defending his father?

"Talk to him about it. Tell him how you feel."

"I'm not jealous," Carter said. "I mean, I don't think I am. I've felt jealousy, and I don't think that's what I feel. If it was one of my friends, say, Hector or Allen or Chuck, sure, then I'd be jealous. But Kevin?"

"Jealousy doesn't always have to be felt for yourself," Hayvenhurst suggested.

Carter tilted his head.

"You think about it."

"You talking about Shannon? Jealous for Shannon? But how? She's dead. Why be jealous for her? I don't get what you mean."

"I can't tell you Carter. You need to determine this yourself."

"Boy, it seems I've got to do a lot of discovering. Why do we pay you anyhow?"

"I'm not here to tell you what to do."

"I know. I know. Only to lead me to the place where I discover a choice needs to be made. You're a mirror, not a 'mirror, mirror on the wall.'"

Hayvenhurst smiled and stood up. "Well, it's time to wish you a merry Christmas, Carter. I will be out of town in a couple weeks, so we won't meet again until the new year. Here, I got a little something for you." Hayvenhurst handed Carter a present wrapped snugly, unable to betray its identity.

"A book," Carter blurted. His eyes widened. "Can I open it on Christmas. I mean, it won't offend you if I don't open it here?"

"Of course not." Hayvenhurst walked Carter to the door. He wrapped his left arm around Carter's shoulder and hugged him. Carter looked up, wondering the doctor's intent. He usually shook his hand; that was all. But Hayvenhurst wore the same gentle stare Carter had always received upon his departure. Perhaps it was his way of saying, "Don't just have a merry Christmas, but a very merry Christmas."

Carter smiled. "Thanks. Thanks a lot."

He left the office, unlocked his bike in the grocery parking lot across the street, placed his first Christmas gift into his backpack, and rode south two miles to the mall. He leaned the bike against the wall of the Christmas specialty store and ran inside to purchase the three mechanical Christmas figurines and to make arrangements for their delivery.

All business taken care of, Carter rushed out of the store, saddled his bike, and pushed through his first several pedals while seated. Raising himself off the seat, he quickened his pace, breathing heavily through a growing grin.

Deck the Halls

Carter ascended the ladder to his attic seven times, placed seven large boxes on the garage floor, and then climbed his way back to the top rung and grabbed another box. Dust encircled his head, his frequent coughing not disrupting his pace. Hanging from his hair and glasses were strands of accumulated dust, giving his thick brown hair the appearance of gray.

As he laid out ten light cords in parallel formation, he estimated two hours were required to finish. It was a challenge to maneuver around his father's tools. Trying his best to retain the state his father had last left the garage, it was taking him longer than anticipated. And with the boxes on the garage floor and the light strings strewn onto the driveway, he guessed his parents would not be pleased. So he hoped to be finished before they arrived home.

One last box remained. Carter climbed to the top and looked despairingly at the assortment of boxes strewed around the foot of the ladder. Twelve boxes were below now, some with tree decorations, others with wreaths, one with lights for outside, and another filled with lights for the inside of the house. There was a box full of Christmas music boxes: an angel that played "Silent Night," a reindeer which turned to the music of "Rudolph the Red-Nosed Reindeer," and a tree ornament that played a collection of carols. Another box was made of Tupperware, containing fragile ceramic statues, candles, and special Christmas napkins, plates, and silverware. His stocking and his sisters' stockings were in another box along with the Christmas card rack and tapes of Christmas music his father had taped from radio stations on Christmas Eves over the years.

Carter held his breath as he reached for the final container in the attic, a six-by-eight-inch hatbox. Cradling it between his chest and right arm, he used his left arm to secure his descent. The pounding in his chest grew until he reached the garage floor. He took a deep breath, ran into the house, set the box by the front-door window, and rushed back to the garage. He turned his wrist and looked down at his watch—less than one hour of daylight.

No time to dillydally; no time to fret about how Stuart's parents had already decorated their home; so had Chuck's and Allen's parents. Carter ran back outside and glanced down the street toward Hector's home. It was the only other house in the neighborhood not yet decorated. Feeling optimistic about his chances of winning the competition this year, Carter was hit by the possibility that his hopes were unrealistic. He shook his head, trying to escape the feeling of defeat that was clouding those hopes. Those Christmas figurines were his only chance. Hopefully, the delivery man would soon arrive with them. He had saved his allowance for two years, helped Hector with his paper route, and sold a small portion of his baseball card collection. "It had better be worth it," he mumbled.

He moved the ladder to the rightmost corner of the roof and searched for the first hook on which he could rest the light cord. The first thing he noticed was that his house needed a paint job. His mother had talked endlessly about this with his father, but his father would say that there was not enough money. Good thing too, the painters were sure to have removed the hooks, thus making Carter's job more difficult.

Previous to this evening, Carter had felt the house looked fine. He did not understand his mother's complaint. But as he arranged the assorted colored lights along the home's perimeter, cracked paint fell onto the pavement beneath him. The old light-blue color of the home became visible underneath the sun-dried, yellowish-green tint of the latest coat. Carter tried to ignore this but began wondering why his father had done nothing about it. He did not buy into his father's "not enough cash" excuse. Before Shannon's death, he would not let the house look unkempt or old. Everything had to be in order. It must be, Carter concluded, that his priorities had changed.

If they hadn't changed, then his father would be doing the decorating, or at least assisting. But here Carter was, hanging the light cords by himself. The boredom allowed him to reminisce of more pleasant Christmases. He shook his head, attempting to erase the memories.

He recalled Shannon's voice and saw her deep-brown eyes and eager, kind smile.

A burning filled his chest. He felt perspiration bead on his forehead and his grip moisten around the cords of lights he held in each hand. He wanted to be held, to be embraced, but the only object near him was the decrepit ladder. He dropped the cords and fell on the ladder's top tier. The lights burst, popping as they fell against the wall of the house.

Carter placed his hands on each side of his face and looked upward. Pulling his hair and sliding his hands above his head, he yelled. Wasn't it okay to do this? Wasn't it what Hayvenhurst had suggested?

"Do it because you enjoy it, not because of the memories," Hayvenhurst had said.

"Yeah, right," Carter muttered.

The screech was calming. It relieved some of the tension he felt. "Wow," Carter thought, "he was right."

How humorous he must look to anyone who saw him act like a madman atop the ladder. He chuckled as he replaced the broken lights.

The moment of truth had arrived. One final check confirmed that all attachments had been made and all the lights were snug in their sockets. Carter briskly marched into the garage to test his creation. As the sun had begun to set, he inserted the extension cord into the electrical socket in the garage. A spark darted to the left of his face. He turned to see if the lights were working. They were out of his vision, above the garage, but he could see their faint reflection on the cool pavement, on the bushes along side of the garage door, and on the lawn. A few seconds later, flickering began.

Carter rushed onto the driveway to get a better view. "They're working!" he shouted.

Next he counted the dark spots on the cords where the lights were not lit: "One, two, three . . . six." He replaced four of them and discovered that two of the sockets were defective. This was all right; he was still satisfied with what he had accomplished.

Carter placed a wreath on both sides of the front door and one in the center of the porch-yard gate. Then he began to place items back into the attic and carried the remaining boxes into the living room where he hoped to finish before his parents returned home. Finally, he swept the garage, making sure to rid all traces of dirt and grime left behind by his efforts.

He was in the house arranging all the ornaments within five minutes. He scurried from table, to bureau, to shelf, to desk, placing the decorations where his memory best served. He was done within the next half hour. Six more boxes had been emptied. He carried them back into the garage, climbed the ladder, and placed them neatly in the attic. There was still no trace of his parents.

Carter rushed out onto his driveway, glancing down the street. There were no headlights from either direction. He breathed easier. Up to this point, he had accomplished his goal: no mess, lights up and functioning, boxes neatly put back into place. There were now only four boxes remaining. Three of these would not be opened until the weekend, when Carter and his father would place the tree in the living room, the only task his father would still participate.

The fourth was the box Carter had taken special care of placing next to the front window.

He felt his heart race. Should he open that fourth box, arrange its contents? Carter closed his eyes, remembering the argument Carolyn and his mother had about the box the previous Christmas.

"Why?" Carolyn had asked, "did you not take it down?"

Carter could still see his mother's eyes, studying Carolyn, almost sizing her up, like kids do on the playground before picking a fight.

"Is it Shannon?" Carolyn continued.

"You want it down? You want to put it out on the table, in front of the window, so the whole world can see our family believes in a fairy-tale?"

Carolyn shook her head. "That's not what I believe, Mother. You taught us about our family. Our struggles."

"Enough. Do it if you're going to do it. Leave me out of it."

And that was it. Carolyn actually had successfully stood up to their mother. Carter and she set up the nativity by themselves. Did Carter dare to take on his mother alone, without the aid of Carolyn?

The air was cool and refreshing. It had been two years since Carter felt a tinge of holiday cheer this strong. A chill ran through his spine. The crooked arrangement of the lights caught his attention. He was frustrated, yet amused, at his hapless efforts in filling his father's shoes. Regardless, he had done something he wanted, and had fun doing it.

It was the most optimistic thought Carter had all week. He felt he had accomplished something significant. Such optimism led him to conclude that he should attempt to complete the task awaiting him within the box that remained next to the front-door window. Once again he turned his head both directions to observe traffic near the house—no cars approaching.

He closed the garage door, placed the ladder back against the far wall, ran inside the house, and grabbed a glass of water to quench his parched throat. He threw off his shoes, wiggled his toes, ran down the hallway, and slid to a stop next to the front-door window. Beside him lay the final box. He sat down next to it.

It was wrapped in masking tape that had become infested with dust and lint. He ripped the tape from the cardboard box before he realized that he had no place to throw trash. He hopped to his feet and grabbed the small wastebasket in the hallway bathroom. He wadded up the useless tape and shot it inside. "Two points!"

Carter's right hand rested on one side of the box. His left hand hovered hesitantly above the lid. He lifted it gently, making sure not to disturb the fragile pieces inside, and hoping none had been disturbed by an unwelcome rodent or cockroach, or shaken by a San Andreas aftershock. The pieces on top eased his tension. The tallest shepherd was still smiling contentedly, though it seemed each year his expression was more difficult to distinguish. Next to him was a boy shepherd with a gleam in his eyes that somehow still seemed fresh and unworn; Carter had envied the apparent joy in the boy's face during the last two holiday seasons, its potency contrasted to Carter's own sadness.

One by one, Carter carefully lifted each figure and placed it a safe distance away from his legs—each shepherd, each wise man, each cow and lamb.

Joseph was next and then Mary. Most of the anxiety Carter felt was gone. All the pieces that could have been destroyed, broken, scathed, or snapped were unharmed. In Carter's mind, the final piece, the baby Jesus encased within a golden cradle, could not be harmed. The manger, along with its cast of characters, had remained unscathed another year. He placed each figure alongside the wall next to the front door.

The tissues within which each figurine was wrapped had been scattered across the floor. Carter withdrew each one with such excitement that he had forgotten his mission of cleanliness. There were a few pieces of tissue still in the box. He reached inside, expecting to grab onto something solid. What he discovered sent a shock of nerves through his body. Except for the wrapping tissues, nothing remained. The box was empty.

Carter panicked. He raised himself onto his knees looking all around, making sure he had not already taken out the golden cradle. He shuffled to the line of figures he had placed near the front door, verifying that the gold piece was not there. Carter maneuvered across the floor to the strewn pieces of tissue around him and inspected each. It wasn't there. He returned to the box and reached inside once more—empty! When he turned it upside down, the final tissues floated to the floor.

Sweat beaded on Carter's forehead. His hands trembled. He ran to the three tree-ornament boxes; two minutes later, he had created an unparalleled mess within the living room. Cleanliness no longer a priority, he rushed into the garage, grabbed the ladder, set it up, ascended into the attic, and carried down the eight boxes previously emptied. They contained the decorations Carter felt were ugly enough to keep hidden from the neighborhood. The remaining contents of the boxes soon found their way onto the garage floor.

"Nothing," Carter muttered. "How can this be? I'm dead. Mom's gonna kill me! Oh God, how could this happen? Where is that stinkin' cradle?"

He and Carolyn were the only ones to handle the nativity the previous year. He knew he was the only one who could be blamed. For the next thirty minutes, he searched and researched dining room cabinets, bookshelves, and drawers in every room of the house. He searched each of the eight boxes three more times. Still, he was not able to find it. He fell to the foot of the table that would hold the manger scene. He landed in a cross-legged position, buried his head into is hands and began to scream and yell with all his strength.

He lifted his hands, with them formed fists, and violently hit himself on both sides of the face. Following a brief reprieve, he opened his hands and began slapping his cheeks. Five minutes elapsed before he had drained himself of energy. He walked dejectedly upstairs and fell helplessly on his bed.

Ten minutes passed before he glanced at the digital alarm clock glowing in the darkness. It was seven fifteen. He had an idea.

Carter grabbed his Bible and rushed downstairs to the site of the nativity scene. He cautiously arranged the characters, making sure to do no damage. His design was done in such a way that the position of the baby Jesus was hidden from view. In place of the missing gold cradle, Carter positioned a paper cradle he had colored the previous week with a gold crayon at Sunday school. Following this desperate effort to hide the truth, he refilled the three remaining boxes in the living room.

The first box was completed when he heard the sound of an engine.

"Please let it be Dad, please let it be Dad. Oh God, please," Carter begged.

The car pulled into the driveway and several seconds later Carter heard the ignition shut off. One minute later, he heard the keys rattle, the doorknob turn, and the service door squeak.

At the sound of footsteps, Carter knew it was his mother. She placed her books and purse on the kitchen counter. The refrigerator opened; items were taken out and placed on the cabinet. Carter heard the oven door pulled open and his mother slide something inside. She approached.

Carter resumed his repackaging of the tree ornaments, pretending not to notice her arrival.

"Carter." Her voice was calm. "I thought you'd be done by now. You've been working hard I see."

"Uh-huh," he grunted.

"The lights are pretty. Did you have any problems?"

"Nope."

"There's quite a mess in the garage, Carter."

"Yes, ma'am."

She walked straight past the nativity table, up the stairs, and into her bedroom. Carter breathed a sigh of relief as he continued cleaning the living room floor.

"Carter," his mother shouted from upstairs.

"Yes?"

"I got a call from Principal Gurney today."

Carter stopped his packing. This was news he hadn't heard in months. He could not remember doing anything within the recent past to deserve any type of punishment at school. Mr. Gurney had promised to notify him of any upcoming teacher-parent-type conferences in exchange for Carter's promise to end his campus pranks.

"Any idea what he may want to see me about?" she continued.

Carter had no idea. He had kept his end of the bargain with Gurney. Within the previous three months, not one student had fallen victim to his exploits. None had been deceived, humiliated, ridiculed, or bullied. Principal Gurney had even talked to Carter one day on the playground, congratulating him for his progress. As a result, Carter had come to respect Gurney. He refused to entertain the thought that his principal had broken his end of the deal.

Carter still had not answered his mother's question. He responded the best he could, adding what he considered a bit of humor, hoping it would help lessen the tension. "To congratulate me, maybe?"

There was no response.

He looked up the staircase, hoping her questions had ended. She was standing at the top of the stairs, her hands on her hips.

Carter got the message. "I don't know, Mom. Really, I've been good. For three whole months!" Carter stopped abruptly. The bargain with Gurney had been a secret.

She peered at her son suspiciously. "It may be something about PTA. I hope for all our sakes that's all it is."

Carter waited. Hoping the inquisition was over.

"Go clean the garage before your father gets home. Dinner will be ready in ten minutes."

"Yes, ma'am." Carter cleared his throat and corrected himself, "I mean, Mom." As he raced through the kitchen into to the garage, Carter let out a sigh.

The aroma of a store-roasted chicken greeted Carter as he reentered the kitchen. His mother was preparing a salad. "Carter," she said, "set the table. Looks like we'll be eating without your father again."

Carter washed his hands in the bathroom sink and then began arranging the plates, glasses, napkins, forks, and knives around the supper table. His mother went outside to get the evening paper. She shut the front door.

"The wreaths are looking a bit ragged," she said aloud. "You think we need new ones?"

Carter didn't answer. His only thought was that if she was examining the wreaths, maybe the crèche would be next. He could not see her from his position in the kitchen, but the silence led him to suspect what she was doing. He could feel the pulsating in his chest intensify. Again, he held his breath. Silence. Thirty seconds of it filtered through the house.

He stuck his head out from the kitchen doorway. There she was, standing in front of the manger scene, her back toward him. She was motionless. Extending her left hand into the deep left-hand corner of the nativity, she extracted the paper baby Jesus in the manger that Carter had placed there minutes earlier.

She spoke calmly, "Carter. Come here, please."

Carter stepped from the kitchen, his head lowered but tilted at an angle to catch any hints of how intense his mother's rage might be.

"What is this?" she asked.

"The baby Jesus in a manger," he answered.

"The paper, Carter." Her tone grew stern. "Is this a joke? Are you planning to wrap it as a gift and give it to one of us as a surprise?"

"No, ma'am."

"Let me assure you, Carter Mason, this would not be wise."

"No, ma'am. It's no joke." Carter cringed. He had no refuge but honesty. Still, just as Mr. Gurney's beckoning of his mother was a mystery, so was the missing status of the golden cradle. Neither, as far as he could perceive, was his fault.

"Have you hidden it?"

Carter shook his head.

"Did you give it to somebody?"

Again he shook his head.

"Carter Anthony Mason, look at me!" Her voice had gradually ascended to the threshold of shouting. "Where is it?"

Trembling with timidity, he responded: "I don't know."

"You don't know? Damn you, Carter! This set is over five hundred years old; the gold is worth over one thousand dollars. It's been in our family for over three hundred years. It's irreplaceable."

"Maybe if you and Dad weren't so busy pretending everything was alright around here, maybe if you had helped me decorate last year, it wouldn't be lost."

As soon as he spoke the words, he knew he was in trouble. He wish he could have grabbed them before they reached his mother's ears and put them in his pocket, written them down, and get them out of his system someway other than how he just did.

"This is our fault?"

Carter could not decipher the tone in her voice. Perhaps his words were not too rash after all. Did he dare say more?

"You've made this house into a place neither I nor your father wants to return at night."

A baseball approaching the plate at over one hundred miles per hour, thrown by none other than Nolan Ryan, and striking Carter in the nose could not have hit Carter with as much veracity as his mother's assertion.

"The pranks. The mess. The lies."

Carter interrupted. "I guess the next thing you're going to say is that Shannon's death was my fault. I encouraged her to read all that stuff. If only I had sided with you three instead of going to church with Dad. None of this would have happened."

It was too late. Carter's words were flowing without any effort. He felt an intensity, an uncontrollable urge, to say something to bring his mother to her knees. This was going to be a heavyweight fight, Ali versus Frasier.

"You're the ones who were holding her back. You couldn't see how beautiful she was becoming. All you saw was she wasn't following in your footsteps."

He looked up to see how his mother was taking this, but before he could interpret her expression, her left hand struck Carter's right cheek. A thunderous slap echoed through the hallway.

"Damn you! Your games have come to this. Our most precious memory of your sister."

"I'll pay it back. I'll buy a new one," he whimpered.

"You have gone overboard this time, Carter Anthony."

"I'm sorry, Mom. Really, it isn't my fault. It just wasn't there. Please, believe me!"

"Believe you, Carter. How can I believe you? How can any of us believe you? Your cute gags that fool your friends, that fool your teachers, that fool us sometimes. How can you believe yourself, Carter?"

Carter was outmatched. Tears fell from the corner of his eyes. He tasted saltiness on the right side of his mouth and began to notice blood drop onto the white-tiled hall floor. Touching the right side of his face, he verified that it was the source of blood. His mother's wedding band had cut his cheek as her hand had swept across his face.

She continued. "Get to your room. No dinner! No homework! No television! Now!"

Before Carter turned to go to his room, he said one last time, "It's not my fault. Really. It just wasn't there."

He began making his way upstairs when his mother beckoned, "Oh, Carter."

Some semblance of hope emerged. For a fraction of a second the memory of her loving, forgiving smile raced across his mind. She waited until Carter's tears ceased to flow, and he wiped them to get a clearer view of her. With malice and vengeance in her eyes, she held up Carter's paper baby Jesus and ripped it in halves and then quarters and then eighths. Carter ran upstairs into his room, shut the door quietly, and tried to cry himself to sleep.

A truck arrived at eight thirty. Carter went to the stairwell and watched his mother open the door. He recognized the driver of the truck as an employee from the Christmas specialty store at the mall. He held a clipboard that his mother refused to sign. "Take them back," she ordered. "We changed our minds."

The gold manger was missing. The mechanical figures would not be part of this year's Christmas display. What was next?

He lay awake until ten o'clock. His crying would last for ten minutes; then there would be a brief reprieve of five to ten minutes; then the crying would resume.

"None of this would have happened had God not allowed her to die," Carter whispered vehemently. "It's all His fault!"

"God, please, if you are there . . . help! Please."

Her Father's World

Katherine Mason stared silently at the spot her son had stood. She didn't see it coming, didn't realize she had the potential to do something like this.

When she saw the mark on his face and the blood trickle from the corner of his mouth, her first impulse was to fall to her knees, beg his forgiveness, and embrace him. It took all of her determination to resist.

She had to show him how disappointed she was with what he had done. If she showed any signs of regret, it would cheapen the lesson he needed to learn.

Carter had stood in front of her weeping, begging for mercy, but the emerging turmoil she felt blocked out his petitions. Her heart told her to hold her only son and try to make things right. Maybe the whole incident could serve as a catalyst to get the family to resolve the conflicts that had arisen following Shannon's death. But her mind was instructing her not to give in.

Rather than hug Carter and endure an agonizing session of confession and forgiveness, she ripped the paper manger Carter had made, and ripped it again and again, until it was a handful of tiny pieces of paper. With each rip she convinced herself that what she was doing was right. And once Carter fled upstairs, she was certain.

She wanted to be alone. She had never reacted this way with any of her children and needed time to contemplate what she had done.

"Damn you, Katherine," she muttered, "don't be weak."

The delivery man from the Christmas specialty store arrived to deliver mechanical figures that Carter had purchased; how could he have afforded them? Would he have dared sell the golden manger?

After refusing to accept the delivery, she determined to do something she had not done in years, not since she had married in the late fifties. She walked to the kitchen, turned off the oven, and picked up the keys from the counter. She got in the car and drove toward Los Angeles.

It was still early, early enough to miss the cast of characters she wanted to avoid. Most of the liquor establishments she passed were dingy. She hoped to spot one to her liking quickly, so that she could get on with the business to be done.

During her second year in college, she had first discovered how freeing it was to visit a bar, sit alone at a corner booth, and order a beer. Although most of the patrons seemed to be there to escape an unpleasant reality, celebrate a special occasion, or find some companionship at the end of a long day, Katherine had a different agenda.

Her first experience was at a small pub in Cambridge, blocks from her Radcliffe dormitory. The day had been a typical nightmare. In her literature class she had composed several essays she felt were outstanding, but the best grade she earned was a C+. She had in the past edited some of the male students' essays from Harvard who had the same professor as she, and felt they were far inferior in quality to hers. Yet they always received higher marks.

It was the day her professor returned her essay on Nora Helmer, from Ibsen's *A Doll's House*, that drove her to visit the pub in Cambridge. She received her usual average grade, but included were these comments:

> *Miss Thurman,*
>
> *You appear to have a high regard for Nora and women like her who have taken their chance in a world they know little about. You scoff at the original editors and praise Ibsen for his daring ending. I too agree with you that the editors showed little integrity in not allowing an artist to have freedom in what he*

wishes to portray. However, it would be wise for you to consider that Ibsen's original work, ending with Nora's departure, ends with just that. It tells us nothing of the trials and tribulations a woman such as herself would have had to endure once she left her home.

If there's anything to learn from A Doll's House, *it is that women ought not allow their emotions to determine the choices they make.*

Katherine's initial impulse was to march into his office and preach the sainthood of Ibsen and how his words had helped her survive a tumultuous adolescence. But doing so with her emotions out of control would only prove her professor's point. Instead, she took the last page of her essay to the pub and held it above a candle on the table.

As the lower corner of the page was embraced by the wick's flame, she envisioned the embers of her professor's words disappearing forever.

Her hand twitched, jerking the paper away, the flame making rapid progress on the paper. She threw the paper on the table and extinguished the small blaze.

A thin line of smoke rose from the table as Katherine examined her professor's comments. They remained intact. She picked up the paper and waved it gently, making sure no sparks remained. Then she folded it into quarters and put it into her skirt pocket.

"Is everything all right, Miss," the waitress asked.

Katherine looked at the waitress, feeling a mixture of excitement and remorse for the words she would soon speak. "I'll have a beer."

"Yes, ma'am. You expecting anyone else?"

"No."

Once the waitress returned with the beer and placed it on the table, Katherine placed her hands between the cushions of the booth and her legs. She stared at the mug, frosted, dew dripping from the handle, and wondered if she had what it took. She looked out the window, at her classmates socializing with the Harvard students. Prior to that evening, she had not tasted alcohol, primarily because her mother regularly preached of its dangers and how it was responsible for making her father into the man he had become. She'd read about studies suggesting that alcoholism was genetic. Such a theory seemed reasonable to Katherine, and she had often wondered whether she would be attracted to it after only one taste. She never dared to find out until that night.

She came to the pub with one purpose: to show her professor, and all the narrow-minded male professors on the Radcliffe and Harvard campuses, that she did have control of her emotions. If those studies were correct and she could stop at only one serving, she reasoned that her willpower and self-control were greater than any of the male collegians across the way at Harvard who regularly got drunk.

She eyed the mug respectfully; the thick amber had almost an entrancing quality. Removing her hands from underneath her legs, she extended her arms and wrapped her fingers around the cold exterior of the mug. There was a whiff, an aroma, almost magical, that was caught by Katherine as she raised the lip of the mug to her mouth. It was a fragrance she often would return to during stressful studies, closing her eyes, recalling that first angling of alcoholic liquid to her mouth.

As it entered and moved through her body, she knew its enticement: the refreshing cool of holding the beer on an Indian summer evening; the bitter, yet pleasing, trace it left on her tongue; the burning as it rushed down her throat and spread through her body; the contentment as it settled in her stomach. She closed her eyes and savored the experience. Now she understood her father's addiction. Since her childhood, it was the first time she had anything but a negative thought toward him.

After ten swallows, the glass was empty. Katherine knew those studies were correct. To have another glass was her only desire. But this is why she came: to prove to all men everywhere that, despite her desire, she was in control. She wiped her mouth with a napkin, left money on the table, walked back to her dormitory, and had the best sleep she could remember.

She made subsequent visits to pubs throughout her college years, all with equal success. Whether it was a condescending professor, an insensitive boyfriend, or a memory of the past, Katherine entered with the determination to drink only one beer. With each visit, her desire for alcohol grew, but as her desire grew, so did her determination to prove her strength. She always stopped at one. Often, she remained in the bar after finishing her drink so that she could observe in triumphant disdain the male students, and at times professors, display their weakness.

As Katherine settled into her booth at Rusty's Pub on Sepulveda Avenue in Santa Monica; memories of that first night raced through her mind. Her motives were so clear back then. But now, why was she here? Why had she come?

Following Shannon's death, she often thought of taking up the old habit but felt that, in doing so, she would only be attempting to escape reality, the very thing for which she once condemned others.

After ordering her drink and paying the waitress, she maneuvered the mug toward the center of the table, cradling it. The moisture on the outside refreshed her aging hands, the hands that had hit Carter.

This is what had brought her here. She had promised herself that she would not touch her children the way her father had touched her that Christmas Eve thirty years earlier. Over and over again, the scene of her hand striking Carter's face played in her memory. Before she knew it, the mug was empty. She kept it nestled between her hands, wishing that she had not consumed the contents so quickly. She was out of practice and felt unprepared to face the temptation that now gripped her. Her college years had created incidents in which she needed to prove her emotional maturity and determination, but what was she trying to prove by coming on this night, so many years after her days at Radcliffe?

Again she shut her eyes, gripping the mug tightly and grinding her teeth. "Why are you here, Katherine?" she asked. "What are you trying to prove?"

"Miss," she beckoned the waitress. "Oh, miss."

Her waitress held up her hand. "I'll be right there."

Katherine began tapping her feet. They were moving rapidly, twitching. Her excitement grew. She'd cross the line. No stopping now. The waitress would be there any second, and Katherine would order the first "second" of her life.

"Yes, ma'am?" The waitress stood beside her.

Katherine looked up. She saw her father standing in the corner of the bar, some ten feet behind the waitress. She could swear it was him. She shut her eyes and then reopened them. He was gone.

"What can I get you?" the waitress asked.

Katherine looked down at the mug. She looked back toward the corner where she thought she had seen her father standing seconds earlier. She shook her head.

It was her father. She had to prove she wasn't him. That's why she was here. That's what she needed to prove.

"Are you all right, miss?" the waitress asked.

A surge erupted from Katherine's stomach. Immediately, she stood up, perspiration dripping from her face and arms. Seconds later she sighed and gulped for air before discharging the contents in her stomach. She collapsed onto the booth and rested her head on the table beside the empty mug.

"Are you all right, ma'am?" the waitress asked.

Katherine looked up; breathed deeply, gaining composure; and stood up. "I'll be fine," she ensured. "Where's the restroom?"

Upon her return, Katherine apologized for the mess but inwardly was grateful. Seeing what she had created, and the unpleasant aroma it produced, any desire to have another beer was gone. She left the bar, once more victorious, proving to the world, and herself, that she was not her father.

My Pal

She was five feet seven, slim, dark skinned, and beautiful. Her voice commanded the attention of all with whom she came in contact. And as she spoke, each male student was spellbound and captivated by her splendor. They adored, they listened, and they learned.

"Ancient Egypt is considered one of the greatest and most accomplished civilizations in history. The ancient Egyptians were one of the first to develop an alphabet. They were a people of great intellect who excelled in fields such as art, architecture, mathematics, politics, agriculture, and military maneuvers. Now, before I lose any of you, let me explain what some of these words mean."

Miss Carson paused midway through her introduction to respond to one of her sixth-grade students raising his hand. "Yes, Philip," Miss Carson invited, "you have a question?"

"Where's Egypt?" he asked.

Another student in the far-right corner of the classroom snickered. Miss Carson angled her body toward him. "Charles, Please."

"Yes, Miss Carson," he said, covering his growing grin and trying to muffle his laughter.

She stopped, her hands on her hips. "Charles, please tell us what you find so amusing."

"Well, shoot, Miss Carson, everyone knows where Egypt is!"

"Really?"

"Yes, ma'am." Chuck De Santo added.

"Then maybe I should ask one of you to come show the rest of the class where it is located on the map."

"Sure, Miss Carson." Chuck raised himself from his desk. "Which map do you want me to use?"

"Sit down, Charles," she ordered.

Chuck sat down and shrugged his shoulders, resuming his slouched position.

"Hector," Miss Carson called out, "help us out here." She pulled down a map of the entire world.

"Me?" Hector Romero responded in a high-pitched voice.

Miss Carson walked toward an empty desk against the wall and sat on top of it.

Hector was still seated.

"Hector," she said, "show us where Egypt is on the map."

Hector stood at his desk, looked at Miss Carson, and then shuffled to the front of the class.

Carter was seated on the first seat in the far-left row of the classroom. He lowered his head in anticipation of Hector's pending embarrassment. He glared across the room at Chuck who appeared to be in as much shock as he. Miss Carson was shrewd, but this was beyond her limits. She was using Chuck and Hector's friendship, as well as Hector's general lack of geographic knowledge, to teach Chuck appropriate classroom manners.

She was shrewd all right, but Carter and his three friends respected her more than any other teacher they had ever had. They were fortunate to be in the same class together. It was the first year they had this opportunity, and as a result, they found it difficult to complain about their teacher's tactics. If one of them had the courage to do so, he might find himself in a new classroom the next morning.

Carter figured Miss Carson was not fooled by the likes of Chuck and him. She had already split the two of them as far apart as possible, assigning the rear-right-corner desk to Chuck and the front-left corner to him. Hector sat in the dead center of the classroom, and Allen, the most conscientious among the four, was considered to have the best seat of all: center seat, front row. For as much as they loathed Miss Carson's disciplinary tactics and her harsh homework assignments, Miss Carson was by far the most beautiful teacher any of them had seen, much less had the privilege of being taught by.

As Hector reached for the map, Carter momentarily forgot about his friend's predicament and admired his teacher's slender lips; cherry-pitted dimples; hazel-green eyes; dark skin; and short, brown hair. Her eyes seemed to radiate light; her smile was matchless; her face pure. *How could she be such a witch?* Carter thought. *She knows Hector can't locate Egypt!*

An otherwise excellent student, geography was one subject that escaped Hector Romero. He had exceptional artistic ability and always scored the highest grade on math and science tests. There was just something about geography that bored him. Hector stood motionless at the front of the class, his shoulders slouched, his head lowered. He raised his eyes toward the world map and then looked back down at his feet.

"Hector," Miss Carson started, "you cannot locate Egypt if you are looking at the floor."

"Maybe Columbus was wrong, Miss Carson," Allen Stanowitz announced loudly. "Egypt could have fallen off the end of the earth and onto the floor."

Carter, Chuck, and Allen were the only students to laugh at the remark.

Miss Carson shot a surprised look toward Allen, "That's enough boys. Now Hector, lift your head. Do you know what continent it is on?"

Hector looked to his right at Miss Carson, her legs dangling over the edge of the desk on which she was perched. A perfect picture, Carter thought, of the paradox of their teacher. She was so appealing, so innocent, almost like one of their female classmates up on that desk, but there was something sinister behind the facade.

This was pure torture. Carter blamed Chuck for it all. If he had only kept his mouth shut, Hector would not be up there. Chuck always found a way to put everyone but himself in uncomfortable situations. Allen had tried to salvage Hector's dignity; now Carter felt he should try something to assist his friend.

Miss Carson often surprised Carter. She ran her classroom with a strong hand but would ease her students' tension by showing signs of compassion. She proved this to Chuck and Carter by giving them the opportunity to change their behavior before recommending that one of them be put into another class earlier in the year. She demonstrated more of this compassion when she came down from the desk and pulled down a second map, replacing the world map Hector was studying with a map displaying only Africa, the Middle East, and southern Europe. "Now Hector, can you show us where—"

Just then a voice came over the intercom. "Miss Carson."

"Yes?" she replied.

"Can you please send Carter Mason to Principal Gurney's office?"

Before any of her students had a chance to tease Carter, Miss Carson answered: "Yes. He'll be right there." She motioned with her hand for Carter to leave.

Carter looked to his left, through the windows lining the left side of the classroom. In the distance, he could see the administrative office. He hadn't been there in almost three months. He stood up and walked to the rear of the class. Opening the door and shuffling through the corridor, he kept his eyes fixed on Hector and the map of Africa, hoping to see him make the right choice. Just before he made his turn toward the main office, he looked through the window at Chuck who slapped his forehead with his right hand. Carter jerked his head back toward the front of the class—Hector was pointing at South Africa.

The morning's activities within Miss Carson's classroom served as a reprieve from the torment of the previous evening. Carter replayed the events over and over in his mind. His mother must have been correct in her assumption: he must have intentionally misplaced the golden manger while he was putting away the decorations the previous year. He just forgot where he hid it.

But where? he kept asking himself.

And then there was the slap. His mother had never disciplined him or his sisters with a physical blow. It was always their father who wielded the belt. But this was no mere act of discipline on his mother's part; she had something else in mind. He raised his hand and gingerly touched the welt left by his mother's wedding band.

When he arrived at school in the morning, his friends asked about the mark on his face. He had prepared a response, anticipating questions regarding the torn skin and reddish-blue streak. "I was putting up the Christmas lights," he explained, "and replacing the ones that didn't work after I had attached them to the house. One broke as I was screwing it into the socket and the glass fell on my face. When I reached with my hand to take it off, I made it worse by digging it into my skin." When he spoke it, it sounded reasonable and his friends appeared to accept the validity of the story. If anyone else asked about it, especially the grown-ups at the school, he'd say the same.

Until Hector's humiliation at the front of the class, it was all Carter could think about. Then Mrs. Jenkins, the school secretary, beckoned him over the office intercom. Until that moment, Carter had forgotten about his mother's call from Principal Gurney. As he turned left toward the school office, Carter considered Mr. Gurney's request to see his mother. Abruptly, he turned and headed toward the school parking lot to see if his mother's car was there. It wasn't.

He was closer now to the front entrance of the school office, so he entered through its doors.

"Carter!" Mrs. Jenkins greeted as he entered. "It's been some time. How have you been?"

"Hello, Mrs. Jenkins. I've been all right."

She smiled.

"We've missed you. You should stop by more often. You know you can do that, Carter?"

"Yes, ma'am," he replied with his head lowered. Carter felt that Mrs. Jenkins was the sweetest lady he knew next to Nana Thurman. During the past two years he visited Principal Gurney's office an average of two times per month. Somehow she managed to comfort his nerves each time he sat in the chair across from Gurney's office door. Her gray hair was testament to her years and wisdom. She calmed his fears by talking about baseball or cartoons or anything except what had led him to be sitting in the chair. He was surprised at her keen awareness and accuracy on such matters and figured she must have grandchildren about his age.

She continued, "Carter, have you met our new secretary, Miss Fairchild?"

Carter glanced across the office at this much younger administrative assistant as she turned to glare at him. In her eyes were traces of the fury Carter had created during the early days of the school year.

"Yes, ma'am, I have." Carter waved to Miss Fairchild and quietly said hello.

"Oh, how silly of me," said Mrs. Jenkins. Although she was well over sixty years old, Carter figured her lapse of memory was more a result of her good will and forgiveness than it was of her age. In any case, Mrs. Jenkins seemed to have forgotten, until that moment, what Miss Fairchild certainly had not.

It was the first week of school. Carter and Chuck had spotted the new secretary and decided she would be the perfect prey for their scheme. The two friends rushed home after school on the Thursday of the first week of classes to fetch their skateboards, a shoebox, a roll of masking tape, and a blown up Bozo the Clown punching bag. They hurried back to the school's front parking lot and made sure Miss Fairchild's yellow VW Bug was still there. It was. Five minutes later, just as they had planned, the new assistant secretary left the school office, got in her car, and started the ignition. Carter and Chuck waited anxiously behind a chain-linked fence to the right of the parking lot's exit.

"Are you done yet?" Chuck asked, his eyes wide with delight, his left foot rapidly tapping the ground.

Carter was out of breath, blowing as hard as he could into Bozo's torso. Bozo was almost completely filled.

"Here Chuck," Carter said as he handed the bottom portion of Bozo to him, "the bottom's full already. Put him in the box. Hurry man, she's already in the car!"

"Okay, okay." Chuck grabbed Bozo, placed him in the shoebox, placed the box on top of the skateboard, and wrapped tape around the box, securing it to the skateboard. Next he placed some old rags and T-shirts in the box to secure Bozo's balance.

"There," he announced, "finished!"

Carter took one last deep breath, plugged the breath hole on Bozo's back, and placed his baseball cap atop Bozo's head. Just then Miss Fairchild pulled out of her parking spot and made her way toward the exit. Carter and Chuck inched closer to the curb, hiding behind a large elm tree several yards from the exit. As soon as she pulled onto the driveway, looked to her left, to her right, and to her left once more, Chuck pushed "Bozo on a skateboard" straight into the middle of the street.

It was a perfect push. Bozo was moving at just the right speed to meet Miss Fairchild's path. She had already reached over ten miles per hour before hitting the skateboard and slamming on her brakes. Bozo flew though the air. The shock on Miss Fairchild's face left Chuck and Carter rolling with laughter on the school's front lawn. Bozo was airborne for at least three seconds before being bounced upward again by his impact with the asphalt. The two boys continued their laughter as Miss Fairchild sat motionless in her car. The noise from the brakes and the crash of the skateboard against the VW's front bumper brought a group of teachers and Principal Gurney rushing toward the site of the "accident."

Chuck continued to laugh hysterically before the witnesses arrived, but Carter's amusement gradually subsided as he observed the effect the incident had on Miss Fairchild. She was shaking violently and had a look of horror. It took Carter back to the night of Shannon's accident, reminding him of his parents' expressions. He slowly drew back from the curb.

By the time Principal Gurney and the other teachers arrived, Chuck had rushed home. All questions were to be answered by Carter alone.

Three months later, Carter's shame remained and he could tell that the new secretary was still shaken by the episode. He sat in silence and attempted to apologize to Miss Fairchild through a sympathetic grin.

Mrs. Jenkins broke the silence. "He'll be with you in a minute, Carter. In the meantime, what did you think of the World Series? The Dodgers came up a little short. It seems they can never defeat those Yankees."

Carter shifted his attention to Mrs. Jenkins, glancing back every few seconds at Miss Fairchild. "Yeah. My dad says they've only beat them twice."

"What about Philadelphia? The last two years they couldn't make it past the League Championship Series. They have a pretty good team though."

"They always choke. They always will," Carter said. "Carlton's pitching and Bowa's fielding are the only two consistent things on the team. Sure they can win a hundred-plus games, but they can't win the big one."

Mrs. Jenkins didn't seem to know specific stats, so Carter felt his analysis of the Phillies might end the dialogue and give him enough time to ask the question weighing on his mind. "Mrs. Jenkins," he asked, "did he say what he wants? I mean, did I do anything wrong?"

"You mean, you don't know?"

Carter shook his head.

"Why, Carter! He's arranged a meeting with you, your mother, and Miss Carson."

"Miss Carson?" Carter mumbled. He began to replay the last week in his mind. He could remember doing nothing of any consequence during the last week or the last month, nothing since the Bozo incident with Miss Fairchild. Principal Gurney had called him into his office the morning after the accident and warned Carter that if anything like that occurred again, he would be transferred to Ridgemont Elementary, the district alternative school for disruptive students. Carter knew he had to change. Attending Ridgemont would be worse than Miss Carson's threat of removing him from her class.

Still, he was in the dark. He began studying Principal Hal Gurney's office door, dreading the moment it would open. The nameplate read Principal Gurney and not Mr. Gurney, a fact that enabled Carter to differentiate between the homonyms *principle* and *principal.* He figured it would be easy to remember the slogan "Hal's my Pal" as a way of remembering the correct spelling. Carter smiled at his genius and original rhyme. Then the door opened. Hal Gurney appeared.

"Carter. Glad to see you. Come right in."

Carter rose from his chair and entered the office. Before returning to his desk, Gurney gave some instructions to Mrs. Jenkins regarding Carter's mother. Carter tried to eavesdrop but could not make out the details.

"Yes, sir," Mrs. Jenkins replied.

Gurney reentered his office and shut the door. "Have a seat, Carter. Make yourself comfortable."

Carter obeyed, choosing the only cushioned chair in the office.

"How have you been, Carter?"

"All right, sir."

"You seem a bit edgy. Is anything wrong?"

"No, no. Nothing is wrong," Carter said defensively. "I mean. Well, shoot. Yes. I do feel a little strange."

"Tell me about it," Gurney invited.

Carter looked at him suspiciously. His tone of voice resembled sessions with Dr. Hayvenhurst. Carter continued, "This whole meeting. I mean, this is the first time I've come to your office without any idea why I'm here."

"Let me put you at ease, Carter. You haven't done anything that has broken our bargain. Nothing, of course, that I am aware of." He stated this as half question and half fact. "Is there anything of which I should be aware?"

Carter shook his head.

Gurney continued with a grin, "No stopping the classroom sinks with butcher paper?" He paused to give Carter an opportunity to respond.

Carter shook his head.

"No splashing mustard and ketchup on the bathroom walls?" Carter shook once more.

"Cutting girls' hair with scissors? Pasting paper ribbons on a classmate's dress? Grinding white crayon into another student's milk?"

Carter was growing irritated. Gurney was recalling each prank Carter had orchestrated as though he admired his creativity.

"And the sulfur tablets in the water faucets or clowning around on skateboards?"

Carter had heard enough. Gurney was having too much fun. "No, Mr. Gurney. You know I've stopped all that stuff!"

"I heard you dressed up as Mrs. Bates for Halloween. That must have been a sight."

Carter placed his hand under his legs, eying his principal with some anger.

"You still enjoy all that?" Gurney asked.

Carter narrowed his eyes. "Sure."

"I'm telling you, Carter, that stuff's not healthy. Too much of anything is not healthy."

Carter grimaced.

"Something wrong, Carter?"

"It's all the advice, sir. You're beginning to sound like my shrink."

Gurney looked disappointed. Carter wondered whether he should have just kept quiet. Maybe Gurney was just trying to be sympathetic and ease the tension. The last thing he needed was to make Gurney his enemy. Carter felt his hands moisten, beads of sweat dripping underneath his shirt.

"Well, Carter," Gurney continued, "let me tell you why you're here. Seeing that you've kept your end of the bargain, I am all the more glad to have called you in here early."

Early? Carter thought to himself. *Earlier than what?*

"You've done well, Carter. And I want to thank you as well as say how proud I am of you. Your classroom behavior, as well as your behavior on the playground, has improved immeasurably." He paused.

This made no sense at all. *Then why am I here?* Carter wondered.

Gurney continued. "That is exactly why I am in a bind. You've kept your end of the deal; I want to keep my end as much as possible. Your mother is due to arrive any minute. You deserve to know the circumstances which brought this about."

Again he paused, allowing Carter time to digest the news. Carter's stomach turned. He was beginning to feel guilty for something he was not even aware he had done.

Gurney continued. "Miss Carson is concerned. It has nothing to do with your behavior. Like I said, your improvement has not gone unnoticed. She is concerned about you."

Carter, flustered, confounded, and perplexed, shook his head in disbelief.

"It has to do with the writing project Miss Carson assigned."

"Sir?" he asked, "I got it back yesterday."

"Well, Carter. That's why she's concerned."

"Concerned?" Carter blurted. "'Bout what? My C+? Does she want to change my grade?"

"I haven't read it myself, but Miss Carson did read me a portion. I'm a bit shocked over your negative feelings, Carter. I'm uncertain about the inspiration behind your project. At first I thought it was your pranks being portrayed more creatively through writing."

Carter interrupted. "But now you realize what a real lost case I am. Why is honesty so abhorrent to everyone?"

Carter could tell Gurney was taken aback by Carter's blunt response. It was a look he often saw on the face of Dr. Hayvenhurst. It was a look he enjoyed creating on the face of any adult with whom he spoke. Carter sat, his arms crossed, waiting for Gurney to continue.

Gurney cleared his throat and drank some coffee. "I'm not saying that you're wrong, or weird, or anything like that, Carter. If indeed this is how you feel about the holidays, then I want you to be assured that you are not alone. Many of us have a dark memory from the past. Unfortunately, you experienced yours at a young age."

The phone rang. Gurney picked up the receiver, "Yes, please, I'll be right there. Have her take a seat."

He replaced the receiver and continued, "Try to enjoy something this season, Carter. A football game. A meal. One of the presents you get. That may help."

Gurney leaned back in his chair. "Your mother's here. Should I let her in?"

Gurney remained seated, waiting.

Carter wondered what would happen if he did not give his principal approval to open. He waited several seconds before nodding.

Gurney rose from his chair and placed his hand upon Carter's shoulder. Softly he said, "If at any time you want the floor, just signal me. I'll silence the others."

Gurney opened the door. "Mrs. Mason, it's good to see you. Please, come in."

Carter's mother entered as she shook the principal's hand.

"Tell Miss Carson to knock before she comes in," Gurney instructed Mrs. Jenkins.

"Please, have a seat." He offered the seat next to Carter.

Carter studied the arrangement of chairs in front of Gurney's desk. He was glad he had not chosen to sit in the center. Soon Miss Carson would be joining them. He shivered at the thought. It would be bad enough; no need to be sandwiched.

"I was just telling Carter how much we miss seeing him in the office. His behavior has improved greatly."

"Until now, apparently," she said. "What has he done this time?"

"To be honest, Mrs. Mason, your guess is as good as mine."

"I don't understand," his mother said. "I received a call."

"Let me explain," interrupted Gurney.

"Yes, please do."

"Miss Carson requested the meeting."

With his mouth open wide, Carter looked at Gurney. Why was he not telling his mother the details he had just told him? What's more, he remained undaunted by her antagonism. His admiration for Gurney grew.

"Did she bother telling you what she wanted to talk to me about," Carter's mother inquired, "before dragging me here?"

"I'd like her to explain it herself. I had Mrs. Jenkins set up the appointment."

"I'm sorry," she said, "I still don't understand. Is this normal procedure?" She looked around the room, emphasizing each word, before continuing, "Arranging a parent-teacher-principal-student conference without letting the principal know the rationale for such a meeting? That does not seem appropriate."

"Under normal circumstances I would agree with you, Mrs. Mason."

"Normal circumstances?" Katherine repeated with irritation.

"Yes. Miss Carson insisted that it was urgent, being the holidays are around the corner."

"The holidays!" Carter's mother exclaimed. "What do the holidays have to do with my son?"

"Miss Carson will be here any minute," Gurney said, "I'd rather she be the one to—"

"It's about my Christmas project, Mom" Carter muttered.

"Carter," she ordered, "be quiet."

Carter looked to Gurney for defense, but he only returned a sympathetic smile.

"Now," his mother continued, "isn't Miss Carson a first-year teacher?"

"Yes."

"And you set up this meeting based upon her recommendation? An unproved, untried rookie?"

"I trust she is competent," Gurney responded.

"Competent? Based upon what evidence? How could you know? Do you spend time in the classroom? Do you look at the papers she grades?"

"I interviewed Miss Carson. I interviewed over half of the teachers presently employed at this school. We have received state and federal recognition for our students' progress and faculty involvement. I would not have hired Miss Carson if I believed her to be anything but competent. Yes, I spend time in the classroom, and no, I do not look at the papers which she or any of my other teachers grade. That is their job, not mine."

For the first time since she walked through the door, Carter felt his mother had lost control of the meeting. He felt more at ease. The office was silent. Carter smiled cautiously.

The lunch bell rang, issuing forth a burst of energy onto the campus. The roar of voices and shuffling feet resounded in the hallways as Carter's classmates rushed to the playground. "It's lunch recess," Gurney announced, "Miss Carson should be here shortly."

The three sat silently until Gurney asked, "So, is the family doing anything special for Christmas?"

Carter could tell that his mother was still trying to deal with Gurney's polite rebuke seconds earlier. Although he was sure Gurney's question was addressed to his mother, he took advantage of his mother's stupor.

"I don't think so. We haven't gone anywhere for a couple years."

"Nowhere," his mother confirmed. "Too busy."

"You must be busy. We haven't seen you at any meetings lately. We miss your input at PTA."

She changed the position of her legs and raised herself in her seat. "Yes. Things at home," she said softly.

Gurney reached across his desk, grabbed a pen, and wrote something on the legal-sized notepad near his phone. "Carter has been exceptional, Mrs. Mason." He raised the notepad; on it was written a large 3.

Gurney continued. "For three months, I have received no complaints about Carter."

Carter could tell his mother was genuinely surprised. Her head cocked back, her eyes widened, and she made a strange muffled laughing sound.

Gurney's eyes shifted to Carter. He seemed sympathetic. His mother's laugh, albeit low in volume, spoke loudly to Carter, and apparently Gurney also, of his mother's disbelief that her son could accomplish three months of good behavior. Such a display of low esteem was humiliating, and Carter felt he had ammunition to fight back.

"Mr. Gurney," Carter announced loudly, "I forgot to tell you." Carter began scratching the cut on his right cheek.

"What is it, Carter?" Gurney asked.

"Last night my mother hit me . . ." Carter paused long enough to get the desired effect. "With some really great news! She just finished finals last night and will be getting better grades than I will this semester! Isn't that wonderful!"

"Yes. Yes it is," Gurney responded.

Carter felt his mother's eyes staring at the side of his face.

"Congratulations, Mrs. Mason! I wasn't aware that you returned to school. What are—" Gurney was interrupted by Miss Carson's knock.

He got up from his seat and invited her to sit down next to Carter's mother.

"Thank you," Miss Carson replied. "Mrs. Mason," she said before sitting down, "it's nice to see you again." Then she turned to Carter as he became lost in her deep hazel-brown eyes.

He swallowed nervously, "Hello."

"Miss Carson," Gurney said, "I was explaining to Carter and his mother that I am not aware of any misbehavior on Carter's part since the incident with Miss Fairchild. I did inform her of the urgency with which you felt a meeting was necessary, and that I thought it was better if you explained the situation since you see Carter on a daily basis."

"Thank you." Miss Carson shifted her weight toward Carter's mother. She seemed intent. Carter imagined her rehearsing the night before, fearful of this confrontation. He felt sorry for his teacher, but in a morbid way, looked forward to any confrontation that may occur between these two women he feared and admired.

His mother's eyes were rigid as Miss Carson began to speak. "I'm sure you're aware of the Christmas project Carter has been working on."

"Yes, and I'm sure that none of his sentences ended with dangling prepositions."

Carter looked to the floor. Already, his mother was digressing. He shook his head, covering his eyes with his right hand.

Miss Carson continued, "Yes. There were no dangling prepositions, there were no run-on sentences, no fragments, very few grammatical errors; as a matter of fact, it was a very well-written paper."

"Great!" his mother announced.

"Did you read the paper?"

Carter shifted his eyes to his mother, his hand still covering his brow.

"No, I did not," she answered.

"I see," said Miss Carson. She shuffled her papers. "Well then, this meeting may be rather difficult."

"You just told me that it was well written. There must be something else that made you call me down here."

"The problem is what he wrote about. The assignment was to share a pleasant memory of the holiday season, not to ridicule the holidays." Miss Carson pulled out a copy of Carter's assignment and handed it to his mother.

She read the first three or four of Carter's commentaries about popular Christmas songs. The look on his mother's face, a bent frown on one side of her mouth and a raised lip on the other, told Carter that she was on the verge of laughter. He knew she approved.

"And you have a problem with this?" she asked while handing back the assignment.

"Yes. Frankly, Mrs. Mason, it worries me. You have a wonderfully bright son."

"Thank you."

"But—"

"But what?"

"His writing is dark. I'm fearful of what he may be holding inside. It's not healthy."

"I don't understand," Katherine exclaimed. "You're telling me that because my son is a cynic, you called me away from work. Is that what this meeting's about? Do you realize you have students in your classroom who cannot read books that Carter was reading when he was seven years old?"

"I'm sure that's true, Mrs. Mason, and that—"

"Don't teachers have enough to keep them busy than to worry about their students' philosophy of life?"

She paused. Carter knew she was on a roll and ready to enter a soapbox sermon he learned to love growing up around the Mason dinner table.

"I know my son isn't perfect. I'm not sure what perfect entails, but what you are so worried about in my son's character is a trait I admire. Unlike most of us in society, he is not willing to accept the pollyanna solutions our schools try to teach our children. He doesn't accept the simple answers spoon-fed at school or church. At least he thinks. He thinks! He writes what he thinks. So, if Carter's cynical essays are the primary reason you called me here today, then I'm afraid you have wasted your time, Mr. Gurney's time, my son's time, and my time!"

No one said a word. Carter looked at the clock on the wall behind Gurney's desk, wondering how many seconds would pass until someone would break the silence.

"Well," Gurney began.

Miss Carson interrupted, "I'm sorry you feel this way, Mrs. Mason."

"There's no need to apologize. I live in a world of reality. There's no need to feel sorry for me, or my son. Now, is there anything else?"

Principal Gurney looked at Miss Carson, apparently waiting for any further reasons for bringing Carter's mother to the office.

Miss Carson was not finished. "As a matter of fact, Mrs. Mason, there is more. I don't think you realize the changes going on with Carter."

"He's my son. I see him every day."

Carter felt like interjecting some commentary on the amount of time each day, but knew it would not serve him well to do so.

"Change?" his mother exclaimed, "Principal Gurney just informed us that Carter's behavior has improved dramatically."

"Yes," Miss Carson continued, "as much as we all disapproved of Carter's previous charades, since he has turned over a new leaf, well, he is not the same person."

Carter was touched. He turned toward Miss Carson and began admiring her as more than a teacher, she was a friend who cared.

"He no longer smiles like he used to; there are no longer any smart remarks that add life to our classroom during lessons; he doesn't play during recess and PE with as much energy and enthusiasm as he once did."

"And you know all this based on four months of observing my son?"

"I have noticed a steady decline, yes."

"Fine. My husband and I will make sure he starts watching Disney on a more regular basis."

It seemed nothing had been accomplished. Miss Carson had one more card left. "There is one last thing," she said.

"What is that?" Gurney sighed.

"I found these inside Carter's jacket this morning."

Carter shot up in his chair. There before all their eyes, Miss Carson held an unopened pack of Camel cigarettes. Carter had kept this habit so well hidden during the past year that neither his father's sense of impropriety nor his mother's sense of salubrity had been offended.

Now, it was being revealed. Carter had never been this careless. He had never taken cigarettes with him to school. That morning was no exception. He tried to piece together how they arrived inside his jacket. After several seconds of wondering, he figured Chuck must have forgotten his jacket and placed the cigarettes inside Carter's for safekeeping. Carter had asked Chuck not to do this, but eventually, Carter would find the cigarettes there again. As his luck would have it, on this particular day, Miss Carson had found the pack before he did.

All eyes in the office were fixed on Carter.

"Carter?" his mother asked. "What is this?"

"They're not mine, I swear!"

"Carter, you better have an explanation," warned Gurney, who was now sitting with perfect posture and wore the look Carter grew to fear over the past two years. "Whose are they?"

Any pause on his part would suggest a fib; Carter began speaking as soon as Gurney finished.

"Mel's."

"Mel? Mel who?" the adults all asked.

"The crossing guard," Carter explained.

"What are you doing with his cigarettes, Carter?" asked Gurney.

"He dropped them this morning. He had just helped me across the street and started to help some other kids get across when I saw them fall out of his pocket. I yelled at him, but he couldn't hear me above the traffic and all. I figured that I could give them back after school."

All the adults looked at one another, it seemed to Carter, trying to confirm if this may be a reasonable explanation. Mel was a safe target, a likeable school employee, who always referred to Carter as "Pres," because of recently elected Jimmy Carter. If Carter could reach him soon enough, he was sure Mel would agree to backup his canard.

"I have seen him smoking," Gurney said. "But, Carter, next time, bring them straight to the office. Understand?"

Carter nodded.

Miss Carson did not move. She said nothing.

Carter's mother was silent but wearing a queer smirk on her face. It appeared as if she was on the verge of breaking into laughter.

Principal Gurney seemed convinced of Carter's innocence. Perhaps it was his desire to confirm that Carter's reformation on the school's campus was complete, or perhaps he just wanted to defend him in an otherwise defenseless position. Whatever the case, Carter left the office unscathed. Gurney shook his three guests' hands and excused Carter to lunch. Miss Carson left the office with a frown. She wished Carter's mother a merry Christmas and headed back to the faculty lunchroom. His mother wished Gurney a nice holiday and thanked him for his concern.

As Carter was leaving the office, his mother beckoned him with a wave of her hand. "Carter," she said as she bent at the front desk and began writing something down on a piece of paper.

"Yes?"

She finished writing, folded the note, and handed him the paper. "Here. I'll see you tonight," she warned as she left through the other side of the office.

Carter hesitantly opened the folded slip of paper. Each written word announced pending doom:

> *Mel Tomlinson is what we have come to affectionately call a stoner. Based upon extensive conversations with his mother (a very reliable source), Mel does not smoke packaged cigarettes. He would consider it an insult to his intelligence. Mel likes to construct his own "smokes!"*
>
> *See you tonight.*
> *Love,*
> *Mom*

The Ring

Carter left the main office grasping the paper on which his mother had written. He stopped to read it, making sure he understood its implications. Four times now he had read the note, each time with a heightened anxiety, nerves racing from the base of his neck to his toes.

He knew what had to be done. The halls were empty; he could hear the rumble of his classmates in the distance. How he wished to be any one of them, away from this mess. He closed his eyes and took a deep breath. He imagined being in Dr. Hayvenhurst's office. What would he suggest? A scream? What good would that do now?

It was hopeless. Opening his eyes, he spotted a trashcan at the other end of the hall, glittering silver in the clear December sunlight. He walked to it, ripped the note in half, and raised some of the disposed lunch fragments, nestling it among them.

As he walked to the asphalt area of the playground, he searched for Mel Tomlinson, found him, and whispered into his ear, "Gurney's gonna ask about some cigarettes Carson found in my jacket."

Mel held up his hand. "No problem. I'll handle it, Pres."

Carter grinned in gratitude.

One fear was settled, but there was one more thing to take care of before lunch ended.

A group of boys were playing kickball near the perimeter of the grass field. He walked with determination toward the center fielder. As he grew closer, he removed his glasses, placed them in their brown container, and put them in his pocket.

"Hey, Carter!" yelled the pitcher. "You wanna play? You can be up after me!"

Carter did not answer. He continued walking toward the center fielder as the other players in the field greeted him.

"Hey, Carter," said the center fielder, "what's up?"

All play stopped when Carter pushed the center fielder down on the asphalt, creating a loud thud.

"Hey. Calm down, man. What was that for?" Chuck DeSanto asked.

"You put Camels in my jacket again."

"Yeah, so what?"

"She found them. Miss Carson found them!"

"Is that why they called you into the office?"

"How many times have I asked you to stop doing that?"

"Listen, Cart, it's not my fault," Chuck pleaded.

"Oh no? Then whose? Do you know my mother was there in the office? Carson just pulled them out in front of my face. In front of my mother!"

"Hey, look, they were bound to find out sooner or later."

Carter did not know what to do next. Pushing Chuck onto the asphalt was not enough. He needed to be punished. A crowd encircled them. Allen rushed over to Chuck, helping him off the asphalt. "You all right, Chuck?"

Allen turned to Carter. "We okay here, guys?"

"Heck, yeah!" Chuck replied, "I don't know what Cart's problem is."

"Carter?" Allen inquired.

Carter burrowed his eyes. Inside his chest a surging, pounding flood was fighting to be released.

Allen raised his head. "It's over now," he shouted to the other students. "Go back to your games and grub!"

Murmurs of disappointment sounded as the other students dispersed.

"What was that all about?" Allen whispered.

"Carson found my cigarettes in Carter's jacket!" Chuck answered.

"You're kiddin'? What did you tell her, Carter?" Allen asked.

Carter looked Chuck directly in his eyes, shrugging his shoulders.

"Yeah, Cart. What did you tell her?" asked Chuck.

Carter raised his eyebrows.

"Tell me you didn't tell her they were mine!" Chuck ordered.

"Why? What are you frightened of? Your father? Being suspended?" Carter asked. "You have no idea what it's like to pay for your own mistakes, do you? It's always your dad's fault or Tony's fault. Even when you get caught, someone else pays the consequences. This morning it was Hector; now it's me!"

"So you finked on me!"

"And what if I did?" Carter asked, "How is that any worse than my parents finding out?"

"When I go home, my parents are there. That's the difference," Chuck answered with clinched teeth. "I won't hear the end of it! Your parents, Carter, they don't care what you do! As much as you dance around, trying to play the good guy these last few months, you've fooled nobody! Tell me, have they noticed or said anything to you about how you haven't been getting in any trouble? Do you think they really care if you smoke?"

"That's enough!" Allen held his hand in the air, instructing Chuck to stop.

"Oh, look. Little Carter is crying!" Chuck mocked as tears fell from Carter's eyes. "Who's going to wipe your tears, Cart? Mama? Papa? Sis?"

Allen turned his back to Carter and pushed Chuck lightly. "That's low, Chuck. Cool it, man."

Carter leaped forward and struck Chuck's face with his right fist. Blood sprayed from Chuck's nose onto Allen's right sleeve. Before Chuck could respond, Carter leaped on Chuck with full force, pushed Allen out of the way, and wrestled Chuck to the ground. The crowd of students reassembled as Carter flayed Chuck's face with blows from both hands. Chuck pushed Carter away and jumped to his feet. Carter rolled over twice before getting back up. A group of kids held Allen down on the ground, making sure this fight would not be interrupted.

The two exchanged blows for one minute before Mel Tomlinson arrived, pushing his way through the crowd of students and grabbing Chuck. Carter ran toward them, pulled Chuck from Mel's grasp, and landed five more blows on Chuck's chest. Mel grabbed Carter's left arm with his right hand and dragged him to the office while his left arm was wrapped around Chuck, carrying him against his torso.

Pink Presents

Wreaths hung on the two entry doors, their scent filtering into the boardroom and joining the pine aroma created by the company's seven-foot Douglas-fir placed in the corner. The tree was adorned with multi-colored lights, their blinking rhythm dancing among the fresh branches. There were ornaments from the past twenty years scattered throughout the tree, made from silver, gold, and crystal and embossed or engraved with the company emblem and the year it was created. Garlands stretched the entire length of each wall. A sturdy mahogany table with fourteen chairs filled the center of the room, and a fully loaded bar—though no bottles were currently opened—was on the back end wall. On the wall opposite the bar was hung a mounted audio-visual unit.

It was a pleasant environment to hold company meetings. The boardroom was on the top floor of a sixteen-story building. Windows lined one side of the room, giving a wide-angled view of the hills surrounding central Orange County. Pictures of previous board members and photographs of Orange County at the turn of the century hung on the wall facing the windows.

The meeting had begun at eight thirty; it was almost noon. At the north end of the table sat the seven owners of Talbot Construction, three on the left and four on the right. The CEO, Bruce Richardson, sat at the head. Richardson's departmental managers filled the remaining chairs and his secretary, seated along the windows, recorded the minutes of the company's year-end meeting.

Sue Chandler, the one female board member, seated near the middle of the table, had spoken the most during the last hour. She was subtle at first, but her tone was growing fatalistic. Except for the papers shuffled, there was little sound or movement in the room. She removed her gold-rimmed glasses after a brief study of the report she held in her other hand.

She made eye contact with the managers as she spoke. "Each of the reports you have provided show a steady decline in profits during the past two years. Your staff is still the same size as when business was booming five, six years ago."

"Sue, please!" pleaded Bruce Richardson. "We've been through this."

"Interest rates are out of our control," explained Frank Thompson, one of Richardson's managers. "The more they increase, the higher the cost of financing. The higher the cost of financing, the less likely people will buy a new home and the more costly it is for us to build."

"That doesn't address our concern," Chandler said, her attention fixed on Richardson.

Charles Smith, another board member, interrupted. "We understand business is slow, but this is not attributable to any of you or your departments. We've been here over three hours, heard arguments for and against, but in the end we must make the difficult decision. We cannot rationalize keeping the current number of employees in the face of the recession."

Doug Mason took a deep, silent breath. He had yet to make any comments, had been asked for no clarification on points other managers made, and felt no need to participate in the morning discussion. Until now.

He despised meetings, especially meetings like this, the purpose of which would lessen the workforce and thereby make his job, and all those remaining at the company, more difficult in the wake of those who would be released. He had held his emotions at bay and felt he was now prepared to offer his opinions, hiding as much of his emotional zeal as possible.

"The problem is how we approach the recession," he started, "not the recession itself. We must think long-term and not succumb to the temptation of managing based on short-term forecasting."

He studied the board members, and his fellow managers, all seemed intent, waiting for him to continue. This was a common reaction by the employees at Talbot when he spoke. Doug felt that this was not a result of his fellow employees perceiving his comments as profound, but that because he spoke so little, they felt obliged to listen whenever he did speak.

He continued: "In the past, we have had such large profits and revenue that managing expense was a minor concern. We weren't careless with our spending, but we had less incentive to be thrifty. Today, we find ourselves in a recession, in an economy that is experiencing not only less growth but inflation and high unemployment."

Doug noticed Sue Chandler straighten her posture and lean forward. He sensed her frustration and impatience. All he had said up to this point was a simple paraphrase of the previous three hours. He had offered no significant input. His heart pounded; he felt nerves tighten in his throat.

He took another deep breath. "We have two options: we can panic in the face of these trying times or we can take advantage of the situation. Utilizing short-term survival strategies such as laying off workers or pulling investments is panicking. If we hang on to our current staff, we have time to train them to do other functions. This will provide us with more highly skilled employees so that we can cut down on the number of subcontractors. None of us need reminding that this is one of our larger expenditures. In addition, keeping our current staff will increase company morale and create a more dedicated workforce. When we get through the recession, we will be stronger, stronger than we are now and stronger than our competitors."

Perspiration soaked Doug's shirt, and sweat lined his palms. No longer were those seated around the table looking at him; each was focused on papers in front of them. He knew where this meeting was headed, but he refused to give up.

"We must look to the future. Retraining new employees in one or two years, when business picks up, will be too costly. Think of the lost profits. An individual who is already trained contributes immediately as opposed to the new employee who will require hours and days and weeks of training. We must think long-term and not panic."

There was another moment of silence. Doug folded his hands and rested them on the table.

Alex Kasey, another manager, patted him on the back and whispered, "Nice try, Doug."

"Do we have a motion?" asked the moderator, Bill Newman.

Sue Chandler made it, "I move that Talbot Construction cut back its workforce thirty percent by January fifteenth of the coming year."

"Do we have a second?" Bill asked.

"Second!" declared another board member.

"All in favor say aye."

All but one board member joined in.

"All opposed, nay."

"Nay," a quiet voice announced. It was Jim Talbot, a twenty-five-year-old minority shareholder and the only son of the company's founder.

"The ayes have it. So moved. Do we have a motion to adjourn?"

"So moved," said a tired voice.

"Second?" the moderator asked.

"Seconded!"

"All in favor?"

"Aye," all said in unison.

Doug gathered his documents while the others shook hands and exchanged holiday wishes. He stood up, hoping to leave unnoticed. Jim Talbot approached from behind and taped him on the shoulder. "Thanks," he said. "Dad would have voted with me, too."

"Your father was a great man," Doug said. "Good head for business, great heart for his employees."

Jim Talbot seemed surprised to hear the kind words. "Thank you," he said.

Doug shook his hand and looked outside the boardroom, into the office corridor, and toward his secretary's desk. "Merry Christmas, Jim," he said, waving as Jim turned to leave.

"Merry Christmas, Mr. Mason."

Doug looked back over his shoulder, making sure he was not needed, and then stepped from the boardroom and briskly walked toward his office.

"Doug, you know what this means?" Bruce Richardson called from behind.

Doug grimaced. He stopped near an empty office, still yards away from his secretary's desk, unsure of what Richardson might say.

"We'll have to put your plan on hold," Richardson continued, "until business picks up. Sorry, pal."

Doug turned to face his boss, trying to communicate to Richardson with respect that such comments ought to be held to a whisper. "When business picks up, we won't have time to implement the plan."

"I know, I know. I was there. I heard you, Mason."

"Heard, but not listened," Doug said with a smile.

"We're the lucky ones, Mason. We go last!"

"For now."

"You've got to be more optimistic, pal. Look at us; we're at the top. Remember ten years ago? We thought we'd never make it!"

"We survived because Talbot once valued their employees."

Richardson raised his finger. "Hey, Mason. Careful. That could be construed as insubordination."

Doug was familiar with Richardson's humor; no threat was meant. But making a joke in light of the layoffs was not amusing. Doug offered a polite grin and began to walk closer to his office.

"Sorry, Bruce," he said, "I've got a lot on my mind."

"You better get these subcontractors on your mind. No more of your fancy cross-training ideas. Go to lunch, take a few days off, and then start making those calls."

"The list is on Karen's desk," Doug said. "She started the calls this morning."

"Of course she did," Richardson said, scratching his head. "And what if we all agreed with your plan in there? You had her start calling before the board made its decision?"

Doug turned toward Richardson and raised his eyes.

"Why do you even bother, Mason?"

"Stubborn. Someone had to try."

"Stubborn is good. Too stubborn is foolish."

"Considering the consequences, it would have been foolish not to try."

Richardson held up his hand. "All right. All right. No more argument." He lowered his hand, placed both hands in his front pant pockets and sat atop one of the lateral file cabinets. "Now, what about the holidays? You going anywhere?"

"My holiday vacation is coming to work," Doug answered as he picked up a stack of mail from his secretary's desk.

Richardson began clapping his hands. "Hurrah," he started, speaking to Karen Jones, Doug's secretary, "Mason is our office Ebenezer." He laughed loudly. "You're hopeless, Mason. Hopeless."

Doug looked up from a letter he had opened.

"Hey, Mason," Richardson said as he hoped off the file cabinet and walked toward his own office. "You goin' to lunch?"

"Not today. I need to get started on those subcontractor interviews."

Richardson waved his hand, signaling his frustration. "Bah-humbug."

Doug directed his attention on his secretary. "Karen?"

"Yes, Mr. Mason?"

"I'll be eating lunch in my office. No calls for the next hour."

"Yes, sir."

Karen Jones had been his secretary for thirteen years. He hoped she would not be one of the victims of the pending layoff.

"There's a stack of applications for your review," she announced. "I've scheduled ten interviews for the next two weeks."

"Ten? Already?"

"Would have been eleven, but one already called back to cancel."

Doug saw the stack on the file cabinet behind her. "Those them?"

He walked to the cabinet, picked them up, and thumbed through the pile, eager to shift attention away from layoffs.

He turned and walked toward his office.

"No calls for an hour," he reminded.

"Yes, sir."

The refrigerator beside his lateral file cabinet was old and rusted, but it kept his food cold, colder than any of those new foreign models. He pulled out his lunch, laid it on the desk, and walked to the window. Pushing the blinds up, he hoped to have a clear view of the surrounding communities and the coastline.

Though he had yet to see it himself, Richardson had told him that he once was able to see all the way to Long Beach. It had been the day after a strong Santa Ana wind—no smog in the basin, no clouds in the sky—creating the perfect conditions to see the *Queen Mary* resting in the harbor. That would not be possible today. Doug squinted and moved closer to the window. Clouds, mixed with a tint of brown orange, filled the sky to the horizon. He couldn't see the harbor, the coastline, or the *Queen Mary*.

He turned from the window and walked back to his desk. He sat, twisted in his swivel chair toward the file cabinet behind him, opened the bottom drawer, and pulled from it an audiocassette. He placed it in a small recorder. Seconds later Prokofiev's *Peter and the Wolf* played softly as he took the first bite of his sandwich.

As he finished eating, Tchaikovsky's *Nutcracker* began. He propped his feet on the desk and closed his eyes. A noise in the adjacent office caused him to stir. He closed his eyes once more but only for a short while, until a plane flying over the building disturbed him. He watched it descend toward the airport in Santa Ana.

He dropped his feet and placed his head facedown on the desk. The "Dance of the Sugar Plum Fairy" chimed, and he grinned. Now he could rest.

His foot, however, was shaking. His shoulders were tense. His arms grew numb from the weight of his head resting on them. He raised his head, realizing he had a headache and was drained of energy. Seeing the stack of papers on his desk and the subcontracting bids he would need to study the rest of the day, he looked away in disgust.

Work was where he went to escape; somehow it was becoming as burdensome as the rest of his life. He ground his teeth and slammed the desk with his fist. He had tried, but it was of no use. His efforts to relax always led to reminisce, never rest. Placing both hands over his face, he closed his eyes. The tears fell seconds later; his body trembled, his face red. Somehow, this worked. It was humiliating to lower himself to such methods, but minutes later he was asleep.

Ten minutes into his nap, he was awakened by a knock. Gathering his senses, he walked toward the mirror in the closet, straightened his tie, wiped his eyes, and opened the door.

"Karen? What is it?"

"I'm sorry, Mr. Mason. You said no calls, but your son's principal is on line six. Says he can't reach your wife."

"And, did he say what he wants?"

"Well. Yes, sir."

She seemed uncomfortable, waiting for further instructions. "Well, Karen. What is it? I'll find out eventually."

"He's been expelled, sir, and they require a parent to take him home."

Postmark: Santa Ana, California

December 14, 1977

Dear Carolyn,

News Flash! Things suck around here! Looking forward to seeing you. I'll have someone to talk to at least. Mom is either at work or school. Dad is working overtime every night and on Saturdays. School sucks. I got a C+ on my Christmas writing project. Miss Carson, my teacher, says I was too negative. I was so negative that she set up a meeting with Principal Gurney and Mom.

Everything was going all right at the meeting until Carson pulled out a pack of Camels that Chuck put in my jacket. I covered for Chuck by saying that the cigarettes belonged to that guy Mel Tomlinson you went to school with. I was able to inform him of my situation before Gurney questioned him. He knew where I was coming from and covered for me. But that's the least of my worries. As you know, Mom's pretty chummy with Mel's mother. To make a long story short, she knew I was lying but said nothing during the meeting in the office.

I was so ticked off that I got in a fight with Chuck. We both got suspended for a couple days, and Dad had to pick me up. After shaking his head and saying two to three times, "I don't know what we're going to do with you, Son," he didn't say a word the rest of the way. Neither Mom nor Dad spoke to me the next couple days . . . but what's new?

I began this letter as I sit in front of the Christmas tree. Dr. Hayvenhurst says I should not focus so much on the past, but as I look at the colored lights, blinking on and off, the memories of you, Shannon, and myself on Christmas Eve—it is all so haunting. Do you remember how excited we would get? Just before we'd go to bed? Mom would give us each a new pair of pajamas, and we would be so anxious to put them on, rush to your room—the only day any of us would want to sleep in the same room with one another. At some ungodly hour, we would wake up and sneak down to the fireplace and inspect our stockings. It felt so wonderful. We'd use our flashlights, grab the stockings, and return to your room to see what we got. Later we'd open our gifts—the most fun of all! But it always ended. Bummer!

As soon as I begin to enjoy these memories, I think of Shannon. That's when I get those fits, the ones only you and Hayvenhurst know about. I was on the verge of entering one as I was writing this letter, but Dad inadvertently saved me by interrupting my writing and inviting me to join him on one of his runs.

I jumped at the invitation; getting away from the memories of Shannon and the past is not always so easy. I hadn't talked to him since he picked me up from school on the day I was suspended. I hopped on my bike and pedaled beside him.

I wrote the rest of this letter as soon as I returned home, while it was all still fresh in my head.

Dad doesn't usually talk much on his runs. I guess Dad just doesn't talk a lot, period. Less and less it seems as time goes by. But tonight, he had an agenda. First, he informed me that I was grounded for a week because of the fight with Chuck. Second, he wanted to know why I smoke and how long I've been doing it. I told him, "I don't know," and, "About a year and a half." He gave me a lecture about how bad it is for my health, that my body is the temple of God, that I am shortening my life span each time I inhale, that I may be killing brain cells and thus decreasing my intellectual capacity, and on . . . and on . . . and on . . . Then he moved on to my lie in Mr. Gurney's office. If I lied in the office, how can they trust anything I say? Dad was specifically suggesting the worst news flash that I have yet to tell you.

The night before the meeting in Gurney's office, I decorated the house. While I was setting up the manger, I discovered to my honest amazement that all was present and accounted for except Shannon's golden baby Jesus. HONEST, CAROLYN—I HAVE NO IDEA WHERE IT IS!!!!

Mom accused me of playing one of my tricks or losing it, but I know I did nothing with it. I even began thinking that maybe I did hide it last year, just as she was accusing me, but I am sure I would remember doing so. Whatever happened, none of us knows where it is.

This leads me to Mom's decision which Dad was trying to explain to me. I had purchased three mechanical Christmas figurines (a boy and girl on a seesaw, Santa, and Rudolph) to add to our Christmas display. I was able to purchase them by saving my allowance money since before last Christmas and selling some of my baseball cards. I've been determined to regain the Christmas decoration title in the neighborhood competition. But in light of recent events, Mom would not, or could not, or did not want to believe that I had been so thrifty. She believes that I hawked the baby Jesus so that I could buy my decorations. Dad thereby informed me that unless I can produce the golden cradle, my three mechanical friends will not be part of this year's display and that I would have to ask the shop for a refund.

Thus, when you arrive here next Saturday, you will see only the patent disarray of lights lining the perimeter of our home. We will have lost for the third consecutive year. Boo hoo!

Dad's pace on his runs does seem to be improving. I find myself having to pedal harder to keep up with him. Then again, that could be attributed to my smoking! As we approached Euclid, Dad told me to go home, that Mom might be worrying about me. I thought to myself, Sure! *Dad often made this request, and up to this evening, I had graciously accepted his invitation, since I was already tired after four miles. But tonight, I was in no mood to be obedient, so I started toward home and turned around to follow him. He ran a couple more miles and stopped at Orangethorpe Park. I rested on the corner across the street. He walked toward a bench and sat down. It was dark, and there was no one else in the park. Dad looked around to make sure of that. He buried his head into his hands and began to shake. I felt ugly inside. I was spying on him. How often does he do this? Is this what he has been doing on all his runs?*

I'm freaked out, Carolyn. Mom is surviving fine; though I don't like what she has become, she seems to be happy with work and school. But Dad seems so sad. He is still spending at least one day a month with Kevin. That spooks me! He never used to spend time with any guy that either you or Shannon dated; now he spends about two hours each month with the guy who killed our sister! It doesn't make any sense!

I often find myself wondering how things might be if Shannon were still here. I can't talk to Mom or Dad, so I'm going to tell you. She was going to tell me something that night she died. You know—you heard her—just before the two of you got in that fight. I wish I knew what it was! I know that she was beginning to believe in God and that you weren't agreeing with the road she was on. But whatever it was, it seemed to make her happier as time went by. She always said that she was searching for some meaning to life, and for a couple months prior to her death, she kept saying that she was "getting closer" . . . whatever that means. I know you don't believe in God or church, but I'm not sure enough yet to make that decision. I'm still going to church with Dad, and I'm still attempting to make Mom proud by bad-mouthing everything I'm learning there. I think Shannon found something in the middle of what Mom or Dad wants each of us to believe. Dr. Hayvenhurst wants me to decide on my own.

I wish I could see you more often. But I'll see ya next week. Let me know how things are going in "Loony Ville" up there. How's practice? Are you enjoying your classes? Any cute girls for me?

Love,
Carter

P.S. Wish me good luck on Thursday the twenty-second, the night of the decoration competition. I'll need it!!!

Postmark: Oakland, California

December 17, 1977

Dear Carter,

I'm glad you decided to write! I was anxiously awaiting your next letter. I'm sorry to hear how things have worsened at home. You've been forced to face harsh realities early in life. I know many classmates, ready to graduate this June, who have not experienced the trauma that my eleven-year-old brother has endured the past two years. The regents of the University of California can hand a degree to anyone who meets certain requirements, but that does not mean they are qualified to live, survive, and contribute to fellow humans in this world of uncertainty.

The last thing you want to hear right now is your older sister's soapbox sermons, so I will try to get to the purpose of my letter. First of all, to fill you in on what's going on up here in Berkeley, things have really mellowed. My fellow comrades, as Dad likes to refer to us, are finding issues more difficult to address. One of our favorite targets, the Republican White House, is now gone. Nixon, of course, resigned, and Ford failed to overcome the principles of your namesake, Mr. Carter.

Fighting for traditional civil rights issues is no longer a priority. Women's rights seem to be the vogue cause. If I seem a bit cynical toward these advocates of civil rights, it's not because I don't agree with their philosophy but their senseless abandon of everything else in life. Many of the so-called leaders up here are so irresponsible, Cart. They are failing classes because they claim they have more important causes in which to invest their time. Their motives are so good, but they don't always think. How can they affect our world without an education? And how can they be educated if they refuse to listen to their professors or do their studies? I'm still as sold on the left as I've ever been; I'm just becoming more aware that the narrow-mindedness on my side of the aisle is just as prevalent as on Dad's side.

I find myself in a unique position up here. I am probably the only student on campus whose two main priorities are to increase two different types of ERAs. Softball practice is going well, and I feel ready to start beating up on those opposing pitchers' earned run averages, but I am also working hard at increasing awareness of the Equal Rights Amendment here on campus and throughout the Bay Area community. Some of us have arranged to go to Washington, DC, next summer. Do you want to come? Although both houses have approved it, it still needs to be ratified.

Now to the main reason I wrote back so soon: your problems with Mom and Dad. Although they don't surprise me, they do worry me. I'm not as concerned with our parents as I am with you. You are young and impressionable. That's one reason I've always been upset at Dad for filling your head so early with his religious beliefs. Dad has his reasons for believing what he believes, but you have no basis for sharing his beliefs, Cart, unless of course that is truly what you want. Sure he's your father and you respect him, but you've got to make your own decisions, just like your shrink is telling you to do. Mom's just plain bitter. Stay out of her way and just hope she comes out of it. I know she can be a witch, because I can be as big a one as she. Just try and stay out of her way!

Do you remember the trip I took to the East Coast to visit Harvard and some other colleges a couple years ago? When I got home from the trip, Dad and I got into that big argument. I never told you what we argued about that day. I never told you about what I learned on my trip back East. I want to tell you now, Cart, because I think it may help you understand Dad much better. Based upon our argument that day, I know he doesn't plan to tell you anything. Please, let what I say to you remain confidential. I tell you for your sake. For my sake, please don't mention it to him; it may just make matters worse between the two of us. I know I can trust you!

I began to get very curious about that Barney fellow who used to call Dad frequently. I had talked to him briefly on the telephone a few times over the years, but my earliest memory of Dad's conversations with him occurred when I was about five years old. I recall how sad Dad's face got whenever he would talk to him on the phone. That's when I first noticed "the valley" that forms on Dad's face whenever he is disturbed about something. "The valley" always seemed deepest when this Barney fellow called.

When I asked Mom what was making him so sad, she would say, "He'll be all right, Dear. Don't worry. Daddy will be all right." The calls continued, and every time the result was the same—Dad's sadness and the deep "valley."

Several years ago, when I had a minimum day at school, I had got home before Mom brought in the mail. There was a letter addressed to Dad from Barney Kyle. I took the mail inside the house, wrote the return address on a piece of paper, and put the paper away in a safe place. I convinced Mom and Dad to let me research the schools back East by myself with the rationalization that the independence would prepare me for college life. Although this was true, my ulterior motive was to pay a visit to Mr. Barney Kyle. And pay a visit I did.

He lives in Alton Bay, New Hampshire, in a quaint two-story cabin. When I arrived it was raining and cold, so he invited me in without any question as to who I was. He did not ask me any questions at first; he waited for me to explain my purpose for the visit. I was blunt. I explained that my father is Douglas Mason, a graduate of Boston University, and my mother Katherine Mason, formerly Katherine Thurman, a graduate of Radcliffe. I came to New England to visit some campuses that I am interested in attending. While I was here, I thought I would pay a visit to the man I've talked to on the phone over the years.

"You mean he's never told you?"

I suspected something shocking, but his tone made it sound almost traumatic. He invited me to sit down, and made me a cup of coffee. The man was so sweet, Cart, almost cute. He had a full head of grey hair; was short and stocky, but not plump; had silver bifocals; and wore jeans and a flannel shirt. I thought of him as a clean-shaven, underfed Santa Claus.

As I began to drink the coffee, I noticed the pictures on the walls and fireplace mantle. One in particular caught my attention. It was a young man holding a baby girl in one arm and hugging a young lady with the other.

Cart, brace yourself: chills ran up and down my spine when I recognized the young man to be Dad. But who was this woman? It certainly was not Mom. The young woman in the picture had short brown hair, was much taller than Mom, darker, and less muscular; in fact, she was very thin. But beautiful! And the baby, Carter—what a doll!

Then it hit me: If that's Dad and that woman is not Mom, who is she? What is her relationship with my father? And who is that baby? Me?

I placed my coffee mug on the table and slowly walked to the picture on the mantle. Sure enough, it was Dad; and most certainly, the woman was not Mom. I looked over at Mr. Kyle for an explanation. I must have looked like a lost puppy!

He smiled compassionately and explained that the young man in the picture is Dad and that the young lady is not my mom. The young lady was his daughter and the baby was his granddaughter.

But that was not the biggest surprise, Cart! Mr. Kyle went on to tell me that Dad and his daughter, Sarah, had fallen in love while both were running for Boston University's cross-country team. Their passions led them to have a baby, and they were planning to get married. One week before the wedding, Dad and Sarah, along with their daughter, Ashley, were driving from New Hampshire back to Boston when Dad veered into the side of a hill. The collision killed Sarah and Ashley while only slightly injuring Dad.

I was stunned. I couldn't speak. Mr. Kyle let me sleep at his cabin that night. I was too frantic to drive back to the city. He woke me early the next morning, a Sunday, and invited me to church. Get this, Cart: He was wearing a black robe! The guy's a minister!

It's no wonder Dad is the way he is! When I got home from my trip, I told him what I had discovered. I wanted to let him know that I cared for him and that I was sorry. But why hadn't he told any of us? He erupted when I told him what I had done. He said that it was none of my business and that things from the past should be left alone. I told him that if things should be left alone, then why does he punish himself by trying to perform penance every day? Why does he live with this past guilt and base every action and decision upon that one act? I accused him of being a hypocrite, as much in regard to his religion as to his politics, and that his whole life was one big lie. He told me never to go behind his back, never to tell you or Shannon, and to reconsider my agnosticism. I told him, "NO WAY! . . . I want no part of your religion, your empty faith, and your cruel God that does not even exist!" The yelling you heard that day was along those lines.

I don't feel much differently today than I did then, Cart. I want you to know that I love Dad, but he is living a lie. Christianity, Judaism, Islam, whatever, is a tool to make the common people feel guilty so that they are more controllable by those in power. You are free, Cart, do not let Dad's mistakes affect the rest of your life! In light of what has happened to Shannon, you may think I'm cruel for saying these things. I know, I've thought about that myself. If I could take back the words I spoke to Dad that day with the knowledge of what would happen to Shannon only one month later, believe me, I would. I am sorry any of this happened. Dad's first tragedy is making the second all the more difficult. That is why you see him crying on park benches on his evening runs; that is why he works so late at night; that is why he spends so much time with Kevin. Guilt controls his life. Carter, do not make this same mistake!

This letter has turned out to be much longer than I anticipated. I will see you in a few days . . . hopefully! As of right now, I do not have a ride home. It seems I can always get a first date, but once the guy goes out with me and hears my views, he never wants to see me again. Word spreads fast; nobody is responding to my request for a ride home on the twenty-third. Any ideas? If worse comes to worst, I'll take the train.

Good luck on the twenty-second! Beat Stuart and his brothers! Haven't they won it three years in a row? You'll have to tell me all about it.

One last thing, Carter: STOP SMOKING! Of all our family, I want you to be the one around when I am old, so take care of yourself!

Love,

Carolyn

Lights

Winter was a day old.

December 22 had arrived.

Just two weeks ago, Carter had had plans to win back the championship for his family at the neighborhood decoration contest. Now, his only realistic hope was to escape the humiliation of coming in last.

The rules were few and had evolved throughout the years. The primary element was that each family could not vote for itself. Instead, the participants ranked the other competitors, the scores ranging from one to eleven if there were twelve entrants, one to ten if eleven entrants, and so on. Using open ballots minimized strategic or ulterior-motivated scoring.

Mrs. Hardaway, Stuart's mother, distributed this year's ballots. Carter extended his hand as she walked passed, "Thanks, Mrs. Hardaway," he said softly. He looked down at the sheet of paper. It contained ten bold lines and, next to each line, a number from one to ten. The name Mason was typed in bold capital letters in the upper-left corner.

Carter glanced at the other families—mothers holding infants, fathers holding toddlers, older siblings holding the hands of their younger brother or sister. He shifted his attention to the brightly lit homes, one moment looking to his left and then to his right and then behind, confirming that he had little chance of winning. He lowered his head, bit his lower lip, and looked back down at the paper he had just received. Though the rules disallowed it, he wrote his family name below the tenth line on the sheet. He drew a bold line underneath and wrote the number eleven next to it.

No family had been able to defeat the Hardaways for three consecutive years. Mr. Hardaway, an engineer at Hughes Aircraft, and his wife, an interior decorator, put together a masterpiece with the help of their four sons. The three older sons had graduated high school, but the youngest, Stuart Hardaway, was still at home, in the eighth grade, living up to the expectations his teachers had of the Hardaway family. He was the oldest of Carter's friends and seemed to have more responsibilities since entering middle school, not allowing him to participate in as many of the neighborhood football and baseball contests as he once did. Carter missed Stuart, for no other reason than being the only one who could stand up to Chuck.

The only proven competition to the Hardaway family had been Carter's father. Carter had previously looked forward to the competition, assured that his father would create one of the better displays. He liked helping, taking directions to do whatever needed to be done. He would look at their home in pride, knowing he had taken part in creating what might be the best-decorated house. But now he was on his own.

Chuck and Tony DeSanto, along with their parents and three younger sisters, were an annual entry in the Christmas display, but their efforts always appeared half-hearted. The DeSanto males would announce early in December that this would be the year they would win. Each year they would stare at the other homes with wide eyes. Although their father was a well-respected drama professor at the university, his artistic abilities did not carry over to the family's Christmas decorations.

The Romeros were a simple family. Mrs. Romero was a widow, so her oldest son, Hector, served as the man of the house, caring for his two younger brothers, younger sister, and two younger cousins, while his mother and aunt worked at night. Their house would not be decorated until a week before the competition and with no extravagance.

The only Jewish household on the block was that of the Stanowitz family. Mr. Stanowitz was on the city council. This fact more than any other prompted many of the residents to encourage him to compete. He accepted the invitation politely and had given the neighborhood a fresh look each holiday season. His family decorated their home entirely in blue lights. Somewhere, a menorah would be displayed, one year on the roof, another year on the front gate, and one year on the lawn. They won the prize in the early seventy's, just before the Mason-Hardaway rivalry began.

These were the expected entries. Each year there would be additional families that would enter but for one reason or another decide not to participate the following year.

Carter reached his hands deep into the front pocket of his hooded sweatshirt. The cold bite of the winter air caused a brief shiver. He wished he had worn a jacket with more protection. His neighbors seemed fine, though they wore no more layers than he. Perhaps his chattering teeth were the result of nerves, not of the weather.

"Ladies and Gentlemen," Stuart's father announced, "let us begin."

Carter waited until the neighbors congregated in front of the first house. It was Hector's home. Carter stood near the back of the crowd.

No explanation or specific description of what to look for was necessary. There were no oohs or ahhs, just the scribbling of pencils writing the Romero's name next to the number they would rank.

Down the street, the crowd of eleven families shuffled. They spent a few minutes at each home to determine a new ranking of the houses viewed.

As the crowd assembled in front of the Mason home, Carter stood with Allen, Hector, and Stuart in the middle of the street, behind the group of neighbors. "Mom didn't let me keep the robots," he whispered.

Carter hoped for sympathy, some words of comfort.

"That's not the worst of it," he continued, "I got some lights ripped off this afternoon."

The string of lights along the house were haphazard: two lights lit—empty space, three lights lit—two empty spaces, one light lit—three empty spaces.

"Chuck?" Hector asked.

"Chuck," Carter answered.

Stuart placed his hand on Carter's shoulder. "It looks all right," he said. "You did a good job."

"For doing it yourself," Allen added.

Carter looked at his home and then down at the ground, swinging his left leg and lightly kicking the curb in front of his house.

The crowd moved on to the remaining four homes. The DeSanto home had a decorative assortment of lights blinking in a chaotic sequence. There was no rhythm or meaning, just lights everywhere.

The pencils moved once more as the rankings were adjusted.

The Stanowitz home was dressed in its traditional blue. The haze seemed to rise from their roof, lights strung not only on the perimeter of the house but also along the sides and top of the home. The menorah was on the face of the garage door and the Star of David was atop their roof.

The pencils moved; the erasers wiggled; the rankings were adjusted once more.

Finally, the crowd assembled in front of the reigning champions' home. The previous year's winner was always judged last. An array of lights danced in sequence among the shrubs of the Hardaway home, in the trees, on the house, along the doorways and gates, silhouetting the chimney. On their lawn was a scene from Dickens's *Christmas Carol*, Scrooge holding the hand of Tiny Tim. On top of the roof, Santa Claus was perched with a full set of reindeer. Rudolph appeared to be flying, Santa's sleigh angling upward as though on the verge of taking off from an airport's runway. Finally, the family had created a nativity ensemble in their porch—cattle, sheep, shepherds, the three wise men, Joseph, Mary, and the baby Jesus. A brilliant star shone directly above the manger.

As erasers wiggled and pencils reorganized the standings, Carter turned away, his eyes quickly filling with tears.

Ten minutes later, the voting was tabulated and the Hardaways won for the fourth consecutive year. The DeSantos finished fourth, the Stanowitzes finished third, the Romeros finished tenth, and the Masons finished last.

Eggnog was served, along with hot apple cider and cookies, as neighbors quickly forgot about the rivalry and wished one another a warm holiday. Carter left early. Knots had formed in his stomach. He felt queasy and weak. He said good-bye to Allen and Hector, congratulated Stuart, and walked home.

He opened the door. The house was dark.

One stair at a time, one step after the next, he walked up to his room, closed the door, crawled into bed, removed his glasses, and pulled the covers over himself. Seconds later, he struggled under the covers, maneuvering his legs to remove both shoes. He raised the covers and kicked them away.

For one hour, he turned his torso side to side, picked up the pillows, and fluffed them, trying to find some way to sleep. He stared at the digital clock in disgust; it was ten thirty. In one smooth motion, he rolled from under the covers and onto his knees.

"God," he began, "I guess You've been wondering where I've been. I'm wondering the same about You. I hoped it would be different tonight, that things would begin to change. If only I could have won. With or without You; it didn't matter.

"Were You there? Were You watching? Do You care?

"I'm sick of all this: You let Shannon die; my parents can't stand me unless I pretend to agree with them about school, or church, or anything. So I've learned to pretend.

"I don't like that. I've learned to behave the last few months, but what good has that done? Not only have I been blamed for doing something I did not do, but I get in trouble for something Chuck did. And then we get in a fight, and tonight he ruins any chance I had of winning.

"Maybe Carolyn and Mom are right; maybe You are not up there! If You are, why let all this happen? Do You think it's funny? I'm here saying all this because I have nowhere else to go. How stupid and foolish I am if You are not up there to hear me! But I'm going to ask anyway.

"They say at church that if I ask, I'll receive, so here it goes: please, show me what Shannon found out two years ago. That look on her face as she walked through the front door—she seemed so happy. Before that, she was always so sad. She was going to tell me something that night, before she and Carolyn got in that big fight, but she never got the chance. What was it she found out? What was she going to tell me?"

He pressed his hands against his forehead and released a welcome yawn.

"That's all I'm asking. If You're there, if You care, let me know what Shannon discovered."

Carter pulled himself off the floor, rolled back under the covers, and fell asleep.

BOOK III:
THE CRÈCHE

Black Holes

Carter poked his head from beneath the bed sheets, jerking from the sweat-saturated cloth. He pulled off his California Angels sweatshirt and held it to his nose. Pressing his eyes shut, he waited for the stale perspiration to lose its punch. The window behind him shook violently, as though on the verge of breaking free from its panes. He turned and watched the vibrating glass settle to stillness. Grinding his teeth, he raised his shoulders as the window began shaking with greater intensity.

"Not happening," he muttered, "not happening."

He walked to the window. Leaves floated by; atop pockets of air, birds struggled to stay their course, losing, it seemed, all control of their wings. It was as though he were looking into an aquarium, witnessing the effects water currents had on its inhabitants.

He hung his head, "It's not fair. It's just not fair." Hoping his words would somehow convince the weather to amend its way, he continued: "I hate the Santa Anas. I hate the Santa Anas. I hate the Santa Anas."

The room held an electric staleness that was already weighing heavily on his mind. He'd likely have to endure this all day, perhaps tomorrow as well. He reached for the alarm clock that rested on his clothes bureau, hoping to turn it and see he had another hour to sleep. As he touched the clock's face, a sharp prickled jolt from the electrically charged metal darted through his body. He kicked the cabinet on which the clock rested, stubbing his toe. The clock tumbled from the cabinet and Carter kicked it midair across his bedroom and against the wall.

Content with his solid contact, assured that he had communicated his frustration with all that had produced the unwelcome shock he had received seconds earlier, he searched for the clock that had ricochet off the wall, onto his bed. He reached for it and read its face: seven o'clock.

One of the branches from the avocado tree tapped the glass of his bedroom window. Tempted to throw the clock at the window, he took a deep breath and tossed it onto his bed. In its place, he picked up the sweat-saturated sweatshirt he had just taken off, began swinging it as though it were a sling-shot, and then released it as it's velocity reached a point he felt would adequately express to the window his disappointment with it, the avocado tree, and the weather outside. As it made contact with the window, a subtle, dull contact was heard, hardly satisfying Carter's intent.

He turned to his dresser, pulled open the middle drawer, and pulled on a whitewashed pair of jeans.

This would be torture, the whole day. Having to attend school on the day before Christmas Eve was bad enough, but he'd been prepared for this when he saw the class schedule in September. But there were things for which he couldn't prepare: the wind, his last-place finish the night before at the neighborhood Christmas gala, the missing golden cradle. It didn't appear that God had heard his prayer.

Carter looked into the mirror as he buckled his pants. He turned in disgust at the scent of his skin. It was dry and tingly but held a feeling of being on the verge of breaking into a cold sweat. He felt like crawling out of his skin, rolling it up, and throwing it into the hamper. He gritted his teeth. "I hate the Santa Anas."

There was nothing he could do about the wind. There was nothing he could do about his last-place finish. But maybe, Carter remembered thinking during his prayer the prior evening, he could do something about the lost golden manger. If he couldn't find it, maybe he could buy a new one. He recalled seeing one similar in a jewelry shop at the nearby mall, but it cost over five hundred dollars. And even if he could find enough money to purchase it, he would not be able to replace the sentimental value of the lost piece.

Or could he? Hadn't Shannon broken the original? Didn't that offer their mother an opportunity to forgive? And didn't she forgive? Couldn't she forgive again? Could he bear the piece not being acceptable? Could he bear not being forgiven after putting so much effort into purchasing a new one?

He had few options, all of which would result in more disfavor from his mother. That piece at the mall had to be bought.

"Carter, come eat your breakfast!" his mother shouted from downstairs.

He looked into the mirror, grinning, "Come eat your breakfast." He picked up his brush and combed his thick hair. "It will get cold, Carter," he mimicked.

He stopped combing, long enough to examine his haphazard attempt at dressing: a worn pair of jeans, a dirty T-shirt underneath a wrinkled flannel, a pair of glasses coated with layers of grime and tears. Shrugging his shoulders, he turned from the mirror, took off his glasses, and wiped them on the portion of the T-shirt hanging below the bottom edge of his flannel.

He put his glasses on, bent to his knees, reached under his bed, and opened a shoebox full of his best, most valuable baseball cards. He took out three stacks, about a hundred cards per pack. They were each wrapped in a plastic sandwich bag and held in place by a rubber band. Underneath the rubber band was a small piece of paper that had a dollar amount written on it. One read $250; another, $175; the last, $100.

These were conservative amounts. Careful not to deceive himself, Carter needed to know for certain how much he could get at a minimum for these cards. He hoped for more, but these totals were far below market value.

Still, he needed assurance. He placed the cards into the front pocket of his backpack and walked cautiously into Shannon's bedroom. He knew where she had kept her collection, but had never dared touch it. He reached to the top shelf in her closet and grabbed the old cigar box their father had given her to store her best cards. He opened the lid and looked over his shoulder, assuring himself that his mother was not behind him.

He knew what he needed and found them immediately at the top of her collection: a sixty-one Mantle, ten sixty-five Steve Carltons, four Ted William cards from the late forties, and a Babe Ruth from his final days on the Boston Braves.

Carter took a deep breath. He grabbed the sixteen cards, placed them into an empty sandwich bag that was in the box, and quickly stuck the bag into his shirt pocket. There was no turning back now. Closing the lid, he placed the box back onto the top shelf, as close to its prior location as he could remember. As he began to shut the door, the box toppled over the edge of the shelf and the remaining cards sprayed across the closet floor.

Carter lowered to his knees and collected the cards strewn as far as Shannon's bed. He looked outside the room, toward the staircase, hoping the box did not make a loud enough sound to raise his mother's curiosity.

As he searched for any cards he may have missed, he saw one facedown that had landed on top of a pile of books in the closet's corner. Despite his urgency and fear of being caught, a facedown card still held enough intrigue to take the time to flip it and admire the picture on the other side.

But as he turned it, his attention was diverted to the cover of the book on which the card had rested: *A Pilgrim's Progress* by John Bunyan.

"That's the one written by the giant," Carter said softly, recalling his discussions with Shannon. He had tried to read it a year ago but still could not understand most of it. Shannon's commentary, written in the margins, was of no assistance. This must be another copy she had. He opened the cover and flipped through the pages. Somehow it did not look as threatening as the copy he had somewhere in his room, the copy Shannon had lent him about a month before her death. Maybe he could try reading it during class and be more successful this time. Most of the day would be devoted to show-and-tell presentations, and Miss Carson would be doing her grading, unconcerned what he was doing so long as he was quiet.

Again, Carter looked behind into the hall, hoping his intrusion into Shannon's room had not been discovered. He reached behind for his backpack and placed the book inside the same pocket as his cards.

He placed Shannon's box of cards back onto the top shelf and closed the closet door. In his hand, he still held the card that had been atop the book. Finally, he looked at it: Boots Day of the Montreal Expos.

"I'd like to boot this day out the window," Carter whispered as he placed the card in his front pocket with Shannon's more valuable commodities.

Cautiously, he shut the bedroom door and closed his eyes, leaning against the wall just outside of Shannon's room. He took three deep breaths, hoping to calm the anxiety and minimize the guilt. He touched his shirt pocket; feeling his heart race made him more anxious, but the bulge in his pocket, created by the cards, gave him an inkling of hope, a moment of comfort. "Carter," his mother shouted again, "come get your breakfast."

He opened his eyes and walked to the stairs. The house was like it was any other morning, silent and orderly. Only two years ago, these same halls were filled with activity: Carolyn and Shannon rushing through their morning routines and their mother beckoning the three of them downstairs to eat their hot breakfast. He smiled, imagining his sisters rushing in and out of the bathroom as he waited patiently on his bed, reading or studying the statistics on the back of his newer baseball cards.

Carter chuckled. "Come eat your breakfast, before it gets cold," he mumbled. "Get cold? How can cold cereal get cold? When was the last time she made a hot breakfast? Oh, let's see. A year? Two years? Boy, I better hurry before that hot breakfast from two years ago gets cold."

He walked slowly down the stairs, dragging his feet and contemplating whether to avoid his mother and go straight to school.

He'd done it before and gotten away with it but not on a day she was offering him breakfast.

As Carter reached the bottom of the stairs, his father came out from the library, holding an open folder with some papers. On most days, his father had already left. Why was he still here?

Unsure if his father had seen him, Carter studied his expression. He appeared lost in thought. Carter squinted, hoping to recognize what he was reading. He could make out the logo of his father's company embossed on the outside cover of the folder. Carter remained still, uncertain as to what he should do next. He had hoped to leave the house unnoticed, but his mother was beckoning him from the kitchen and his father was standing just a few feet from him. Still, Carter wasn't sure if his father knew he was there.

"Was that you I heard, Son?" his father asked without looking up from the papers.

Carter swallowed nervously, trying to remember what he was muttering while he descended the staircase, and relieved that his father was not upstairs when he was in Shannon's bedroom.

His father finished reading the document and closed the folder.

"Work?" Carter asked.

His father approached Carter. "I heard you speaking."

"On the stairs, you mean?" Carter stalled, looking to the kitchen.

"That's right."

"I was just mumbling."

"You know your mother doesn't like mumbling."

Carter covered his mouth, attempting to hide the grin his father's comment produced, but his efforts only made him break into laughter.

Carter cleared his throat, hoping it could somehow disguise the laughter, somehow cause him to stop the laughing.

He was afraid to look at his father, but once he did regain composure and stop his bout of laughter, he did look his father in the eyes. What he saw was not anger, not disappointment, but something more alarming, something he could not recall seeing on the face of either of his parents. It was as though his father, the man he had always looked up to, was just another schoolmate on the playground whom Carter and his friends had played a prank on. He was hurt.

"I mean the mumbling, Dad," hoping a clarification as to what he found so humorous may appease the effect his laughter had had on his father.

His dad's stare grew intense, moving it seemed from offended to impatience.

"The mumbling, Dad. It's the mumbling that you say Mom doesn't like. That's what made me laugh."

His father remained still, waiting.

"It's just funny. I mean Mom complaining about my mumbling. At least there's sound coming from my mouth."

Carter kept his head lowered and his eyes raised, recognizing that his confession probably wouldn't help clear the tension or any hurt his father felt.

Nothing, there was no reaction.

Carter bit his lip, wishing he could get some read on how his father felt about him. The expression of hurt was gone. In its place, his father appeared distracted, unaware that he was having a discussion with his son.

His father raised his nose. "That's strange. Wait here." He walked past Carter toward the kitchen door and pushed it open.

"Where are the pancakes, Dear?" Carter heard him ask.

Carter shook his head, dropped his backpack to the floor, and sat in the chair near the front entrance of their home. He leaned back.

He wanted to leave, get out of the house, do something, anything, but remain here. It was a humorous thing, Carter thought. Minutes earlier he dreaded having to go to school on Christmas Eve's Eve; now he couldn't wait to get there.

He straightened himself in the chair, leaned forward, and placed his head in the cup of his hands, bracing his arms between his head and thighs. He thought about his plans for the day. Once school was out, he'd rush to the baseball card shop, make his deals, and head straight to the jewelry store in the mall.

"Another change in plans," he heard his mother announce. "Where is he?"

"Honey, this is not going to help. I thought we agreed—"

"Douglas, please. You have no idea."

"Now, Katherine, we were going to make peace."

"Every day it's something new: a frightened school secretary, cigarettes, a fight with his best friend, losing Shannon's manger, and now this. There is no peace with that boy in the house!"

Carter raised his head, unsure of what he had done to create this new ire.

"His little games have got to stop. He's playing us for fools. He thinks that because we are never home, he has free reign over this house. Over everything in the house. Even his attitude."

"Katherine, both of us are out of the house, more than before. We had to expect he would grow a bit more independent."

For several seconds, there was silence. He hoped his father's words convinced his mother to forgive whatever offense he had unwittingly committed.

But his father spoke again. "It was your idea to start working."

Carter grimaced.

"Your lunch is in the refrigerator," she said. "You can cook yourself some eggs for breakfast."

"Now, Honey . . ."

"No, Doug. Let's stop before we say anything more we'll regret."

Carter had heard enough. It was the same old story. If it wasn't quiet, there was arguing. He turned his head to the front door, considering the wisdom in departing.

He stood up and swung his backpack over his shoulders. As he reached for the doorknob, His attention shifted to the manger scene in front of him. For a moment, he was comforted, recalling the Hardaway's portrayal of the nativity scene they had arranged on their front porch. It had been so surprisingly comforting, so beautiful, and so perfect.

But then, here before him, was his family's manger scene—nothing in comparison. There were no bright colors, no fancy lights, not the golden manger that his mother had accused him of stealing; just some old, worn-down pieces of wood. But after tonight, if all went as planned, there would be a new golden cradle, a cradle that just might convince his mother to forgive him, just as she did Shannon ten years earlier.

As he gazed at it further, he turned from the front door, dropped his backpack to the floor, and feel to his knees at the foot of the table.

"One, two . . ." he counted. "Where's the other one?" Carter searched for the third wise man and then realized two of the shepherds were missing also. His body shook; beads of sweat formed on his temples. Mary and Joseph were gone.

He stood up, moved the figurines still on the table, and made sure pieces had not fallen. He searched under the table and glanced quickly around him.

In disbelief, he shook his head, closed his eyes, and began to laugh. "This is nuts!" he whispered, being careful not to alarm his parents.

He looked behind him, around him, and under the table again. This had gone too far. It was useless; someone was out to get him, and as far as he was concerned, they had won. He was tired of feeling guilty for things he had not done.

He jumped from the floor, picked up his backpack, and opened the front door. He patted his shirt pocket and took Shannon's cards out, making sure they were still there. "I'll definitely need you guys now."

Shaking his head, he turned back toward the nativity and hummed the theme music to the *Twilight Zone.* Next, he spoke with his best Rod Serling imitation: "An innocent boy accused of losing missing Christmas figurines. He's mischievous and enjoys playing pranks on others. But he's as surprised as any over the disappearance of one Mary, one Joseph, two shepherds, and one wise man. Could he be the victim of circumstance? Or could he have just entered . . . the twilight zone?"

"Carter!" shouted his father. "Come here!"

Carter shut his eyes tightly, lowered his head in defeat, placed the cards back in his pocket, and slowly shut the front door, not wanting to give any indication to his parents that he was on the verge of leaving without their permission. He knew the inquisition he was about to face and would not allow them to begin their questions.

He entered the kitchen, stoic and numb.

"Go on, Dear," his father invited.

"Wait," Carter announced. "I have something to say. It's a confession, really." Carter looked up. Neither of his parents looked pleased, but he had gripped their attention.

He continued. "I lost all control. My faculties have left me. I mean, I didn't know what I was doing. There they were, right in front of me, calling to me, 'Come here, little boy. Come here, Carter,' they beckoned, 'Come here.'

"The temptation was too great. So, I stole them. I took the king. I took the two shepherds. I took Mary. I took Joseph. I sold them all. I haven't decided what I will buy with the proceeds, but maybe I could afford a pack of gum. I've found that hawking Christmas figurines is a lucrative enterprise."

Carter glanced over his mother's shoulder, noticing the ticking of the clock on the wall behind her. Seconds continued to pass; the only sounds he could hear were the movement of the clock's second hand and the wind outside. He shifted his gaze to his mother, studying her eyes, noting the burning calculation they revealed, and surprised that her wit had yet to produce a response to his sarcasm.

The stupor his words produced served as a momentary reprieve. Then the telephone rang.

Setting his eyes on his mother, his nerves reawakened and his heart's pace increased with each passing second she let the phone ring. Finally, after six rings, she picked up the receiver.

"Hello. Mason residence."

She looked down at Carter, fixing her eyes on his. He knew he had not escaped her wrath.

"This is she," she informed the voice on the other end.

Her voice transformed into a soft whisper. She angled her body away from Carter and his father as she asked short, quiet questions.

"When? How long has she been awake? Is she still up? I'll be right there."

She hung up the phone and grabbed her purse. "Doug," she announced anxiously, "Mom's up again. It's been ten minutes already. Can you take care of this?" she asked, pointing toward Carter.

"Of course. Call me as soon as you have a chance?"

"Of all days," she muttered before turning to Carter's father and hugging him tightly. They embraced for what seemed to Carter an eternity, in light of the tentative state of his grandma. It was a welcomed sight; he couldn't remember the last time he had witnessed affection between them.

She kissed his father, and then walked toward Carter and kissed him lightly on the forehead. Another shock. He couldn't recall the last time she had kissed him at all. "We'll finish this tonight," she said slowly enough to convince Carter that he had little hope of relying on his grandmother's consciousness to erase from his mother's mind the fact that five more pieces of the crèche were missing.

Awakenings

Katherine Mason stepped on the accelerator, pushing the needle to fifty miles per hour. Her hands trembled, her fingers tapping the steering wheel. She may not get there in time, she told herself. She had to drive faster, fast enough to arrive before her mother's memory again relapsed.

Ten times during the past year, this had occurred. Nana Thurman would wake, her memory temporarily returning. She would be aware of her surroundings, her condition, and her identity, only to return to an almost unconscious state minutes later. On three occasions, Katherine made it to her bedside in time to be with her, to be really with her. How appropriate it would be, if she were able to visit with her mother again two days before Christmas.

It was a blessing, giving Katherine hope that someday the woman she admired might return. It was a curse, reminding her that Nana would probably never fully recover.

She turned the car into the rest home's entrance, memories of her childhood racing through her mind. Her mother had made it so livable, so comfortable, and so loving. Growing up, she realized how different their lives were from other families' and how difficult her mother's life was compared to the mothers' of her classmates. As she reached adulthood, Katherine grew more aware of the heartaches and pain her mother had endured. Why couldn't she rise above her own difficulties like her mother had? Why was she unable to shower her children with the affection her mother had shown in the midst of adversity?

With the image of Carter, standing in the kitchen minutes earlier and attempting to rationalize his actions, she wasn't sure where she had gone wrong. She knew he had grown more independent, wiser, and was now forming opinions of his own—attributes she hoped all her children would acquire. So why feel guilty? He was becoming just what she had wanted him to be.

Still, they had lost touch. Once Shannon died, she stopped tucking him in bed. Why? Was she too self-absorbed in sorrow to care for her child still living? By the time she realized the gulf between them, she was already toiling on her master's and working part-time. She had commitments to keep; she didn't have the luxury she once had to be the type of mother she would want to be. She wasn't sure Carter would want it that way.

And then, there was Carolyn. She left for college eight months after the accident and had become the woman Katherine had always envisioned. She was beautiful, confident, caring, realistic, and scholarly. There was nothing Carolyn would not be able to accomplish. Two times each week, she would call to get updates on Carolyn's classes and the softball team. "Fine, Mother. Everything is fine," was always her answer. Then she'd ask, "How's Cart, Mom. Is he doing any better?"

"He's all right," Katherine would answer, but Carolyn would begin asking deeper questions, as if she knew the tension in the home. "Mom," Carolyn once urged, "he's your son. He's hurting. He's got no one but that shrink. You were always there for Shannon and me. Just talk with him."

The words echoed in Katherine's mind, haunting her as she pulled the keys from the ignition. Why was she so afraid of talking with her son? She knew that Carter and Shannon had formed a strong union during the last two years of her life. Perhaps Carter had a more intimate knowledge of who Shannon was than she did. Was she jealous? How childish—something her mother would have easily risen above.

But her mother had something she didn't have: faith in God. And Katherine suspected that it was this faith that had helped her mother through it all. But there was a price for her mother's faith—denying the truth. How could her mother believe in a God who allows all the human tragedy that exists in the world? How can an all-powerful, all-loving God allow her mother to be beaten by her father? How could he allow a daughter to die so needlessly in a car wreck?

It disturbed her that she'd become so bitter since the accident. She knew that her bitterness was aimed at a higher power. Was this an indication that she really did believe in God? This consideration was frightening. Her entire life was based on the premise that no deity existed, that men and women are in complete control of their lives. The slightest possibility that a higher power could exist left her feeling vulnerable.

She shut the car door and rushed through the line of parked cars to the front of the rest home. She signed her name to the visitor's register and made her way down the corridor to her mother's room.

Outside each doorway, she read the nameplates of the residents, wondering how many would receive visits from family over the next week. She wasn't ready for this; she came to see her mother, not to care for her mom's hundred or so lonely neighbors.

She stopped in the middle of the long corridor.

Where was she?

A hallway?

Which hallway?

A strange, distant, but somehow familiar feeling of total helplessness overcame her. She felt like crawling up into a ball in the corner of the building.

She looked behind her. Finding no comfort in the eyes of the rest home's employees, the helplessness grew in intensity. She was a child again, her eyes wide, her body shaking, staring at the door that separated her from her mother and father. She closed her eyes as she heard the shouts, the hits.

A man coughed from the room at which she had stopped. She opened her eyes and looked down the hallway. She ran, and as she drew closer to her mother's room at the end of the hall, she remembered that night, two years earlier: the swinging doors, the sympathetic stares of the doctors and nurses, the body of Shannon lying motionless under thick hospital blankets, her eyes shut and her mouth solemn.

Finally, at the rear of the building, she came to the plate reading Margaret Thurman. The door was open, and a nurse was at the bedside.

"Katie," a frail, but excited voice announced.

Katherine dropped her purse on a chair near the door and rushed to her mother. She grabbed her hand. "How are you, Mom?"

"It's been awhile," Margaret said in a weak whisper. "I know you've been here while I'm sleeping. The nurses tell me you've come. You're a good daughter, Katie."

Katherine smiled, attempting to keep her tears from showing. She looked at the nurse. "How is she?"

"She's a trooper. She's doing fine." The nurse patted Margaret softly on the shoulder. "I'll leave the two of you. We can talk later, Mrs. Mason."

"Thank you," Katherine answered.

"Pull up a chair, Katie," Margaret said, "I need to talk with you. I'm not sure how much time I have this go-around."

Katherine looked at her watch. "It's already been twenty minutes, Mom. That's—"

Margaret sat up to interrupt. "Not now, Katie," she said sternly. "I have something to say."

Katherine was stunned. Her mother had just awoken from memory relapse and here she was, speaking in a tone that she hadn't heard since her college years. "What is it?"

Pushing herself up, it seemed her mother's arms would snap from the tension, the bones visible beneath the hanging, famished flesh. Katherine would have offered assistance, but knew her mother would have refused it. Margaret pushed herself higher, turned, and looked Katherine in the eyes. "It's them, Katie. They're here."

Katherine shook her head. "I don't understand, Mom. Who's here? Who are 'they'?"

Margaret's smile grew, and her gaze seemed to leave the room.

This was it, Katherine thought. She had heard of people entering a peaceful state just before dying and seeing people from their past. Here it was, the day before Christmas Eve, the same day Shannon left the house before dying in the early morning, and now her mother. Katherine grasped her mother's hands tighter.

"I'm not imagining this, Katie. Everything they told me when I was a little girl is true. Everything I told you. I know you chose not to believe it. I honored your wish; I told none of the children; they know only that it has been a family heirloom. Nonetheless, they're here and they've come to help."

Margaret squirmed and squinted. Katherine could feel her mother's tense hands. She didn't have much time.

Her mother's stare grew more focused. "You lied to me, Katherine Melody Thurman. I know you were trying to protect me, but you lied just the same. Of all people, I thought you would never—"

"What are you talking about, Mom?"

Margaret held up her hand. "Don't deny it, Katie. They wouldn't be here if it wasn't necessary. Whatever has happened to the kids, they've come to help."

Katherine looked away. Her mother had asked about the family on the three occasions before, but the last thing she was going to do, was tell her mother that one of her granddaughters had died. And yet somehow she knew, or at least she knew something was wrong. Was it mother's intuition? Who had told her? How could a seventy-eight-year-old woman in her condition find out something like that?

Margaret's voice faded. "I know, Katie, because they're here. They never came unless it was urgent."

Katherine looked back at her mother, whose eyes were widening by the second. Suddenly, she remembered. She knew to whom her mother referred.

Before Margaret could say more, her eyes shut. She was asleep. Katherine gently rested her mother's hands on the sides of the bed, kissed her on the cheek, and whispered, "I love you, Mama. Merry Christmas."

Katherine left her mother's bedside and was overcome by a daze. She was in her car now and thought she had talked to the nurse. She was unsure of how much time passed since she had left her mother's bedside and unable to recall the walk down the home's corridors or the specifics of any conversation she may have had with the nurse.

She shook her head and placed the key in the ignition.

Fortunately, there was no work or school-the entire day was free. She would go to the mall and do the Christmas shopping she felt necessary. She drove into the street and seconds later onto the freeway.

"They're here," she said softly as she drove, remembering the words her mother had spoken minutes earlier. "They've come to help."

She swerved the car to the right, came to a stop in the emergency lane, and buried her face in her hands.

It wasn't even nine o'clock and already she had had enough of this day. Five more pieces of the crèche were missing, and her mother had awoken to announce, "They're here."

Last Call

The sun fought its way through the dense morning fog covering San Francisco Bay. Recreational sailors maneuvered past commercial vessels waiting to enter the Pacific. Already the distant streets were filled with traffic, rushing to make business deals before the long holiday weekend or to purchase gifts.

Kimico Turnboldt could see the traffic jamming the bridges as she stopped to rest, hands on hips. She took a deep breath and looked at her watch, then bent over, placing her hands on her knees and taking more deep breaths. This was what made life worth living. She smiled and pointed upwards, saying softly, "Thank you."

For a late December morning, the sun was working unusually hard. The sweat accumulated quickly after she departed campus, saturating her Berkley Athletics sweatshirt. She turned and walked slowly to the traffic light. It was red, but there was no traffic approaching from either direction. She pushed the small button on her watch to resume the time, and started a light jog.

On most days, the Berkeley campus bustled with life from the early morning hours of one day to the early morning hours of the next. But on December 23, the few cars that did remain on campus belonged to the collegiate athletes who were either still in bed sleeping, or on their morning runs.

Kimico turned into the east entrance of the campus, passing empty dorms, empty classrooms, and empty parking spaces. She glanced at her reflection off the library windows, proud that she had shed the fifteen pounds her coach had suggested back in September. She would stop to admire herself, or at least slow down a little, but she would not feed such vanity, so she accelerated to the steps of her dormitory and immediately dropped to the grass to begin three sets of one hundred sit-ups.

After a long shower, she packed her suitcase, anticipating the welcome she would receive when she got off the plane in Montgomery. Her heart raced as the images of her younger brothers and sisters, cousins, and parents rushed through her memory. She hadn't been home since last December, and she had regretted more than once staying in Berkeley to take those summer courses. But it was necessary to stay on the team.

As she packed her suitcase, she occasionally glanced at her sleeping roommate. She smiled, grateful to know someone so intelligent, honest, and athletic. Her roommate was probably the most beautiful woman she had known; she seemed to have it all. Yet, somehow she was not envious. There was too much sorrow in her life. Why would she want to trade places with her? A sympathetic grin crossed her face when someone knocked on their dorm-room door.

"I'll be right there," she whispered loudly, being careful not to wake her roommate. Kimico shuffled to the door and cracked it just enough to squeeze her muscular torso into the dorm's hallway.

A young female swimmer stood a few feet away, brushing her hair. "Phone call for Mason."

"Thanks," Kimico said. She paused and grinned, still holding the door. Looking back at her roommate, she pursed her lips, swung the door open as far as its hinges allowed, held it for several seconds and, with all the strength in her right wrist and forearm, slammed the door shut.

Her roommate shot up. "What the . . . what's going on?" she shouted.

Kimico returned to her bed and resumed packing. "Phone call, Sleeping Beauty."

Carolyn Mason rubbed her eyes while she was still under the covers. She yawned and stretched. "Couldn't you have just tapped me on the shoulder?"

Kimico smiled.

Carolyn didn't move.

"Are you going to answer it?" Kimico asked.

"Answer what?"

"The phone."

"You're serious?"

"For goodness' sake, Mason, why do you think I woke you? If I were you, I'd get my tail in high gear. It could be a ride home, girl."

"You're a dreamer, Kim," Carolyn mumbled.

Kimico studied Carolyn as she dragged herself from beneath the bedsheets, her long, well-toned legs barely covered by the Philadelphia Philly T-shirt she wore as a nightgown, "It ain't gonna happen," Carolyn continued. "No drive home. I'll take the train."

Carolyn stretched her arms and took a deep breath. "I've had that notice on the board for over a month. Nobody called until I took my name off it."

"How'd that work out?" Kimico asked.

Carolyn ran her hands through her hair and eyed Kimico with impatience. "Guess," she answered and then shuffled into her slippers and walked out the door into the hallway.

"Hey, Mason!" Kimico called out. "You going out like that?"

"What?"

Kimico shook her head. "You just don't get it, Mason. Guys see a woman like you, dressed like that—and, man, forget it. They lose all semblance of self-control."

But Carolyn had left.

....

The phone's receiver was still hanging freely by its wire coil. Carolyn picked it up. "Hello?"

"Is *these* Carolyn Mason?"

"Yes." Carolyn rubbed her eyes, still wishing she were asleep.

"*Yoor* postcard notice on the *commoonity boolleetin* board—I see that *yoo* are in need of a ride home for the holiday."

"Yes." Carolyn's eyes widened, intrigued by the caller's accent.

"*Doo yoo* still need *assistants*?"

"Assistants?" Carolyn asked, a hundred images running through her mind, images of the caller, of a ten-hour drive alone with him. There was something in his voice that enticed her and made her feel on edge. She could feel her heart beat with more authority.

"Yes, a ride? *Doo yoo* need *assistants getteen* home?"

"Yes. Yes, I do. I'm sorry. I mean . . ." Carolyn frowned and then leaned back on the wall, twirling the phone's cord.

"I am leaving in one hour. Would *yoo* be *readee* by this time?"

"Yes," Carolyn said quivering. She held her hand up, in front of her face, and observed it shake. A bead of sweat fell from her forehead. "Yes," she repeated, "I'll be ready."

"I *weel* see *yoo* at eight *twentee. Veery* good?"

"That will be fine." Carolyn hung up the phone, still leaning against the wall and now smiling. She fanned herself with her hand and sighed. Breathing deeply, she straightened her posture and walked calmly back to her room.

Kimico had just closed her suitcase as Carolyn reentered, closed the door behind her, and went straight to the bathroom.

"Well?" Kimico asked.

Carolyn splashed water on her face, looked into the mirror, and smiled, her heart still rapid. "You were right, Kim. It's a ride home."

"All right, Mason! You scored in the clutch! What did I tell you, girl?"

"When do you leave, Kim?" Carolyn asked as she reentered the bedroom.

"That anxious to get rid of me? You don't plan to do anything with this guy before driving home?"

"C'mon! I promised you."

"Yeah. You've been a good girl, Mason—when I'm here to watch over you. But what about them nights you ain't here? Where you've been then?"

Carolyn went back to the bathroom, collecting her toiletries and packing them in a small bag.

"And what's that goofy smile on your face, girl? You look like you're in love."

Carolyn looked at Kimico suspiciously through her image in the mirror. Then she studied it herself to see if Kimico was correct. She was. Carolyn shook her head and bit her tongue, hoping to erase what she had just seen.

"I'm telling you, Mason. Girl, you better get wise to these men. One day you'll run into one—"

"Give it a rest, Kim. How long do you think it takes for word to get around campus that Mason won't do it in her room 'cause her roommate doesn't believe that stuff should be done? They start to think I'm like you."

"Don't blame that on me, girl! Everybody knows Miss Mason got a mind o' her own. She don't need some black, backward, Alabamy backstop telling her whom she can and can't see. I just said, 'Don't do it here.'"

Carolyn finished gathering her things in the bathroom and put them on her bed. "I suppose you're right about one thing, Kim: no guy wants a girl who has a mind of her own or who can play better ball than he can. I've been blessed with both."

Kimico dropped her suitcase at the foot of the door and sat on the corner of her bed. She lay back, folding her arms behind her head.

"Anyhow," Carolyn continued, "this guy doesn't seem to be my type. I don't even know his name."

Kimico tilted her head toward Carolyn. "What type is that?"

Carolyn was at her closet. "Which dresses should I take?"

"Yellow," Kimico answered. "Guys drool over long-haired brunettes wearing yellow."

Carolyn turned, narrowing her eyes.

"It's Freudian, ya know, like, subliminal. The yellow and black makes guys think of us as bumblebees. They want to see how long they can play with us before getting stung."

"You've got to be kiddin'!"

Kimico stood up and brushed her hair back. She angled her hips, placed her right hand on her right side and then rested her left hand behind her head. "I'm a brunette. I know."

Carolyn eyed her curiously. "I don't know, Kim. I'm not planning on going out with anyone."

"So, what about this guy? You say he's not your type. What's that mean? I didn't think there was a man that wasn't your type."

"He talked strange. Precise. From the East, maybe."

"Eastern accent. Hmm. Love them New York-Boston boys!"

"No. Not from the East Coast. Eastern . . . Eastern."

"You mean, as in the Middle East?"

"Yes." Carolyn turned, noticing Kimico's widened eyes and smile. "You find that humorous?"

"You like foreigners, Mason. I know you, girl. Anything that isn't typical, that's your type. You may say you're not interested in this guy, but you can't fool me."

"A man's a man. It doesn't make any difference where he's from."

Kimico's grin grew. "It does to you, Mason."

"Doesn't your plane leave soon?"

Kimico glanced at her watch. "I've got an hour. Besides, I wanted to talk."

Carolyn sighed, placing her hand over her eyes. "Not now, Kim. I've got a lot on my mind."

"I know, Mason. That's why I waited 'til you had no choice but to listen. You're a busy woman. You've got to make time for the crucial things in life, girl."

Carolyn dropped her hands from her face. Kimico was no longer smiling; she wore her serious stare. Carolyn learned to accept this side of Kimico's personality. There was little about Kimico that got on Carolyn's nerves; she was clean, organized, and polite; had a wonderful sense of humor; and was modest and intelligent. She was the hardest hitting member of Berkeley's softball team and had a stronger throwing arm than even the catcher on the men's baseball squad. She understood

Carolyn's athletic competitiveness and unwillingness to settle for second best. Following their freshman year, Carolyn convinced herself that it was in her best interest to remain Kimico's roommate for as long as possible. Enduring her sermons meant not having to risk getting a roommate who did not have all of Kimico's attributes.

Kimico put on her coat, walked toward Carolyn with open arms, and embraced her. "Now. I want you to have a wonderful time at home with your family. You hear me, girl?"

Carolyn tried to communicate her impatience with a wry smile.

"Give that brother of yours a big kiss. Let him know how much you love him. He needs it! Give your dad a chance, Mason; he could teach you something about Christmas. Try to patch things up. He loves you, girl! And spend some time with your mom, Mason. She's hurting. She may not show it, but she's got some serious luggage.

"Is that it?"

"No way, girl. The most important thing of all . . ." Kimico waited and smiled.

"What's that, Kim?"

"I love you, Sister!"

Carolyn smiled politely, returning Kimico's hug with a couple light pats of her hand on Kimico's back.

"Carolyn," Kimico said, "look at me." Kimico extended her arms and held Carolyn by her shoulders.

Carolyn tapped her foot, shifting her attention from her closet to Kimico. "What is it Kim, I've got to shower. You've got a plane to catch."

"You're a smart one, Mason. I've been on a lot of teams and never have I played with a girl as savvy as you. You have the knack, that instinct and common sense that the coaches can't teach."

Carolyn ground her teeth; something was brewing.

Kimico released her grip on Carolyn and shot her arms out, exclaiming, "And how you pull off those grades with the little time you study is beyond me. It's like you remember the stuff after only one sitting and have no need to go over it again. You read for the fun of it. I've never met anyone like you, Mason. You're funny that way."

Carolyn shifted her weight from one leg to the other and eventually rested herself against the bedpost. This was unbearable. It was awkward, to say the least, to receive such affirmation from a teammate from whom she had only minutes before received rebuke for her liberated sexual lifestyle. She tried hard not to appear rude by keeping eye contact.

She noticed Kimico's eyes widen. Carolyn held her breath. *Here it comes.*

"Mason, you've used your brains to be the best on the softball field and in the classroom. Now it's time to really put that brain of yours to the test. You're so convinced Christmas is a waste of time. You disagree with your father and ridicule all those, including myself I presume, who believe in God and invest their lives seeking Him. I've always wondered how a smart girl like you could dismiss religion so easily. It makes more sense than you give it credit, Mason. Look past your hang-ups and listen to logic, just like you do in class and on the field."

Carolyn wasn't sure if she was finished.

"You hear me, Mason?"

"I understand." She'd say anything to get Kim out the door.

"Good. You know I love you, girl. I wouldn't say any of this if I didn't love you."

Carolyn gave a subtle tilt of her head, communicating some appreciation of her roommate's intentions.

"Good," Kimico smiled. "Have a safe trip and enjoy your vacation." She picked up her suitcase and headed toward the elevator.

"Merry Christmas," Carolyn called out. "I'll see you in a few weeks."

"Adios!" Kimico shouted as the elevator doors shut.

Show-and-Tell

Miss Carson knew how to run a class. Carter figured her to be a natural dictator, one of those teachers who only need stare at a student to regain control of a situation. More than once, during the early months of the school year, Carter had been the recipient of that stare. Her glaring eyes, lowered head, and straight-lined mouth were threatening enough. They not only forebode disaster, but also erased her otherwise attractive features. To be a compliant, well-behaved student was in Carter's best interest, for he not only averted her wrath but also gleaned her beauty.

From September through December, Carter learned to appreciate his teacher's professionalism. Although he wished she was more light-hearted and would ease up on the workload, he had to admit that he had never enjoyed school more than he did as a sixth-grader. And Miss Carson's unwavering control of her class had a lot to do with it. But on December 23, the final day of school before the two-week holiday, he began to see a more relaxed side of the woman he admired.

The entire day was full of activities: playing games with holiday themes, making crafts, singing carols, and eating donuts covered with white, red, and green sprinkles. The spelling test was comprised of words from popular Christmas songs, and the history lesson focused on the traditions of Santa Claus and the Christmas tree. The surprise of the day's activities created a joy in Carter he hadn't felt since the Christmas before Shannon's death. All of it helped take his mind off the problems awaiting him at home and the uncertainties of how things were going to develop. Would Carolyn make it home from Berkley? Was Nana okay? Would he be able to sell enough of his cards to buy a new piece for the crèche? No, now it was six pieces he needed to purchase. Would he have enough for six pieces?

Miss Carson had scheduled the remainder of the day with show-and-tell presentations. The more timid students of the class were scheduled to present; the ones who tried to put off the pending horror of presenting something before their peers. Carter could tell his classmates were growing restless. He was amused by Carson's attempts to add excitement by contributing bits of information to each of the presentations. But it was not helping.

He felt sorry for Hector, who was the final student scheduled to share. But he also knew what Hector was going to show the class, and was eager to see how his classmates would respond.

There were still four more presentations before Hector. The boredom was unbearable. Carter reached under his desk and cautiously opened his backpack. He looked toward Carson, who was grading papers. He took out the book he found in Shannon's closet, *A Pilgrim's Progress*, and began to flip its pages, before realizing the sandwich bags with his baseball cards had fallen to the floor. He quickly reached down and placed them back inside the backpack. He hesitated to look around, not wanting to tip-off any of the other students the value of the cards.

He took a deep breath and tried once more to find some interest in his classmate's presentation. Taking a deeper breath, he lowered his head and began searching Shannon's book for pieces of her writing that may make sense.

Immediately, Carter stopped when he saw his name written in bold: "CARTER WAS RIGHT!"

He looked up, certain that his excitement was noticed by others in the class. Other than the narration of the student currently sharing his insect collection, there was only the shuffling of feet under desks. Again, Carter looked to the rear of the class. Miss Carson still was grading papers.

He studied Shannon's words further.

> *It's not just the hill that both characters are climbing that's similar between the two books. Both Camus and Bunyan agree that there are "fake" Christians. Carter, thank you! You led me back to this piece of Brit Lit that I once thought useless.*

He read Shannon's words once more to confirm his sister's glowing report.

Carter shook his head, recalling how lost he was when he attempted to read the book one year earlier. What prompted Shannon to write such a commendation?

Shannon's words of gratitude were written next to the text of John Bunyan's *Pilgrim's Progress*:

> *You did well to talk so plainly to him as you did; there is but little of this faithful dealing with men nowadays, and that makes religion so stink in the nostrils of many, as it doth: for they are these talkative fools, whose religion is only in word, and are debauched and vain in their conversation, that being so much admitted into the fellowship of the godly do stumble the world, blemish Christianity, and grieve the sincere.*
> *(The Pilgrim's Progress, John Bunyan, Penguin Classic Books, 1987, p.76)*

"I do understand some of it," Carter muttered. At least he recognized that whoever spoke these words was not pleased with some so-called Christians, just like that Camus fellow in the Sisyphus book. He was encouraged to look further. Flipping more pages, he stopped when he found another of Shannon's notes written in the margin:

> *There are so many wrong ways. Which is the right way? Is there one truth? And which way, if any, leads to it?*

Carter read the narrative next to this piece of Shannon's writing. The two main characters had been misled on their journey by a "flatterer" who deceived them, convincing them that he would lead them on a "safer" route.

> *"Come hither, you that walk along the way,*
> *See how the pilgrims fare, that go astray!*
> *They catched are in an entangling net,*
> *'Cause they good counsel lightly did forget:*
> *'Tis true, they rescued were, but yet you see*
> *They're scourged to boot: let this your caution be."*
> *(Pilgrim's Progress, p. 117)*

Again, Carter was pleased he understood the poem. But such a harsh penalty for making a mistake, for taking what Shannon called, a wrong way? Can the penalty for choosing a wrong way be so harsh?

He continued to read as Hector's turn grew closer. He would be next. Carter looked back down at the book; a large star was placed next to a passage on page 46, underlined, and circled.

> *There I hope to see him alive, that did hang dead on the Cross; and there I hope to be rid of all those things that to this day are in me an annoyance to me; there they say there is no death, and there I shall dwell with such company as I like best. For to tell you truth, I love him, because I was by him eased of my burden, and I am weary of my inward sickness . . ."*
> *(Pilgrim's Progress, p. 46)*

Carter stopped. His eyes widened. Next to this same passage, Shannon had written, "Can he remove my burden? Can he cure me of my sickness? My pride?"

Never had Carter imagined the possibility of either of his sisters uttering, or writing, such words. Shannon actually seemed to be contemplating the life and the death of Jesus and that perhaps there was some value to it.

Hector rose from his desk and walked to the front of the class. Carter was lost in thought. He wanted to listen to Hector, but he also wanted to read more of Shannon's notes. His eyes met Hector's; he could tell Hector was nervous. It was as though Hector was asking for his assistance. With his eyes, Carter attempted to assure him that all was good, that he would do fine. Hector returned a doubtful grin.

As Carter reached down to place the book back into his backpack, his fingers touched the outer edge of the book's pages. It felt as though one of the pages was missing. Carter looked more closely, wondering why he had not noticed this particularity before; one of the pages was folded on the top-right corner.

Carter glanced at Hector and was hoping he could quickly read something on that page without offending his friend. At the front of the class, Hector was still arranging his items for presentation.

Carter opened to page 107.

> *Thus by the shepherds, secrets are revealed,*
> *Which from all other men are kept concealed:*
> *Come to the shepherds then, if you would see*
> *Things deep, things hid, and that mysterious be.*
> *(Pilgrim's Progress, p. 107)*

Renaissance Flannel

Hector cleared his throat. He held a worn, wrinkled grocery bag. Carter smiled, closed the book, and folded his hands on top of his desk.

He knew what was in that bag and felt certain his fellow students would be enthused to discover what it contained. Besides him, only Chuck and Allen knew what was inside.

Carter recalled weeks earlier when Hector was asked to identify Egypt in front of the class. He knew his friend would fare better today. What Carter admired most about Hector was his modesty. Probably the most talented, responsible, and mature among their circle of friends, Hector often undermined himself when asked to do anything that might show how far ahead of his peers he actually was.

He was amazed at how much Hector did outside of school. Following his father's death in Vietnam, Hector was a wage earner, delivering daily papers to over two hundred customers from whom he had to collect monthly payments. He helped his mother and aunt run a small flower shop three to four nights each week, and still found time to play with his neighborhood friends.

In school, Hector knew shortcuts to math problems and understood scientific theories in textbooks that contained words most of the other students could not pronounce. He was in the best physical condition of his class because of the many miles he rode his bike. But none of these attributes held a candle to Hector's greatest talent. Carter grinned in anticipation as Hector reached inside the bag and removed two manila envelopes.

Hector started his presentation: "Today I have brought . . . today I will present . . . I'm going to show you some sites around our school that most of you will recognize."

Several students giggled. Chuck kicked the desk of a girl laughing in front of him. "Hey! Cool it!" he ordered.

"Charles," Miss Carson requested, "keep your legs to yourself."

Chuck crossed his arms and slouched in his chair. He looked toward Carter and shook his head as Carter's eyes met his. A slow, subtle, sinister grin grew on his face as he turned his attention from Carter back to Hector.

Carter bit his lip, wondering what Chuck was up to.

"Continue, Hector," Miss Carson invited.

"Thank you." Hector unclasped one of the two envelopes and took out a sheet of paper.

"As you can see," Hector continued, "this may appear to you as just another ordinary piece of notebook paper. Upon which you will write another set of notes. Another set of math problems that must be figured. Another essay due tomorrow. But, when I see a blank piece of paper like this, I don't think of these things. I think of pictures, of action, of a tree blowing in the wind. I think of a right fielder diving for a catch near the foul line, a bird landing on a telephone wire, a boy fishing in Eisenhower Lake, an airplane flying overhead, a beautiful Christmas tree with lots of presents underneath."

The giggles had stopped. Hector held the attention of each student. Miss Carson leaned back in her seat. From the same envelope, Hector withdrew a stack of papers.

"This is my little sister flying a kite," he explained as he held up his first sketch. "I thought it was funny, her tiny body being tossed by the wind almost as much as the kite. That's why I drew this one." He placed the picture on the table in front of him.

"Hector," Miss Carson said, "please pass the pictures around, so the class can get a better look." She glanced up from her grade book as Hector passed his first picture. "And class," she continued, "be careful handling them. Remember, Hector has spent a lot of time on these."

"Show us another one, Hector!" shouted Chuck.

"Yeah, Hector. Show us another one!" Allen echoed.

"I drew this one after Chuck, Carter, Allen, and I got home from an Angels' game last summer."

The sketch showed the intensity on a pitcher's face as he delivered a pitch toward home plate. The stands around him were full. The scoreboard on the giant *A*, shown behind him and read

	R	H	E
YANKEES	0	0	1
ANGELS	2	5	0

The pitcher's right arm was at its apex; his surge forward seemed to burst from the page.

"Wow!" exclaimed one boy in the middle of the classroom.

"Awesome!" said another.

"He looks so real!" said one of the girls in the front row. "Who is he?"

"Who is he!" shouted Chuck. "Any dope knows who that is! Just look at his number, stupid!"

"That's enough, Charles," ordered Miss Carson.

"Number thirty? So what? What's that mean?" the girl continued.

Miss Carson sighed, "Hector, can you tell the class who is the subject in your drawing?"

Chuck laughed. "You mean, you don't know either?"

Miss Carson cleared her throat. "Hector, please tell the class who pitched four no-hitters during the last four seasons and who led the American League in strikeouts through most of the 1970s."

Chuck turned in his seat.

"It's Nolan Ryan," answered Hector.

"Did he pitch a no-hitter that day?" asked another student.

"No. I just made the scoreboard up to make the picture more exciting."

"That's cool!" a few students said.

"Hey, Hector," Allen raised his hand, "show us some more."

"Yeah, Hector, show more!" repeated other students.

Hector shared twenty of the twenty-one sketches he had brought with him.

"When do you draw them?" one student asked.

"At home after I finish my paper route, during recess if it's raining, before I go to bed, during social studies class . . . sometimes."

Miss Carson did not seem to mind the confession. She appeared more relaxed than she had since the show-and-tell presentations began.

Carter looked around the class. Most of his classmates had their mouths open and gazed at Hector, smiling, giggling, and listening to his description of each sketch. After briefly describing one, he passed it around for the entire class to see close-up.

"Are there any more questions for Hector before the lunch bell?" Miss Carson asked. A few seconds of silence followed. "Very well," she continued. "Let Hector know how appreciative we are for sharing with us his drawings. His pictures are very entertaining. Thank you, Hector."

"Thank you, Hector," several students responded in the midst of their applause.

"Wait a minute!" Chuck shouted.

Miss Carson slouched. "What is it, Charles?"

"I have another question."

Hector looked at Charles with wide eyes. He shook his head, begging Chuck not to do what he was about to do.

"Go ahead, Charles," invited Miss Carson.

Chuck sat up on his knees. "What's in the other envelope?"

Hector placed both his hands in his back pockets, shifted his weight nervously from one leg to the other, removed his hands from his back pockets and put them into his front pockets.

"What's in the other envelope, Hector?" repeated Chuck with a beguiling smile.

"Yeah, Hector. Show us what's in the other envelope!" another student requested.

A chorus of voices rose in the room. "C'mon Hector. Show us. Let us see."

Hector looked to Miss Carson for assistance, but she seemed as curious as her students to discover what the second envelope contained. Then Hector looked at Carter. He shook his head and whispered, "You don't have to do it. Just ignore them."

Lowering his head, Hector picked up the envelope. "Well . . . it's . . . it was supposed to be . . ." He raised his head and looked at Miss Carson. "It's a gift. A Christmas gift. A card, really. For Miss Carson."

He slowly walked to the rear of the room and handed the envelope to her. As he walked back, Chuck slapped him on the back, "That a boy!"

"Oh, Hector, how sweet!" Miss Carson stood up and proudly held the envelope.

"Open it, Miss Carson," students begged. "We want to see!" She looked to Hector. He nodded his head slowly. Silence filled the classroom as she withdrew the solitary page of paper from the manila envelope. Her eyes widened as they made their initial contact with the drawing. A few seconds later, she blushed. "Hector!" she said in awe. "I don't know what to—"

"Let me see!" Chuck insisted, leaping from his desk and grabbing the paper from his teacher's hands. "Look, everybody! It's Miss Carson! Hector drew Miss Carson!"

Chuck held the paper high for the entire class to see. It was far superior to the twenty other drawings Hector had already shown. He had captured all of Miss Carson's physical traits: her lush lips, her hourglass figure, her stylish short hair, her large eyes, her slightly rounded chin, her medium-sized nose, and her subtle dimples. In the drawing, Miss Carson was kneeling at a student's desk. The student wore an expression of confusion, and Miss Carson was in the midst of assisting the student to understand. The details of the drawing were amazing, and Hector had not only captured his teacher's beauty in the picture, but also accentuated it to a level that made Miss Carson blush as she attempted to regain control of her class.

"Isn't she beautiful?" Chuck resounded as he laughed heartily, holding the picture high.

"Let me see!" another student asked. A few seconds later, he joined in Chuck's laughter. Soon, most of the students left their desks to get a closer glimpse of the drawing. The room filled with laughter. Only Hector, Miss Carson, and Carter did not join the ruckus.

The dismissal bell rang for lunch. The students rushed to their desks, waiting for their teacher's approval to leave.

"You're dismissed," she snapped. "Don't forget, we'll have dessert right after."

Half the class had left and Hector was still standing in front of the classroom, gathering his drawings. He placed them in his backpack at the foot of his desk.

"Don't worry about it, Hector," Allen said as he walked toward the classroom door. "We were just having some fun."

Chuck wrapped his arm around Hector. "Yeah, Hector. You've got to lighten up. We weren't laughing at you, man; we were laughing with you."

Allen grabbed a football from a box in the back of the room and tossed it to Chuck. "That's right," he added.

Chuck held up the football and pushed it into Hector's torso, like a quarterback handing off to his halfback. "Let's play some ball."

"You in, Hector?" Allen asked.

"Sure," he answered quietly.

Carter called out, "Hey, Chuck!" Carter waited for him to stop and turn before he continued. "I didn't see Hector laughing up there. How could he be laughing with you if he wasn't laughing?"

Chuck swept his hand through the air and raced toward the playground.

Miss Carson was still inside the doorway. Carter avoided any eye contact with her, walking slowly into the hallway.

There was an excitement on the campus that, for a moment, lifted Carter's spirit. In less than two hours, the students would be free—free from assignments; free from tension-filled exams; free from playground rivalries; free to stay up late; free to sleep in; and free from toil. It was a contagious cloud, hovering over each group of students. He saw smiles everywhere he turned, envying the anticipation he knew they felt for the arrival of Christmas morning.

Somehow, even the heated air and dry winds didn't bother him as much as they had in the morning. As he made his way onto the playground, he remembered he had forgotten to grab his lunch from the refrigerator before leaving home. He didn't enjoy eating in this weather anyway. Somehow, the smells and sensations caused by the Santa Anas left him with little appetite. Besides, the events at his home were keeping him preoccupied enough to help him disregard his need for sustenance.

He didn't have time for breakfast, but he did eat a couple donuts Miss Carson had brought for the class. He had skipped lunch on other days in order to optimize his recess time. It was a ritual many students had perfected; they would eat only the items in their lunch that were appetizing and easy to finish quickly, and then rush to play. Carter didn't particularly enjoy skipping lunch, but since he had no appetite, he joined his classmates who were already in the midst of their games.

He headed directly to the area designated for two square. Five minutes later he had already lost twice to the reigning champion, Rex Tolan. Since September, only four students had been able to defeat Rex. Although Carter was not one of them, he was determined to accomplish an upset and be the new reigning champion when the students returned from their vacation in January.

While waiting in line to challenge Rex a third time, Carter looked out to the grass field where Hector, Allen, and Chuck were organizing a football game among the more talented athletes. Less talented classmates were not invited to play. If they presumed to be invited, they were chosen last and ignored the entire game. They would not be given the opportunity to touch the ball unless they recovered a fumble or intercepted a pass, in which case, they would no longer be considered less talented athletes. The next day, they would be chosen earlier; otherwise, they would never return.

Carter guessed he had about two minutes before he could challenge Rex once more. As he waited, he watched his classmates in action. In particular, he paid close attention to his group of friends on the grass field. He looked on sadly as they lined up to choose teams. For the last month, he and Chuck had hardly spoken. And since Chuck was their leader, he had lost most contact with the others also. Only when he went over to Hector's house, helping him to fold his newspapers, was he able to spend time with any of them.

His attention was diverted when he noticed a kid he did not recognize wandering the playground. Carter followed his steps as he moved from the swings, to the jungle gym, to the sandbox, and finally, to the grass field. He seemed hesitant and lost. Certainly, he looked out of place. He was not wearing the same type of clothes as the other kids but an oversized flannel shirt that hung just above his knees. Each step he took seemed an adventure, as if he may trip at any second. He wore a pair of sandals and pants that rose at least three inches above his ankles. He wore no socks and had a dark complexion, and slightly sun-bleached hair that was wavy and long.

Carter amused himself, wondering if that's how kids used to dress in the sixties. The small boy walked toward the kids choosing teams for football. The boy approached Chuck and tapped him on the shoulder. Chuck turned but ignored him. Then the boy began asking other students questions.

Whether it was his stature or his clothes, Carter could not tell, but the small boy quickly became the center of attention. It didn't take long for Chuck to intervene.

Carter felt sorry for the kid. He knew Chuck would do anything to get that football game started. Chuck asked him something and the boy shook his head.

Other students began asking the strange kid questions until Carter heard one of them shout, "Carter Mason?"

Chuck turned toward Carter and pointed directly at him.

"Hey, Carter. It's your turn again," Rex announced. Carter was in a daze, wondering why the group on the field had told this strange kid his name and why Chuck was now directing the boy toward him.

Carter shook his head, stepped into his square and received Rex's serve, returning it safely. Carter and Rex volleyed for several seconds before Carter sneaked the ball into the right-rear corner of Rex's box: Carter one, Rex zero. Carter looked behind him, toward the grass field. The boy was walking in his direction. He turned back around and served an ace into Rex's square. Carter was one point away from defeating Rex for the first time in his life. He would not let this little kid get in the way of his glory.

It was Rex's serve. Sweat and nerves began to grip Carter as Rex returned from chasing down Carter's ace. Rex served the ball into Carter's corner and Carter returned it safely, another long volley beginning. It was interrupted by a loud slamming sound against the blacktop pavement behind them. The ball fell in Carter's square untouched as he turned to see what had caused the noise. The other students in line filled him in on what had happened.

Just after Chuck had pointed toward Carter, the small boy in the oversized flannel shirt began walking in Carter's direction. Chuck then ordered Hector Romero to go out for a practice pass.

"A bomb!" Chuck ordered as Hector began to run. Chuck pumped twice, waving with his other arm for Hector to run further.

Chuck threw the football past Hector straight toward the kid. He had thrown with such speed and at such a high arc, that when the ball made contact with the strange boy's head, it knocked him over and caused him to fall face first onto the pavement, producing the loud smash that prevented Carter from defeating Rex.

Principal Gurney raced toward the boy. Mel Tomlinson had already helped the kid to his knees and was gently holding his head still, making sure he had not suffered a neck injury. Gurney and Mel slowly raised the boy to his feet, holding his hands and walking him toward the health office. Hector was right behind them, dragging his feet, shaking his head, and mumbling.

Convinced that defeating Rex was hopeless, Carter ran to catch up to Hector but stopped short when he heard Hector and Principal Gurney talking. He turned around and found a solitary corner against the school building to sit.

About five minutes later, Carter saw Hector reenter the playground and sit alone on a bench in the lunch area.

Carter stood up and slowly walked toward him and stopped a few feet away.

Hector looked up and waved. "Hey, Cart."

Carter wasn't sure what to say or do. Finally, he sat next to Hector.

"Guess you saw all that."

Carter shook his head. "I heard the kid hit the ground. I didn't see it all."

"That's it, Cart. I've had it. I've had enough of Chuck and his games. First there's that picture of Miss Carson; then hitting this kid with the football."

Carter scuffled the ground with his feet, kicking trash under the table. "That's just Chuck. He's always been like that. Look at the way he treats his own brother."

But Carter stopped as Hector raised his head and looked straight into Carter's eyes.

Carter glanced away when he noticed the tears. "I'm sorry, Hector. I didn't—"

Hector's voice quivered. "It's not what he did to me, Carter. It's not what he's done to you. It's how he uses us for his amusement. Look at that kid. He did nothing. Chuck just wanted to get rid of him and have some fun. I knew what he was up to, but I went along with it anyhow."

"He'll be all right," Carter mumbled. "It can't be that bad."

"No more," Hector choked through his tears. "No more."

Pinto Philosophy

The campus seemed desolate. The steps leading up to the dorm's entrance were spotless compared to the usual chaotic spread of beer cans, potato-chip wrappers, and newspapers. She placed her suitcases on the walkway and sat on the lowest step.

As far as Carolyn knew, she was the only coed who hadn't left for the holidays. The other female athletes had left for the airport or begun their drive home. The absence of voices and the hustle and bustle of college life made the otherwise familiar environment foreign.

She liked it. The silence gave her the opportunity to think. Finals, softball practice, studying, writing papers, and study sessions had filled her time over the past four months. She couldn't recall her last moment of stillness.

Initially, Carter and her parents came to mind. The next few days were unpredictable. Carter's letter painted a bleak picture of the home she once loved, the engaging discussions ranging from sports to politics at the dinner table, and the time in the family library before going to bed. She determined during her freshman year that her parents had done a good job raising their children. Compared to most of her peers, she was ready for the rigors of college life, and she was most grateful for the passions they had instilled in her, particularly politics. But since Shannon had passed away, her parents had become strangers.

She had always felt a certain distance from her father and wondered whether things would be any different had she not announced to him that she learned nothing of value at Sunday school. It surprised her then that her wish not to attend was respected. She was only seven years old, yet her parents had deemed her mature enough to make such a decision. On the steps of her dorm, Carolyn shook her head in disbelief, recognizing that what her parents had done was extraordinary.

They were both wonderfully gifted and intelligent. Then how, Carolyn often asked herself, could they not rise above the death of Shannon? Her mother denied the pain of it; her father was burdened by his guilt of how he could have prevented it as well as the guilt of his own accident two decades earlier. Both of their lives had turned direction. No longer were their children a priority. She had left for college, and Shannon had left the world. Without regard for their son, their father began working more hours and their mother began working a forty-hour week plus attending graduate school at night.

But this was none of her business. She had her own life over which to be anxious. College was demanding and required all her strength. There were the joys and rigors of meeting men, romancing men, enchanting men, and dumping men. And finally, there was her insatiable appetite for controversy. Controversy made life interesting, fun, and exciting. Without it, there'd be no progress, no stimulation, and no life. Controversy is what Carolyn lived for. It was why she chose to attend Berkeley.

Often, she found herself becoming the promoter of rallies and talks, giving it all she got to create a concern among the other students. Her topics ranged from the unjust conflict in Vietnam to the fight for civil rights of minorities and women. But her favorite topic was the presidency.

It had been one year since the country had elected a new president, and already the press was attacking him over the weak economy, a weak cabinet, and an overall weak presidency. "I'd choose honesty over political power and savvy in any of our leaders," Carolyn muttered.

She breathed in deeply and pulled her hair behind her ears as she recalled the restraint with which she had written her last paper. Still, it wasn't enough. She grimaced at the memory of her written words.

> Honesty necessitates strength. It is the true indicator of a man's character when he is able to face the unknown when admitting his weaknesses and mistakes. But, if one is to retain a perception of being strong, invincible, and faultless in our society, he must embrace deceit.
>
> It is a sorrowful state of affairs in our nation. An increasing number of those running for office are elected by running campaigns full of dishonest propaganda, propaganda that most Americans know is not true but accept because it is easier to believe what we want to be true than to wrestle with what is reality.

Carolyn shook her head, wishing she could turn back time, rewrite her paper, and turn it in again. "Too subjective," was her professor's only comment. All her life she had prided herself in sticking to the facts. But here she was, acting like a child and filling her papers with her own opinions of how President Carter was doing a decent job, how the country was a mess, and how it was more crucial for the president to be honest than to pretend that he or his cabinet have it all figured out.

"You're a smart one, Mason." Isn't that what Kimico had said an hour earlier? Yes, but what good are brains when one can't control emotions? Carolyn scolded herself, ashamed of her heated feelings that came across so clearly in class discussions and daily conversations. It was no wonder she had driven away so many men in just the year and a half she had been on campus.

But she had scored in the clutch, just like Kimico had said, securing a ride home she previously thought was not possible. She felt her pulse race as she thought of meeting the man who had offered to drive her home.

"Don't blow it, Carolyn," she said softly. "Stay calm. Be yourself. Control your opinionated, oversized mouth."

Carolyn reclined further on the steps, attempting to relieve the apprehension. Over the last two months, she had begun to feel a prolonged loneliness, something she had never before felt.

She was frightened and not sure how long the feeling would last. As active as she was in campus politics and as successful as she was in class and the softball field, she felt ostracized. She thought how this came about. Being so popular throughout high school and having a successful freshman college year did secure a truckload of admirers and acquaintances. Then why did she feel like such an outsider? Had her attitude changed? Was she an elitist as some of her teammates accused?

"You're too hard on yourself," Kimico often scolded. "You've got to lighten up."

Good old Kimico. Always seemed to say what was on her mind. If you did something great, she'd shower you with praise. But, if you did something of which she didn't approve, she'd let you know in that special way of hers.

There were few things over which Carolyn and Kimico disagreed, although Carolyn would never let her know that. It was her sexual lifestyle that offended Kimico most. Though she knew that sleeping with any man she found attractive was foolish, Carolyn found respite and release from the tensions in her life whenever she entered the arena of pleasure. Kimico had insisted that Carolyn never again sleep with a man in their room, and although this was inconvenient at first, Carolyn grew to appreciate the benefits it produced. The arrangements were more difficult to make and guarded Carolyn from giving in as frequently to her passions. But letting Kimico know this was not in Carolyn's plans. It would offer her too much encouragement to make other suggestions that might limit Carolyn's freedoms.

The one topic they discussed most was family. Kimico's mother and father raised their children with a strong work ethic and encouraged their ten children to dream. Kimico was in the middle somewhere, with two brothers in medical school, another brother teaching, and a sister serving as a deputy district attorney in Montgomery. Carolyn smiled, recalling Kimico's descriptions of her family and imagining the energy and excitement at their gatherings.

But there was nothing wonderful about Carolyn's family. Each conversation she had with Kimico left her feeling depressed and sad. She would have to leave the room, go for a walk, and find a solitary place to think—to think of what she could do to make things better and what she could have done differently.

If she could change anything, it would be to take back the words she spoke to Shannon the night before the accident. How many times had she replayed that evening and the exchange of words in her mind? Shannon was right when she accused her of jealousy. Often, she thought of Kevin. He was far more interesting and fun and thoughtful than any man she had met since.

Why did I break up with him? Carolyn thought as she remained seated on the steps in front of her dorm. *And why did I let my jealousy come between me and Shannon? If I had not broken it off, they would have never spent time together. Shannon would not have been in that car with him. And I would not have gone home with him in that state. We'd both be alive. We'd still be sisters.*

Perhaps this was the type of guilt her father endured. She would not fall prey to his way of thinking, his way of life. The past must be left behind, and she must go on living, learning from the past without being obsessed with it. But here she was, reliving it, immersed in guilt, and feeling sorrow for herself. "Hypocrite!" she sneered.

She stood up, hoping to leave behind her depressed mood, and looked down the drive leading to her dorm; five more minutes until her ride was due to arrive. *Who knows?* Carolyn mused. *Perhaps he may turn out to be more than just a ride home.*

A rumbling of an engine arose in the distance. Carolyn watched a white Ford Pinto approach. As it drew closer, she noticed how worn the car was: dents on the front bumpers, a smashed right headlight, a missing hubcap, and a broken side window on the left-rear passenger side. She closed her eyes and quickly opened them, hoping either that the car was not the one in which she would be riding home or that she had only imagined the car's defects.

The Pinto stopped in front of the steps. Carolyn considered whether she should deny who she was if the driver were to ask. For the moment, she walked toward her luggage. The driver attempted to open his door but could not. He maneuvered himself over the gears and emerged from the passenger-side door. The first quality of the man that Carolyn noticed was the length of his legs. As he rose from his crouched position in the car, he uncoiled. Carolyn saw his shoes were worn and his pants clean but outdated. She closed her eyes, regretting that she had agreed to ride home with him.

A soft breeze rushed past from behind as again she was aware of the empty campus and the loneliness she felt. She opened her eyes as the man straightened his back, his torso and head rising to heights equaled by the members of Berkeley's basketball team. He was thin, but as he closed the door and began to walk toward her, his broad chest and large arms created a rush of blood from her heart.

Carolyn abruptly forgot about the possibility of hiding her identity. She blushed when she first noticed the man's facial features. His skin was dark. He had a strong jaw and East Indian features. His hair was straight and glossy black. He had large, rounded eyes and a perfect nose. He walked with a royal gate. Carolyn stood statue-like as she attempted to catch her breath.

"Carolyn Mason?" the stranger asked, matching the voice she had heard over the phone earlier that morning.

"Yes. That's me." Carolyn's voice slightly cracked. *Stop that, you idiot!* She told herself. *Don't act like a child!*

She felt like she was back in junior high, a flood of emotions racing though her mind, causing strange sensations throughout her body. She forced herself to gain control. "You must be my ride home. I can't tell you how grateful I am for your willingness to have me tag along. Are you sure it's not an inconvenience?"

"I'm at *yoor* service, Miss Mason."

"Please, call me Carolyn."

"I'm at *yoor* service, Miss Carolyn."

"Just Carolyn."

"*Veery* good. I'm at *yoor* service, Carolyn."

He stood still, waiting beside her.

Carolyn looked up, noticing his dark-brown eyes. She gulped. "I thought I'd come down. You know, save us time and all. Save you a trip up all those stairs."

"*Theese* are *yoor* bags?" He moved in between the luggage and Carolyn.

As he approached the suitcases, Carolyn moved back, quickly regretting that she had. He bent over and lifted them up. *"Ees thees eet,* Carolyn?"

"That's it." Underneath his shirt, Carolyn could make out the highly defined outline of muscles as he raised her luggage.

"Then *yoo* are a light traveler."

"You mean for a female?"

"I *meen* for a human *been*. I have friends, male friends, who carry much more luggage than many of my female acquaintances. It *ees* not a matter of gender, Carolyn, I believe *et ees* a matter of *securitee*."

"Security?" Carolyn asked.

"The more garments one packs, the less likely *hee* or *shee* will meet weather that *ees* not suitable to one of the stored garments."

"I see."

He placed the luggage in the back of the car. "Shall we go, then?"

Carolyn sat in the passenger seat as her chauffeur closed the hatchback. She reached for the door and began to close it when she realized he was standing over her. She looked up with surprise.

"I'm afraid *yoo* will have to remove *yourself*," he said.

Oh great! Carolyn thought, *I must have offended him somehow*. She rose quietly.

"Thank you," he announced as he crunched his lanky body back into the Pinto's interior, maneuvered back over the gears and into the driver's side.

Carolyn sighed with relief. "Sorry. I forgot."

Although the car had a noticeably worn exterior, the interior was decent. It was as though somebody had taken great pains to make it clean and comfortable. There was no dust on the dashboard, no grime on the windows, and no dirt on the carpet. A fresh smell permeated the car. Carolyn felt peace. She leaned back.

Somewhere between San Leandro and Livermore on Interstate 580, Carolyn realized she still did not know her driver's name. The thought of her parents, discovering that she was driving home with a foreign man whose name she did not know, was amusing. She cleared her throat, unsure as to the best way of asking the question.

"Oh my!" he exclaimed. "My name! I have not yet introduced myself. *Pleese*, forgive *mee*." He turned to face Carolyn. "My name is Kamal. Kamal Patel," he announced with his right hand extended.

Carolyn shook it. "Patel? You must be from the Punjab?"

"No, no, I am not. But I do have family there. You have been to India?"

"No. In high school, I had a friend named Patel. When we studied India, she told the class her family has many relatives there."

"*Yees, yees*. My family does originate from the Punjab, but we moved long ago."

Kamal steered the Pinto into the right-hand lane of Interstate 580 in order to enter onto Interstate 5. He traveled at sixty miles per hour. "And *yoor* family? From where *doo* they originate?"

"Both my parents were raised in California, the Los Angeles area. Funny thing is, they didn't meet until they were in college back East."

"That *ees* peculiar."

"They didn't even go to the same school. Mom went to Radcliffe, and Dad to Boston University."

"Then how did they meet?"

Carolyn paused and then chuckled. "My parents did not tell us much about it."

"Maybe they wanted to tell *yoo*, but *yoo* never asked?"

Carolyn smiled and looked to Kamal. “No, I asked. Several times. Then I learned the lesson.”

“The lesson?”

“They’d give me some general answer like, ‘We met in Boston,’ or ‘back East.’ When I asked them to be more specific, my mother would turn away and my father would say, ‘Another time, Dear.’ If I was persistent, his temper would flare. None of us liked Dad’s temper.”

“So *yoo* did not discover?”

“Oh, I found out.”

Kamal looked at Carolyn. She saw he did not understand.

“My parents would never tell me; that much I knew for certain. Neither of my parents have any brothers or sisters, so I had no uncles or aunts to ask. Mom’s mother was our only grandparent still living, and I’m not sure she knew the details. But I figured that sooner or later I’d run into someone from their past, someone who could tell me.”

“And did you?”

“I met him a couple years ago in New Hampshire,” she answered. “He knew my father. I guess he was a sort of mentor. You see, the man I met is a pastor of a church up there and my father’s very religious. Anyway, he narrated to me the sequence of events that led to my father and mother falling in love. I don’t want to bore you, so to make a long story short: She fell in love with my father the first moment she saw him, at a Harvard-BU track meet in which Dad won his mile race by more than ten seconds. She introduced herself after the meet, and they were carrying on a good conversation until my father’s girlfriend surprised them from behind with displays of affection.

“My mother must have felt immensely dejected at that point, for just moments earlier this girl had won her third event of the day. To make matters worse, she was beautiful. I saw a picture of her at the man’s house; she was stunning! Poor Mom!

“Anyhow, things didn’t work out between my father and this other woman. Dad was so depressed that he gave up running and focused on his studies. He tried to get away from the BU campus as much as he could, so he would study at Harvard's library. That's when he saw Mom again.

"One day as he had just finished studying, he was walking past the women's softball game against Dartmouth. There was Mom, on third base. He stayed to watch the completion of the game but was too timid to approach her. He didn't have to; Mom had seen him sitting in the stands by himself and made it a point to talk with him after the game. The rest is history."

Kamal looked at Carolyn. "I *doo* not understand."

"What do you mean?"

"*Theese. Theese ees* a marvelous story! Why would *yoor* parents not want *yoo* to know about it?"

Carolyn looked away and shrugged. "Maybe they don't want us to think it's that easy."

They entered the Grapevine in the midst of Carolyn's narration. Already two hours had expired. Carolyn wondered if she had talked too much. Had she asked enough questions? Did he think highly of her?

She wanted to look at Kamal, without his noticing. During their conversations, she had tried to steal glances of his profile, but doing so was too distracting, causing her to lose her train of thought. She wanted time to study his features and determine whether he really was as handsome as the last time she had glanced over at him.

She hadn't been this nervous around a man since her first date with Kevin. *This is ridiculous*, Carolyn thought. *I've got to make a move.*

"I must warn you," she alerted.

Kamal looked over. "*Yees*?"

"Sleeping in cars is genetic. There's no Mason worse than me, except maybe my brother. We were always falling asleep in the backseat on vacations. So, unless you mind driving the next one to two hundred miles in silence, I recommend we find another topic to discuss."

"All right," he said. "You mentioned your brother. How many siblings do you—?"

Carolyn interrupted. “Not family, please. It’s just that I’m going to be home for the next eight days; I don’t need reminding.”

“All right. Then school?”

“Boring. The classes, I mean. The activity on campus—that’s where the real excitement is. Sometimes I think the students get more done than the professors. And we’re the ones paying them.”

“*Yoo doo* not find your classes interesting?” he asked.

Carolyn shook her head. It was her first chance to look at him, to really look, to study. He was concentrating on changing lanes, trying to maneuver past a convoy of commercial trucks. His sideburns were neatly cut; his face smoothly shaven; his eyebrows thick but fine. His eyes, oh, his eyes!

He passed the convoy and steered back into the slow lane.

She had a monopoly, a seven-, maybe eight-hour window of ownership and opportunity. She chased the tension out through the ends of her fingertips, her toes, the top of her head, just as she did before each of her games.

Kamal turned, Carolyn’s eyes still studying his. If she hadn’t cleansed herself of the anxiety, the pressure, she probably would have shifted her eyes elsewhere, but she was a gamer; she kept them focused on Kamal, and he kept them focused on her.

“So the classes, you find them boring?” Kamal resumed.

She placed her hand on his right knee and then held it palm up. “What are they teaching us, Kamal? In history and English, we’re learning things that I knew in high school. In my math class, they teach us theories that most will not use again. I’m not saying the classes are useless; I just haven’t found something that really intrigues me.”

“Nothing?”

“Well, I do find the most relevant classes to be the physical sciences. Therein lies the solution to many of our problems.”

“Then *yoo* are a chemistry major?”

“No.”

“Physics?”

“No.”

"Biology?"

"No. I am not majoring in any of the sciences."

"Then what?"

"I haven't declared. I'm only a sophomore. Sure the sciences have value, but look at our world, Kamal. I mean—"

Carolyn paused, conscious of where she was headed—into another of her speeches. She'd do her best to cut it short. After all, the more she looked at Kamal, the less talking she wanted to do.

"You know," she continued, "the poverty, the crime, the corruption in governments all over the world. Then there's the child abuse, rape, discrimination, and the remnants of what our national leaders conveniently called a conflict instead of a war. I'm overwhelmed. How do I decide on one major? I want to help out with all these problems, but where do I start?"

"That *ees* a good question. But you must remember, you are not alone; we have one another."

Carolyn liked how that sounded—"We have one another." She sat silent a few moments considering whether he meant anything beyond what surely he intended.

She shook her head. "What about you? You look older. I mean, more mature than an ordinary undergrad."

"Perhaps."

"Then you are a graduate student?"

"Of sorts."

"Your field? What are you studying?"

"Philosophy."

"That was your major?"

"It was."

Right then, she felt something she had not experienced since arriving at Berkeley. There had been moments when her passion to be touched by a man was so great that she took the initiative by wrapping her arms around his neck, hoping he knew what to do next. But never had she forced herself to make no advance, take no initiative. Kamal had not responded to her hand on his knee. She was still trying to calculate what that meant. But something more pressing was grasping for her attention. Kamal was a philosopher, or at least one in training. She yearned more to hear his ideas than to find out how he might respond to her ivory arms.

"How did you decide on Philosophy?" she asked.

"*Eet* was not *soo* much a decision, Carolyn, as *eet* was a direction."

Carolyn shook her head. "I don't understand."

"My whole life, since I was child in India, I remember asking many questions: '*Why* do so many people beg, Mama?' '*Why* does the earth shake so violently?' 'If there are so many hungry people in our land, *why* do we not eat the cows like those in the north? Like Papa's family?' 'Why does Papa's family not like your family? *Ees* it because you are Hindu and they study Zoroaster? And if so, why should that matter? You and Papa rose above that.'

"And there were the deeper questions: '*Why* am I here?' '*Why* is there no hope?'

"*Yoo* must understand, Carolyn, I have searched my whole life. I chose philosophy because it was the logical field for me to study."

Carolyn wondered whether there was something, other than softball, in which she excelled at naturally. Something like Kamal's questions, which made sense for her to pursue.

"What makes it so logical?" she asked.

"The study of philosophy itself, or my decision?"

"Your decision."

"Like you said before, Carolyn, there are many problems in our society and in our world. How can I help others with their problems when I am uncertain of the solution myself? I had to discover the solution."

"*The* solution? Or *a* solution?"

"*The* solution," Kamal repeated.

Carolyn shook her head. "I don't understand."

"The solution to the question, why am I here? *Eet's* the fundamental question of life. We all ask *eet* one time or another, in one form or another."

Carolyn pushed herself up in the car seat and looked directly at Kamal. "You mean, what is the meaning of life?"

"Precisely."

Carolyn kept her eyes fixed on Kamal, his head grazing the bottom of the car's ceiling. She was safely away from her passions. She eyed him cautiously before asking her next question. "And you? You know this meaning?"

"I do."

Carolyn chuckled in disbelief, shaking her head. "A philosophy major! No, wait, a philosophy graduate who admits that life actually has a meaning. That is what you're saying?"

"*Eet* is."

Carolyn brushed her thick hair behind her ears. Her skepticism mingled with intrigue, and she asked with a wry smile, "Then tell me, Dr. Patel, what is the meaning of life?"

Kamal turned, looking at Carolyn. "Now?"

His eyes fed the desire she held for him. Her smile grew, and a moment later, she nodded.

"But, I am hungry. I could better answer your question with full stomach."

Carolyn had not eaten all day. She looked at her watch. It was already eleven thirty. Suddenly, she felt hunger. "It's past breakfast."

"Then we will eat the lunch," Kamal announced. "Look! Denny's is five miles ahead in Kettleman City." He pointed to a billboard advertisement. "Will that be satisfactory?"

Carolyn's warm sensation grew. This was going to be a magical ride home. She hoped it would never end. "That will be fine," she answered, imagining what life might be like with such a man.

Window Shopping

She settled in the classics aisle. The aroma of unturned pages with fresh print and binding helped relieve tensions created at work, and school, and home. Going to the library did not help. It was too stuffy, and as much as they might attempt to minimize it, it was too noisy. Frederick's Bookstore was quaint, quiet, and contained the widest variety of quality literary works from the past and present.

It was five minutes past noon. She had entered the store around ten thirty. Her first stop was the wall on the left-hand side of the store. She walked straight to the shelves containing do-it-yourself manuals, pulled one out, and tucked it underneath her left arm. Next, she made her way over to the sports section where she spent less than one minute to find a suitable biography. Within the next three minutes she went from the biography selections at the back of the store to the new fiction releases near the front and then to the romance aisles and then to history. At each location she withdrew one or two books. By the end of her twenty-minute spree, both hands were full of the family's Christmas presents. She sighed, placed the stack of books in an empty cart, and pulled it behind her until she came to the two aisles of classic literature.

Initially, she flipped through a couple Balzac novels, but she was not in the mood to read Balzac. Then she glanced over some of Melville's work; *too mundane*, she thought. Then it was Joyce—*too esoteric*; Dickens—*too depressing*; Steinbeck—*too real*; the Russians—*too bloody*. It seemed the spark which each of the works had previously possessed was gone. She spent at least ten minutes trying to absorb herself within each story, but none could hold her attention. Not one could keep her from thinking about her mother, her son, and her dead daughter. Not one could assist in relieving the anxiety produced by her mother's words hours earlier.

It took one hour to drive the five miles from the rest home to the mall. The traffic was not heavy, nor had she made any other stops at stores. Her first thought was of Carter. She would drive to the school and intervene, or intercept, or somehow prevent his encounter.

She upbraided herself for feeling anxious about what she had previously believed to be a silly myth, a family legend. She drove past the school, knowing that if she attempted to do anything, she'd appear psychotic, crazy, and paranoid.

After driving past the school, she considered returning home, but she still had most of her shopping yet to do. Then she noticed a car in her rearview mirror and realized she had seen that same car behind her minutes earlier, on the other side of town.

She turned left. So did the car behind her.

She turned right. So did the other car.

A couple minutes later, she turned left; the car behind her went straight. At first, she was relieved. Her hands moist with perspiration, she lowered her head in shame.

As a child, it was fine to believe such stories about her family and about the characters of the crèche coming to assist in difficult times. But she was an adult, a wife, and a mother. She was a graduate of Radcliffe College, currently working on her master's degree. How could a woman of her intelligence react as she? And there were more pressing matters over which she should be investing her time: how to patch up her relationship with Carter, how to make this Christmas better than last year, and what to make for dinner.

She would not allow it to happen again. She would not allow herself to believe that she had anything to fear.

She turned the car and drove toward the mall.

Forty minutes later, during which three more cars in her rearview mirror persuaded her to alter course, she finally arrived at the mall.

Now, in the midst of the aisles in Frederick's Bookstore, she was growing frustrated, unable to lose herself in the pages of the books she loved. She raised her eyes in desperation and sighed. She'd give it one more try.

As her eyes returned to the book, she noticed a man in the biography section diagonally across from the classics. He was handsome. He looked familiar. Their eyes met. She looked away.

Slamming the book shut, she felt powerless to escape from the paranoia that anybody she may meet could be one of them.

The man walked to the reference aisle directly across from her. He looked at her, stared at her. He was too close. She turned her back to face the rear wall. The sweat intensified. Her body shook.

"Katherine," she heard a voice call, "Katherine Mason."

She turned toward the voice. It was Betty Thompson, a fellow PTA mother. "Betty."

"Those all yours?" Betty asked, pointing at the cart Katherine had filled with her family's Christmas presents.

"Yes," she answered, keeping watch of the man who had been staring her down.

A little girl walked up to him, holding a book. She held it high, as if to hand it to the man. He did not notice her.

"His daughter," Katherine said softly, releasing a long sigh.

"Katherine?" Betty asked. "Is everything all right?"

Katherine smiled, again chiding herself, but relieved at the sight of the child who had now gotten the man's attention.

"Yes, Betty. I'm sorry. My mind is full of—"

"No need to explain, Katherine," Betty interrupted, "Five kids, three brothers, seven nieces and nephews, in-laws, my husband. I've barely started. I'm going nuts, Kate. I don't know how I'll finish all this stuff by tomorrow. The turkey, pies, the cleaning, going to church tomorrow night and then again on Sunday morning. Wouldn't you know it, Christmas on a Sunday! I still have to wrap the presents too! The list goes on and on and on."

Usually, Katherine would have been irritated at Betty's subtle arrogance and disregard for the trouble at the Mason home, but today, with all that was running wild through her mind, she was numb to Betty's words.

"You here alone?" she asked Betty, surprised that with such a large family, not one of them would be with her.

"Sally's in the back, looking at some children's books."

"Sally?" Katherine asked, her eyes widening.

"She's my youngest. Five years old."

Katherine turned, looking for children at the rear of the store. There were none.

"What's wrong, Katherine?" Betty asked.

"Your daughter? Sally? Is that her?" Katherine pointed at the little girl talking with the man. The man was now kneeling, eye level with the girl, turning the pages of a book and reading to her, his hand resting on her shoulder.

Betty raced toward the two of them. "Sally," she shouted.

Sally looked back and waved, inviting her mother to join them.

Katherine pushed her cart, following Betty.

"Mama," Sally announced loudly, "listen to this story. It's so funny."

"Come here, Sally," Betty ordered. "What have we told you about talking with strangers?"

Katherine shut her eyes. Again, her fears awakened.

"But, Mama, he offered—"

Betty pulled her daughter behind her and approached the man. He was smiling. His smile was peculiar and beguiling, almost obscene.

"Ma'am?" he asked.

"You lay your hand on my daughter again, I'll call security."

The man shrugged and walked out of the store, the smile not leaving his face.

Betty turned to face Katherine, holding Sally's arm tightly. The look on her face was terror, guilt, and relief.

Katherine placed her hand on Betty's shoulder and pushed the cart toward the cash registers. One thing was certain, whoever that man may have been, he certainly could not have been "one of them." His expression told of his unwholesome intentions. Although Katherine was relieved of her fear, she could see the turmoil Betty was enduring. "Let's get a bite to eat."

Betty was shaking, looking behind, and holding Sally's hand tightly.

Katherine purchased the books in the cart and walked toward the east end of the mall with Betty and her daughter. She looked down at Sally. The innocence of not knowing why it may be so dangerous to talk with a stranger wouldn't cross her young mind. She was still smiling, even after her mother's continual reproach after leaving the store.

It was the excitement of the season. Christmas was only two days away. Katherine guessed this to be the source of joy she saw in Sally's eyes and smile, her skip, her humming. Forty years ago, that had been her: holding her mother's hand, coming home from the Christmas Eve service in Baltimore, coming home to a man full of rage and alcohol. For most children, it takes a few years to erase the smile now on Sally's face; for Katherine, it took a few minutes.

Still, the innocent smile radiating from Sally gave Katherine a glimpse of what it was like to be young and full of hope. She had forgotten how that felt, and yearned for more than a glimpse.

"Mommy! Mommy!" Sally shouted. "Toys! Toys! Can we go in? Please! Please!"

Betty looked to Katherine as her daughter tugged her arm. "You don't mind?" Betty asked.

"I'll go to Sears," Katherine said. "I'll meet you here in ten minutes."

"Better make it fifteen," Betty warned as she gave in to her daughter's tug.

Katherine walked toward Sears but, just before entering, waved her hand through the air and sat down on a planter in the center of the mall. No more shopping was necessary. She took her Christmas list from her purse and crossed off the items purchased in the bookstore.

She picked up her bag and walked down the corridor. Next to reading, this was once her greatest joy—window after window: jewelry store, shoe shop, records, book store, men's clothing, women's clothing, novelty, toys, food, candy, and appliances. She once found respite when visiting the mall: stopping in front of each store window and tasting within her mind the feelings associated with owning the object behind the glass. Would she want it? Could she buy it? Should she buy it? How much? What would Douglas think? And if the object was undesirable in her opinion, the question always was, What would possess someone to purchase such a thing?

It was a game she used to play with her daughters, asking the questions, imagining the joy of owning and purchasing each item, as they raced through the mall, hand in hand, smiling and giggling and enjoying life. As she passed the toy store in which Betty and Sally had entered, she observed mothers with their daughters. The sights and sounds were haunting, beckoning her to recall the images of walking hand in hand with Shannon ten years earlier and of her tiny eight-year-old daughter pointing excitedly toward a teddy bear, a doll, or a toy nutcracker. As she grew older the excitement was over a cute dress or pretty shoes.

Ten minutes passed since Betty and Sally entered the toy store. Katherine continued her walk. The glass of the store windows seemed especially clear; the colors inside bright and cheerful. Again, the wonder of Christmas, as a child, passed through her memory. She thought of that Christmas in Virginia, looking out the window, snow falling, the crèche placed on the table in front of the window.

She stopped in front of the jewelry shop in which she and Doug had arranged for the repair and plating of the cradle that Shannon had broken ten years earlier. There was one gold piece on display that resembled her family's heirloom. She studied it, making sure it was not the one Carter had misplaced or stolen. It was not.

She was disappointed, hoping for concrete evidence to dispel the lunacy racing through her mind.

"I could buy this one," Katherine said to herself. "We could surprise Carter, just like we did Shannon. Make things right, or at least better, and let him know we still love him. I still love him."

For the third time in just a few minutes, that Christmas joy struck Katherine. This time it struck with such ferocity that she was determined—determined to buy the gold cradle, give it to her son, and once again be a good mother.

She entered the store.

"Kate!" a voice shouted from behind. It was Betty. "Kate!"

Katherine rushed toward her. "What is it, Betty? What's wrong? Where's Sally?"

"I don't know. She's gone! I don't know where she is! I looked all through the store. I asked all the employees. She's not there!"

A Gentleman's Agreement

The small boy in the oversized flannel shirt was taken to rest in La Vista Elementary School's health office. There he fell asleep.

The dismissal bell woke him amid loud shouts echoing the halls of the campus, children racing down the corridors, backpacks in one hand, crafts and holiday treats in the other.

He sat up and examined the activity. The expressions of joy and excitement on their faces mirrored the happiness within him. He jumped up and down, smiling and waving his hands at the other children as they passed the window.

He had never been in a room like this. All around him were strange objects he'd never seen. He studied the eye chart, placing his finger on each letter and running it across the surface of the paper. He opened a drawer and took out a wiggly object with two ends and a bright shiny metal circle at the point where the two ends met. He placed it back in the drawer, afraid that his handling it may get him in worse trouble than he had already gotten himself. There were extra-large wooden sticks, a tiny glass instrument with shiny metal at one end, and a box with thin paper coming out the top of it. The objects were enticing, but he restrained himself from touching any of them for too long.

He noticed a faint noise echo through the room, like water dropping from a tall tree. He turned toward a washbasin and saw a water droplet fall from a long silver arm coming out of the wall. He walked toward it and scratched his head. He pulled a chair over, climbed on top, and reached for the knobs. It took thirty seconds for him to discover how to handle the knobs. The rapid issue of water from the faucet frightened him at first, but soon he started playing with the water and splashing it throughout the office.

The door opened and the man who had escorted him to the office entered with another boy. "Mr. Gurney," he gulped. He was frightened at first and reached toward the knob to shut off the water. He twisted it in the wrong direction, increasing the water's rapid flow. Kicking with his legs and running in place on top of the chair, he panicked. The speed at which the water came out of the silver arm continued to increase. His fidgeting grew more rapid until Gurney turned the knobs, stopping the flow of water.

Gurney chuckled. "I'll say this, Carter, he sure acts like a Mason."

The boy was not sure of Gurney's intentions. He eyed the man nervously as he opened a cabinet, took out a roll of paper towels, and began cleaning up the mess.

"Carter," Gurney beckoned for assistance.

"Here, let me—" the boy offered.

"No, no, no. Take a couple of these. Dry yourself off."

The boy took the towels from Principal Gurney, jumped off the chair, and began patting his arms with the towels.

"Carter tells me you're cousins."

He was confused. "Cousins?" he asked.

"Yes, from back East," Gurney asked as he continued wiping water from the counter.

The boy remained silent, looked at the other boy in the room, and realized what was happening. Somehow he had found the boy he had been looking for earlier on the playground. He wasn't sure how, but sure enough, there he was, standing behind the man cleaning the counter. The man had addressed the other boy as Carter; that must mean it was him.

The boy smiled. "Yes. The East. At least I think. Let's see, there's that, then the ocean . . . Yes, I'm from East."

Principal Gurney sighed as he finished cleaning the counter. "So, you're from the East Coast. Came to visit the Masons for the holidays? That's nice."

"Yes, sir," the boy responded.

"I'm Principal Gurney. And you are?"

"My name is David, sir."

"Well, David, I hope your head is all right. You have a nasty bump there."

"I'll ice it as soon as we get home." Carter insisted. "Let's go, David. My mom's waiting for us."

"Just a minute, Carter." Gurney held out his arm as Carter walked toward the door. "I need to talk with you two."

Carter lowered his eyes.

Turning toward David, Gurney asked him to take a seat in one of the three chairs against the office wall. He motioned Carter to do the same.

"Now, normally I would ask both of you a lot of questions to discover what happened out on the playground this afternoon. And normally, I would also be asking Carter why he invited his cousin to come onto the school campus during the middle of the day. But, in light of the time of season and the time of day, I will allow an exception." Gurney winked at Carter as he said it. "In return I want you both to promise me that you will have a wonderful Christmas."

The boy was confused, unsure how to respond. He looked at Carter.

"Is it a deal?" Gurney continued.

Carter shrugged his shoulders.

"Carter?" Gurney asked.

Carter stood up, extended his right hand, and shook hands with Gurney. "Sure."

Then Gurney turned to face David. Gurney extended his right arm. David looked behind at Carter who motioned, instructing David to extend his right arm. David smiled, turned, and reached for Gurney's hand.

Gurney patted him on the back. He led the boys out of the health office, around the secretary's desks, and to the front door.

"Merry Christmas, Carter!" an elderly lady said.

"Merry Christmas, Mrs. Jenkins," Carter said softly.

"Who is your little friend?" the elderly lady asked.

"His name's David. He's visiting from back East."

"Oh?"

"I've got to go, Mrs. Jenkins. I hope you have a wonderful holiday. Bye."

"Why thank you, Carter. What a nice thing to say."

David saw how Carter's comments were greeted by the elderly lady. "Merry Christmas," he echoed.

As they walked away, Gurney offered one last encouragement, "Oh, Carter. You've kept your end of the bargain. Santa knows!"

"Thanks," Carter muttered, "but he stopped visiting our house two years ago."

Family Reunion

"Who's that?" David asked.

Carter looked down at David as they stepped onto the playground's blacktop area. "Mr. Gurney? He's the principal."

"The principal, and Santa?"

Carter studied David for a few seconds. "Why were you looking for me?"

"I was sent to look for you," David answered.

"By my mother?"

"I don't know your mother."

"But you know me?" Carter asked. "How do you know me?"

"Chuck showed me who you are."

Carter stopped walking. The two of them were on the grass field. Several students lingered on the campus, also making their way home. "You know Chuck?"

"I met him today!" David explained.

"You sound exited about that."

"Sure!"

"He's the one who hit you on the head."

"Oh no. It was that ball."

"He threw the ball!" Carter realized that this fact was not significant to David. "He meant to hit you!"

Still David did not seem to mind.

"Doesn't that make you mad?"

"He showed me who you were. If he hadn't hit me with the ball, maybe we would have never met."

Carter shook his head as he began slowly walking across the field. "So your name's David?"

The boy smiled.

"Do you have a last name?"

"You mean like Mason?"

"Your last name's not Mason. You're not my cousin. I made all that up."

"Why?"

"Why? Why what? Why aren't you my cousin? I suppose because neither of my parents have any brothers or sisters. I can't have a cousin. It's impossible!"

"Why did you make it up?"

Carter looked down at David, narrowing his eyes.

As he thought of what to do with this kid, how to get rid of him, they exited the large grass field of the school onto the sidewalk leading to Carter's home.

"Hey, Carter! Who's your new friend?" Chuck DeSanto shouted. Standing with him were Allen and Hector.

Chuck walked up to David and rubbed the back of David's head. "How's the noggin, little fellah?"

David grimaced as Chuck rubbed harder.

"Stop it, Chuck." Carter ordered.

"Who's gonna make me?"

"He's done nothing to you. Leave him alone." Carter said calmly. He wrapped his arm around David, turning him toward his home.

Chuck stopped rubbing David's head and wrapped his arms around both Carter and David. After a short struggle, Carter almost broke free, Chuck still clutching the collar of Carter's shirt. Carter quickly turned, releasing Chuck's grip. He felt Chuck hit his chest, making one last effort to grab hold of him.

Losing total control of Carter, Chuck wrapped both his arms around David's waist, and raised him on his shoulders. "Maybe I'll throw him into the Redford's backyard," he announced, "Theodore will take care of him!"

Carter's eyes widened. Allen laughed. Hector ran toward Chuck.

But Chuck had already raised David to the top of the brick wall separating the Redford's backyard from the sidewalk. Chuck began whistling. "Here, Theodore," he beckoned.

Soon a deep barking emerged. Allen stopped laughing as Chuck gently leaned David over the edge. The pit bull's bark grew louder.

"I don't believe this!" Carter exclaimed, "the kid's gonna die down there!"

Allen and Hector rushed to the base of the wall where Chuck was barely holding on to David.

Hector pleaded, "Chuck! Look at the kid; he's not half your size. Give him a break!"

"Get Carter over here to defend him. Hey, Carter! Come save your little friend!"

It was surreal. The whole day seemed like a dream, one bad omen after another. Carter reached into his shirt pocket. Just feeling the edges of those sixteen baseball cards, protected by the thin plastic sandwich bag, helped him make it through the day. He had a purpose, a task to accomplish, that offered some hope for normality back at home.

When Hector was humiliated in the classroom that morning, he reached inside, felt the cards, and sighed. After each loss to Rex, as he waited in line, he tapped his pocket, verifying that they were still there. When he saw Hector crying, he placed his hand over the pocket and felt the bulge the cards created. When Gurney asked him to come to the office for the small boy who had been hit, Carter lowered his head and took solace when he saw the cards in his pocket.

Now, as he reached inside, he felt nothing and saw nothing; the pocket was empty. Several feet away, at the base of the Redford's wall, an empty sandwich back was tossed by the weakening Santa Ana's. Carter turned toward the grass field, hoping to spot a trail of cards that somehow fell from his shirt. Chuck's laughter grew more hysterical.

Carter examined his pocket for a hole. There was none.

"Carter," he heard Chuck call, "you looking for these?"

Carter turned.

Stunned, Carter stared, his eyes wide and reddening. The cards were not only in Chuck's hand, but also no longer in a protective sandwich bag.

How? Before he could process the tactics Chuck had used to get Shannon's sixteen baseball cards, Carter raced into the street and onto the sidewalk, realizing that the hand in which Chuck was now displaying the cards had seconds earlier been all that kept David from falling off the edge of the wall.

"Careful, Chuck," Allen screamed.

"I'm only having some fun, Al. Lighten up! Where's that Stanowitz humor?"

"The kid, Chuck," Allen continued, "the kid."

"Oh, stink," Chuck turned, placing the cards in his left hand, rolled his torso onto the top edge of the wall, and reached down.

Carter leaped and climbed the wall, hoping to help David. But he was too far away. Only Chuck could help.

David had grabbed hold of a decorative ledge once he toppled over the wall. Chuck reached down with his right arm and grabbed hold of David's left hand. Carter eyed the cards in Chuck's left hand, recognizing this was his chance to get the cards back without a struggle. But any attempt to do so might jeopardize David's safety. Chuck was the only one who could save David from Theodore's jaws.

David's tiny body was hanging from the ledge near the top of the seven-foot backyard wall. Theodore leaped toward David, his tongue swaying back and forth and his saliva flying through the air.

Allen and Hector climbed up the wall next to Carter. There was nothing they could do. David's only hope was if Chuck could retain his grip and muster up enough strength to pull David back.

Theodore's barks grew increasingly louder. His leaps grew higher as Chuck's grip grew less secure.

"C'mon Chuck. You can do it!" Allen chanted.

"Hang on, David," said Hector, "Chuck will save you." Carter was silent, eyeing Chuck, eyeing David, then Theodore, then the cards.

Perspiration on Chuck's left hand was soaking the cards, sure to decrease their value. Carter ground his teeth. Perspiration on Chuck's right hand provided enough lubricant to loosen his grip on David.

With one last desperate surge, Chuck pulled David's arm as his tight-clasped hand slid past the boy's fingertips. Chuck fell backward. Thumps sounded on both sides of the wall simultaneously.

Carter jumped down, hoping to grab the cards from Chuck. Chuck was covering his ears with his hands, the cards still in his left hand.

Theodore's barking grew louder. Carter turned from Chuck and looked up at Allen and Hector.

Hector jumped from the wall and raced toward the Redford's front porch. "C'mon, Cart," he beckoned, "let's knock on the door."

Allen jumped down also, shadowing Hector. Carter was about to join them when he realized Theodore was no longer barking. He glared at Chuck.

Chuck, with voice shattering, announced, "Oh no! My dad's going to kill me!"

Hector raced back toward the wall, leaped to the top ledge and looked down. He immediately smiled, and his distinct laugh filled the air. Allen and Carter rushed to the wall, beside Hector, and joined in his laughter.

"They've gone mad!" exclaimed Chuck. "You guys are sadistic!"

"You're not going to believe this, Chuck," Allen said. "That kid is petting Theodore. He's petting him and wrestling with him."

"You mean he's okay?"

Mrs. Redford entered the backyard breathing heavily. "Oh, my! What are you children up to now? Baseballs, toilet paper. You've gone too far this time."

"My dad's not going to kill me after all," Carter heard Chuck mumble below him.

"Oh my goodness!" Mrs. Redford exclaimed. "Are you all right? How did you get down here? Let me see you!"

After a cursory inspection, she wondered out loud, "For goodness sake! The angels must be watching over you, boy! He's capable of harming men ten times your size!"

When David emerged from the Redford's front door, he was carrying a sack of Christmas cookies. He shared them with his four new friends. Carter, Hector, and Allen partook gratefully, but Chuck questioned, "What was that? A joke? What are you trying to pull over on us, little fellah? You from the circus or something? Who is this guy, Carter?"

Carter partook of the cookie begrudgingly. Though he was relieved that nothing had happened to David, his concern over the sixteen valuable cards that Chuck still possessed overshadowed any joy a cookie would normally bring. He ignored Chuck, swallowed the cookies fragments, and began to take another bite when he realized how and when Chuck got the cards from his pocket. It was just minutes earlier, when both he and David where entangled in Chuck's grasp. When he pulled away and felt Chuck's hand hit him on the chest, Chuck must have been reaching for the cards. Obviously, he knew they were there.

Carter gulped. A frightening possibility shot through his mind, causing greater anxiety. If Chuck knew about the sixteen cards and was able to snatch them, what about the ones in his backpack?

He swung the pack off his shoulders, fell to the ground, and unzipped the section where he had placed his three hundred cards that guaranteed him at least five hundred dollars. They weren't there.

He looked up. Above him were Allen and Hector. Hector looked confused; Allen was shaking his head, grinning.

Chuck had raced down the street toward his home, laughing.

In one hand he held Shannon's sixteen cards; in the other, three packs wrapped with plastic sandwich bags and a rubber band. "Hey, Cart," he yelled, "come and get 'em. Come and get 'em, you stupid geek. Bringing these to school. Only you, Carter. Only you!"

Carter hung his head. An empty feeling near his heart brought him close to tears.

"Let's go, Allen," Chuck screamed. "You comin'? We're gonna be late."

Carter looked to Allen. "Get them for me, will you? I need them bad! Please."

"You going with the jerk?" Hector asked Allen.

Carter looked at Hector, surprised. He'd never heard him speak like that about anybody.

Hector continued. "You saw what he's done here today. To me this morning. To this kid. To Carter."

"So," Allen chimed.

"Don't think your turn's not coming."

"You threatening me?" Allen stepped closer to Hector.

Carter jumped to his feet and held out his arms, trying to calm his friends. "What is this, guys? What's happening to us?"

"Chuck's right about you, Cart, you're a loser," Allen started. "Always have been. True colors are finally shining through. Only an idiot would bring cards that valuable to school. Only a loser would get caught with cigarettes in his jacket. Only a loser would get in a fight with his best friend."

The commentary was thunderous. Numbing. Carter could not believe what he was hearing. Allen, neutral Allen, so hesitant to make a comment, positive or negative, about anything, much less anybody, had just spouted the most insulting words Carter had ever heard spoken.

"Leave, Allen," Hector instructed. "Get outta here."

"You're siding with Cart? You wanna be a loser too?"

Hector pushed Allen with both his arms, convincing Allen to obey.

He did, running in the wake of Chuck's path to his house.

Carter stared after Allen, knowing any hope of getting back his cards was diminishing. That empty feeling grew more numbing.

"I forgive you," he heard David say.

Carter turned his head, studying David, unsure if he heard him correctly.

"That's what I'd say," the small boy continued, "hits them like a brick every time."

Carter shook his head. "I've got to go. Hector, man, I have no idea what to do. It's over. It's all over." Carter buried his face in his hands.

"Forgiveness," David repeated. "You release it. They've got to deal with it. Why burden yourself?"

Carter peaked through his hands, amazed that this kid would not shut up. He saw Hector nod; it seemed reluctantly at first but then, a few seconds later, as though he agreed with what David was saying.

Carter raised his brow, staring down Hector. He had to get those cards back. He had to get to the store and buy five additional pieces plus the golden cradle. He had to get rid of this kid. Forgiveness? What did that have to do with anything? He needed help. He'd ask for Hector's aid. He hoped this forgiveness nonsense would not interfere.

David seemed enamored with Hector. Carter shook his head and whispered, "Don't encourage the kid. I need your help."

"So, how do you two know each other?"

"I don't know," answered Carter. "We haven't gotten that far yet."

"Well, where does he live?"

"Back East."

"And we're walking him home?"

"Oh!" exclaimed David. "I'm staying with my brother."

Carter closed his eyes in defeat. "Your brother? Here? In Fullerton?"

"We came together," David announced.

This was getting worse by the second. This kid was getting him in deeper trouble than Carter could manage to get in himself. He had no time to find this kid's brother. He had already lost a valuable hour with him already.

"Where's he at?" Hector asked.

Carter placed his hand over his eyes. Hector was not cooperating.

"At the university," David answered. "He told me to meet him at the university."

Carter and Hector looked at each other quizzically.

"Cal State? That's pretty close," Hector said.

"Quite a hill too," Carter added, dreading more lost time.

"Hey, Cart!" Hector shouted. "We'll run into them!"

"What are you talking about?" Carter was disgusted with everybody at this point. Even Hector wasn't making sense.

"Mr. DeSanto. He's the drama professor. Tonight's the big play."

Carter's eyes lit up. Tony and Chuck had traditionally helped their father as stagehands. If he could get Mr. DeSanto on his side, possibly threaten Chuck that he would tell his father about his exploits, then he might be able to get back his cards.

Carter placed his backpack around his shoulders. "Let's go!"

"I've got my route," Hector announced.

Carter shook his head, determined to see this new plan come to fruition. "Make a deal. We walk David to Cal State, and I'll help you deliver tonight. I'll do half!"

"It's a deal!"

Carter and Hector shook hands.

The two friends raced toward State College Boulevard, leading to the entrance of the University, when they noticed David still standing behind them. His right hand was extended. He appeared to be waiting for something.

"What is it, David?" asked Hector. "You want another cookie? There are none left."

"The deal!" David exclaimed. "Don't I need to move your hand like the man in the office? We moved each other's hands."

Carter motioned to Hector. "Just do it."

Bury the Hatchet

When he stepped to the starting line during his high school and college years, whether the race was around a track, through a grass field, or up and down dirt paths, the greatest challenge was just before the gun sounded. Within seconds after the race began, once he settled into a pace, he felt calm within his chest and the anxiety diminish. When he stepped to the front of a meeting, whether he was a student or an executive, the challenge was to emerge from all the physiological reactions his body produced when faced with uncertainty—the racing heart, the perspiring hands, and the dry throat.

The monthly meetings he had arranged with Kevin followed the same pattern. When the accident occurred, it was clear what he had to do: he had received forgiveness; therefore, he must forgive. He had been shown compassion; therefore, he must be compassionate. He had received encouragement from Barney Kyle; therefore, he must encourage Kevin Hatch. But as clear as these expectations were, the pending encounters with the man who was responsible for his daughter's death was not.

A week prior to each of their monthly meetings, he scrambled to come up with issues they could discuss, fearing silence and awkwardness would fill their hour together. During their first few lunches, he had intended to verbalize that he had forgiven Kevin, but saying 'I forgive you' seemed too contrived. So he decided he would show it rather than say it.

As he walked into the café, he looked to the rear booth; it was vacant. He felt the corner of his mouth rise and forced it back, erasing the grin.

"Mr. Mason," the elderly owner welcomed with a warm smile, "your booth is ready."

Doug raised his hand, "Hello, Gil."

"There are two of you, no?" Gil asked, pulling two lunch menus from behind the front counter.

"He's here?" Doug asked.

Gil motioned Doug to follow him to the rear of the café. "He arrived 'bout ten minutes ago. Was just sitting here in front. Thought I'd let him sit in the usual spot. Went to the men's room just before you walked in."

Lowering himself slowly to the booth, Doug grabbed the menu Gil was holding in front of him. Gil placed the other menu across from Doug.

"Would you like to hear the specials?"

"I'll have the usual."

"Very good, Mr. Mason. And the young man?"

"We'll give him a few minutes."

"And for drinks? A glass of water and a coke?"

Doug ran his hands over his eyes. "That's right."

As Gil walked away, Doug pushed the menu to the side and folded his hands on top of the table.

He heard the bathroom door open and restrained himself from looking over his shoulder. He grabbed his menu, reached for Kevin's menu, placed it behind his, and evened their corners by tapping them on the table.

"Mr. Mason," Kevin said softly.

"Kevin." Doug stood, pushed a smile, and shook Kevin's hand. "Do you know what you want?"

"Same."

"Gil," Doug beckoned, "I think we're ready."

A waitress arrived at their table at Gil's direction. "Hello, fellas." She looked up from her order tablet. "Feeling adventurous today?"

"Kevin?" Doug asked, holding out his hand, inviting him to go first.

He didn't answer.

"Kevin?" Doug said a bit louder.

Gil arrived with the drinks, handed Doug a glass of water and placed the soda in front of Kevin.

Kevin wrapped his hands around the glass and rubbed his fingers across its surface, clearing it of condensation.

Kelly, the waitress who had served Doug the past five years, cleared her throat.

Doug looked up and saw concern in her eyes.

"Give us a minute—" Doug started.

"Burger and fries," Kevin softly said, his eyes still fixed on the glass of soda.

Kelly wrote his order and then turned to Doug. "Cobb salad?" she asked, grinning as she finished writing his regular order.

She placed the tablet into a front pocket of her apron. "I'll be back with some bread."

A motorcycle sped past the café and stopped at the light. Doug looked over and envied the man in shiny, black leather, tassels dangling from his felt boots. Doug had never been on a motorcycle, but he envied the man—he was alone, hindered only by a red light. As soon as it would turn green, the road extended forever and the man on the motorcycle could ride to the horizon.

No such freedom existed for Doug. Kevin was sitting just a few feet away, a young man in turmoil, in need of some words to help him through the anguish. But whatever those words may be, Doug did not know them. He was fearful of saying anything that may make Kevin feel worse.

Kelly arrived with a basket of bread and placed it in the center of the table.

"Is something wrong, Mr. Mason?" she asked.

Doug looked up. "No, Kelly. Thank you."

She left to take an order at another table.

"Kevin," Doug started, unsure of what words he would next speak, "you think Denver is the real deal?"

Kevin shifted his eyes upward, tilted his head, and shrugged. "I think they'll beat Pittsburgh on Saturday, but they won't make it past the Colts or Raiders."

Doug nodded, not in agreement with Kevin's assessment of the Denver Broncos' chances of advancing in the NFL play-offs, but that Kevin's somber reply confirmed his suspicion that something was troubling Kevin more than when they had last met.

"Even with their Orange Crush defense?" Doug asked further, hoping that his innocent line of questions may reveal something more.

Kevin briefly made eye contact with Doug and then looked past him.

"The two NFC games on Monday," Doug continued, "make the day after Christmas a bit more bearable."

Kevin again looked at Doug, this time with a tint of excitement. "You taking Carter to the Rams game?"

"No," Doug answered, scolding himself for not thinking of this himself, certain that Carter would have been genuinely surprised to have received the tickets Christmas morning.

"Los Angeles is doing well," Kevin continued. "The Dodgers in the World Series, though they lost to the Yanks. Now the Rams have a chance to make it to the Superbowl."

Kevin spoke in a subdued monotone, confirming that something was terribly wrong. Usually, any sport-related dialogue served as a welcome diversion and their banter was exchanged with exuberance, bordering on passion at times. It was the only topic Doug felt comfortable discussing with Kevin. Somehow, he'd have to find a way to transition into deeper dialogue.

"I've been curious, Mr. Mason," Kevin started, looking up and making what seemed to be forced, deliberate eye contact.

Doug tensed. He feared Kevin's next words.

Kevin cleared his throat. "Why are we here? I mean, why do you ask me here each month?"

Doug crossed his legs, reached for a piece of bread, placed it on his napkin, picked up his glass of water, took a sip, and studied Kevin over the brim of the glass.

"I've been thinking about this for a long time," Kevin continued, "at first I appreciated it all, you being so nice to me. It was as though you were letting me know that you forgave me. If the man I hurt the most forgives me for what I have done, than why am I constantly reliving the horror of that night?

"I replay it over and over again in my mind. I can't sleep at night. I know you're trying to help me move on, but I can't. I just can't, Mr. Mason. I took Shannon's life. I killed her."

Kevin's eyes were moist with tears. He used his napkin to wipe the streams falling down his cheeks. The distinct sound of sneakers on pavement, Kelly's sneakers, approached their booth.

"Cobb salad for the young man," she said.

Doug was about to correct her when she continued, "and a hamburger and fries for the younger man."

Doug looked up, hoping Kelly was perceptive enough to sense the tension at their table.

Kevin pushed his plate aside as soon as Kelly left for another table. "I didn't grow up in a religious home, Mr. Mason. Don't know if it's worth my time. But I learned in college from one of my philosophy profs about why Jesus had such an impact; it was forgiveness, mercy, love. I've lived in a world without those things. Sports has no room for any of that stuff. My father left when I was a little kid, so my coaches served as my role models all through high school and into college. Each wanted me to succeed in anything I put my hands to. None of that forgiveness stuff was in my upbringing. I couldn't understand it. Forgiveness, what did it mean in the everyday world? What you've shown me cracked open a window to a world I never thought existed."

Doug felt a faint pulsing grow in his forehead, creating a burning sting behind his eyes. He took a deep breath, determined to control the dam of tears.

Kevin pushed his plate further from him and covered his eyes with both hands, his elbows on the table. "I can't do this any longer. I don't deserve your love, Mr. Mason. I know you mean well, but each time we meet . . ."

Doug reached across the table and lightly touched Kevin's shoulder. "It's okay, Kevin. I understand."

Kevin looked up, his eyes red.

Doug continued. "The first couple years are the most difficult."

Kevin straightened his posture and wiped his eyes.

"I've been there, Kevin. I know what eats away at you each night."

Kevin grabbed another napkin and blew his nose.

"You can't erase it. None of it. What's done is done, and the haunting memories are potent, relentless. There is no relief, and what's worse, you know you don't deserve any relief, so wanting the relief makes you feel even worse."

"How did you know?" Kevin asked softly, leaning across the table.

Doug studied Kevin, calculating the wisdom of revealing his past. "We all make mistakes. We all have regrets."

Kevin leaned back, waving his hands, the most animation he had shown. "But does it go away? Does it ever go away?"

Again, Doug reached across the table. He opened his hands and rested them, palms facing up. Once their eyes met, Doug motioned for Kevin to place his hands in his. Slowly, Kevin rested his hands atop Doug's palms.

Two decades earlier, a man had sat across from Doug, arms extended, their hands joined. He had spoken those words Doug had avoided speaking to Kevin. "I forgive you Douglas Anthony Mason," Barney Kyle had said. "Your best way of thanking me for this gracious gift is to live in freedom—free from guilt, free to pursue your dreams, free to love, free to invest in the lives of those you love."

He would soon speak similar words to Kevin. He had failed to live up to Mr. Kyle's request; he sincerely hoped Kevin would embrace the message, believe it, and live it out. Twenty years of regret and guilt and nightmares were something he hoped Kevin would not have to endure.

Doug wrapped his fingers around Kevin's hands and tightened his grasp. Inwardly cursing his hypocrisy, he announced, "I forgive you, Kevin. I forgive you."

The Meaning of Life [1]

Kamal accepted Carolyn's invitation to pay for lunch. Every trait of this man was appealing. Now he appeared undaunted by a woman paying his meal. Surely such a man would stand by a woman who pursued what society said she could not pursue; surely he would support her in any endeavor she had.

They maneuvered themselves back into the white Pinto and continued heading south on Interstate 5. Los Angeles was only three hours away; traffic would soon be thickening with holiday travelers.

Kamal accelerated onto the freeway and, after several lane changes, once more settled into the slow lane. "Very satisfying," he said softly, stretched his torso, and took a deep breath.

"You ate steak." Carolyn announced.

"I did. And how was your hamburger?"

"But aren't you Hindu?" Carolyn grimaced after she heard the words, resenting her presumptuousness and stereotyping.

Things had gone so well during lunch. They discussed families, childhood, and hobbies. She enjoyed listening to him. She enjoyed watching him use his arms, his hands, and his face to emphasize or

---

[1] Much of the dialogue in this chapter is inspired by the apologetics text written by J.P. Moreland, *Scaling the Secular City*, published by *Baker Book House* in 1987. Specific ideas originated by Moreland and others are noted.

clarify his message. The longer he spoke, the longer she could watch and study him.

There was a moment, before their meals were served, when Kamal was sharing about his love for travel, that Carolyn looked away from Kamal's face, drawn by the image of his hands. How she longed to be touched by him. She felt ashamed for such a deep longing, unsure of what her passion meant or why she felt any shame. Such longings for other men had never produced remorse. She shifted her weight in the booth, purposefully keeping a distance between them and hoping this would assist in controlling her usual tendencies. But the longer they talked, the more she had to restrain herself.

And for all her efforts, successful as they were during lunch, she blurted something as stupid as, "But aren't you Hindu?"

Kamal showed no sign of being offended.

Carolyn leaned forward, looking into Kamal's eyes, to see if she could read anything that might suggest she was being too forward. He looked at her inquisitively.

She felt safe to continue. "But isn't it true? I mean that Hindus, at least most Hindus, are vegetarians?"

"Actually, *eet* fits in quite well with our discussion prior to lunch."

"Eating meat constitutes the meaning of life?"

"No, no," Kamal answered quickly, "that *ees* not my suggestion. My journey in discovering life's meaning led me to forego some of the laws I had previously felt obligated to keep."

"I see." Carolyn looked ahead at the road. She contemplated the similarity of Hindu laws with her father's religious beliefs.

"Carolyn," Kamal started. Carolyn liked the way he said her name. "What do you believe?"

"What do I believe?" she repeated.

"Yes. About life, about our reason for being here?"

"I suppose to help make society a better place in which to live."

"But why? Why is that your purpose?"

"History proves it's the best way to insure civilizations to prosper and endure—through good times and bad—to protect the sanctity of human life. I'll do everything within my power to protect an individual's rights."

"Rights? What grants an individual any right? Who are you to say that another human *ees* violating the rights of any other human? On what basis do you justify your zeal for civil rights? Could not the individuals you accuse of violating another's rights be just as correct in asserting that you are violating their right to pursue success?"[2]

"I understand what you're suggesting, but doesn't this road eventually lead to anarchy?"

"An individual's rights are relative unless you have some starting point to determine what rights all individuals share, a basis of sorts. If humans were left to discover this basis on their own, well, then we'd end up with anarchy. What I'm trying to suggest is that humans alone cannot come to know what these rights are, nor the basis of these rights, nor the purpose of their existence."

"I see. You're talking about God, or a god." Carolyn tried hard not to sound skeptical, to keep an open mind.

"You're not fond of the idea?"

Carolyn looked straight into Kamal's face. She wanted to be careful not to offend his beliefs as she had so many others'. "It's not a question of how fond I am in regards to his or her or its existence. The question is, `How can he exist?' In the midst of a world of pain and oppression, how can anyone claim that a divine being exists? It makes no sense!"

"Oh, but it does, Carolyn! It does!"

Kamal said this with such assurance, such passion, that Carolyn felt an array of emotions pass through her body, causing her skin to break into a hybrid of sweat and bumps. She resented Kamal for his apparent certainty, respected him for his ability to express what he believed, but pitied him for his naivety. She felt a longing for her father, feeling as though he needed to hear this. Carolyn was certain that no god existed.

---

2 Examination of morality and differing views on the meaning of life: *Scaling the Secular City*, J.P. Moreland, pages 108-115

Her father never seemed sold on his religion; he seemed faithful but not certain. Kamal appeared different.

He continued, "The existence of God makes more sense than any theory man has formulated in the sciences, philosophy, or theology."

"And you discovered this? You can prove this?" Carolyn asked, trying hard to hide her cynicism.

"I can."

"How?" she added. "You going to pop him out of a hat?

Kamal chuckled lightly and turned. He looked directly into Carolyn's eyes, replaced his grin with a stern countenance, and appeared as though he was on the verge of making a profound announcement. His serious demeanor was frightening; Carolyn was curious as to what his next words would be.

"I want you to think of a library," he requested.[3]

Carolyn was bewildered. "A library?"

Kamal continued, "A library. I want you to picture in your mind a library with an enormous number of books. In fact, this library has an infinite number of books, all with black hard covers."

He paused, looked at Carolyn, and waited. "Do you have a picture of the library in your mind?"

Carolyn did not see any point in arguing. Besides, she enjoyed logic puzzles; at least that's what it appeared Kamal was up to.

"Got it?" Kamal asked.

Carolyn went back in time, recalling the family vacation through the District of Colombia ten years earlier. She imagined the size and scope of the Library of Congress. Within it, there was a myriad of shelves filled with books, more than she could count. She obediently imagined them all having black hard covers.

---

[3] Moreland, *City*, p. 23, based upon the work by William Lane Craig, *The Kalam Cosmological Argument*, Macmillan, 1979, pp. 6-7.

"Now, before we go on, we must clarify the type of infinite we are talking about. Are you familiar with the terms *absolute* and *potential* infinite?"[4]

"Sure!" Carolyn answered. "Freshman calculus. A potential infinite is what we use in mathematics. It is a series of numbers that has a beginning but no ending. It goes on forever. An absolute infinite, however, is a series of numbers or events with no beginning or ending. It extends forever in both directions."

"Excellent! Now, what would happen if your library contained an absolute infinite number of red books as well as the absolute infinite number of black books already there?"

"We'd have a library of absolute infinite size." Carolyn answered.

Kamal chuckled as he veered a bend in the highway. "Yes, I guess that would be true. But suppose a curator asked this question: 'Do we have as many black books in our library as we do red books?' What would you say?"

"No! That would be ridiculous! We could never count them!"

Kamal continued. "Suppose further that you could withdraw all the black books; couldn't we say, based upon the definition of an absolute infinite, that the total number of books is still the same?"

Carolyn shrugged in agreement. "Based upon the theory, yes, the number of books would be unchanged. If there is an infinite number of books, it's illogical to suggest that the number of books can be split in half."

"Exactly! Common sense tells us that this cannot be true. How can we take away an infinite number of objects and still have the same number as before? It's not logical. We do not experience absolute infinites, because they do not exist in the real world."

Carolyn raised her head, being sure she understood. "I'm with you so far."

---

4 Discussion of Absolute and Potential Infinites as well as presentation of Kalam Argument: Moreland, *City*, pp. 18-42.

"Think, Carolyn. The theory says an absolute infinite has no beginning and no ending. If such a theory is impossible, then there must have been a beginning—a beginning to our universe, to our solar system, to our planet, to life."

"But just because we don't experience absolute infinites, does that mean they don't exist?"

"Perhaps they might. But even if one did exist, the present moment in which we are now talking could have never arrived. Since there would be no beginning to start from, events could never traverse to any particular moment in time as we know it."

Carolyn brushed her hair behind her ears. She looked out the window, watching the horizon.

"If you are still not convinced, consider the second law of thermodynamics. What does it say?"[5]

Carolyn turned back toward Kamal. "That all events and all objects lose energy and order with time. Everything moves toward chaos. If a bottle of perfume is opened within a room, its scent is dispersed throughout the room until it fades away. Once the bottle is opened, it is impossible to reverse the process. You cannot gather the scent and replace it back into the bottle."

Kamal smiled as Carolyn spoke. It filled her with a pride she had long since forgotten from her days around the family dinner table.

Kamal interrupted her memories. "In your illustration, the initial action is opening the bottle, correct?"

"Sure."

"Likewise, the universe, most scientists agree, is expanding. Eventually it will run out of energy, approach maximum randomness, and expire."

"Definitely!" Carolyn exclaimed. "We can't move backward. All of nature follows the second law. Anything that did not, would be above the law, would be supernatural, would be—" Carolyn caught

---

[5] Moreland, *City*, pp. 34-35

herself before saying the word. Her eyes widened as she realized a new dimension of possibility.

"Ah, but you are jumping ahead, Carolyn. If the universe had been here forever, as the absolute infinite theory suggests, then the universe would have expired an infinite time ago. But since the universe does still exist, then it must have had a beginning."

Carolyn shrugged her shoulders and tilted her head, granting Kamal his theory.

"So," Kamal continued, "if you can accept that all events do have a beginning, then we must next deal with a great paradox that follows this conclusion."

Carolyn had been thinking this very question seconds earlier: "How could the beginning have occurred if there was nothing before it?"

"Exactly," Kamal said with some surprise.

Carolyn continued, "The conditions must have been present in order for the beginning to occur. Then these conditions reacted with one another to cause the beginning."[6]

Kamal shook his head. "Do you exercise?" he asked.

Carolyn peered at Kamal, squinting and abashed by his sudden change in direction. "Sure, almost every day. I have to."

"Why do you have to?"

"To be in shape for our softball games, to keep my coach off my back, to be better than my opponents."

"Who decides to do the exercise? The running? The throwing?"

"Me, of course!"

"Not your health?"

The question confused Carolyn.

Kamal went on. "Not your strong legs? Your dedication? Your diet?"

"I don't understand."

---

6 Moreland, *City*, pp. 38-42

"These are your conditions Carolyn: your health, your frame of mind, your motivation, your diet. They are not the agent that causes you to exercise; they are the conditions that enable you to exercise. You, Carolyn! You are the one that causes the act of exercising to begin. Only you can make that decision."

"So what you're saying is that some agent out there, call him God, call her Mother Nature, is responsible for all this?"

"That's it, you've got it!"

"I may understand it. But that does not mean I accept it. Shoot, Kamal, I may agree the Republican Party exists, but that doesn't mean I'm going to vote for one of them!"

"Indirectly you have just confessed a belief in God."

"I don't deny that ideas of god exist. I deny that a god exists. Granted, you can call your agent that caused a beginning to be your God; I call that agent evolution."

Kamal nodded. It was a pleasing nod, not condescending; it was as though he agreed with her logic.

"Yet," Kamal said, "some people do claim that there are those who create God in their minds and their imagination in order to cope with life's hardships. But even if this is true, that does not make God's existence any less real than your disfavor with the idea."

Carolyn shifted her weight toward Kamal, tucking her left leg under her right, elevating herself in the car seat. "For argument's sake, let's say your supreme agent exists. Then why all this evil in the world? If he is so supreme, why does he allow the world to continue on the path it is taking? Why does he allow us to live in such a messed-up society? Is he sadistic? I mean, let's be honest. Look at us, Kamal! This world is a mess: innocent children massacred in Vietnam by teenage American boys with a blind trust in their government; millions dying of cancer; civil unrest caused by religious factions that claim to know this Divine Agent of yours. How do you reconcile an all-powerful God with this obviously imperfect world?"

"Oh no, Carolyn, you need to look at it all from another angle! This God is powerful enough! His power is unimaginable!"

"Then why doesn't he do something?"

"Power can only do those things which power can do."

"What is that supposed to mean? Power can do anything."

"Can it?"

Kamal paused before continuing. "If you were all powerful, Carolyn, there would be certain things you could not do."[7]

"That makes no sense."

"Let's say for example, Carolyn decides she wants to make a circle into a square. I'll grant that she could do that, if indeed she is all-powerful. But, it would be entirely different for me to claim that Carolyn could make a square circle. You see the difference?"

Carolyn tilted her head, granting him his point.

"Likewise, there are many things God cannot do. None of which are any indication of a lack of power on His part. He cannot make a square circle anymore than he cannot cease to exist. These are not limitations on his power since power is not relevant to them. Therefore, when God made man, he created him in his likeness, so the Bible tells us. He created man with the freedom to choose. He could choose to love the being that created him, or he could reject his creator. God could not create a free human who could not sin any more than He could create a square circle, for that would be to make free creatures who were not free. Since evil is traceable to the freedom God had granted his creatures, evil is no more evidence to the limit of God's power than is His inability to make a circle with four sides."[8]

"You were actually taught this stuff at Berkeley?"

"No."

"Back home then? In India?"

"There and elsewhere. I traveled much during my formative years."

"It's interesting. I'll grant you that. But how do you relate it all to life's meaning?"

---

[7] Moreland, City, pp. 26-28, 66

[8] Moreland, City, p. 66

"God's desires become our purpose. His will becomes our aim in life."

"And how do you discover that purpose?"

"By seeking him."

"And if you find you are seeking the wrong god? If you are a Buddhist, say? A Taoist? A Muslim?"

"A Hindu?" Kamal said with a wide grin.

"Very well, a Hindu."

"I measure the facts made available to me. Just like I presented them to you. I adjust my former beliefs accordingly. It's a growing process. The more I seek him, the more my life changes."

"You seek a god who may not exist. I will use the powers I know I possess to change things in this world I know are wrong. You tell me which makes more sense?"

"The two choices you present are not mutually exclusive, Carolyn. You can have both."

"Seeking a god who is not there only takes time away from helping other people. There's too much to do and not enough time for me to waste on such a gamble!"

"Why's that, Carolyn?"

"I look at my father. He's invested so much in seeking this Divine Agent of yours. It makes his life miserable. Don't get me wrong; you seem content—I guess you've known where to draw the lines—but my father is constantly trying to better himself: do more deeds, give more money, go to church more often, pray for his wife and kids more . . . that sort of thing."

Kamal interrupted. "I think I understand. But it's not a matter of my knowing where to draw a line. The question is not about performance. If it is, that person is seeking the wrong God, a god who does not exist. God is perfect. Therefore, none of us can perform to his level of acceptance."

"Then why do you bother pursuing him?"

"I pursue Him because I believe He has already accepted me. You see, Carolyn, God has made us acceptable not by the works we perform but by his mercy and forgiveness. I seek Him because He has given me so much. I want to know this Divine Agent better because of what He has given me."

"You're talking about Jesus now. I know all that stuff. We have those lunatics up at Berkeley too."

"There's an element of truth in all fanatics, Carolyn. That's what makes them successful. Just because there may be people misrepresenting Jesus Christ, don't make the mistake of disregarding Jesus Christ himself."

"Then you are a Christian! And all along I thought . . ." Carolyn stopped.

Kamal did not request her to complete the statement. Carolyn suddenly recognized her hypocrisy. She was as guilty of narrow-minded bigotry as those she regularly condemned. She had gained a genuine respect for Kamal's intelligence, but as soon as she learned that he was a Christian, she considered him to be a nitwit.

She hung her head, straightened her legs, and stared out the window.

She thought of her father. He used to read to Carolyn and her siblings many of the stories in the Bible. How silly they sounded. Almost like the Aesop's Fables cartoons that she and Shannon watched when returning from school each day—good lessons and morals but of no historical value. But, if what Kamal had told her were true, what did it mean for her father? Had he never discovered this mercy of which Kamal was talking? Neither Kamal nor her father was right as far as she was concerned, but which of the two had a correct view of their God?

Secure

Katherine grabbed Betty's arm and raced into the toy store, pushing her way through the crowd near the cash register. "A small blonde girl, six years old. Have you seen her?" Katherine asked one of the employees ringing up a sale.

The employee shook her head, making no eye contact with Katherine, as she totaled a customer's purchases.

Katherine turned to another employee. "Excuse me."

The employee looked up, frustration in her glare.

"My friend. Her daughter. Has any—"

"I am sorry, ma'am," the young woman said, "but no, we have all searched the store."

The woman looked at Betty.

Fear grew in Betty's eyes.

Katherine looked away, uncertain what to do next.

"I did explain to your friend," the young woman continued, "many children either are taken to the concierge by other adults or find their way themselves."

Betty was growing pale. Katherine would have to handle this on her terms.

"It's located at the center of the mall, just a couple hundred yards to the right. We'll keep our eyes open for your daughter. If we see a lost girl, we'll send her to the booth with one of us."

"Thank you," Katherine replied.

Katherine, still holding Betty's arm, led her back into the mall's corridors.

"Betty," she directed, "you go to the booth; I'm going to the flower shop on the other end of the mall. One of my neighbors owns it. She may have an idea."

Betty remained motionless, as if she hadn't heard Katherine's directions.

Katherine looked at her, growing frustrated by her friend's apparent ease at losing this child. It was amazing, Katherine thought, that Betty's four elder children had survived unscathed and could all be accounted for.

Katherine placed her hands on Betty's shoulder and looked her in the eyes, "I'll meet you at the booth in five minutes," she said slow and stern, "okay?"

Betty still did not respond.

Katherine grabbed her by the arm and walked briskly to the concierge booth, dragging Betty behind her. There were two booths side-to-side in the central atrium: Santa's Workshop and the concierge. "This must be it!" Katherine shouted above the noise of shoppers.

"You tell them about Sally," Katherine directed. "Describe her. Tell her where you were. Tell her about the man in the book store."

Katherine paused, making sure Betty understood. Betty's eyes awoke when Katherine mentioned the man. "Thank you, Kate," she said.

"I'll leave my bags with you. I'll be back in five minutes." Katherine waited for Betty to show some sign, confirming she understood the plan. Betty stepped closer to the concierge, extending her neck, and waved her hand, trying to get attention from one of the employees.

Content that Betty was on board, Katherine turned and raced through the mall to Rosa Romero's flower shop. The terrible thought of Sally being taken by the man in the bookshop spurned her to reach Rosa's store in less than two minutes.

Rosa informed her that the concierge would notify security and that security would watch all exits. Although Rosa insured Katherine that she would watch closely for Sally, there was little more that could be done.

Katherine sighed, thanked Rosa, and raced back toward the concierge.

She recalled announcements regarding lost children being made earlier in the day, while she was still in the bookstore. She hoped to soon hear a description of Sally over the mall's speakers. There was none. Had Betty even reached the front of the line?

Scenarios of what may happen to Sally raced through Katherine's imagination, increasing her anxiety and sympathy for Betty. As she approached the line that had formed at the concierge, she could not see Betty. There were now five women waiting in line, all wearing the same terrified stare that Katherine was feeling.

She turned around, searching the perimeter of the mall's center, hoping to spot her friend.

On a bench, across from the concierge, sat Sally. Betty was kneeling, her hand resting on Sally's knee. She was looking up, listening to a woman dressed in a mall uniform.

Katherine breathed deeply and smiled. She walked up to them.

Betty was listening intently to the woman, one moment gazing at her daughter and then back at the woman.

As she approached, Katherine heard the woman's soft, eloquent, and kind voice. She was young, probably around the same age as Carolyn. Her face full of acne; she was nonetheless very pretty.

Katherine would let the woman finish speaking before she interrupted.

"From one generation to the next," the young mall employee said, "he has shown his strength and scattered the arrogant, giving them up to the imagination of their hearts. He defeats rulers and builds up those who are lowly. He feeds the hungry, but sends the rich away empty-handed. He helps his people and is merciful. Always merciful to his people . . ." She paused, lowering her head.

Interesting, Katherine thought, wondering whether this young girl was reciting poetry, maybe a sonnet from Shakespeare. It sounded familiar, though she couldn't quite place it.

Katherine cleared her throat.

Betty turned around, "Katherine!"

Sally stood on the bench, waving. "Hi, Mrs. Mason."

Katherine smiled. Sally was unharmed and happy.

"What happened?" Katherine asked, turning her attention to Betty.

Betty stood, gesturing to the young mall employee. "This young lady intercepted them."

"Them?" Katherine asked with widening eyes.

"The man in the book store," she clarified.

Katherine began weighing the possibilities of what may have happened if this young woman hadn't intervened.

Betty continued. "He was holding her hand, just about to exit, when she struck up a conversation with him."

Katherine turned to the girl. "What did you say?"

"I asked him if his little girl had visited Santa?

"He said, 'no'. Then I bent down and asked Sally if she'd like to visit Santa."

"I said, 'yes,'" Sally announced.

"That's right," she said, smiling at Sally. "As we turned to go back into the mall, the man ran out the doors."

"He got away?"

Sally was shaking her head rapidly.

Betty was smiling. "Apparently she had arranged with security to detain him, depending on his reaction."

Katherine grinned at the girl's crafty plan, approving of her efforts. "But how did you know?" Katherine asked the young lady. "How did you know something was wrong? That Sally wasn't his daughter?"

"Recognition of low estate," the girl explained.

Katherine looked at Betty, uncertain of what that meant.

Betty shook her head and shrugged. "It's what she was explaining when you walked up. Something about being able to perceive when someone is doing something against the will of another. Helping them because you were helped. She recognized this in Sally, I guess."

Sally and the young girl were playing a game with their hands, clapping them against one another. Sally was teaching her what to do.

"To tell you the truth," Betty whispered, motioning to Katherine to come close, "I can't process anything right now. I can't stop thinking about that man, if he had gotten through those doors."

Betty's eyes were moist, her nose dripping.

Katherine reached into her purse and handed Betty a pack of tissue.

"Thank you, Katherine. Thank you for your help."

"You need anything?" Katherine asked, feeling helpless, not sure how she could comfort her friend.

"We've got to go to security. The police should be there by now. We've got to answer a few questions."

"Would you like me to come?"

Betty grabbed Sally's hands. "No, Katherine. We'll be fine. I've messed up both our days. We'll do lunch after the holidays?"

"That'd be nice," Katherine answered.

Betty hugged Katherine and thanked her once more.

The mother and daughter walked hand in hand toward security.

"Bye, Mrs. Mason." Sally called out. "Bye, Mary," she waved to the young mall employee.

The young employee waved back at Sally.

Katherine turned with haste, eyes wide, studying the young woman. With all that had transpired, Katherine's fears from earlier in the day had grown dormant. At Sally's annunciation of the mall employee's name, they had awoken.

She turned to Katherine.

Katherine looked at her, rage filling her mind. She had been cornered, tricked, and blindsided by this young woman now standing beside her in the center of the mall.

If this was it, if this is the beginning of what her mother had promised, she did not want it. Before this moment, her whole day was filled with fear and thoughts of how to avoid possible confrontations. Now that a confrontation had begun, fear was replaced with anger.

But hadn't she made this same mistake throughout the day? Four times in the car? The man in the bookstore?

She would ask this girl some questions, confirm that it isn't she. Then the rage would melt back into fear. And the fear, once the holidays had past and none of the encounters her mother had promised occurred, she could concentrate her attentions on making things right with Carter and on bringing her home back to the way it had been prior to Shannon's death. The day's events had served as a catalyst, waking her from the coldness she had let develop in her home. She would not let this continue. She had failed, but she would change and make things better for her husband, for Carolyn, and for Carter.

But first she must confirm that this girl was not one of them.

"You were of great assistance to my friend," Katherine began.

"Losing a child can be frightening," she said.

Katherine gulped.

"You've children?" Katherine asked, wincing.

"I do."

Katherine wasn't sure what to ask next and why she was asking her anything. Again, she remembered the cars earlier in the day. They eventually turned or went in a different direction.

"I wasn't married." Mary continued.

"Oh?"

"I was engaged, but I wasn't married!"

Katherine gave a gentle sigh, hoping this meant that the young woman was not whom she feared.

Mary continued, "You can imagine the stir it caused in my family. My brothers wanted to know who was responsible for it. Of course my parents were ashamed. My father could not understand the lack of reason I had used. My fiancé, well, he was such a good man."

"You mean it wasn't him?" Katherine asked, hoping to hear answers to her questions that were contrary to the scriptural accounts of the nativity.

"No, it wasn't him. I tried to explain to them that it wasn't my fault and that it wasn't his fault either, that it was nobody's fault. They didn't understand. Perhaps they couldn't understand. They wanted nobody to find out. But eventually, we couldn't hide it. My fiancé married me even though he knew the child wasn't his. I don't think there would have been another man who would have done that. He comforted me in midst of all the gossip and encouraged me that what we were doing was right."

"But the father? Did the father ever know?" Katherine asked.

"But there was no father! That's what made it all the more difficult. How do you explain that to your parents? Your friends? Your fiancé?"

Katherine shut her eyes. Each of the girl's answers were confirming her fears. How could this be happening?

Mary continued, "It's in these most difficult moments that I grew to recognize what was really important. All of us have a choice how to react to difficult times: we can blame God or come to him for help. It is during those times of difficulty that the greatest things have happened in my life. You see, if I hadn't endured those nine months, if my husband would not have endured those nine months by my side, neither of us could have experienced the wondrous joy we felt when our son was born."

Katherine bit her lip, uncertain of what to do. Mary's words were clear; there could be no other explanation. That she allowed the conversation to get this far was beyond excuse.

"Are you all right?" Mary asked.

Katherine looked at her and studied her. Certain that her rage was evident, Katherine told herself to relax. She turned, looking around the mall for an escape.

She needed to gain control of the situation. Though she had feared this encounter since her mother's warning and though she had taken courses of action to prevent such encounter from occurring, she had failed.

"Mrs. Mason?" Mary asked. "Is something wrong?"

Katherine looked to her left and to her right. She turned and looked behind her. So many people in the mall, in its stores, and in its corridors. And yet, this girl had found her. This girl had tried to speak to her of things she would otherwise choose not to hear.

"Mrs. Mason?" the girl asked again.

Katherine looked her in the eyes.

Mary did not lower her gaze. Katherine thought of her childhood and how the girl's expression resembled that of her own mother so many years ago—full of compassion, yearning, and desire to assist with a child's struggles.

"Mrs. Mason?" she asked once more.

Katherine shook her head, turned, and left the mall.

Big Brother

The probability was diminishing. Each new event of the day was decreasing the likelihood of replacing the six missing pieces from the crèche.

His head began to hurt as they left for the university. He continued to be conscious of the pounding in his chest, aware that each new beat of his heart was more or less equal to one less second he had in achieving his tasks. It had been likely that he would have gotten the funds necessary from the cards he intended to sell, but that was before Chuck's sweat saturated the once pristine cardboard edges of Shannon's collection. There was no certainty of how much, if anything, he would now get for those. And he hoped Chuck did not have enough time to devalue his own personal collection. If he had, this trek with Hector and David would prove to be the final leg on this day of vanity.

Carter rethought this conclusion, realizing with greater remorse that he would still have five to six hours with his family once he arrived home. The only escape was sleep—laying his head on the pillow and, if lucky, finding it easy to slumber.

He shook his head constantly, occasionally looking up to see if either Hector or David might offer some consolation in word or expression.

There was none.

Hector charged ahead, seemingly anxious to finish this chore of finding David's brother, to get Carter's cards, and to return home to his paper route. David followed him, running with all his strength to catch up and then stopping to regain his breath and then running again to catch up to Hector.

Carter was falling behind. He wondered if he would be able to run at their same speed if he hadn't been smoking during the past year.

The gap was widening. He could hear Hector shout, "You did all right last night, Carter. The house, I mean. It wasn't bad." Hector looked over his shoulder, reached for David's hand, and pulled him into his stride. "If it makes you feel any better, we came in tenth."

"We used to come in first," Carter shouted between breaths, amazed at how fast Hector was running. "Even Chuck and Tony did better than us."

"Who's Tony?" he heard David ask Hector.

"Chuck's bro," Hector answered.

"What's a bro?"

"Brother," Hector answered. "He's Chuck's younger brother."

Carter stopped. He could not continue at this pace. He bent over, breathing heavily, amazed that David now seemed to have adapted to Hector's speed.

"You all right?" Hector called back.

Carter held up his hand, signaling that he was okay. He was appreciative of the good time they were making. Chuck would be getting a ride to the university from his mother; he was sure to be there already.

He waved his hand for Hector and David to continue. "I'm right behind you guys. Just keep going."

A minute later, Carter felt nauseous. Something had to be done to slow down Hector.

He stopped again. "Sorry, guys," he shouted, "can we just walk real fast. I can't keep up."

Hector looked at his watch and shrugged. "Sure."

Carter, still breathing heavily, bent over, hands on his knees, looked up at David, and pointed at Hector. "You should have seen this guy this morning."

David's eyes widened, studying Hector.

"It was great!" Carter exclaimed as he briskly walked up to them.

"What? What was it? What did he do?" David asked.

"Show him Hector. You've got them with you, don't you?"

Hector took out a few of his drawings and showed them to David.

Carter's plan was working. Looking at the pictures would require walking. No more of this fast-paced running.

"These are wonderful!" David said. "What's this?"

"That's Nolan Ryan," Hector answered. "He's a pitcher for the Angels."

"Oh?" David said with a confused stare.

"You like baseball?" Carter asked as he stepped ahead of his two friends.

Hector and David followed.

"Baseball? What is it?" David asked.

Carter was curious as to how Hector may answer.

"Well, it's a game," Hector started.

Carter interrupted, "Actually, it's a ball. The game is named after the type of ball used. You mean you've never played baseball?"

"You've never watched it?" Hector inquired.

David shook his head.

Carter looked back at Hector, communicating his curiosity. He read the same curiosity in Hector's gaze.

They entered the university campus, Carter feeling some optimism of accomplishing something toward fixing all that had gone wrong.

"Almost there!" David informed. "Just around the corner!"

"Cool!" exclaimed Hector, again looking at his watch, "It's only three thirty."

"Let's see," Hector announced. "It'll take us about another ten minutes to get home, maybe ten minutes for you to get the cards. Then you can meet me at my house after you buy your stuff. I'll start folding the papers; then it will only take an hour or so to finish with your help. Then maybe you can eat over tonight!"

Carter envied his friend. The rest of Hector's day was planned. There were no uncertainties, no curveballs—a day filled with fastballs, and Hector appeared anxious to step into the box and have his way with the pitcher. Carter, on the other hand, felt like he did when Chuck would be pitching against him, knowing that whatever Chuck decided to throw, he would not be able to hit.

The sun was shining bright with only white strips of clouds scattered overhead. It was over eighty degrees. Though the Santa Ana winds had left the Southern California basin, the stale, muggy scent of the dry heat still whistled in the air. Carter smiled, remembering how foreboding that morning had been, seeing the wind blistering outside his bedroom window. Now there were signs the winds were over; there was a subtle cool filtering the air. Maybe there was hope.

"Well, here we are," David announced. "My brother said to meet him here."

Carter and Hector stopped. They turned toward one another and at the same moment said with amazement, "This is the Performing Arts Center."

"Your brother's a student?" Hector asked.

"An actor?" Carter interrupted. "Or maybe he's just helping Chuck's dad with some of the props?"

David didn't answer; he had already entered the theater. Carter and Hector followed him inside.

It had been three, maybe four months since Carter had last been within the walls of California State Fullerton's theater. Before he and Chuck had their fight, he was an invited guest to each of the opening performances of Mr. DeSanto's campus productions.

Today, the theater looked different, naked almost. There was something obscene about seeing the entire theater in lights without any glamorous props or costumes. The curtains were down, and all those on stage wore street clothes.

Carter sat on the aisle seat in the last row. Hector sat in front of him, and David remained standing next to them, in the middle of the center aisle, standing on the tip of his toes and tilting his head to the left and right.

Chuck was seated with his younger brother near the front, to the left of the group of actors. Allen was not in any of the seats. That was a relief. Carter assumed the two of them would be coming to the theater together, now he would only have to deal with Chuck.

Two men were off to the left part of the stage, engaging in what appeared to be an intense disagreement. Carter recognized one of the men to be Chuck's father. Whatever their debate, Mr. DeSanto's wishes were sure to be granted. He was in charge of the Drama Department and well respected by the art community throughout Southern California. At least that is what Carter deduced from his mother's high regard for him. Whatever he was telling the other man certainly would be obeyed.

Seconds later, the other man hung his head and Mr. DeSanto turned in haste, waving an invitation for another man to join him on stage. Carter jerked his head and saw this third man approach from the opposite side of the stage, his face hidden from view by the darkness of the stage overhang.

"You've got fifteen, maybe twenty minutes," Chuck's father told him in his deep, bellowing voice.

"Thank you," the man said.

"Don't push it," Mr. DeSanto warned with pointed finger, "and don't disappoint me. I've stuck my neck out on this."

Mr. DeSanto turned his attention to the group of actors waiting in the front two rows. "Sorry for making you wait. But this is an opportunity I could not let pass. Something I rarely do. All of you know how much control I demand of our productions, but this, this opportunity, I knew I'd regret not taking."

There was a silence. Carter wondered what was happening. What could cause Mr. DeSanto to lighten the hold of his iron fist?

"This play," Mr. DeSanto continued, "this has been performed by all of you at least once. I've been the director for twelve years. Most of us have seen numerous productions, heard the story, sung the songs, read the narrative in the Bible. For myself, I know that on more than one occasion, I have grown numb. I've taken for granted what we portray here, upon this stage.

"I'm not asking any of you to reconsider any religious beliefs you may have, only to do what I've asked you to do in any of our other productions—to put yourselves in the shoes of your character. As Atticus Finch so aptly put it, Carl?" Mr. De Santo extended his arm to one of the actors sitting in the front row.

Carter recognized him as the man who played the lead role in *To Kill a Mockingbird.* The student answered on cue to Mr. DeSanto, "Not to judge another person until you walk a mile in his shoes."

"Precisely," Mr. De Santo answered. "So, I am doing something this afternoon that I have never done, ever considered to do. Something my esteemed colleague thinks is a waste of time, but which I hope will enable each of you to reconsider the mundane attitude we are all tempted to bring to tonight's performance."

Silence filled the theater. Carter looked at Mr. DeSanto, respect growing with each passing moment. It was as though he was using the silence to accentuate the words he would next speak.

"A man walked into my office this morning, unannounced, uninvited," Mr. De Santo said. "But I welcomed him. Why? Because I had a flat tire on my way to work, and it was this man who helped me fix it and make it to my morning classes so that I could administer some final exams that many of you enjoyed throughout the day."

Some students laughed as Mr. DeSanto spoke, but he continued before the laughs faded. "Later in the day, in between the exams, this same man arrived at my office, and I invited him to sit. We spoke of what I will now let him tell you. I knew that I would be a fool to forego this opportunity. For when he spoke to me this afternoon, I felt his words were as powerful a portrayal of that first Christmas as any production I have directed or seen. How he knows what he knows, who he is, where he comes from. Well, these questions are irrelevant for us at the moment. What is relevant is that he has the ability to create images that I believe will aid each of you tonight. I urge and expect you to give him your utmost attention."

Mr. DeSanto turned to the right-hand stage and held his arm out. "Josh, you're on."

Carter blinked and his eyes widened as the man beckoned by Chuck's father walked out from the darkness and onto center stage. His facial features became clearer in the light. His clothes, though larger, were of the same arrangement as David's. His hair, his eyes, his skin color—all like David.

Carter tapped Hector on the shoulder as he looked up at the proud gaze of David.

"That's right," David announced, looking behind at his new friends and then pointing toward the stage. "That's right. Josh is my bro."

Carpenters

Doug Mason trudged the office stairs, each step causing him to wonder how he found the energy to run his twenty to thirty miles each week. The dry, biting air carried by the Santa Ana winds ushered in several annoyances: skin that itched, hair that needed constant attention, and eyes that watered. These irritants clouded his day more, seemingly accusing him with menacing smiles and reminding him that he was incapable of emerging from his past, of finding an escape from his guilt, and of being a good husband or father.

He had fallen asleep the night before with some hope that his wife would try to make peace with their son. That failed. And Carter made matters worse by misplacing, or stealing, five more pieces of the crèche.

There was the call from the nursing home in the morning, and Katherine later called from the mall, notifying him that her mother had again relapsed.

Finally, there was the uncertainty of when Carolyn would arrive home.

He reached the top of the stairs and drew a deep breath, closing his eyes and reaching for the bar that pushed the stairwell door open. He felt a dizzy spell and opened his hand, supporting himself against the door. Stars clouded his vision. He waited for it to pass and placed his hand on his temple.

He straightened his tie and pushed open the door. As he made eye contact with his secretary, Karen Jones, he forced a smile. "Any messages?"

"None," she said. "But, your two o'clock is here."

"Oh?"

"He's in the bathroom. Nice gentleman. Very friendly."

"Jacobson, isn't it?"

"Yes, sir."

Doug searched through his mail basket. "Send him in once he comes out."

"Very good, sir."

Doug entered the office while reading an advertisement. He left the door open and sat in his chair behind the desk. He flipped through the booklet when he heard a light knock.

"Doug Mason?" the man asked, his voice piercing the silence with excitement.

"Yes, come in. Please, have a seat."

The man shut the door and walked toward Doug.

Doug stood up, extending his hand. "You must be Mr. Jacobson."

"Thank you for taking the opportunity to meet with me. Being the holidays, I know you must be keeping yourself busy even outside of the office. This time of year; it's magnificent. Really, it's my favorite."

Doug tilted his head, calculating what this man could be up to. His smile seemed genuine, but the way he paraded into the office caught Doug off guard. He felt like he was meeting a title industry salesman at a party, attempting to assume that sense of familiarity that could lead to future business relations.

Jacobson sat on the edge of the chair in front of the desk. "I'm sorry," he said, "did I interrupt?"

"No, no, you didn't. I was just reading here about the latest computers." Doug held up the thin booklet. "It seems they'll make us obsolete. Probably put me out of work."

Jacobson chuckled, "These new machines. They're everywhere."

Doug reached underneath his desk and placed the ad in the trash.

"You have special plans for the holidays?" Jacobson asked.

Doug shook his head, "No."

"No relatives from out of state?"

"I have a daughter at Berkeley. She arrives tonight, we hope. My wife and I are only children. No aunts, uncles, or cousins for the kids. Just the four of us."

"You have two children?"

"A boy and a girl."

"Children are a blessing." He paused and seemed to be lost in thought.

Doug wasn't sure how or when to begin the interview.

Jacobson looked up. "How old is your boy?"

"Eleven." Doug felt an urge to look at the clock across the office but did not want to be rude.

"Eleven," Jacobson clapped his hands and roared with laughter. "He's at the age!"

"He's a handful." Doug smiled politely, becoming irritated with the wasted dialogue. He studied Jacobson further; he was still laughing, though the intensity had diminished, following his commentary on the unique nature of adolescence. His eyes canvassed the office, and he inched back in his chair. He chuckled some more with a constant smile.

Doug reached for a folder and removed the application Jacobson had completed. He read portions of it and then looked back up.

"Eleven," Jacobson muttered, "an exciting age for a child at Christmas."

Doug put the application back into the folder, closed it, and laid it back on the desk. The irritation he had felt moments earlier was gone, pushed aside by an amused curiosity. Doug slid back in his chair and tilted the swivel back. "I'm afraid Carter grew out of that a couple years ago."

"His name is Carter?"

"Just like our president," Doug added.

"Interesting name."

"Actually, he's named after one of my wife's favorite college professors. He was a genius. Our son has got a pretty good head on his shoulders, when he applies himself."

"I'm sure he'll come around. Kids have a way of surprising."

Images of Carter's antics raced through Doug's memory. For the first time, he saw them as a testament of youthful vigor rather than dark rebellion.

"I suppose you have a list of questions for me?" Jacobson asked.

"About the job, yes," Doug straightened his posture, inched up in his chair, and opened the folder again. "You understand what we're looking for?"

"Yes, sir. I've gathered from recent articles in the paper and talk around the sites that business is declining. I imagine your company is looking for quality labor for reasonable prices."

"You seem to have a good grasp of the industry."

Jacobson shrugged. "Not really."

Doug expected him to say more. He had never had an applicant sell himself short. He eyed Jacobson curiously before continuing, trying to determine whether he had the necessary credentials before investing any more time in the interview.

"The work being done by our company is presently located in South Orange County," Doug said. "I don't suspect that would be a problem. From your application it says your expertise is carpentry. Can you describe some of your past jobs?"

"Most of my work is done by me or with the help of my sons."

"A family business?"

"Well, no, not exactly. Most of my past work was done with the help of my sons—furniture, cabinets, chairs, dining tables."

Doug turned the pages of the application and studied it closer, hoping to find a reason to hire Jacobson.

"Did I say something wrong?" Jacobson asked.

"The paper," Doug began, "we tried to make it clear in the newspaper that we were looking for carpenters who have subcontracting experience."

"Oh," Jacobson said. He reclined in the chair, apparently not understanding that he was not qualified to even apply for the job.

"There must be some misunderstanding," Doug continued. "Don't get me wrong; I'm a carpenter myself. It's a hobby of mine. But we're looking for large-scale carpentry contractors. You know, framing homes, lots of homes."

"Oh, I've built many houses."

"But do you own a business? How many employees work for you?"

Jacobson looked confused. "I work for myself."

Doug picked up a pencil and tapped the yellow legal pad on his desk.

"Is that a problem?" Jacobson asked.

"I'm afraid it is."

Jacobson smiled.

His eyes again canvassed the office. He did not seem to understand the awkwardness of the situation and remained seated as though he were waiting for Doug to ask more questions.

His eyes eventually fixed on the shelves behind Doug's desk. "Amazing!" he said.

Doug turned to see the object of his admiration. "It's a boat. A ship really," Doug announced, "used in the War of 1812." He picked it up and handed it to Jacobson. "You see, my wife and I are history fanatics. I try to sculpt objects that have historical significance."

Jacobson leaned forward holding the ship carefully and resting it in both hands. He stood, walked to the window, and held it to the sunlight. "You made this?" he asked. "It's beautiful. So intricate."

"Thank you."

"What type of wood did you use?"

"Oak. I find it strong enough to withstand accidents but soft enough to sculpt with little difficulty."

"Amazing!" Jacobson said again. "Do you have other pieces?"

"Not here I'm afraid. I keep most of my work at home."

Jacobson turned from the window, walked briskly back to Doug's desk, handed the boat back to him, sat down, leaned forward, and asked, "What's you most treasured piece?"

Doug chuckled. He felt his face flush. "You're serious?"

"I know I must seem awfully forward, but I love the smell of freshly sawed wood, the feel of a smoothly sanded surface, the logical process in proceeding with a task, the creativity with which we can express ourselves. That is carpentry, Mr. Mason. And you are very good at it!"

Doug bowed his head in gratitude.

"So, which is it?" Jacobson insisted.

"Well, I guess it would be our dining room table. It was an anniversary gift for my wife. I used mahogany."

Jacobson sat back a few inches in the chair and placed his arms on the rests.

"And you?" Doug asked, wishing to divert attention.

"That would be our first home."

"You built your own home?"

"Many times."

"By yourself?"

"You bet. My kids weren't old enough. There's nothing like a home. There's nothing like building one. You and I have a great gift, Mr. Mason. Our lives are invested in activities with concrete goals and objectives. We see our projects finish before our eyes. We see the joy our projects bring to others.

"The home is where a child's character is formed, where the rational for their actions can be traced. Take myself for example. If you worked with me for any length of time, you would begin to wonder what causes me to act the way I do. If you knew what was going on in my home, well, there would be your answer. I think I've learned more as a parent, more about myself, than all the years before I had become a father. I learned about how deeply selfish I am by nature and how lonely life can be."

"Lonely?" Doug asked. "With all your sons?"

"I didn't always have a full house, but even with all the children and my wife, life's circumstances can leave you feeling very lonely. I can't count all the times we had to move just after establishing relationships with our neighbors. We lived as aliens. Perhaps the worst was when our first son was born. We were traveling, and my wife was pregnant. There were so many tourists that all the hotels were booked. She gave birth outside. Can you believe that? I delivered my own son outside, under a canopy. Two years later, after we had made some friends, we had to move to another country. I had to find work in a land where the people did not speak our language. Years later, when we began to adjust again, we moved back to another town with other people and other customs. All over again, the cycle of loneliness began."

"We've been fortunate, lived in the same house since our first child was born." Doug reached in his pocket and peaked at his watch. The early discovery of Jacobson's lack of qualifications still left ten minutes before the next scheduled interview. He reclined in his chair.

"Do you ever feel lonely?" Jacobson asked.

Doug raised his brows, not sure he understood the purpose of the question. "I guess. Everybody does at one time or another."

"Loneliness," Jacobson murmured. Then he fixed his eyes on Doug. "There's no time worse to experience it than the holidays."

Doug tried to show no reaction.

"Do you know when I feel loneliest?" Jacobson continued. He moved forward in his seat. "It's the fear of not measuring up. You know, those times when you look back and see what you've done and what you haven't done, consider what you are expected to do by your wife, your boss, your children, your society, yourself, only to come to the conclusion that in light of your past failures, you're doomed. 'I'm only a carpenter!' I find myself shouting. How can so much be expected from me?" Jacobson stood up, pacing the floor. "It leaves me feeling so helpless, so lonely."

Doug stared at Jacobson, studying him. He was not sure how to react to his commentary. But with each word Jacobson spoke, it eased the turmoil brewing in Doug's mind since his lunch with Kevin. He was happy that another man understood how it felt and what it meant to fail, and to hear him express it so openly, with such honesty and no shame.

Jacobson turned from the window. "You have children, Mr. Mason. A daughter at Berkeley, a good school. She must be intelligent and a good worker. Probably many other positive qualities. Am I right?" Jacobson held out his arm, inviting Doug to answer.

"Well," Doug paused, "sure."

Jacobson paced some more, one moment speaking to Doug, the next, shuffling toward the window and then toward the door. "What do you do?" he continued. "How do you feel, when it strikes you? When you begin to realize that this son or daughter of yours is facing issues that you have never dealt with? He or she needs advise, and you can't offer it because you've never been at the point where he or she has arrived."

"I suppose you seek another parent's advice."

Jacobson pointed toward the ceiling. "Ahh," he said, "but what if they don't know either? Nobody knows! My point is this: your ignorance leaves you with an awesome awareness of how empty you are! How shallow and incapable of being a father!"

"But none of us have an answer for everything," Doug announced, feeling some frustration that Jacobson should be aware of such an obvious fact.

"But do you see my point? Have you ever felt inadequate as a father?"

Doug owed Jacobson no answer. He felt anger toward Jacobson for presuming he could ask such a question and for presuming such dialogue could be exchanged with a stranger. He kept his mouth shut long enough for Jacobson to begin another inquiry.

"Or how about this scenario? You are involved in some project, a marvelous plan that will benefit all society. It could be a housing project, an office building, your own child, maybe. While completing the task, unbeknownst to you, you discover that you are responsible for the deaths of twenty children!"

Doug furrowed his brow, wondering what type of horrid past this man had lived.

Jacobson continued. "The guilt can paralyze. Believe me, I've been there. Not being a wise enough father. Not sharing in the pain of all those parents whose children were murdered. Guilt is always knocking, waiting for me to welcome it. Waiting for me to surrender."

Doug's anger subsided as he recognized Jacobson's struggle. He seemed content, perhaps happy. Maybe he had found a way to conquer his guilt. Some insight he could share. Doug leaned forward and asked, "And . . . and, do you? Do you surrender to it? I mean, do you surrender to the guilt?"

"I have," Jacobson confessed.

Then he struggled just as Doug. He could offer no assistance. Rather, Doug would have to find words to console Jacobson, just as he consoled Kevin minutes earlier.

"But still," Doug began, "guilt isn't all bad. It keeps us honest. Without it, our society would be in a state of chaos. Without it, every man would do whatever he pleased."

"Look around us," Jacobson answered, "look at this world. Does guilt stop any of us? We can grow so accustomed to functioning alongside of it that we lose consciousness of it. Guilt is not a remedy; it is only an indication that we are in need of a remedy."

Jacobson's face grew stern. He looked at the ceiling and then at Doug. "Do you believe in God, Mr. Mason? I don't mean the god of dos and don'ts we learn about in synagogue and Sunday school, the god who lays down the law and punishes all those who disobey. That's not God. It's an attribute of God, sure, but he's much more than that."

"I guess. Sure."

"He's the remedy, Doug, not guilt. The blunders, the mistakes, the shortcomings, the sins of our past; all of them must be surrendered to this God who has the power to deal with them. He can get rid of them; he can excuse them; he can forgive them. I know what it's like to live with guilt, and I know what it is to live by grace. If He forgives my sin and accepts me with all my shortcomings, then why can't I? When I trust him to deal with me in this world, better than I can deal with myself, that's when life gets exciting. That's when you live free, unhindered, with a joy you not thought possible."

Jacobson stopped. He seemed finished.

He held out his hand, waiting for Doug to stand up. "Well," he said, "I've taken enough of your time. I know you have more interviews and would like to get home before the holiday traffic."

Doug stood, relieved that Jacobson initiated his own exit. "Yes, yes, I do."

"It was nice talking with you, Mr. Mason."

Doug began to extend his hand across the desk, but changed his mind and walked out from behind his desk to walk Jacobson to the door. "Thank you for coming. Sorry we could not work something out."

"Oh, I almost forgot," Jacobson placed his briefcase on top of a file cabinet next to the door. "I brought something for you. Now, it's not a bribe. We know that, since it's clear I won't be getting the job."

Jacobson chortled at his humor. "I try to brighten people's Christmas." He handed a small rectangular box to Doug. It was wrapped in a brown-colored, generic-looking Christmas wrap. Around it was a neatly tied red ribbon.

"Thank you," Doug said, taking a quick inventory of his office, searching for something to give Jacobson. He saw the ship and stepped toward the shelf when Jacobson left the office.

"Merry Christmas!" Jacobson said to Doug's secretary as he walked down the hall.

Doug looked from the ship, to the gift, to Jacobson walking toward the elevator.

"Your three o'clock is here," Karen Jones said from her desk. "In the restroom," She smiled. "I guess they like to freshen up. Not too different than us ladies."

Doug turned and walked toward her desk. "Strange man, Jacobson."

"Sir?" Karen asked.

Doug decided not to entertain any further dialogue. "My next appointment," he instructed, "don't send him in right away."

"Yes, sir."

"I'll buzz you when I'm ready," he called out before turning and closing the door.

"Yes, sir."

Doug returned to his chair, set Jacobson's present on the desk, and stared at it. He turned toward the window and stood up. He walked slowly, as if not wanting to disrupt what he saw outside his window.

There were no clouds. There was no smog. The wind had stopped, but it had left in its wake a basin free of the pollutants that daily deterred him from having a view of Southern California's beaches. The pale orange haze was replaced by a pristine blue to the coastline and to the horizon, past Catalina. Long Beach Harbor was in clear view. He could see what he had always hoped to see—the *Queen Mary* sitting on her watery throne, her bold black bottom, her bright red smokestacks, and her sparkling white trim.

He walked closer to the window. The tri-colored ship was whispering a message to his heart that somehow he had missed all these years.

Black—the color of sin; red—the color of his blood; white— the color of being made clean.

First Kevin and then Jacobson and now the ship—three reminders that his suffering was his choice. There was another option.

Barney Kyle had spoken the words twenty years ago. Doug spoke similar words to Kevin just over an hour earlier. Jacobson testified that it was possible.

Now, for the first time, he heard a voice outside of his own consciousness. It wasn't audible, but he knew whose it was.

"Where you're at right now," it said, "is just fine. There is no need to do anything more than accept my acceptance. It is sufficient. Nothing more is required."

The message was clear. His head had understood the theology, but somehow, his heart had failed to grasp the significance.

Still, he hung his head and turned back to his desk. He looked to the floor.

He turned again, the clear view of the ship still present.

Accepting this offer had a price: acknowledgment that the past twenty years were in vain and that it took twenty years to recognize this.

Again, he turned to his desk. He sat in his chair and picked up Jacobson's gift, tossing the small brown package into his briefcase.

He pressed the intercom button.

"Karen," he said, "send in my three thirty."

Within Another's Shoes

He had already allowed five minutes to pass without making a move. It was ten minutes to four o'clock, and he not only had to get the cards back from Chuck, but then he had to find a way to arrive at the card shop before five, sell the cards, and race to the jewelry store before it closed.

Too many things could go wrong. Too many things had already gone wrong. How could he be sure to get the value he needed from the cards? The owner of the shop would certainly perceive Carter's anxiousness to sell and therefore not offer fair market value. There was no assurance that he could get the cards from Chuck. He needed Chuck to be distracted, something, or someone, that would divert his attention long enough for Carter to grab the cards from Chuck's backpack. But, Carter suddenly thought of something more frightening: What if Chuck left the cards at his house? What if he had not brought them with him?

Carter lowered his head, ashamed, angry, and frustrated. Why hadn't he considered this possibility? But, as Carter looked at the clock, realizing he had let five minutes pass without making any attempt to accomplish his goal, he rose from his seat, walked slowly passed Hector, gently grazing his shoulder, letting him know that he was making a move, and cautiously advanced two rows ahead of where Hector was seated.

He stopped, wanting to make sure that his movement had not drawn attention from Chuck or anyone else in the theater. Fortunately, the speaker, David's older brother Joshua, was engaging the actors, in a way that Carter himself had been lost in his monologue, costing him those five precious minutes.

"Wait!" someone shouted.

Carter froze.

Fear to make any movement prevented him from looking to his left or right, in hopes of discovering that the command was directed to someone other than himself.

Seconds of silence passed until the voice spoke again. "Be not afraid," it said loudly.

Carter felt some relief, not because the voice had said, "Be not afraid," but because he now recognized who spoke the words. It was Joshua.

Still, the fright was enough to convince Carter to sit on the aisle seat, now three rows in front of Hector. At least some progress had been made without his presence being noticed by Chuck.

He took several deep breaths as Joshua continued speaking.

"Be not afraid?" Joshua spoke it now as a question, raising his tone as if the statement was incredulous. "Imagine," he continued, motioning to the group of actors, "every night, for over ten years, for some of you maybe twenty or thirty years, you work outside in these fields. You are familiar with the most subtle sights and sounds—the wind blowing through the grass; a chirping cricket; water trickling, sometimes racing, through stone-bed streams and paths; frogs bellowing in the distant marshes; a horse's neighing; the rusty wheels of a chariot growing nearer on the main highway leading to the city. As for the sights, you long for those evenings when the moon shone bright and full, but even on those rare nights, clouds from the nearby sea would often keep you from having a clear view of the land.

"Silence was king out there," Joshua explained. "No music, no radio, no television. Just the sheep, walking back and forth, grazing, bleating.

Carter's eyes fixed on Joshua. He walked from one end of the stage to the other, raising his hands to expound his points. Then, for what seemed a minute, Joshua did not speak. Carter heard voices behind him. He looked back at Hector and David. They were now sitting next to one another and whispering. Carter attempted to grab Hector's attention, to encourage him to cease talking, but Hector seemed too preoccupied and did not respond to Carter's gestures.

He decided to make another move for the cards. As he began to rise from his seat, Joshua once again shouted and raised his arms above his head, spread eagle.

"A brilliant light that had no business being there shone all around. And in the middle of that light was a figure, the figure of a man."

Joshua lowered his arms and sat on the stage, his legs dangling over the edge. He seemed less intense. "Now all of you have an image in your mind of how you believe an angel may appear. It may be from a Renaissance painting, a Christmas card, or a show you have watched. Even two thousand years ago, the people had conceptions—preconceived ideas of what angels may look like. Even they, like you today, would be frozen with fear in the presence of one.

"So when this angel speaks, 'Be not afraid,' you must think of what your reaction would be. A simple nod? Saying, 'Okay, I believe you. Let's go, guys.' And with a wave of your hand you do what he instructs?"

Joshua shook his head. "You listen to him. You listen in awe, your mouth open, your nerves rattling, your skin still shivering and moist with perspiration. For if you are not dead already from the fright you had just experienced in seeing the light and seeing this being, then he must intend no harm to you."

Carter knew there was no turning back. Time was not on his side. But two things kept him from making any further advance: First, he sensed the moment was not right. He was just a couple rows from the center of the theater, and his movement may be an interruption to what was transpiring on stage. He would not only then be seen by Chuck, but also be the cause of ire by all the actors and Mr. DeSanto. Secondly, Carter wanted to hear the rest of Joshua's narration.

He hunched over in his seat and sighed. He began to feel defeat enveloping him.

"'I bring you good news of a great joy which will come to all the people.'" Joshua had stood back up and began pacing the stage again, keeping eye contact with the actors. "'For to you is born this day in the city of David a Savior, who is Christ the Lord. And this will be a sign for you: you will find a babe wrapped in swaddling cloths and lying in a manger.' And suddenly there was with the angel a multitude of the heavenly host praising God and saying, 'Glory to God in the highest, and on earth peace among men with whom he is pleased!'"

Joshua paused.

Carter felt a window of opportunity, if only he could move forward and not break the silence. He made it down three more rows unnoticed.

"This is crucial," Joshua focused his attention on the group of actors who would play the shepherds. "Somehow, you must find a way to express to the audience the urgency you feel to obey the angel's command to go to Bethlehem. The passage says that they went with haste. They found the baby and their parents . . ."

Carter knew the story. Feeling he had little more to glean from Joshua's insights, he quickly moved forward two more rows, turned to his left, and moved across the center aisle to the left-hand side, six rows directly behind Chuck. He did this with such ease that he was surprised at how close he now was to Chuck. He moved forward one more row and slowly sat in the reclining theater seat. It squeaked as he rested into place.

Chuck looked over his shoulder and spotted Carter. Immediately, Chuck reached for his backpack and placed it on his lap. He raised his chin, squinted his eyes at Carter, and looked at his father.

Carter too looked at Mr. DeSanto and then back at Chuck. Of course, why hadn't he acted on this earlier? Before entering the theater, Carter had hoped to somehow get Mr. DeSanto on his side, but on seeing Chuck's father on stage, interacting with his students, such a plan seemed pointless. Interrupting Mr. DeSanto would not make him an ally.

He studied Chuck further; his profile reflected trepidation, fear, that somehow his father might not be pleased with Carter's cards being in his son's backpack. Carter began formulating a new plan, a way to inform or at least cause Chuck to think that he would inform his dad of what his son had done.

But still, the time was not right. Joshua continued speaking to the actors.

Carter's hands grew moist. He had to act but was afraid to make himself an annoyance.

Next, Joshua spoke to the actress who would portray Mary. "By far the most difficult role," Joshua explained. "More than any other person, she understood the significance of the child she had just given birth to. Yet she still had questions. If this child was really the Messiah, how capable was she of raising such a significant person in the history of her people? Furthermore, the angel said that he was Emanuel, God with us. Was she then to believe that she had just given birth to God himself?

"Yes, we know she believed this; the Gospels record as much," Joshua explained. "But, once again, try to reflect on the immense responsibility, the uncertainty of all that went through her mind."

The actress nodded.

But Joshua did not seem content. "All this on top of the inconvenience of giving birth in a stable. The smells of the cattle, the discomfort of hay prickling you as you lay, going through contractions, your perspiration unending, nearing complete exhaustion."

Again, the actress nodded, this time more emphatically, convincing Joshua to turn his attention to the actor who would play Joseph.

Joshua began to explain to the actor that Joseph shared not only the questions running through the mind of Mary, but also questions of pride and shame. "Pride that was injured because this first son was not his; shame that he felt this pride."

Carter was desperate. Regardless of any word that Joshua may speak, he could no longer listen and wait. As he rose, Chuck and Tony began to shove one another. Mr. DeSanto quickly walked to his sons. His presence was enough to bring a momentary peace.

Carter looked at Mr. DeSanto. Their eyes met. Carter waved his hand, smiled, and sat back down.

Shaking his head, Carter knew his moment had passed. He blew it. He lowered his head in defeat.

Out of the corner of his eye, he saw Tony slug his older brother in the shoulder. Carter looked at Mr. DeSanto who did not appear to see his youngest son's assault.

Carter jerked his head back toward the two brothers in time to see Chuck stand and slug his younger brother in the stomach. A loud thud echoed through the theater, followed by Tony's struggles to silence his sobs.

Joshua had lost the attention of all the actors. Mr. DeSanto raced to his sons and dragged them to the rear of the stage.

From Carter's seat, he could see what transpired among the DeSanto family. He looked around in dismay, at the actors and stage hands, hoping they could see what he saw, but not only could they not see because of the angle of their seats, but also Joshua had begun his concluding remarks and regained their attention.

Already, Chuck's father had slapped Chuck across the face three times. Chuck was holding up his arms in defense, attempting to stop any further blows. Tony had raced to his father, and began pleading with him to stop. Mr. DeSanto held Tony tightly around his waist and threw him to the floor.

Still, Chuck did not cry. He stood stone-faced, making no eye contact with his father but looking at some point, it seemed, far away, outside the walls of the theater.

The Hammer and the Light

It was over.

Joshua coached the actors, received light applause, and walked to the rear seats of the theater, joining his younger brother David.

All hope of getting the cards was lost. Had he been alert, Carter would have risen from his seat when Chuck and his brother were scolded by their father, opened Chuck's backpack, and taken back the stolen cards.

As he drew near to Hector, David, and Joshua, he heard Joshua speaking in an excited whisper. Hector was leaning forward; David was standing, fidgeting, and rubbing his hands as his brother spoke.

"Carter," Hector shouted, "come here! This is cool!"

Whatever Joshua was speaking seemed to be the cause of Hector's excitement. Carter, hoping it involved some plan to get back his cards, quickened his pace and slid into a seat across the aisle from Hector. Just then Allen walked through the center doors.

"Hi guys." Allen waved. "Where's Chuck?"

Carter recalled the hurtful words Allen had spoke a couple hours earlier. He felt uncomfortable, not wanting to acknowledge Allen's presence.

"He's up front," Hector answered, "but I wouldn't go up there."

Allen looked to Hector and then Carter. "Why? What's up?"

"Chuck's dad laid it to him a few minutes ago," Carter answered. He looked at Allen. His eyes seemed to beg for more details.

"He'll be okay." Hector waved his hand. "It's Chuck. He always lands on his feet."

Allen did not appear convinced. He looked to the stage, his eyes darting from left to right, as he slowly sat in the seat behind Hector.

"Hey, Carter," Hector announced, "Joshua was telling us about Christmas."

"Yeah, I know. I heard him."

"No, but before there was a Christmas. Before Jesus was born."

Carter narrowed his eyes, studying Hector. "How can there be a Christmas before Jesus?"

"A long time ago," Joshua started, "before there was a New Testament, but after all the people and events you have learned about from the Old Testament—great men like Noah, Abraham, Joseph, Moses, David, Samuel."

"Samuel," Carter said softly, thinking of Nana reading the story of the boy prophet.

"All these men and women had several things in common," Joshua continued.

"They were all Jewish?" Allen asked.

Joshua looked at Allen and smiled. "No, not all of them. Each was used by God to do some great act, an act of deliverance or an act of awakening. Whatever it was, the act was to help the Jewish people—to help them succeed, to help them defeat their enemies, to help them through difficulties such as famines and droughts, to help them please God.

Allen stopped looking to the front of the theater. His eyes were fixed on Joshua. Carter could tell his curiosity had been captured. Still bitter over Allen's hurtful words spoken outside the schoolyard, Carter observed with envy his friend's enjoyment. Allen once had apologized for things which did not require an apology; now he did not appear to recognize the potency of the words he had spoken.

"But like all humans," Joshua continued, "the Jewish people were not perfect. As often as God granted deliverance or success, the people would soon forget Him. They took Him for granted, not thanking

Him for His deliverance, forgetting that it was He who blessed them. They thought His help was no longer needed. As a result, they got themselves into situations in which they became victims of stronger nations with wicked kings whose only aim was to oppress and use the Jewish people and their land for their own gain. This happened again, and again, and again. Most of the heroes you read about in the Old Testament looked forward to a better day—a day when God's deliverance would be complete and final, a day when God would not only deliver the Jewish people, but would also provide deliverance for all the other nations."

"And?" Allen asked.

Hector interrupted, "Was there a deliverer?"

Although Carter felt some intrigue for Joshua and his narration, he was nowhere near as excited as Hector and Allen appeared. He was busy thinking over his failures throughout the day. The more Joshua spoke, the more his friends listened, the longer he would have to sit in the theater, dwelling on the fact that he had lost over five hundred dollars worth of baseball cards and still not found or replaced the golden manger.

"Tell them more," David pleaded with his brother. "It gets better."

Joshua leaned against the row of seats behind him and patted one of the upholstered seats, inviting David to sit. "You're making me nervous, little brother. Have a seat."

David obediently sat as Joshua continued. "This cycle continued for hundreds and thousands of years: receiving God's blessings, forgetting God and relying upon themselves, suffering under the hand of wicked nations, seeking for God's deliverance, God once again delivering, once again blessing.

"Then one day, there was a great king. You probably have learned about him in school. He was an emperor, Alexander the Great. He conquered most of the world, including Israel. After he died, his kingdom was divided into four sections. Israel was part of one section, the Seleucid Empire. Another section was the Ptolemaic Empire. Egypt was part of this second section."

Hector raised his hand, smiling, "I know where that is!" Carter imagined the great emperor. During a recent lesson, Miss Carson had introduced the class to the young conqueror. Carter had been fascinated that someone could rise to great power at such a young age. He inched forward in his seat, eager to learn more.

"These two empires fought constantly for over a hundred years. The Jewish people were caught in the middle. Then the most wicked of all the emperors, Antiochus the IV, insisted that all Jewish customs no longer be practiced. Any Jew that disobeyed would be put to death. He set up an idol of the Greek god Zeus in the temple. Many of the Jews obeyed Antiochus's orders; others refused and fled to the wilderness. But there was one man, a priest, named Mattathias who had five sons, who stood his ground, refusing to obey the emperor's order.

"Mattathias was so angry that he killed a fellow Jew who was worshiping the idol. Later, he killed some of Antiochus's servants.

"These actions led to revolts led by his five sons. Antiochus's soldiers tried to defeat them, but God continued to grant deliverance to his people."

"Maccabees," Allen said. "You're talking about Judas Maccabees."

"Who's that?" Hector asked.

"Never heard of him," Carter added.

"C'mon guys," Allen said, looking at Hector and then Carter. "It's what Hanukkah is all about."

Carter looked at the brothers. "Really?"

"Why didn't you ever tell us?" Hector asked.

"Yeah," Carter added, "this is a cool story."

Allen raised his shoulders. "You never asked."

He turned in his seat toward Joshua. "He was the middle son, right?"

"That's right. And you know what 'Maccabees' means?"

Allen shook his head. "It's just their name. The family name."

"It means *hammer*." David stood up, pounding the seat in front of him. "*Hammer*."

Joshua patted him on the back. "So named because he hammered, or defeated, all the enemies of the Jews."

Two streams of thought were now battling for Carter's attention. The first was excitement. This Maccabees fellow accomplished what the shepherd boy David did when he defeated Goliath, what Daniel did when he was thrown into the den of lions, and what Joseph accomplished in Egypt. All faced overwhelming odds and emerged victorious. Could Carter possibly hope to experience similar deliverance? The second stream of thought was to piece together how this story had anything to do with Christmas, for that is what got Hector so excited in the first place.

"Wait 'til you hear the rest!" David enticed.

"But how does all this have anything to do with Christmas?" Hector asked.

"You mean," Allen started, "you mean, the two are related? Hanukkah and Christmas have something in common?"

"That's how we got started talking," Hector said. "Just before you and Carter got here, they were telling me about the world before Jesus was born, the Jewish world. How they were waiting for a great king."

"Very good." Joshua pointed at Hector with his hand. "Very good, Mr. Hector."

David clapped and then patted Hector on the back.

"This Judas Maccabees," Joshua continued, "continually came up with ways to defeat the Syrians against overwhelming odds. Historians may say that it was because of his brilliant battle strategies, but the Jewish people then, as many Jewish people today, believe that it was God's hand that gave them victory. Just as God miraculously parted the Red Sea, or brought down the walls of Jericho, so God led Judas Maccabees and his army to victory."

Carter felt a thunderous, affirmative "Amen" echoing in his head. He smiled and inched up further in his seat, hoping to receive further confirmation that there was hope, hope for even him.

"All had not been won, however," Joshua warned. "The temple was still occupied by foreigners, and in it, was a statue of a Greek god. Judas was determined to bring this to an end!

"After the people devoted themselves to prayer, they raided the temple and destroyed all the idols. They repaired portions of the temple that had been destroyed, and they began to offer incense and sacrifice to God like they did before Antiochus arrived on the scene. The nation was so appreciative, so grateful, they spent a whole day burning sacrifices to God. All this happened on the morning of the twenty-fifth day of Kislev, or December on today's calendar. On this day, everybody worshipped God, knowing it was He who had given success over their enemies. But one day was not enough to express thanks to their God. So they extended the celebration another seven days. They decorated the temple with gold crowns and shields; they repaired the gates and the priest's chambers; they lighted lamps. Judas and his brothers decreed that an eight-day celebration should be kept year after year.

"That's why we call it the Feast of Lights," Allen said. "Or Hanukkah. I have heard most of that, but I didn't know about the names of the emperor and all the other stuff the Macabbees did."

"But what happened after?" Hector asked. "Did the Hammer become king?"

"No," Joshua said. "Sadly, what happened in the years after the festival followed the same pattern Jewish history had in previous years. Judas's followers relied on their power, and Judas himself forgot about God, became arrogant and less grateful. Eventually, he died in battle. All but one of his brothers died premature deaths by violence. Once the last brother, Simon, died, family conflicts caused more chaos for the Jewish nation. Children put their own mothers into prison, in-laws murdered one another, and in the end, the people splintered into factions. They had greater freedom, but the Roman Empire was soon to take that away."

"Then why celebrate at all?" Carter asked. "Why is a victory that was so short-lived remembered for so long?"

Carter looked at Allen, hoping not to have offended him. But Allen was nodding, apparently wondering the same.

"It's the symbolism, Carter," explained Joshua. "The feast of Hanukkah is a symbol of hope for Jewish people everywhere. It marks a true miracle in the lives of our ancestors. God provided a deliverer, and we continue to hope for the ultimate deliverer, what we call a Messiah, one who will deliver us and our decedents forever."

"And the lights?" Hector asked.

"They represent hope," Joshua answered, "the hope of a Messiah who will light the way?"

"But," Hector began, "but wasn't Jesus the Messiah, the king they had looked forward to?"

Allen shook his head. "That's not what we believe."

Allen looked at the two brothers. They were silent. "You guys are Jewish, right?"

"We are," Joshua agreed.

Allen continued, "Then you agree, Jesus is not the Messiah?"

"Do you remember how I said that many of the people you read about in the Old Testament had two common traits?" Joshua asked.

"I think so," Hector answered.

"What were they?"

"God did great things through them," Hector said.

"And?"

Allen raised his hand. "And they looked forward to a greater deliverance."

Carter glanced at Allen. It was strange; somehow that biting bitterness he had felt minutes earlier had lessened. The camaraderie he usually shared with Hector and Allen had returned.

"A greater deliverer!" Joshua clarified Allen's answer. "Each of them realized their humanity. They understood and believed the promises that God had given to their forefather Abraham, that he would bless the whole world through the Jewish nation. It's appropriate that Christmas is celebrated on the twenty-fifth of December, so close to the Jewish Feast of Lights. Although the Messiah was actually born during the spring, it is appropriate to celebrate his birth during the same season as Hanukkah."

"In the spring?" Hector repeated in unbelief. "But Easter is in the spring!"

"You sound so sure of that," Carter said skeptically, looking at Joshua, "as if you were there!"

David moved closer to his brother, standing beside him and his head only slightly above Joshua's waist. "You heard my brother earlier? Up on stage?"

"Yes," Hector answered.

Carter recalled Joshua's description of the weather that night. It would have been balmy and cool, he had explained to the actors, but not cold as one would think of a winter night.

"What's all this about?" Allen asked. "What happened on stage? What did I miss?"

"You see," Joshua began, "that baby was the Light. Not just one light on the menorah, but the ultimate light who delivers us from any foe, even the strongest. He was, and is, the Messiah we had been looking for back then. That is why we celebrate both Hanukkah and Christmas. God has been our nation's deliverer, yes. That is why we celebrate Hanukkah. But of greater importance, God has now ensured the entire world of deliverance. That is why we celebrate Christmas!"

The lights of the theater dimmed and some of the actors left through side exits, others walking up the aisle. Carter stood up, trying to spot Chuck. Maybe there was still a chance of getting the cards. He looked at the clock. It was after five.

Although Joshua's stories offered hope, all they accomplished in the real world was to divert Carter's attention so that nothing could be done to salvage his day.

He lowered his head, his chin sinking to his chest.

"What's wrong?" David asked.

Hector placed his hand on Carter's shoulder. "Cart. You okay?"

Carter ground his teeth and shook his head. There was nothing left to do but go home and endure whatever his parents had decided would be his punishment.

He buried his hands in his front pockets, kicked the ground, and turned toward Allen, Hector, and the two brothers.

Allen walked toward the stage, looking over his shoulder. "I better go see if I can help Chuck." He turned back around. "See you guys tomorrow?" he directed the question at Hector and Carter.

"Cart," Allen started, paused, and then walked back toward the four of them.

Carter looked up.

Allen lowered his eyes. "Sorry. Sorry 'bout this afternoon. You know, with Chuck."

Carter smiled. Something, at least, had not changed for the worse.

"Nice meeting you two," Allen shook the brothers' hands.

"One minute, Allen," Joshua pleaded.

Allen looked at the older brother.

"David?" Joshua beckoned.

David wore the same smile that first grabbed Carter's attention on the playground. He had seen it throughout the day and realized now that he may not see it again. In the midst of all the day's disappointment, this small kid amused Carter.

David reached inside a grocery bag that Joshua had carried with him from the stage. He handed a small box to Allen.

"For, for me?" Allen stuttered.

"For you," David answered.

Allen bowed his head. "Thank you."

The two brothers bowed their heads in return. "Happy Hanukkah."

"Happy Hanukkah," Allen replied. He turned, walked slowly to the front of the theater, looked at his gift, then back at the brothers, waved one last time, turned, and called out, "Chuck. Hey, Chuck."

"And for you two," Joshua announced.

David reached inside the bag and handed a present to Hector.

Hector ripped it open. It was a set of drafters' and artists' pencils.

Hector held the set with outstretched arms, turning them at all angles. "How'd you guys know?"

Carter could see the gift was valuable. The strangeness of it all was that they could not have chosen a more perfect gift for his friend.

Although Hector's mother would have liked to purchase such a set, Carter knew she would not be able to afford the quality of the pencils that Hector now held.

"I can't accept these. I don't know how to thank you."

"Using your gift for what God intends shows the greatest gratitude," Joshua said.

David's smile widened as he reached inside and handed another gift to Hector. "This is for Chuck."

Carter's heart leaped, it seemed, to his throat. How could this kid so willingly offer a gift, and with a smile so large and genuine, to the jerk who intentionally hit him on the head with a football and almost fed him to the Redford's pit bull?

David reached into the bag and held one last gift. "This is for you, Cous'." David winked as he held it in front of Carter.

Surprised at the gift, surprised at the mist he felt in his eyes, he reached for the gift, saying nothing.

Joshua crumpled the bag and handed it back to David. "Remember, Carter, what we spoke of today," he said. Remember what you have heard. Remember what you read in class this morning: 'Thus by the shepherds, secrets are revealed, which from all other men are kept concealed.'"

Carter bit his lip; he had read those same words in Bunyan's book, just hours earlier, prior to Hector's show-and-tell presentation. Here was a man whom he had just met, reciting these same words, somehow privy that Carter would know their significance.

He held the present bashfully at his side.

"Well, Carter," Hector prompted, "aren't you going to open it?"

He shook his head.

"You don't mind?" Carter asked looking at the brothers.

"No, not at all," Joshua answered.

"You'll like it!" David announced, looking up and smiling at his big brother.

"My papers!" Hector shouted, turned his wrist, and looked at his watch. "We've got to do my route!"

Carter followed Hector's motions, shaking the hands of both brothers. As Hector exited the theater, Carter lingered, wanting to express gratitude for the gift or to say it was a pleasure meeting both of them, but he couldn't think of the words to say. He looked at the two brothers, his eyes meeting theirs. He was fearful of Joshua mostly for speaking the exact words printed in Bunyan's book. He wasn't sure what that meant. Perhaps it was just coincidence.

"Thank you," he finally said in a soft voice, grinning to express more gratitude. He waved good-bye, turned, and raced after Hector.

Big News

There was a rhythm Hector entered, which always frustrated Carter and made him a little envious whenever he assisted with his friend's paper route. It was a gentle reminder at how adept Hector was at tasks and how inept he was; how responsible his friend had become at twelve years old and how irresponsible he still was. Regardless, he enjoyed these times, witnessing this kid become immersed in such a mundane activity, excel at it, and do it with unconscious pride.

Carter could not imagine having this responsibility each day, the expectation to stuff the papers, fold the papers, and deliver the papers. On some days, thin paper, spattered with grocery advertisements and various other ads, was required to be wrapped within the newspaper itself. Hector called these *inserts*; Carter referred to them as *a pain.* There would be days when there were no inserts; those were the days on which Hector could finish his route within an hour and then join the neighborhood gang for some football, basketball, or baseball. However, there were days, and their frequency increased as the holidays drew near, when the number of inserts could be five or six. Advertisements from department stores, furniture warehouses, discount drug stores, auto retailers, and real estate agencies, all required Hector to invest an additional amount of time when folding his papers.

He arranged the inserts, along with the newspaper itself, in stacks surrounding him, in a curved, crescent-shaped pattern. The newspaper would be at the leftmost end of the crescent; the inserts to the right of it, arranged by thickness. The heaviest insert would be just to the right of the newspaper; the lightest, farthest from it.

As they approached their neighborhood, the street light across from the Romero's home shone down on the stacks of paper, casting short shadows on their driveway. With Christmas Eve the following day, there were six inserts to feed into the main paper. This was the first time Carter would help Hector on a day like this.

Hector sighed at the sight of them and blew through his lips, lifted the garage door, flipped the light switch on the far wall of the garage, returned to the driveway, picked up the first stack, and carried it into the garage.

Carter admired his friend in action and, on most days, would have been content to remain a spectator while Hector labored, but, since Hector had gone out of his way to try and help him get back the cards from Chuck and since Carter was in no hurry to return to his house, he welcomed the idea of filling the next hour with manual labor.

Each of the bundled stacks was held in place by a bright yellow plastic band. Going to all seven bundles, Hector released the tension in each band by breaking the plastic seal, creating a pop that echoed in the Romero garage. Somehow, this sound always gave Carter a warm feeling inside.

Next, Hector arranged the stacks in his patented crescent-shaped order and sat on the inside of the curve. Carter smiled, thinking of how his friend resembled a percussionist in Kiss, Styx, or Led Zeppelin.

With his right hand, Hector fed the lightest of the six inserts into the next lightest and then into the heaviest, and finally all the inserts into the newspaper itself.

"Carter," Hector said as he finished the first paper, "I forgot the rubber bands."

Carter raced to the tool chest, on top of which he remembered Hector kept a large Folgers coffee can filled with the rubber bands that would secure the fold in each paper.

He raced back to Hector, opened the lid, and handed the can to him. "What do you want me to do?" he asked.

Hector wrapped a band around the first paper, threw it across the garage floor, and began the process of feeding the inserts one into the other.

He finished the second paper, a third, and a fourth. Carter did not want to disrupt his progress.

Once he had finished ten papers, Hector instructed, "Get my bag and start placing them in the order I like."

"Okay," Carter answered, hoping he knew the pattern to which Hector referred.

"And Carter," Hector continued, taking the time to make eye contact, "today one isn't enough. These burgers are huge," he announced, holding up the monster newspaper he had just finished folding. He threw number twelve into the growing pile, "I'll need you to fill two bags and, if you can, help me deliver."

Carter was thrilled to have another excuse for delaying his return home. He ran to the other bag hanging on the wall at the other end of the garage, grabbed it, and raced back to Hector.

The bold aroma of the fresh newspaper print excited Carter. He placed one paper on top of another in the canvas bag that would rest on top of Hector's banana-seat bicycle. He was smiling and thought how odd it was for him to be happy. Thoughts of Chuck, Nana, Mom, and Shannon quickly erased the smile

"Hey, Cart?" Hector asked.

Carter had finished one side of the bag but was afraid that he had made a mistake. But Hector wasn't looking at him; he was still in his rhythm, feeding one insert into the next.

"Yeah," Carter replied.

"That Joshua. He got me thinking."

On the way home from the university, Carter could not recall any conversation with Hector. Carter had been preoccupied, attempting to refrain from letting his emotions become visible, wondering, at times dreading, what other awful event may occur, and contemplating the useless nature of life and how correct Shannon's friend, Albert Camus, was in asserting as much. Carter was in no mood for conversation; he was appreciative that Hector had not been in one of his talking fits, making conversation about any mundane occurrence he saw. It wasn't that Hector irked Carter when he talked endlessly, for most of the topics about which he talked also interested Carter, but tonight, Carter was in no mood to engage in such dialogue.

Hector's excitement on any subject was evident when he spoke: When he was sitting, his legs would move rapidly, tapping the ground and knocking against one another. When he was standing, or walking, his hands would constantly be rubbing against one another.

Now Carter remembered seeing these same agitated features, minus the talk, on their way home. At one point, Carter realized he was walking alone. He looked back and saw Hector's silhouette under the bright moon. It appeared that he was having a conversation, his lips moving and making some muttering noise, and his hands doing their thing.

Carter stopped packing the bags. He glanced at Hector, wondering what Joshua could have said that made such an impression on his friend.

"Thinking?" Carter echoed Hector's question. "About what?"

Hector stopped folding the papers. "Did I ever tell you about the last time I spoke with my dad?"

Carter froze. He shook his head.

"I was five. We had just finished dinner. My two sisters were there, at the table, but they weren't old enough to remember him."

Hector had never spoken to Carter about his dad. He wasn't sure how to react, or what to say, so he continued to fill the canvas bags with the papers as Hector spoke.

"It was the night he left for Pendleton. A couple weeks later, they shipped him to Vietnam. It was the last time I saw him."

Hector was looking at the floor. He did not appear sad, or solemn, but wrinkled his eyes like he was trying hard to remember.

"He walked up to me while I was eating some ice cream, squatted, and looked into my eyes, like he was about to say the most important thing he had ever told me. I remember thinking that this was when he'd tell me there was no Santa, or wondering if I had forgotten something bad I had done and he was going to discipline me.

"What he say?" Carter asked.

"He placed his hand on my shoulder and then my head and then my shoulder again. I guess he was waiting for me to finish my ice cream.

"'Hector,' he finally said when I put the last spoonful in my mouth, 'I won't see you for some time.'

"I don't remember what I did, and I don't remember a whole lot of what else he told me that night."

Carter raised his eyes, wondering if Hector would resume folding the papers and what this story about his father had to do with Joshua.

"Don't remember a whole lot," Hector muttered as he picked up the next insert, "except one thing."

Carter stopped packing again. He studied Hector, anticipating his next words.

"He called it 'the big news.'"

"Big news?" Carter repeated.

"That's it." Hector paused and then continued, "He told me that important men are in the newspaper, men who run countries, who have lots of money, and who do amazing things. 'All of them,' he said, 'they are the news.'

"Then he tells me that no matter what any man or woman may do, no matter how hard anybody tries, it can never make everyone happy. There will always be fighting. 'They're waiting for the big news,' he told me, 'Son, we're all waiting for the big news.'"

Hector had resumed the rhythm of folding the newspapers. The movement of his hands, the feeding of inserts, and the wrapping of rubber bands around the folded bulges replaced his otherwise fidgeting hands when he entered into one of his monologues. Carter could see it in his friend's eyes; he was on the verge of expounding.

"Remember what Joshua told us? That before there were any Christmases, the Jewish people were waiting for a Messiah. Someone, just like my dad told me, who seeks to change the world, make it happier for everyone. No fighting, stuff like that."

Now, he understood the connection between Hector's father and Joshua. He was following Hector so far.

"A week or so ago, I asked my mom why does God allow so much wrong in the world. 'Has Jesus failed to accomplish what he had intended by coming from heaven? Did he die on the cross for nothing?'

"So I asked her. And she tells me, 'Hector, Jesus didn't fail.'"

Carter studied Hector. He hadn't realized his friend struggled with these same questions.

"What did your mom say?" Carter asked.

Hector looked up, confused. "I told you. She said, 'Jesus didn't fail.'"

"I don't get it," Carter confessed.

"I didn't either," Hector announced, "until today."

All the papers were folded. Hector jumped to his feet and began filling the second bag with the folded newspapers remaining on the garage floor.

"You mean," Carter asked, "he didn't fail?"

Hector shook his head. "No, it's not that he didn't fail to do all those things; that's not the problem. The problem is that we expect him to do all those things. We thought we knew why he came, but we were wrong. Just like Joshua was telling us about the Jewish nation before Jesus. They were expecting someone to defeat the Romans, just like those five brothers defeated their enemies. We are expecting Jesus to defeat our enemies, cure all sickness, take away all poverty, make everyone happy."

Carter finished filling the first canvas bag, lifted it, and placed it on Hector's bike. "Then why did he come?" he asked.

"Mom says that there is nothing more evil in this world than the human heart."

"So?" Carter said.

"He came to take that evil out."

“Yeah?” Carter waited for more explanation.

“I’m just guessing here,” Hector said, “but I bet it’s more of a miracle to change my heart than to take away all sickness, rid the world of poverty, and defeat my enemies.”

Hector had finished filling the second bag and placed it on one of his sisters’ bikes. “You don’t mind riding a girly bike, do you, Cart?”

Carter shook his head. He had begun recycling Hector’s words, wondering if they may be valid, how his parents may respond, and how Shannon may answer the questions racing through his mind. He was oblivious to how he may appear on a pink Schwinn.

Menagerie

Walk away.

Don't turn around.

Don't turn back.

Find the car. Open the car. Stick the keys in ignition. Drive home.

Wrap the presents purchased from the bookstore.

Cook dinner.

And wait.

It was so clear, not easy, but clear. Forget about the girl in the mall. Forget about what she had said. Forget about whom she had feared her to be.

But what of the rest of the family? How was she to insure that none of them would encounter any of these unwelcome visitors?

Any abnormal attempts she may make to intercept or interrupt the chance meetings could cause her family to place more significance on the encounters than if she made no attempts at all.

She felt overwhelmed, uncertain as to whether she should warn her husband, drive to Carter's school, and phone Carolyn. Though they each knew of the crèche's history with the Thurman family, none of them knew of this special attribute. She resigned herself to do nothing, nothing until any of them tried to enter her home. She would not allow this.

She hoisted the bags upstairs and dumped the books onto the bed. One by one, she wrapped each book and set it aside, weighing the options of what she would cook for dinner. As she reached for the final book to wrap, she discovered a small rectangular box that did not look familiar, that she had not purchased.

She opened it.

She turned the small box upside down, emptying the contents. A worn, wooden, manger figurine fell into her other hand, one of the five she had discovered missing in the morning.

It was Mary.

She bit her lip and closed her eyes and breathed deep.

She breathed deeper and held her hands on the side of her temples.

The wooden nativity piece prodded her head. She lowered her hand, opened her palm, and glared at it.

She placed it back into the box, placed the box into one of the bags that had been full of books, and threw the bag into the corner of her closet.

If she could focus on dinner, if she could make peace with Carter, if she and Carolyn could have a deep, long dialogue, and if she and Douglas could share intimacy tonight, then the box was irrelevant. It would stay in the closet and life in the Mason home could turn back in the direction of normality.

She would make her home as it used to be without the help of the miraculous or supernatural but with her strength, with her determination, with her wisdom, and with her love.

Knowing she did not have the necessary ingredients in the house to make dinner, she rushed down the stairs, wrote a note explaining her absence in case Carolyn got home, grabbed her purse, and drove to the nearest grocery store.

Although he would be back to work within three days, he left the office feeling a freedom akin to the last day of school before summer vacation.

His drive home offered some respite from the day's turmoil: there was little traffic, the radio stations were all playing Christmas music, and it seemed each song was from an artist in the forties and fifties, causing him to reminisce of his childhood and adolescence, creating an anticipation he had not felt in years.

As he turned onto his street and pulled into the driveway of his home, he remembered Jacobson and Kevin. He remembered the antagonism between him and Carolyn, his distance from Carter, and the growing divide between him and his wife.

He pulled his key from the ignition, reached for his briefcase, and walked slowly through the garage and into the kitchen entrance. A note was taped to the kitchen door leading to the rest of the house. It was from Katherine.

She had gone to the store to buy groceries for dinner.

Doug looked up.

There were no sounds in the home.

He pushed through the kitchen's swinging door and surveyed the living room.

At the foot of the staircase he sighed, feeling drained yet recognizing the opportunity before him. He prodded himself up the stairs into his bedroom; stripped down; threw on a pair of shorts, a pair of white socks, a long-sleeve T-shirt, and his worn pair of running shoes; jogged down the stairs and through the front door; and headed north to the trails of Brea Hills.

Carolyn offered to pay for gas. Kamal accepted. She had paid for his meal and paid now for his fuel. It was her way of saying thanks. She considered herself fortunate. Not only did she get the ride home for which she had previously given up hope, but also the time spent on the journey was enjoyable. Among other things, she wished that somehow it could be extended.

Kamal steered the car back onto Interstate 5 as Carolyn replayed the phone conversation she had with her mother two minutes earlier. Her mother had just returned from the grocery store when she picked up the phone. As she spoke, she was unpacking groceries, removing pots from the cupboard, speaking with a vigor Carolyn had not heard in two years. Carolyn informed her that she was on her way and that it may be another one to two hours, depending upon the traffic. Her mother assured her that they would not begin the meal without her and looked forward to her arrival, that there was much she wanted to discuss.

Carolyn sighed, recalling a brush of her innocent youth, hoping her mother's excitement was indication that their home had recaptured a portion of the Christmas magic she experienced as a child.

Carolyn looked at Kamal. He seemed curious.

"You're smiling," he said.

"I am?" Carolyn needed no mirror to substantiate Kamal's observation; she felt the sensation, the relief that the heightened corners of her mouth created.

"We'll be home within two hours," she said softly.

These words echoed though the car, awakening Carolyn from her brief encounter with joy. "Two more hours with Kamal," she thought, "only two hours."

She could spend the rest of life with this man and not tire of hearing his voice, looking in his eyes, discovering life by his side. Still, she had made no physical advance and knew if she did, she'd regret it. How then could she prolong their time together? How could she ensure that she'd see him again?

Turning in her seat and brushing her hair behind her ear, a nervousness growing in her bosom, she asked, "Kamal?"

He looked at her. "Yes?"

"What are your plans for dinner?"

After finishing with his share of the paper route, Carter slowly walked toward his house, still wrestling with the words Hector had spoken earlier. It was a relief; somehow Hector helped him forget about the events of the day and the inquisition awaiting him once he walked into his home.

As they peddled through the neighborhood, Carter throwing papers to the houses at which Hector directed, he could not make sense of the words Hector had spoken: "It's more of a miracle to change my heart . . ."

If Hector was right, if Jesus came to chase the evil out of people's hearts, then Jesus had failed, at least as it concerned Carter. First, there was Chuck; Carter hated him for all that he had done: the cigarettes, the mocking of Shannon, the humiliation of Hector and David, and the stealing of his baseball cards. Then, there was his mother; more than once did he wish that she was the one who had died, not Shannon. There was the anger he still felt toward Allen, the shame for his father, and most of all, the resentment and hatred for God, for it was he who allowed all that had transpired over the past two years.

Carter knew and recognized each of these facts of his life as things that should not be in his heart. The good doctor helped him to acknowledge their presence but did little to help him rid them from his mind. As he thought of Chuck, or his mom, or his dad, or God, he felt in his chest a heaviness pushing down on all his organs—his heart, his lungs, his stomach.

Hayvenhurst could not help him get rid of these thoughts. Carter had failed. And if Hector was right, if Jesus could do it, then why was all that hatred and anger still lingering within him?

Looking up into the clear night sky, visible because the Santa Ana winds had chased away the usual clutter of smog and clouds, more stars were visible, more than Carter could ever remember seeing. Perhaps, Carter thought, people are like stars—so many; some are forgotten by God; some don't get their hearts fixed; some do.

He reached the driveway of his home and noticed a worn Ford Pinto parked on the curb. He looked toward the front door and heard lively talking and laughter coming from inside. He looked back at the car when he recognized Carolyn's laughter.

He hadn't had a run this refreshing in over a year. Two hours and fifteen miles after leaving his home, he felt he could go another five or ten miles.

He was free out here, free to let loose the turmoil and burdens he carried from the office and home and free to contemplate the questions created during the interview with Jacobson.

Here was a man, carrying memories of guilt and of feeling insufficient and incapable. Yet he was happy, content, and free. How did Jacobson arrive at such a place and after twenty years Doug Mason had made no progress and felt no relief, no peace, no joy? Doug felt the strength and power still residing in his legs and lungs. Physically, he was invincible, compared to the weakening character and spirituality he felt within. Consciously fighting the frustration within his psyche, he quickened his pace, pushing his strides to a point where he felt on the verge of flying.

With each stride, Doug's pace heightened, reaching almost a sprint. He felt his youth return as he turned onto his street, his home just yards away.

Carter skipped from the courtyard to the grass and onto the sidewalk when he heard the familiar gait of his father's running rapidly approach. He turned and saw his father come to a halt and lean forward, resting his arms on his legs, breathing heavier than Carter was used to seeing.

"Dad?" Carter called out.

He held out his left hand, signaling Carter to wait or signaling a greeting, or maybe both.

Carter walked toward him. "Carolyn's here. Must have come in this car."

Carter's father straightened his posture and looked at the white Pinto to which Carter was pointing.

"They're inside?"

Carter looked back toward the front door, nodding.

"You go in. I'll be there in a few minutes. Need to catch my breath."

Carter did want to go inside, see Carolyn, and have her rush to him, hold him, and squeeze him tight. He was hopeful that would be her reaction. But he felt he could not let this moment pass. He would wait until his father was no longer breathing heavily, and hoped that he may be able to answer the question tormenting him.

His father rose from his crouch. "Carter?"

Carter looked back toward the house and then back at his father. His breathing was almost normal.

"What is it, Son?"

He didn't know how to say what he was thinking, how to express his deep longing for an answer to his question.

His father's curiosity seemed to grow the longer Carter delayed. He walked up to Carter and held his chin, tilting his head upward.

Carter could no longer hide the tears.

"Carter? Son? What is it? What has happened?"

"Nothing," Carter answered. He shook his head, wiped his eyes with the sleeve of his shirt, and then cleared his throat.

He swallowed, still not sure what words to speak. "How come," he started nervously, "how come Jesus hasn't changed my heart?"

Once he spoke the words, he could not take them back. He was relieved when he heard them come from his mouth, so relieved that he asked further, "How does He change it?"

He wiped his eyes again, waiting for an answer.

At first, his father's eyes were fixed on Carter. Then they wandered, seeming to look beyond him, somewhere behind him, far off, maybe at all those stars Carter had noticed minutes earlier.

Maybe, he didn't know either.

Pokeweed and Priests

It had been a long shot; Carter hoped his father would have some insight into Hector's commentary. He had let seconds pass in silence, allowing him time to think.

His dad released his hand from Carter's head, brushed his shoulder, stepped back, and sat on the ledge of the planter behind him. His shoulders were slouched, his eyes were downcast, and "the valley" between his eyes was growing. Carter wouldn't exactly describe it as a smile, but his father raised the corners of his mouth as if he was thinking, frustrated, and just as lost as Carter felt.

"It's Christmas," his father said in a low voice.

Carter was not sure if his father spoke these words to him or was just making a general comment. So he waited.

"It isn't supposed to be like this," his dad continued. "How'd I miss it all these years?"

"Dad?" Carter asked quietly, raising his hand atop his head and scratching it, unsure of what to say or what to do.

His father shook his head, as if waking from a nap. "Go inside, Son," he instructed. "Tell your mother I'll be there in a few minutes."

Carter obeyed and walked through the porch. He looked back toward his father, recalling the night he saw him crying on the park bench. He turned and opened the front door. Immediately, aromas enveloped him that he hadn't sensed in years: bread baking in the oven, basked with butter; some type of meat roasting; a potato dish simmering; and assorted vegetables steaming on the stove. Before he had a chance to take a deep breath through his nose, Carolyn raced from the dining room with wide arms to Carter and hoisted him to the ceiling. Once she lowered him back to his feet, she kissed him lightly on top of his head.

"Come," she said excitedly, "we're playing cards. Dinner is still cooking; Mom's playing too."

"Mom, playing cards?" Carter whispered. He trailed behind, holding Carolyn's hand as she led him into the dining room.

Carolyn glanced back with a grin, "And a guest."

Carter looked up, skeptical that his mother would partake in a game of amusement.

Carolyn was correct; his mother was at the table, sitting in the chair usually reserved for Carolyn. Carolyn was seated in Carter's normal spot, and the guest was seated in their father's chair.

His mother seemed lost in the study of the cards she held fanned in front of her face. She raised her eyes and invited Carter to sit. There was no hint of pending repercussions for the events that had transpired earlier in the day. Still Carter chose to sit next to Carolyn, as far from his mother as possible.

Here, Cart," Carolyn stood, guiding Carter to sit in her place, "you sit here."

Carter obeyed, stealing another look at his mother. Her eyes were darting from the guest, to Carolyn, and back to the cards she held.

Carolyn held out her hand toward the guest who was now standing, "This is Kamal."

The guest, who was very tall, taller even than Kevin, stood up and bowed, extending his hand.

Carter shook it.

"Kamal," Carolyn continued, "this is my brother, Carter."

Kamal extended his hand. "Very nice to meet you, Mr. Carter."

Carter smiled, restraining a giggle. He looked at his mother. Her eyes were fixed on Kamal.

"Walk around, Cart," Carolyn instructed. "You sit here, next to Kamal. He hasn't played poker before and like you, needs reminding of which hand is best. I'm letting him use the encyclopedia, just like we let you use it."

Carter studied Carolyn, amazed that she offered him the use of *World Book Encyclopedia*'s P. On all other occasions, he had to beg for use of it.

He sat next to their guest and glanced at the listing of poker's various card combinations: royal flush, straight flush, and all the way down to two pair and one pair.

"We'll let you in on the next hand, Cart," Carolyn explained. "We're in the middle of this one."

Carter inched forward, glancing at the cards Kamal held. He glanced back at the list of poker hands in the encyclopedia. Kamal held a Christmas tree cookie in his hand but did not seem intent on eating it. He placed it on a large green-and-white plate in the middle of the table, "One Christmas tree," he said, "and I'll increase it by one snowman." Kamal reached down and took a snowman cookie from a paper plate at his elbows and placed it on the large green-and-white plate in the middle.

Carter smiled. He studied the table further. Both Carolyn and his mother had paper plates, similar to Kamal's. His mother's plate seemed to have the most cookies, Carolyn seemed to be doing all right, but Kamal's plate was almost empty.

"I'll meet your tree and man," Carter's mother announced, her face without expression, "and raise you one bell and two angels."

Carolyn dropped her cards to the table. "I fold."

Kamal gazed at his cards, glanced over them at his opponents, especially Carter's mother, studied the list in the encyclopedia, and looked back to his five cards. He lifted one bell cookie and his last two angel cookies and placed them on the large plate.

Carter's mother placed her cards on the table. "A pair of twos."

Kamal chuckled, "A pair of twos."

"Now what?" Carter asked.

"We look at the remaining cards," Carolyn explained.

She propped herself up in her chair and studied Kamal's hand, "An ace, a ten, and a six."

Carter stood up and pointed. "And Mom has an ace, a jack, and a four."

"Mom wins," Carolyn announced, shrugging and offering a conciliatory grin to Kamal.

Kamal sighed but didn't seem too distraught with the defeat. He had only five cookies remaining on his plate.

Carolyn went to the kitchen and returned with another plate of cookies. "Carter, you'll start with five of each. Angels are worth the most, then the trees, snowmen, and bells—in that order. Okay?"

Carter pulled the chair closer, sat on his knees, leaned forward, and rested his elbows on the table.

After Carolyn dealt, Carter picked up and studied his five cards. Nothing. An assortment of valueless cards with no common suite or valued sequence: a two, a four, a six, an eight, and a ten. Not one face card, only five multiples of two. He sighed, realizing he failed to hide one of his many "tells." He looked up at Carolyn, and she was grinning. Such a lack of control on his part would have previously produced some expression of disapproval from his sister, but something was different about her today. Can college change the way older siblings treat younger siblings?

"Carter, it's your bet," Carolyn announced.

He formed a fist and tapped the table as though he were knocking on a door.

"What's he doing?" Kamal asked.

"That's his way of saying, 'Pass.'"

"He doesn't have a good hand?" Kamal asked.

Carolyn grinned.

"Two angels." Kamal placed them on the center plate.

Carter looked at Kamal and was impressed with his bold bet. He looked at Carolyn, wondering how much worse a player Kamal could be.

Again, Carter's mother met Kamal's wager but this time did not raise the ante.

Carolyn also joined, wagering two angels.

If Carter was to remain in this hand, he'd have to forfeit two of his cherubs. He wanted to play but knew he'd have other chances with better cards. He placed his cards on the table. "I fold."

"I'll take two cards," Kamal said.

Carolyn tossed him two, and Kamal placed one at the far end of his hand and one in the middle. He seemed pleased with the one card at the end and indifferent toward the one he placed in the middle.

As Carter shifted his gaze toward his mother, she seemed to recognize exactly what Carter had. She too asked for two cards. When placing them into her hand, she gave no indication of their value.

Carolyn took one card.

Another round of wagering began. His mother's face was rigid, and Carter noticed his mother study their guest, her eyes filled with the anger and displeasure he had come to know too well.

The ensuing wages once again emptied Kamal's plate; he was betting it all.

"What have you got, Mom?" Carolyn asked as Kamal had made the final bet and dumped his remaining cookies on the jackpot.

"Three of a kind. Three queens."

Carolyn laid her cards down, "Two pair; aces and fours."

Kamal laid his cards. "A three, a six, and three Kings," he announced.

When he said it, Carter's heart leaped; he hadn't realized he was rooting for Kamal. He clapped once, announced "Hurrah!" and began to clap again. His mother pushed her chair from the table and stood up, her face filled with rage and her eyes fixed on Kamal.

"Mom?" Carolyn asked.

Carolyn turned to Carter, who was looking as confused as he felt.

"Mom?" Carolyn repeated.

Their mother turned toward the kitchen and then toward Kamal. "Damn. Damn it all," she started, shaking her head.

"Mother, is everything all right?" Carolyn once more questioned.

The front door opened.

Carter heard his father shuffling in the hall, probably removing his running shoes.

"Carter," his mother ordered, "let your father know I'm in the kitchen and dinner will be ready in twenty minutes."

Carter did not take his eyes off his mother and was grateful she was not looking at him, relieved that her eyes remained locked on Kamal. "Okay," he answered.

"Carolyn," she ordered, her eyes not moving, "please direct our guest to the front door."

Carter looked to Carolyn. Her eyes burrowed.

"Clean this up," their mother said, pointing to the cards and cookies strewn across the table. She turned and entered the kitchen.

"What the . . . ?" Carolyn said, turning to Carter, contorting her body, and waving her arms. "What was that, Cart? Is this normal?"

Carter raised his eyes, unsure how to answer.

"Smells good," Carter heard his father say from the hall as he entered the dining room.

"My prodigal from Berkley," he said, wrapping his still-moist arms around Carolyn and embracing her lightly.

"Hi, Dad."

"And who's our guest?"

Carter looked at Carolyn, but she was looking back to the kitchen.

"Kamal," Carter answered. "He drove Carolyn home."

Kamal stood up and shook their father's hand. "Very nice to meet you, Mr. Mason. You have a wonderful family."

"I'm sorry, Dad," Carolyn started, "how rude of me. Yes, Kamal drove me home."

But again, Carolyn's attention seemed drawn to the kitchen. "I'm going to see if Mom needs any help."

"Very good," Carter's father said, "and is Kamal staying for dinner?"

"Yes!" Carolyn answered, looking over her shoulder, pushing open the swinging door, and entering the kitchen.

"Well, it sure smells appetizing," their father continued.

"Mom said it would be ready in twenty minutes," Carter announced.

"You will both need to excuse me then," his father said. "I will take a quick shower and be down as soon as I can."

Carter watched his father ascend the stairs. He turned and looked at Kamal, who was still standing where he had shaken his father's hand. Kamal stood motionless. Carter felt sorry for him. Certainly, he must be confused, uncertain whether he was supposed to leave or stay as it appeared Carolyn wanted.

Carter reached for the empty card box in the center of the table and began to gather the cards.

"Can I assist?" Kamal asked.

"No," Carter answered, "I've got it."

Next, Carter picked up the cookies and cleared the table of crumbs, unwilling to let any of his mother's orders left undone. Holding one plate full of cookies, he took one step toward the kitchen. He looked at Kamal, still standing, and then back at the kitchen door, before setting the plate back onto the table. Again, he looked toward Kamal and toward the staircase and sat down.

Aware that his mother wanted their guest to leave, he did not know what to do next. He invited his guest to sit, opening his hand to the chair across from him.

Now what? How was he to entertain their guest? Carter reached for the encyclopedia, which was still open to the poker-hand rankings. On this same page, he noticed a word that offered a brief reprieve: "Pokeweed."

It was the entry directly beneath the description of Poker, on page 533. He recognized the word, for he had turned to this page often, but had never paid much attention to it.

At first sight, he thought of what an appropriate nickname it would be for Stuart Hardaway, the eldest of his group of friends. Stuart had just entered middle school and stopped hanging out to play with the rest of the kids on the block. Though he was a good athlete, tall, strong, and had good coordination, Stuart was slow, the slowest runner on the block, maybe the slowest runner Carter had ever seen. If only he had made the connection when Stuart was still playing with the gang; the nickname would have stuck, and Carter would have been congratulated for discovering it.

Then, for the first time, he began reading the description of pokeweed:

> *Pokeweed is a tall, branching perennial herb with greenish-white flowers and deep purple, juicy berries. It flourishes in waste places and along roadsides . . .*

"Hmm," Carter muttered, thinking of how the greenish-white flowers nestled with the deep purple reminded him of Christmas.

He read on:

> *The stem of the pokeweed grows 4-10 feet high . . .*

"Just like a Christmas tree," Carter whispered.

> *The plant has a brilliant appearance in fall, when the leaves become red and the berries ripen.*

Carter's interest was growing deeper.

> *The berries, together with the poisonous roots, are used in medicines that treat skin and blood disease, and relieve pain and inflammation.*

"You see congruence?" Kamal asked.

Carter looked up at his guest.

Though he was struggling with the elementary definitions and theorems he was taught in geometry, he did understand congruent angles, congruent lines, and congruent circles. He understood to what Kamal was referring, pleased that someone else, a grown-up no less, saw what he saw.

"Tell me," Kamal invited.

"The colors," Carter said excitedly, "green, white, red, purple—they're all part of Christmas."

"Anything else?"

Carter smiled, "Four to ten feet. Most of the trees on the lots are between four to ten feet. That's funny!"

Kamal seemed to be waiting for some further insight.

Carter shrugged, wondering what he might have missed. "I guess," he started, "I guess that's it."

"Read down here," Kamal invited.

Carter looked down to where Kamal was pointing and then continued to read aloud:

> *Pokeweed seeds are poisonous, and the leaves are frequently mottled by a virus disease that may be carried to flowers and vegetables by insects.*

"But," Carter said, "just above, it says that pokeweed cures some diseases."

"That's right," Kamal said.

"How can something that is poisonous cure disease?"

"Another congruence," Kamal answered.

"Really?" Carter asked. "To what?"

"To Christmas."

Carter shook his head. "I don't get it. What do poison and Christmas have in common."

"It's the baby."

"The baby?" Carter asked. "The baby Jesus? Poison?"

Again Carter shook his head. "I don't see the connection."

"Think of the baby grown up," Kamal invited. "What happened to him?"

Carter tilted his head, trying to understand. "You mean the cross? The cross is the poison?"

Pursing his lips, Carter strained to complete the logic. "Is that it?"

He certainly hoped not. He had left Hector's house, longing for his heart to be changed. His father had not been able to answer his question. Speaking with Kamal gave him a sense that some light could be shed on the subject.

"Is there more?" Carter asked.

Kamal turned his body, directly facing Carter. He cradled the encyclopedia in his two enormous hands. "Close your eyes, Mr. Carter," Kamal instructed.

Carter closed them.

Kamal continued. "Imagine one of your best friends betraying you."

That was not difficult. He thought of Chuck.

"Now imagine people telling lies about you."

Again, Carter had no problem with this: all the missing pieces of the manger and his parents assuming it was his fault.

"Because of their lies, you are sentenced to die."

Carter opened one eye; that was something to which he could not relate.

Kamal held out his hand, inviting Carter to continue playing along.

He obeyed.

"Leather whips whose ends are cut to form nine strips or tails. The ends of each tail fitted with tiny sharp bones, stones, glass shards. With these whips they swing at your back with all their strength. Thirty-nine times, leaving your skin torn and bloody. They place a cloak on your back and press a crown of thorns onto your temple, mocking you, causing the thorns to dig into your scalp. Minutes later, when the cloak has coagulated with the damp skin and blood all over your body, they rip the cloak off your back . . ."

Carter jumped at this description, thinking of the stinging pain created by his mother pulling a Band-Aid from his skinned knee.

"The pain Jesus endured was the poison," Kamal concluded. "Somehow he overcame the poison and used it to heal, just like the medical world has learned to harness the poison of pokeweed to heal disease."

"You mean heal our hearts?" Carter asked.

"Here," Kamal reached out his hands, giving the encyclopedia to Carter.

Carter looked up, waiting for instruction.

"Turn to 'Priest.' P-R-I-E . . ."

Carter was fully aware of how to spell the word. He flipped through the pages, hoping to prove this to Kamal before he finished its spelling.

"Priest," Carter announced, "one who serves as a mediatory agent between man and God."

"Continue," Kamal instructed, "read on."

"In the Catholic Church, the official to whom one confesses."

Carter looked up from the book, hoping Kamal would clarify.

"When you need your heart changed," Kamal began, "when you need it healed, the first step is acknowledging you need change."

Sitting up straight in his chair, eyes wide, Carter anticipated Kamal's next words.

"Carter!" Carolyn beckoned from the kitchen, pushing open the swinging door, her arms holding five plates. "Help me set the table."

"Just a minute," Carter pleaded, "Kamal and I are talking." Carolyn held out her hand, instructing Carter to remain quiet. "Just set the plates. Keep talking."

As she turned to go back into the kitchen, she almost ran head-on into her mother. She was carrying a tray of bread.

"What's this?" her mother said, pointing with the bread in her hand at Carter and Kamal. "Why is he still here?"

"Mother!" Carolyn shouted. "What's your—"

"You left him here alone!" their mother shouted. "I told you to show him out."

"He drove me home, Mom."

"Damn you. He's still a boy. He's impressionable."

"But Mom," Carolyn pleaded.

"Get away from him now!" she directed the order at Kamal, maneuvering past Carolyn and speeding toward him. "Get out of my house!"

Carolyn's face flushed. She raced to Kamal, who had stood up and gone behind the chair.

He did not appear offended, not even surprised. He moved gracefully.

"No," Carolyn begged.

"Don't touch him, Carter Anthony Mason," his mother ordered. "He's not welcome here. None of you are."

Carter heard his father walking down the stairs, racing almost. "What's going on down there?"

Although his father looked at his mother, awaiting explanation, his mother's eyes remained fixed on Kamal.

"Our daughter's ride home is leaving," she announced.

"So soon?" Carter's father asked, his eyes seeking explanation. "I was told he's staying for dinner."

Carolyn grabbed Kamal's hand, looking up into his eyes.

Gently, he pushed her away, extending his arms. He bowed to her and then to her parents and finally to Carter.

Carolyn turned to her mother and then to Kamal. Back and forth she turned, unable to find words to remedy the standoff. Kamal walked himself toward the front door, Carolyn following and pleading that he stay.

"Can I at least walk you to the car?" Carter heard her ask.

"Here," he said.

Carter wanted to see what was happening, but his mother remained at the head of the table, apparently waiting for the door to shut and Carolyn to return alone.

The door shut. Carolyn walked slowly back to the dining room. She strangely resembled Shannon; her hair was disheveled and a sorrow was in her stare.

She looked at her mother, holding a small box in her hands.

"Do you have any idea, Mother? Do you have any idea . . ."

She looked up at her mom. "I haven't experienced such joy since our days around the supper table growing up. What was that? What's going on?"

Her mother did not respond; her eyes were fixed on the box Carolyn held.

"What just happened in here?" Carolyn continued.

"Katherine?" Carter's father pleaded.

Still focused on the box Carolyn held, she made no response and no recognition of the inquisition from Carolyn or her husband.

"Katherine," this time their father spoke with stern tone, "what were you thinking?"

"Give me that box," she ordered Carolyn.

Carolyn held it up, turned it in her hand, studied it, and looked to Carter and their father. "What?"

"Damn it, Carolyn, give me the box!"

Carter's father turned quickly and raced up the stairs, tackling two on each stride. Within twenty seconds, he raced back down, breathing heavily and holding two boxes of equal size with the one Carolyn held.

"Carter?" Carolyn asked, her eyes fixed on their mother, "What were you and Kamal talking about?"

Carter swallowed nervously, looked at their mother, and lowered his eyes.

"Carter!" Carolyn ordered. "Tell us what you two were discussing!"

He peered at his mom and at Carolyn. "Pokeweed," he answered.

"Pokeweed?" Carolyn repeated as she turned, her eyes telling Carter she needed further explanation.

"That's right," Carter continued slowly, his eyes moving from his mom, to Carolyn, to the floor, and back to Carolyn. "Pokeweed and priests."

Torn Curtain

"That's enough," Carter's mother shouted.

Carolyn held up her right hand. "Let him continue!"

"Open the box," Carter whispered to Carolyn.

"What?" Carolyn said with some annoyance, looking down at him.

"Open the box," Carter pleaded, not daring to look at his mother as he asked the question.

"But why?" Carolyn asked.

Carter walked to the chair in which he sat to play poker, bent over, and reached for his backpack. He unzipped the front pocket and removed the box he had received from David and Joshua. "I got one, too."

Carolyn looked at the box held by Carter and then the two boxes held by their father. She reached her fingers to open the lid of the box she held.

"Don't you dare," their mother ordered.

Carolyn's stare darted to her mother and then to the box and back to her mother. Then, as she looked at Carter, she opened the lid and turned the box upside down, and out came the worn wooden wise man.

Immediately, their father opened both boxes he held, and Carter felt as though a thousand-pound weight had been lifted from his shoulders as both Joseph and Mary were taken out of their respective boxes.

"Hurrah!" he shouted.

"Carter Anthony Mason," his father ordered, "did you arrange this?"

He looked at his mother, fighting hard to keep from smiling and unsure as to why this turn of events caused her such dissatisfaction.

"No," he turned to his father. "No I did not."

"Let me see it," he whispered to Carolyn.

Carolyn handed it to him.

As soon as Carter held it, he knew—its weight, the ridges and texture of the aged wood. "This is it!"

"Is what?" Carolyn asked.

Carter ran to the front door, inviting Carolyn to follow. "Our wise man."

"Of course it is," Carolyn said.

Carter stopped. He looked back at his sister.

She continued. "What I can't figure out is why he would take it and put it in a box and then give it to me as though he had bought it."

Carter shook his head. "No. You don't understand." He placed the wooden piece in its place. "It was missing this morning."

"This morning?"

"Look." Carter turned back toward the table, pointing down at the crèche. "Dad has Mary and Joseph, but we're still . . ."

He stopped when he heard his mother race toward them. She held out her arm the same way she did two weeks earlier, when she hit Carter across the face. Carter turned his head, closed his eyes, raised his shoulders, and waited for contact.

But the doorbell rang, and Carter felt a rush of air brush past his face as his mother grabbed the knob and opened the door. It was a UPS delivery employee.

Carter opened his eyes and saw a look of horror on Carolyn's face. Her eyes fixed on the subtle welt still visible under Carter's right eye. Carter knew immediately that Carolyn understood.

He looked at the box he still held, opened it, and found exactly what he suspected: two shepherds—one, a young boy; the other, an adult.

From behind, his father wrapped his arm around Carter's shoulder and handed him the wooden pieces of Mary and Joseph.

Carter took the pieces and placed them in the nativity. Now only one piece was missing.

Their mother was busy, speaking with the UPS delivery man.

Carolyn walked to Carter and whispered, "Who gave you that box, Cart?"

Carefully, Carter glanced up at his mother, who was still in dialogue.

She glanced back and momentarily focused on the now almost fully populated manger and then at her family. "UPS delivery to wrong address," she announced. "I'll take it next door."

As she closed the door behind her, Carter felt relief, though he knew it to be short-lived.

There were four people in her life whom she could call family. Three of them were standing behind the door she just shut; one had lost most her memory and was in a rest home just down the road. They should be the ones who receive the best of her time, the best of her efforts, and the best of her love. That morning, she acknowledged her failure to do this during the past two years, and though she intended to begin making amends, her attempts had been derailed by these guests. She had no desire to meet them and no desire to hear the message they came to declare.

Now her family was privy to the special qualities of the crèche and to the secret she had kept even from her husband. The secret she insisted her mother keep from the children. But she wanted no more of it. It had infested her life from her earliest memories. Others might think it miraculous to be visited by such folk; she did not. And she would not allow her family to know more of its history.

When she first opened the door, she was relieved, for the presence of the UPS man had given her not only the opportunity to open the door instead of slapping her son across the face but also an escape from the revelations occurring within her home.

"I have a package," the middle-aged UPS driver had announced.

"It's kind of late," she said.

"Yes, ma'am. Last day before the holidays. You know how it is. Sign right here, please."

Katherine did not take the pen from his hand. Her attention was drawn to the small rectangular brown box he held. It was wrapped neatly with a red ribbon. She didn't dare speak or react in any way that may draw the attention of her family.

"Ma'am? Your signature, please."

She turned toward her family and announced to them that the package was for their neighbor, that she would deliver it to them. She shut the door behind her and then signed the delivery confirmation.

As she signed, the deliveryman laughed.

Katherine eyed him for an explanation.

"I'm sorry. It's not you, ma'am, it's just, well, you should actually consider yourself lucky!"

"Really?"

"I almost didn't get this to you. I didn't see it. It must have fallen out of the truck. I was pulling away, just made my last delivery, and in my side-view mirror, I see this guy running after me. He gave me the box, and on it was your address. Funny thing is I hadn't remembered seeing it throughout the entire day. I guess it was so small."

Katherine looked up and held out the signed document. "Is that it?"

The deliveryman continued laughing.

"Yes?"

"I'm sorry, ma'am, but I have to share this with someone. The irony of it all, you know, it being Christmas."

Placing her hands on her hips, she pressed herself to be civil and show no rudeness to this stranger who had no idea as to the bad news enclosed in the box he had delivered.

"The guy who gave me the box—he was dressed like Jesus. You know, beard, mustache, long brown hair, a little darker complexion, but the same type of clothes you see in the movies. He must be in some play tonight. You should have seen him running behind my truck, trying to catch up to me; could have tripped over his robe."

Katherine fixed her eyes on the deliveryman.

"Well," he said, turning and walking to his truck, "you have a nice Christmas."

Katherine followed him out to the front yard, glancing behind, making certain that her family was not aware of what had been delivered.

The UPS driver was still shaking his head, smiling and giggling as he drove off.

She shut her eyes and took a long, deep breath. Eventually, the box would have to be opened, the content removed. With constraint, she opened her eyes and held the box out, in the palm of her hands, her arms extended.

Again, she looked behind, then moved several feet to her right, far enough to be out of sight from the windows of her home. Slowly, Katherine untied the ribbon and opened the lid.

She removed the golden cradle, crumpled the box in her hand, and stuffed it into the front pocket of her jeans. She headed toward the middle of the street, looking for some sign of the man of whom the delivery driver had spoke.

She looked into the sky and would not bow her head.

Walking back to her home from the street's center, cradling the golden manger in the cup of her hands, she whispered, "So this is it? Forty-two years, and this is what I've got. Does this replace my daughter? Am I supposed to be thankful? Where were you? Where were you Christmas Eve when I was a little girl? Where were you two years ago? Now you come! Damn you for not listening to all my mother's prayers! Damn you for letting him do to her what he did! Do you know what I felt? Do you care? To see my mother lonely every day? I was powerless, but you are supposed to be, oh, so powerful! She served in churches, prayed for pastors, gave her money, read her Bible. For what? Today she lies in a hospital room; she can't remember; she can't watch her favorite movies; she can't walk outside in the world she thanked you for each day. She can't read. Or laugh. Or cry. Or think. Are you so powerless not to be able to take her breath away? Or are you so cruel to continue humiliating her and burdening us? What do you do with all your time? If you wouldn't help Nana, why not Douglas! The torture you put him through! Why do you burden him with such guilt? He's only sought to do good! And then Shannon! This will not do! I will not accept! Depart, and leave us alone! We want none of your visits, none of your words, none of you!"

She walked back to the street's perimeter, positioned herself as though she had just fielded a groundball at first base, wound her left arm backward, strode forward with her left foot planted, and with a right-leg stride, launched the golden manger into the sky in the direction of the intersection south of her house, into a row of thick bushes next to the Romero home.

She turned, walked back through the porch, and opened the door.

Carter turned in frustration, looked at the ceiling, and stomped the floor. If he had known who Joshua and David were, who Kamal was, if he had had only more time with any one of them, perhaps they could have explained how his heart could be changed. Still, hope remained. One piece of the crèche had yet to be returned. One more visitor would come, and he was the most important of them all. He could answer Carter's question.

Carter stood on the bottom step of the stairs, facing the front door. Next to him sat Carolyn. A few steps above sat their father.

When Carter's mom opened the door and reentered the house, they all stared at her. "Honey," his father announced, "we need to talk this out. Before dinner. All of us."

She chuckled, shaking her head. "Not now, Douglas. Not ever."

"Katherine. Enough. This is Christmas."

She looked up at Carter's father, fury highlighting all her features.

Carter felt he had something to offer.

"This has gone on long enough," his father explained. "We must work through this."

"Dad," Carter spoke softly, cautious to not enrage his mother further or disrespect his father. "Can I say something?"

He turned to look up at his dad and waited for approval. His dad looked at Carolyn. She seemed to be curious as to what he may say.

"Go ahead, Son," his father announced.

"Remember our vacation a couple years ago?" Carter began. "The one in that French fur trapping town in Idaho, with that big lake."

"Coeur d'Alene," Carolyn added.

"That's it!" Carter said excitedly. "Well, anyway, that Sunday, Dad and I went to church, remember? Shannon followed us. The minister talked about some rich dude who died and a poor guy who lived outside his house who died around the same time. The rich guy went to hell and asked God to send someone—an angel or some saint—to his family, to warn them about hell, how hot it was and all that. And Abraham said that God wouldn't send anyone. Don't you see? Don't you get it?"

Carter looked at the three; his father answered with a shake of his head. His mother, defiant, fixed her eyes on Carter; Carolyn, still seated, looked up, with a faint grin and gleam in her eyes.

"It's all so clear," Carter continued. "God and Abraham did not listen to the man because he was in hell, but God may have granted him the request if he had been in heaven!

"The night Shannon," Carter went on, "the night of the accident. She told me that night . . . she told me that she had something important to share with me. But, but, I could see it in her eyes; she had discovered something. She didn't get the chance to tell me then, so she got help and sent them from heaven. God allowed it, 'cause she's up there, not in hell like the rich man. They came, and they could have answered . . . they could have answered my question."

"Question?" Carolyn asked. "What question?"

His father cleared his throat. "Carter asked me earlier tonight." He paused and, it seemed, waited for Carter to grant him permission to continue.

Carter nodded.

"Carter feels God should be able to change our hearts, and wonders why He doesn't?"

For the first time since coming back inside the house, Carter noticed his mother move. She shuffled her feet and seemed to be searching for a chair to sit on. Her eyes were wide.

Carolyn laid her hand on Carter's shoulder.

Carter shook his head, not looking at his sister. He didn't want sympathy. He wanted an answer. And all these people who had come into their lives throughout the day probably knew it. Yet, all of them had come and gone.

Again, the doorbell rang.

Carter jumped from the bottom stair and raced toward the front door.

His mother stood up. "Don't answer it!" she ordered, grabbing Carter's arm as he tried to pass.

Carter was determined to find some way of maneuvering past his mother to open the door. No way was she going to stand in the way any longer. He knew that the man on the other side of that door could answer his question.

Carter struggled to free himself from his mother's grasp. He looked to Carolyn for assistance, but she seemed confused. His father's eyes were fixed on his mother, looking as though he did not know her. "The valley" on his face deepened.

Carter violently pulled his arm free from his mother's hand and reached for the door knob.

"Carter Anthony Mason, don't you dare!" she shouted

The doorbell rang again.

He felt his mother's hand sweep at his shirt, but Carolyn must have been restraining her, allowing Carter the freedom to turn the knob.

He cracked it, hearing the hinges wind.

Carter blinked. "Hector," he said quietly.

"Hey, Cart. Look what I've got!"

Hector held up five sandwich bags filled with baseball cards.

Carter smiled and looked away, hoping to see someone in the distance behind him. Instead, standing behind Hector, trying to hide, was Hector's youngest sister.

"Don't be shy, Jessica," Hector invited. "It's just Carter. You already know him."

She peered around Hector's leg, looking up at Carter. Her large, round, dark eyes shone with joy. She smiled and then stepped beside Hector.

"Who is it, Cart?" Carolyn called, opening wide the front door. "Hector! I haven't seen you in so long! You're still growing!"

Hector lowered his head, raising his hand. "Hi Carolyn."

"Who's this?" Carolyn asked, lowering herself to Jessica's eye level.

Hector placed his hand on Jessica's back and inched her forward, "This is Carolyn, Carter's older sister."

Jessica's eyes were moving up and down—one second on the ground and the next studying Carter and then Carolyn and then back to the ground. She kept her hands behind her back and stubbornly fought Hector's attempts to move her forward.

"How old are you?" Carolyn asked.

Jessica looked up and held up six fingers. As she released her two hands from holding on to one another, Carter's eyes shot open and his heart began to race. With her left hand, she communicated five of her years; her right hand held up one finger. The other four fingers were wrapped around a golden manger—Shannon's golden manger.

"Carter," Carolyn said, "invite them in."

Carter walked backward into the house, keeping his eyes fixed on the manger.

Jessica finally gave into Hector's prodding and entered the home first.

"Hi Mr. Mason, Mrs. Mason." Hector waved. "Merry Christmas."

"Merry Christmas," Carter's father offered.

Hector bent at his sister's side and whispered something in her ear. She walked slowly toward Carter's mother, holding out her hand and inviting Carter's mother to accept what she held. Carter saw his mother's eyes lower and glisten with moisture. She opened her hand, and Jessica reached up, handing it to her.

She patted Jessica lightly on the head, walked to Carolyn, handed the manger to her, turned, and trudged upstairs.

The crèche was complete. No more visitors. Carter stared at it, thinking its return would be the magical ingredient to make all return to normal.

He glanced at his father, who was still seated in silence. Just seconds earlier, his mother had walked past him, up the stairs, without sign of camaraderie or affection between them. He looked at Carolyn, who was rearranging the manger inhabitants. He turned to the door, which was still open, wishing that someone other than Hector and his sister had been the ones who rang the bell.

He had hoped it was the baby, or at least the child grown up. The baby in the manger had been missing, just like the others. But, unlike the others, he did not visit. Why? There was nobody left to explain how this baby could change his heart?

Again he looked at his father.

Again he looked at his sister.

He looked upstairs at the dim light seeping through the opening beneath his parents' bedroom door.

He looked at Hector.

He looked at Hector and hope reappeared.

Why had he not thought of this earlier?

He shut the door, grabbed Hector's hand, and led him to the library.

"Carter?" Hector asked. "What's up?"

"We need to talk," Carter said, almost skipping to the doors of the library.

"Okay. What about Jessica?"

Carter turned, seeing Jessica join Carolyn at the manger.

Carolyn looked up at Carter, her eyes full of understanding.

Carter opened the door to the library and invited Hector to sit.

"What's up, Cart?" Hector asked once more. "You wanna know how I got the cards back from Chuck?"

Carter shook his head violently.

"Tell me about him. Tell me all you know about Jesus."

BOOK IV: POSTSEASON

Songs of Ascent

Chuck and Carter eventually made up, but within a year, although the friendship between Carter and Hector grew, their time with Chuck and Allen lessened. It wasn't the antagonism between Carter and Chuck that led to this alienation but their habit of attending synagogue with Allen on Saturday afternoons, intrigued by the memory of their encounter with the two brothers, Joshua and David. Hector and Carter's insistence that Jesus was the Messiah for whom they were all looking caused a commotion, leading the rabbi to have a long discussion with Allen and his father. Allen had become curious about his two friends and about the similarities between the two religions, but after the meeting with the rabbi, their friendship gradually transformed into acquaintance.

Rabbi Hoffman delivered a sermon in the spring of seventy-eight that Carter felt summarized his experience. The rabbi read from several psalms. He called them "travel songs" of the ancient Hebrews, which they would chant as they journeyed to Jerusalem three times a year to celebrate festivals. The path was treacherous according to the rabbi—steep, rugged, and filled with dangerous beasts and thieves. The climb would often be in the hot summer months of the Middle East. "One must have been determined and motivated to set off and complete such a journey," the rabbi taught. "These psalms of praise to their God helped remind them of the goal they pursued; it helped them endure the torture they were feeling on the journey."

Such a description by Rabbi Hoffman sparked images of Carter's old friend, the "Sissy." He imagined Sisyphus pushing the proverbial stone up the steep incline. What hope could keep Sisyphus trudging upward his entire life? What hope could keep those ancient Hebrews trudging upwards to Mount Zion to participate in the festivities? What hope could he have that he may one day understand the mysteries beyond his understanding?

Carter grew certain that one day he would stand on the summit of the incline along with Shannon and all the other Sisyphuses of the world. Life was not without meaning. To know God and to seek Him provided the impetus to move through life and through all its potential tortures, doldrums, and failures.

Hector encouraged Carter to submit a narration of the events surrounding the family crèche to Miss Carson in an attempt to improve his English grade. Carter told him that it would sound too crazy but that he would write an appendage to his earlier project, hoping to assure his caring teacher that all was okay.

A Christmas Commentary

by Carter Mason
English/Miss Carson
May 25, 1978

What Child is this, who, laid to rest,
On Mary's lap is sleeping?
Whom angels greet with anthems sweet,
While shepherds watch are keeping?

This, this is Christ the King,
Whom shepherds guard and angels sing:
Haste, haste to bring Him laud,
The Babe, the Son or Mary.

Could not have answered the opening question better myself!

The first Noel the angel did say,
Was to certain poor shepherds in fields as they lay;
In fields where they lay, keeping their sheep,
On a cold winter's night that was so deep.
Noel, Noel, Noel, Noel,
Born is the King of Israel.

I do not agree with the "cold winter's night" part, but the angels did indeed proclaim a historic message to those shepherds. "Born is the

King of Israel!" If only all of us would discover the significance of the angel's message. I know the shepherds did!

We three kings of Orient are
Bearing gifts we traverse afar,
Field and fountain, moor and mountain,
Following yonder star.

O star of wonder, star of night,
Star with royal beauty bright,
Westward leading, still proceeding,
Guide us to thy perfect Light.

With all their wisdom and power and fame, these three guys searched for something even greater than anything they had. They worshipped the little child! What's our excuse? How much greater are we than those wise men?

O holy Child of Bethlehem, descend to us, we pray;
Cast out our sin, and enter in, be born in us today.
We hear the Christmas angels the great glad tidings tell;
O come to us, abide with us, our Lord Emmanuel!

"Enter in."
"Born in us."
"Come to us."
"Abide with us."

Even the name *Emmanuel* means "God with us." The writer was onto something here. This baby, whose birth we celebrate each year, doesn't belong on one day of the calendar, or at a church as much as He belongs inside us. We must invite Him in, however. He won't burst inside without a hospitable welcome.

"Behold, I stand at the door and knock; if any one hears my voice and opens the door, I will come in to him and eat with him, and he with me."

—The baby, after he grew up, died, and became King

Larry Forcey is a former history teacher who now works as an accountant in the title insurance industry. He has published two articles—one illustrates the passion of a fellow baseball fan, and the other is an inner dialogue in which he wrestles with the theology of suffering. This is his first novel. He works and lives in Orange County.

Bibliography

Baseball Reference.com; Philadelphia Phillies, September 15, 1975 entry: http://www.baseball-reference.com/boxes/

Bunyon, John. *The Pilgrim's Progress*, 2nd ed. (New York: Penguin Books, 1987).

Burns, Edward McCall, Robert E. Lerner, and Standish Meacham. *Western Civilization*. (New York: Random, 1980), 482-483.

Camus, Albert. *The Myth of Sisyphus*. (New York: Alfred A. Knopf, a division of Random House, 1955).

Catholic Bible Press. *The New American Bible,* "Apocrypha: 1 Maccabees." Nashville: Catholic Bible Press, a division of Thomas Nelson Publishers, 1987.

Fosdick, Harry Emerson, ed. *Great Voices of the Reformation* (New York: Random House, 1952), 37-41.

Gonzalez, Justo L. *The Story of Christianity, vol. 1, The Early Church to the Dawn of the Reformation* (New York: Harper and Row, 1984), 346-356.

—*The Story of Christianity, vol. 2, The Reformation to the Present Day* (New York: Harper and Row, 1984), 102-109.

Greatsite Marketing Online; entry on "English Bible History—John Hus"; www.greatsite.com/timeline-english-bible-history/john-hus

Ibsen, Henrik, *A Doll's House*. Translated by James McFarlane and Jens Arup. New York: Oxford University Press, 1961.

Latourette, Kenneth Scott. *A History of Christianity, vol. 1, Beginnings to 1500*, rev. ed. (New York: Harper and Row, 1975), 664-675.

Moreland, J.P. *Scaling the Secular City*. (Grand Rapids: Baker Book House, 1987).
Serling, Rod. *The Twilight Zone*, Season 2, "Night of the Meek." Originally aired December 23, 1960.
Webster's Collegiate Dictionary, 9th ed., s.v. "priest."
Wikipedia; Wikipedia's "Florence Baptistery" entry: http://en.wikipedia.org/wiki/Florence_Baptistery
Wikipedia; Wikipedia's "John Wycliffe" entry: http://en.wikipedia.org/wiki/John_Wycliffe
Wikipedia; Wikipedia's "Richard Nixon" entry: http://en.wikipedia.org/wiki/Richard_Nixon
World Book Encyclopedia, 1969, s.v. "Pokeweed."
Zondervan Bible Publishers, "Revised Standard Version of the Bible". Copyright 1946, 1952, 1971 by the Division of Christian Education of the National Council of the Churches of Christ in the USA. Used by permission. (Grand Rapids: Zondervan Publishers).

Song Lyrics

Brooks, Phillips. "O Little Town of Bethlehem." 1868.
Dix, William Chatterton. "What Child is This." 1865.
Gilbert, Davies, edited by William B. Sandys. "The First Noel." (Carols Ancient and Modern, 1823).
Hopkins, John Henry Jr. "We Three Kings of Orient Are." 1863.
Hughes, John Ceiriog. "Deck the Halls." 1784.
Moore, Clement C. "The Night Before Christmas." 1823.
Neale, John M. "Good Christian Men, Rejoice." 1853.
Pierpont, James L. "Jingle Bells." 1857.
Sears, Edmund. "It Came Upon A Midnight Clear." (Christian Register, 1849).
Susan Gregg, ed., *Christmas Orphans*, "Jolly Old St. Nicholas." 1916.
Torme, Mel, and Robert Wells. "The Christmas Song." (Edwin H. Morris & Company, a Division of MPL Music Publishing, Inc. and Sony/ATV Music Publishing, 1946). Used by permission.